MW00784126

beach vibes

SUSAN MALLERY

beach vibes

CANARY STREET PRESS

CANARY
STREET
PRESS™

Recycling programs
for this product may
not exist in your area.

ISBN-13: 978-1-335-40253-0

Beach Vibes

Canary Street Press
22 Adelaide St. West, 41st Floor
Toronto, Ontario M5H 4E3, Canada
CanaryStPress.com

Printed in U.S.A.

beach vibes

1

Beth Nield had no choice but to admit that her sixty-seven-year-old aunt had a much more interesting love life than she did. Actual living proof of that sad fact sat at their shared breakfast table, eating a high-fiber cereal while watching the morning news.

Hunter was a still handsome seventysomething who'd worked for the USPS his whole life, retiring with a very nice federal pension. But his "real" money had come from playing the stock market. She had no idea where the two had met, but this was the third morning this month she'd found Hunter eating a hearty breakfast after a night of, well, nothing she wanted to think about.

Despite the fact that Beth's divorce had been finalized just over a year ago, she hadn't been on a date. As for spending the night with a man, well, she couldn't begin to imagine that ever happening. She'd been telling herself she didn't need that sort of distraction and that relationships were more trouble than they were worth, but thinking about how happy her aunt was these days, she was starting to wonder if maybe she was wrong. Perhaps there *was* something to falling in love. Not that she'd ever had much luck in the romance department—her divorce was proof of that. Her brother hadn't been successful in love, either. Maybe there was a genetic flaw.

Not anything she was going to think about this morning, she told herself firmly as she put her breakfast dishes in the dishwasher and called out a goodbye to Hunter.

While the Los Angeles metro area was known to be a nightmare traffic-wise, Beth had what could only be described as a glorious commute. She lived a mere twenty minutes from where she worked, and the majority of that drive was along Pacific Coast Highway through Malibu. Yes, there were plenty of annoying stoplights, and on the weekends, visitors clogged the roads, but it was difficult to mind when just to the west was the Pacific Ocean.

Although Malibu was known the world over, the LA-adjacent community was in fact much smaller than most everyone imagined. The actual population was less than twelve thousand people, with the majority of the businesses and houses clinging to the coast. There were canyons and hills that stretched east, but the area everyone thought of when they heard the name was within a couple of miles of the water.

Beth made the familiar drive with her windows open and the scent of the salt air brightening her day. The ocean was more lively today with whitecaps visible out to the horizon and seagulls circling overhead. A light breeze danced with the palm trees. This early, the beaches would be relatively empty, but by noon, they would fill with locals and tourists, all eager to enjoy nature's beautiful offering.

When she pulled into her reserved spot behind Surf Sandwiches, the sight of the cheerfully painted one-story building filled her with fierce, happy pride. She might have bought the business out of a sense of obligation and a need to help her brother, but over the years, she'd grown to love the place. When she and Ian had divorced, he'd asked to buy her out of their house. She'd used the money to purchase the vacant storefront next door and had expanded her business, giving her a much larger eating area for customers and a remodeled kitchen and prep area, not to mention additional parking. The latter was a precious commodity in always congested Malibu.

She'd kept the surfboard rack and outdoor shower for her customers who came directly from the beach across the street, and had painted the outside the same bright, cheerful yellow she used on the logo. To make the remodel go more quickly, she'd closed for three weeks, giving her just enough time to second-guess herself and wonder if all her regulars would forget about their favorite sandwiches. But at the grand reopening, there'd been a line nearly around the block, and since the remodel, sales were up thirty-eight percent. Information that would make any small business owner's heart flutter with joy.

She unlocked the back door and walked to the newly enlarged employee space. Big lockers filled one wall, with comfy sofas opposite. During the refresh, she'd added a couple of sets of tables and chairs and had upgraded the Wi-Fi. By giving up space in her office, she'd squeezed in a third bathroom—this one for employees only.

It was barely eight in the morning, three hours before the store opened, but Yolanda and Kai were already hard at work prepping for the upcoming day. Surf Sandwiches was open from eleven until seven. The biggest rush was from about eleven-thirty until one, with a second, surprisingly intense post-school surge, followed by a gentle wind-down until closing.

Yolanda, a pretty, petite brunette with more energy than

the battery bunny and three kids under the age of ten, was her go-to morning person. Despite her tiny stature, she had a killer mom glare that could reduce anyone with attitude to submission in less than three seconds. Even more significant, she wielded the Hobart meat slicer with surgeon-like precision. Even Rick, Beth's actual surgeon brother, agreed Yolanda had mad skills.

"Morning," Beth called as she stepped into the kitchen. "How's it going?"

"Good." Yolanda smiled at her. "Kai's a worker. I don't mind when he comes in early."

Kai, a twenty-two-year-old who'd walked away from family money to surf rather than go to college, beamed at the compliment. "Yo, that's high praise. Makes me want to work harder."

Yolanda winked at Beth, as if silently saying that was the whole point of the words. Then her humor faded.

"We need lettuce. When I went to get it out this morning, I saw it's all rotten."

Beth groaned. "Not the lettuce. What happened?"

Yolanda pointed to the small kitchen where the industrial refrigerator and restaurant-size stove sat. "You can go look for yourself. I salvaged a few bunches, but we're going to need a lot more for the day."

An unexpected but not unheard-of disaster, Beth thought as she went into the kitchen and saw containers of sad-looking lettuce sitting on the counter, the good bunches already off to the side. She calculated the damage, took a couple of pictures with her phone and then pulled the ongoing Costco list from a drawer.

While she ordered most of her supplies from various distributors, like most small restaurant businesses, she relied on a big-box store for backup. She added tomatoes to the list, then returned to the front to confirm they had everything else they needed.

She and Yolanda quickly discussed what she would be buying.

"Let me get in touch with my produce guy. I'll head to Costco as soon as they open."

"We'll be fine," Yolanda told her. "We know what to do."

Beth went into her office, where she quickly booted her computer and the pay system she used. She found two large office lunch orders waiting and immediately forwarded them to the kitchen, where they would be flagged and reviewed. Once Yolanda determined what had to be made, the orders would automatically go in queue thirty minutes before they were supposed to be ready. The improved software had been expensive, but worth it. These days a lot of customers wanted to order and pay online, then just drop by to grab their food and get on with their lives.

She sent a quick email to her produce guy, complete with pictures. She'd been working with him for years and knew a credit would be sitting in her account by the end of day.

She helped with the prep work until it was time to head out with her shopping list. Getting to the closest Costco required a longer and less interesting drive than her commute to work. She listened to the radio and thought about all she had to get done when she returned to the store. Kai would make the cilantro, pumpkin seed and jalapeño pesto, which was usually her job. He was her newest employee, but he was a good hire. She was very fortunate with everyone who worked for her. Most had been with the store over a decade, and turnover was low. She paid well, offered great health care and did her best to be a fair and reasonable boss.

When she'd shut down for the three-week remodel, everyone had been paid their usual amount. She'd even arranged for a special evening at a local movie multiplex where she'd rented the smallest theater and had hosted dinner and a movie for staff and their families. Everyone had had a good time, and a few had mentioned making it an annual event—a reaction that made her happy. Tragically for her, that was the wildest her social life had been since the divorce. Except for work and her recent commitment to volunteering at a local food bank, she was kind of turning into a grumpy hermit, which wasn't her nature at all.

But she couldn't seem to get motivated to, you know, get out and be in the world.

She missed having friends to hang out with. She missed being in a relationship, yet given how she was spending her days, she was very much stuck in a rut of doing nothing. Her aunt was warm and caring, but Agatha had her own life, what with her man friend and a new and oddly successful home business of crocheting custom bikinis.

Beth turned in to the industrial area where the Costco was located and drove toward the sprawling building at the end of the street. As she headed through an intersection, her gaze drifted to a large billboard on her right. Immediately her entire body went on alert as her brain struggled to comprehend what she was seeing. She instinctively turned toward the billboard—and accidently steered in that direction as well. Before she could slam on the brakes, she'd driven off the road, up onto the sidewalk (mercifully empty of pedestrians), stopping less than a foot from a fire hydrant.

It took a couple of seconds for her to start breathing again. Adrenaline poured through her from both the near accident and the billboard itself. She managed to put the car in Park before turning off the engine and getting out to stand on the sidewalk and stare in disbelief.

The billboard was huge and showed a happy couple staring into each other's eyes. Not really noteworthy if she ignored both the fact that the man in question was her ex-husband, Ian, and the heartfelt message next to the photo.

Patti, you mean the world to me. I'm so grateful to have found you. I love you. Will you marry me?

She pressed a hand to her chest, as if to keep her heart from jumping out and flopping around on the road. Her brain was still having trouble processing what she was seeing, and she honestly didn't know what was more confusing to her. The billboard itself, the fact that it was two blocks from Costco, or that her very ordinary, believer-in-a-routine ex-husband had proposed in such an un-Ian-like way. Oh, and maybe the fact that he had obviously moved on and fallen in love with someone else while she hadn't been out with friends, let alone a man.

Ignoring a sudden wave of sadness, she sagged back onto the driver's seat and pulled her phone from her handbag. Within seconds she was on Instagram and scrolling through to find Ian's account. As their divorce had been as low-key as their marriage, she'd never blocked him, and apparently he'd never blocked her, either. Which meant she could see everything he'd posted for the past couple of weeks in color photographs and videos.

If the picture of the two of them holding champagne glasses and smiling at the camera was any indication, Patti had said yes. But instead of staring at the happy couple, Beth found herself searching the crowd of friends that was gathered around them. Friends she'd thought had been her friends as well, back when she and Ian had been married. The three couples had been tight, hanging out together, even taking the odd vacation as a group. But when the marriage had fallen apart, she'd discovered she was actually only the friend-in-law. The other two women hadn't wanted to get together and had finally explained they were picking Ian. At the time, that had hurt about as much as the end of her marriage.

She flipped through more pictures and saw one of Ian and Patti with Ian's large, extended family. The family she'd thought of as her own, appreciating the sheer size and volume of get-togethers. Growing up it had just been her, her brother and her mom. She'd always dreamed of being part of a big family, and with Ian, that had happened. Only once she and Ian split up, her relationship with them had ended as well.

Beth dropped the phone on the passenger seat and stared at the billboard. Ian was getting married again, to Patti—whoever she was. They would have a life, possibly kids. All the things she'd thought would happen when she and Ian had been together. Only they hadn't.

She knew she didn't want him back—their relationship was long over. But she did envy his future, or at least all the possibilities. Ian had kept living his life and looking for ways to be happy.

And here *she* was, in her car, alone and semi-friendless. Except for Jana, a relatively new friend she really liked, there was no one. Yes, she'd done great things with her business, but what about her personal life? Why was she half-parked on a sidewalk, staring at a billboard while on her way to Costco? Didn't she want more?

A sharp pain cut through her—two parts regret but one part intense longing for more than the nothing she'd apparently chosen. She needed friends in her life and possibly a man. While the latter seemed like more than she could comfortably take on right now, the former was doable. She was a good person. She was likable. The friend thing shouldn't be so hard.

She needed more than just work, she told herself. She needed to get out of the house and start doing things. Anything. Beginning right this second. Or possibly after she made her Costco run. But today for sure.

"What do you call a paper airplane that can't fly?"

Jana Mead was already smiling, even as she turned from her computer to the man standing just inside her office.

"I don't know," she said, appreciating the happy anticipation that accompanied Rick's unexpected visit. In the past couple of weeks, he'd stopped by a few times, always with a dad joke and an invitation to coffee or dinner or a picnic. So far she'd managed to resist saying yes to his very tempting suggestions, but even as she repeated, "What *do* you call a paper airplane that can't fly?" she felt herself weakening.

"Stationery."

She laughed. "Okay, I'm writing that one down. I may have to explain the difference between stationary and stationery to the younger ones, but my oldest niece will absolutely love the joke."

"Excellent." He stepped a little closer. "How's it going?"

"Good. Busy, as always. What about you? How many lives did you save today?"

"Just a couple."

Rick was a big-shot surgeon while she was a part-time medical billing clerk who spent her days fighting with insurance companies over coverage. Which one of these was not like the other? He was about five-ten with dark hair and eyes and an aura of quiet confidence. Fit without being too muscled, and good-looking enough to make a woman look twice.

"Impressive," she told him.

He shrugged. "It's just about the training and, you know, some skill."

"I think it's about more than that."

He shoved his hands into his front pockets and drew in a breath. "I've asked you out three times, and you've said no every time. I get it. You're not interested."

He hesitated as if unsure what to say next, which gave her time to want to pound her head against the desk, mostly because she *was* interested. Very interested. When she saw him, she got that *whooshing* sensation low in her belly—the one that made a normally sensible woman want to ignore her vow of "no guys—not now, not for the next ten years" even when she knew she couldn't afford to get involved with anyone.

There were so many reasons. She was the single mother of a precocious four-year-old, she was in the middle of her last semester at community college where the calculus class she was taking was kicking her butt, and she had this job. Dinner with a man? Who had the time?

But more significantly, she just couldn't take the risk. Since having Linnie, she'd tried hard to be careful. Sensible, even. And her last relationship had been so unbelievably bad, she'd vowed no men ever for at least a decade.

He gave her a sweet, sad smile that made her feel like she was making a horrible mistake.

"We work in the same building, so we're bound to run into each other," he continued, his expression earnest. "I don't want you to feel awkward. So I'm here to say I won't ask you out again." The smile widened a little. "But I might still tell you a joke or two."

"I'd love that," she said, trying to ignore the guilt and regret filling her.

If she was going to break her rule, this would be the guy to make her do it. She liked him. He was funny, sweet and kind. She liked how she felt when he was around. But she was stronger than his appeal. She had to be. Woman power and all that.

"Did I do it wrong?" he asked, meeting her gaze. "The way I suggested we go out. I'm only asking because I'm not good at this kind of thing." He offered her a faint smile. "I was the smartest kid in class, and you know how that goes. Then in college, I was on a scholarship, so I spent all my time studying. After that, medical school and residency. The fellowship. I never got a chance to, you know, develop those skills."

She was slime, she thought, coming to her feet. Mean-spirited girl slime. Worse, she was weakening. How was she supposed to resist all that?

"No, Rick. You were fine. I'm just not in a place where I'm comfortable dating anyone." She offered a smile. "There's nothing wrong with you. I hate to use the cliché, but in this case, it really is me, not you."

"Yeah? Did you want to reconsider? We could go on a picnic and alpaca lunch."

Despite her regret and determination, she laughed.

He held up a hand. "Kidding, by the way. Not asking you out again."

This was hard, she thought, wishing there was a third choice, but it seemed dating or not dating were the only two. If only he wasn't so…perfect. She'd always assumed surgeons were arrogant and cold, but he wasn't either.

They'd met by chance at the downstairs coffee place in their shared medical building. She'd placed her order, then had reached for her wallet, but it wasn't in her bag. Embarrassed, she'd started to cancel her order, only to have Rick—standing in line behind her—offer to pay. The clerk had taken his credit card before she could say no.

She'd found her wallet in the passenger wheel well of her car, where it had obviously slipped onto the floor. She'd carried ten dollars with her for two weeks, hoping she would see him so she could pay him back. When she had, he'd asked her to dinner, and she'd refused. But they'd kept running into each other and had even had a quick coffee a time or two. The more she got to know him, the more she liked him. If things had been different, she would have said yes in a heartbeat.

"I had a bad experience," she told him. "I'm still in the feeling burned stage. That's why I don't want to date right now."

"Whatever he did, he was a fool," Rick told her earnestly. "No guy with half a brain would walk away from you."

He hadn't walked, Jana thought grimly. She'd dumped him after he'd slapped her daughter. Four-year-old Linnie had quickly forgotten the moment, but Jana was still living with the guilt of picking such a jerk, and she hadn't been on a date since.

Rick took a step back. "I'll get out of your way. I know you're busy." He turned away, then spun back. "It's just there's something about you. It's like you glow from the inside." He shrugged. "That's all."

Then he was gone.

Jana sat back down, prepared to deal with the next insurance problem on her desk. She was the medical billing clerk for a large derm practice, and patients were forever having issues with their coverage. But her brain seemed unable to focus on her computer screen, and all she could hear was Rick saying, "You glow."

Had a man ever thought that about her before? Her last boyfriend, in addition to slapping her daughter, had seemed to be forever putting her down in little ways she hadn't noticed until she'd ended things. He would never have thought she glowed.

Rick was an age-appropriate, handsome, single guy who happened to be a gifted surgeon. He was sweet, funny and sincere, and he was obviously very interested in her. Did she think she could do better? Yes, her life was complicated, but honestly, was she really going to let him walk away?

She jumped out of her chair and raced down the hall. She spotted him waiting by the elevator. It was his day for office visits, because he was in dark pants, a tailored shirt and a tie. She'd never dated anyone who wore a tie before. She wasn't sure she'd ever dated anyone who owned one.

The elevator doors opened, and he started to step inside.

"Rick! Wait!"

He turned and saw her. In that second, his entire face lit up.

She hurried to him. "If you still want to go out with me, I'd like that."

"Yeah? You'll have dinner with me?"

She laughed. "Yes."

He pulled out his phone. "Can I get your number? Is that asking too much?"

She pulled hers from her back pocket. "It's not, and if you don't have my number, it's going to make coordinating things really complicated."

2

As Beth loaded canned beans on the shelf of the food
bank, she saw an older woman hovering by the rice and pasta.
Tentatively she reached for a box of spaghetti, only to pull her
hand back as if she were afraid of doing something wrong.

A newbie, Beth thought, her chest tightening with sympathy.
No doubt she was confused by the rules and a little ashamed to
be needing the help. Beth quickly finished with the beans and
walked over to greet the woman.

"Hi," she said cheerfully. "Can I help you?"

The other woman ducked her head. "Um, thank you. I don't
know what I'm allowed to buy." She flushed. "I shouldn't even
be here. It's just with my limited income and—"

Beth lightly touched her shoulder. "Hey, it's okay. You're welcome here. Let me explain how this works." She pointed to the red tag hanging from the woman's cart. There was a big 1 on it.

"That's your group number. Ones are generally a single person or a couple. Throughout the store, you'll see signage telling you the quantity you're allowed to take." She pointed to the sign on the shelf in front of them.

"Group one is limited to one large bag of rice and two boxes of pasta." Beth smiled at her. "We just got a huge shipment from our distributor. Take the pasta, please."

The other woman managed a faint smile in return. "It's just me at home. And my cat. I don't need very much."

"Still, we're a good resource. Stock up. I saw some lovely blackberries in the produce section. Oh, and we have cat food and litter in the pet aisle. Meat and dairy are in the back. We're low on cheese this week, but there's lots of chicken."

She looked at the woman. "It's okay to be here. No one's judging you. Honestly, I'm grateful every time I see a full cart of food. This is Malibu. No one should go hungry. We have a reputation."

"Yes, people assume we're all rich and famous."

Beth chuckled. "I don't need to be famous."

The other woman laughed. "Me, either, but I wouldn't say no to rich." She nodded. "Thank you, dear. You've made me feel better."

"Anytime. If this is going to be your regular shopping day, then you'll see me next week. I'm here from two until six."

The woman moved on, and Beth wheeled the empty boxes into the back of the store, where she quickly broke them down and put them in recycling.

She'd started volunteering at the food bank about three months ago, when her business had been closed for the remodel. She'd applied online, passed her background check and been assigned a "training buddy." She remembered how nervous she'd been during her first session. Jana had immediately put her at ease, showing her what was expected and explaining how to deal with their clients.

The work itself was fairly basic. Beth stocked shelves, swept floors and helped out customers. She worked four hours a week and always left feeling better than when she'd arrived. Something she needed today, she thought grimly. In the past twenty-four hours, her emotions had been on a roller coaster. The shock of seeing the billboard and realizing she hadn't done anything to have a personal life had quickly morphed to disbelief, then unexpected heartache, followed by an evening of binge-watching episodes of *Friends* and eating way more ice cream than was healthy. It seemed telling herself she didn't care that Ian was getting married was a whole lot easier than actually not caring. A frustrating admission because she knew her disquiet had little to do with the man himself and everything to do with what she was and wasn't doing for herself.

Her third hour into her shift, she spotted Jana loading butter into the cold case and headed over.

"Hi," she said. "Are we still on for a quick dinner?"

Jana smiled at her. "Yes, please. If you have time."

"Absolutely. See you at six."

She returned to her job, happy their plans had worked out. In the past couple of months, she and Jana had started to become friends. At first they'd chatted on their way to their cars. Then they'd started going across the street to grab a quick coffee. A couple of weeks ago, Beth had offered to bring sandwiches so they could eat on the patio in back of the food bank.

She liked Jana and, given her recent revelation about her friendless state, was hoping they could start hanging out more.

Exactly at six, she walked to her car and took out the small picnic basket she'd brought with her. She met Jana on the back patio, where they settled at a table in the shade. Spring in Los Angeles was unpredictable. It could be foggy and sixty for days at a time or unseasonably warm, as it was now. When it was eighty this close to the ocean, it would be over a hundred inland.

But here on a hill, with an in-the-distance view of the ocean, a light breeze and seagulls strutting around, hoping to get a crumb or fallen chip, it was pleasant.

"Next time I need to bring dinner," Jana told her. "It's my turn." She pressed a hand to her belly. "I missed lunch, and I'm starving."

Beth waved away her comment. "Don't be silly. I own a sandwich shop. This was easy. I pulled together a bunch of leftovers. It was nothing."

Jana watched her unload the cooler. "Your 'it was nothing' is my gourmet feast."

"Then you need to get out more," Beth teased.

Beth set out cans of flavored water, bags of chips, a couple of cookies and two wraps. "Turkey, Brie, walnuts, lettuce, cucumber salsa and a dressing that is my own recipe."

Jana groaned. "My idea of a sandwich is PB&J."

"You have a little girl. Kids like familiar food."

"Yes, and I lack culinary creativity. You're a master at what you do."

"Thanks. We actually have a PB&J menu at the shop where we do very interesting things with what should be a classic sandwich. We can grill it or add bacon or even pickles."

Jana winced. "I get the bacon, but I'm not sure how I feel about pickles in the PB&J."

"Yeah, not my favorite, either. Whenever we add menu items, we do several tastings, first with the staff, then with a few favorite and trusted customers. I'll admit there were some faces about the pickles."

Jana took a big bite of her wrap and groaned. "So good," she mumbled, still chewing.

Beth let her eat before starting a conversation. She knew that Jana had gotten up early to get her daughter ready for preschool before heading off to community college for classes. After that she would have gone directly to her part-time job. From there, she'd come to the food bank for her weekly shift.

It was a grueling schedule that should have sounded off-putting, only Beth couldn't help being a little envious. When she'd been married to Ian, having a kid hadn't seemed like a priority—there was always going to be time. But since the divorce, she'd found herself wanting a family more and more. She didn't regret not having kids with Ian, but she wished she'd had them with someone.

Unfortunately, remembering that brought yesterday's billboard encounter right to the front of her mind and made her sigh.

Jana finished the first half of her wrap and wiped her fingers. "That was perfect. Thank you. I'm less starving and can be more civilized now. What's going on with you?"

"The usual," she said automatically, before unexpectedly blurting out, "My ex-husband is getting married."

Jana drew her eyebrows together. "Does that upset you?"

"No," she said, then paused. "Yes." She shook her head. "I don't care that he's found someone. We're done. It was just the shock of how I found out and realizing he's got a personal life and I don't."

"How *did* you find out?" Jana asked. "Through mutual friends?"

"He proposed on a billboard."

Jana's surprise was almost comical. "As in 'will you marry me' up there for everyone to see?"

"I know, right? Worse, it was by the Costco. That's romantic." She considered the location. "I wonder if they met there. Then it would make sense." She waved her hand. "Whatever the reason, what matters is I wasn't expecting it, and for some reason, the information is unsettling."

"Of course it is. Whether you care about him or not, who wants to see his proposal billboard?"

"Thanks. She said yes, by the way. I saw the pictures on Instagram."

"So you're torturing yourself," Jana said lightly. "Maybe it's time to let the Instagram connection go."

"You're right. It's not I like check in on him. I was just curious this one time." She sighed. "He looks happy, and she's happy. There are pictures of his whole family. We used to be tight, back when we were married. They were nice. But it's not as if they wanted to stay in touch with me after the divorce."

She hoped she sounded matter-of-fact but had a bad feeling a note of pathetic had crept into her voice.

"I'm totally fine," she added briskly. "Things are great with me."

Jana had finished the other half of her wrap and reached for a bag of chips. "I say this with love, but that wasn't convincing. If you're totally over him, which I believe you are, then none of this is about him or the wedding. It's about you and why it's bugging you."

Beth nibbled at her wrap. "It was the shock." She hesitated. "I guess part of it was seeing him with our friends. They used to be our friends, but now they're his and, I assume, hers." Her voice trailed off.

Jana nodded. "I get it. I'm doing a thousand things all the time, and I still have moments when I feel lonely. It's a thing. My life hasn't exactly been conventional. Before I had Linnie, I moved around a lot. Since then I've been scrambling to learn how to be a mom and figure out what I want to do with my life. It doesn't leave a lot of time for me."

"You need a longer day," Beth said. "Just thinking about your schedule exhausts me."

"What about you?" Jana asked. She waved toward the food. "You're a sandwich artist, and you love what you do, but from the little you've shared with me, you don't have much of a personal life. You live with your aunt, which is nice. Multigenerational homes are the best. You hang out with your brother every couple of weeks. You volunteer here. But that's not enough. You need to have things to look forward to. Friends. Possibly a man."

Beth willed herself not to flush. If Jana, who was firmly in the new friend category, could figure all that out in a matter of seconds, how obvious were her issues? Was she secretly wearing a "pity me, I don't have a life" sign?

"You're right, of course," she murmured. "Only now I feel broken."

"Not broken. Not for either of us. Just a little misguided with our priorities. Seeing the billboard was a good thing. It allowed you to see what was bothering you in your life, and now you can fix it."

She was being so nice, Beth thought, and immediately had the strangest urge to blurt out, "Will you be my best friend?" Only she thought that might be a little scary to say *and* to hear. But she liked Jana. They'd clicked from the start and had laughed their way through her training. Beth always looked forward to their quick dinners together.

"You're right," she said. "I need to make changes. The food bank is a start. I really like working here. It's satisfying."

"I agree. So, next up would be what? Dating?"

"I'm not the dating type."

The response was automatic, mostly because she couldn't imagine going out with someone—only where was that coming from? Why shouldn't she be happy with someone? Her marriage to Ian had failed, but that was about them, not the institution. There were aspects to being married she'd really liked. Despite how she was currently living her life, she wasn't by nature a solitary person.

"I don't believe you." Jana studied her. "You're attractive, successful, smart and what? Thirty-five?"

"Thirty-eight, and I'm not smart. I could never do what you're doing."

"Medical billing? Yeah, you could. You're an entrepreneur, so I'm not sure you'd want to, but you could."

Despite her unease, Beth grinned. "No, go to college. I thought I would, a long time ago, but I'm not college material."

Jana frowned. "Why would you say that? You run a business. The day I met you, you'd just finished a class to learn the new software system you were having installed. People you'd met there were texting you, asking you questions, and you weren't the instructor."

"I understood it more easily than some of the other people. The program is very close to the one I had before. I didn't have their steep learning curve."

Jana finished her chips. "I remain unconvinced. Whoever said you weren't smart was wrong, and you need to get that voice out of your head."

Beth responded with a smile, thinking that particular voice had only told her the truth to spare her pain. Rick had always looked out for her. He was three years her junior, and practically a genius. When they'd been younger, he'd been the one to help her with her homework. In fourth grade, he'd understood her middle school math better than she had. When she'd asked him about going to college, he'd gently pointed out there was no way she could make it. A good thing, because she loved owning the sandwich shop.

Thinking that reminded her of why she was upset. "You're right about me not having something to look forward to," she said slowly. "Emotionally, I've moved on from the divorce, but him getting married is a tangible demonstration of how over us he is. I guess I need something similar."

"Without the billboard proposal?" Jana asked, wrinkling her nose. "I don't want to judge."

Beth laughed. "And yet you are. Don't worry. I'm judging, too." She lowered her voice. "It was right next to an ad for a personal injury attorney. Really? You know they came by later and took pictures. They're going to have to edit them for sure."

Jana grinned at her. "I kind of like your style." She leaned forward. "Okay, just say the first thing that pops into your head. What have you always wanted to do but never let yourself?"

"Learn to ride a horse."

Beth had no idea where the unexpected statement had come from, and she immediately tried to call it back. "No, that's silly. There's no purpose in horseback riding."

"So? It sounds like fun. Why haven't you done it before?"

An interesting question. Beth considered her answer. "I wanted to when I was a kid, but Mom never believed in doing normal things. She would have wanted me to learn bull riding instead. When I was an adult, there didn't seem to be time or money. Once Ian and I were married, I guess I forgot I wanted to learn." She paused. "I really don't have an answer."

"Maybe it's something you should consider doing just for you."

"Maybe." Beth wasn't sure she ever did anything just for herself.

"Was the divorce bad?" Jana asked. "I know sometimes they can be really hard to get through."

Beth shook her head. "No. We were both reasonable." She hesitated, not sure if she should say more. Except for her aunt, no one knew what had really happened at the end of her marriage.

"You don't have to talk about it if you don't want to," Jana told her. "I wasn't trying to pry."

"Oh, I know that. It's not you. I guess sometimes it's hard for me to share personal stuff." But she found herself wanting Jana to know. "It wasn't the divorce itself that hurt so much. It was how we got to that place. Ian came to me and said he wasn't happy. He didn't know if he wanted to try to fix things or not. I had no idea he wasn't okay with us, so I was in shock." She shook her head. "Actually, I was scared. I didn't want to lose him or us. I liked being married to him."

"I'm sorry. What happened?"

"We agreed to do all the things. Counseling, long walks on the beach, writing in a gratitude journal." She opened her bag of chips, but didn't eat any as she remembered how she'd thrown herself into connecting with her husband.

"It was a tough couple of months, but I knew it would be worth it. We started having more sex and laughing together. It was working, or so I thought."

Jana groaned. "Oh, no! He didn't agree with you?"

"Nope. We met with our counselor to assess where we were. I went on and on about how wonderful everything was and how I was so much more in love with Ian than I'd ever been." She drew in a breath and ignored the sense of having been a fool. "He said he hadn't changed his mind. He was still unhappy, and he wanted a divorce. I moved out two days later."

"I'm so sorry. No wonder his getting married is bothering you. How dare he be happy!"

Beth managed a smile. "I'm over him. It took a while. The remodel helped by being a really big distraction." One she'd been grateful for. "I don't think about him or us or want to go back." She thought about what her friend had said. "But you're right. I haven't made much of a life for myself. Seeing the billboard was a wake-up call. I've made good changes in my business. Now it's time to make a few changes for myself."

"Absolutely." Jana raised her can of flavored sparkling water, and they toasted. "Good for you. Think about the horse thing. Oh, and the next time a hunky guy asks you out, say yes."

"There aren't any hunky guys hanging around. But should one appear, I'll consider it." She smiled. "Okay, enough about my drama. How are you doing?"

Jana pressed her hands to her chest. "I'm loving Dex Thursday."

"Excuse me? What's a Dex Thursday?"

Jana laughed. "That's right. You don't know about my odd

little family. Dex is my brother Teddy's best friend. They've been finishing each other's sentences since they were nine. Dex had some issues with his folks, so he moved in with us." She frowned slightly. "I guess he was maybe fourteen when that happened. Anyway, he's like another brother to me, and he's an uncle to my brother's kids and to Linnie."

She took a bite of her cookie. "A few months after Teddy lost his wife, Dex started taking his kids to hang out at his place on Thursday nights. They order in and watch movies. It became a thing. Well, Linnie's been seeing this and begging to go, but I thought she was too young. When she turned four, she announced she was more than ready to be with her cousins. Dex agreed, and now we have Dex Thursdays. He picks Linnie up from preschool, gets Teddy's kids and does his thing."

She glanced at her watch. "He has them home by seven thirty."

Beth stared at her. "Wait a minute. You're saying Thursday afternoon is the only day of the week you don't have your daughter, and you're using your free time to volunteer at the food bank?"

Jana looked surprised by the question. "I was volunteering before, but I had to arrange for childcare. This makes it easier."

"You're a better person than I am," Beth murmured.

"Hardly. I have to volunteer. It's kind of in my blood. My parents are currently in Africa with their church, building a school. It's how Teddy and I were raised." Jana waved her hand. "You're making it more than it is. Besides, you're a giver, too."

"I volunteer four hours a week, and I've only been doing it a couple of months. That hardly makes me a giver."

"No way. I don't agree." Jana's voice was firm. "You brought me dinner. A couple of weeks ago, I mentioned how I went directly from my last class to my job and there wasn't ever time to get lunch. You instantly wanted to feed me. You're very much a giver—you simply show it differently."

Beth squirmed at the praise. "It was a sandwich."

"Technically, I believe it was a wrap, and it was delicious. You saw someone in need and you responded. You should give yourself a little credit."

"Not something I'm comfortable doing," she said before she could stop herself. "And here we are talking about me again. Your turn for a little psychoanalysis. Why do you deflect the conversation from yourself?"

She asked the question lightly, as much to tease as to seek information. She liked Jana and wanted to get to know her better.

"I'm a single mom who's working part-time and going to college. I spend every second of every day scrambling. I find your life calm and serene." Jana laughed. "Something I can only aspire to."

Calm and serene? Did she really mean boring? Because that was how Beth was starting to feel about herself.

"Calm is overrated. Embrace the chaos."

"I'm trying." Jana drew in a breath. "Okay, I'm just going to say it. I haven't told anyone yet, and I don't know how I feel about it."

Beth leaned forward. "Now I'm intrigued."

"A guy at work asked me out, and I said yes." Jana shook her head. "I don't date. I had a really horrible breakup about a year ago. It was shattering. Before that, I was dealing with being a new mom and figuring that out. I want to do the right thing for my daughter. I want to be strong and a role model."

Beth didn't understand. "Why would you worry about that? Look at all that you're doing. You're admirable."

"I'm not. I've screwed up a bunch. In the past—with guys. In high school, my teachers begged me to consider college. They wanted to help me get into a really great school, but I said no. I wanted to take a different path. So here I am, pushing thirty, living with my brother, working part-time, dealing with classes and my four-year-old. Sometimes I think I've done it all wrong."

"You haven't. I'll remind you, I'm living with my aunt. And hey, you said multigenerational households were the best."

"I was trying to make myself feel better."

Beth had to admit she was a little relieved to find out Jana wasn't perfect, but she didn't like her friend having doubts.

"You deserve a little fun in your life. If you like the guy, go for it." She paused. "By that I mean go out on the date. Not, you know, *go for it* in any other sense."

Jana grinned. "You mean no sex on the first date? I agree."

"You said you work with him? Is dating allowed?" Beth didn't know the ins and outs of corporate policy when it came to dating, and she'd never had to deal with an interoffice romance at Surf Sandwiches.

"Oh, it's not that. The derm office is in a medical building. The guy isn't from the practice. He works in another one." Her smile softened. "He's sweet and funny. Very attractive. I told myself not to give in, but he said he thought I glowed."

Beth felt a whisper of envy way deep down in her gut. No man had ever said that about her. "You absolutely have to go out with him."

"That's what I thought." The smile returned. "He wears a suit. I've never dated a man who even owns a suit."

"Ah, so he's successful."

"Very," Jana said, her voice teasing. "Hmm, maybe I should embrace the whole 'when in doubt, marry money' thing."

Beth grinned as she raised her can of sparkling water. "Absolutely. To the rich guy. May he fall madly in love with you."

3

Jana pulled into the wide driveway in front of her brother's one-story ranch-style house. The big rambler sat on an oversize corner lot. After moving in right before their oldest was born, Teddy and his late wife had built a separate office and treatment room for Teddy's business.

There was no ocean view in this residential part of Malibu, no movie stars or paparazzi. Just older homes with plenty of bikes and toys scattered in the front yards. Teddy's house had been built in the 1970s. The inside had been mostly updated, but the high beamed ceilings and layout were a reminder of another time.

Jana pulled into the large garage, careful to keep to her side. Her small SUV fit in easily, but Teddy's classic Corvette had a special place in his heart, and she didn't want to get too close and risk a door ding. Her brother parked his Suburban outside.

She went into the house, pausing for a moment to embrace the silence. It was far from the norm, and just for a second or two, it was lovely to hear…or not hear. A quick glance at her watch told her she had about twenty-five minutes until Dex returned with all four kids. As soon as that happened, the decibels would hit jet-engine level, but until then, she would take advantage of the quiet.

She turned left, past the living room and kitchen. Beyond them was the large family room, and just past that was the "guest" wing she and Linnie called home. Two bedrooms shared a good-sized bathroom. In the hallway was a small alcove with a built-in desk where Jana did her homework.

She sat and pulled her laptop from her backpack. She wanted to double-check her grade on the last calculus homework assignment. If she had the B she'd hoped for, she would have a bit of a buffer going into the next few weeks.

She logged into the community college and quickly accessed her grades from calculus, then smiled when she saw the B+ by her most recent assignment. Thank goodness. She'd gotten a D on her first homework assignment—a grade she'd never seen before and one that had caused her to start visiting the math lab. Calculus was the toughest class she'd ever taken, but she was determined to do well. If she was accepted to the UCLA nursing school, her acceptance would be conditional. She would be expected to keep up her grades during her last semester at community college, and that meant passing both her classes with at least a B−.

After backing up her notes, she closed her laptop, then looked at the paper academic calendar she'd pinned to the wall. She had her calculus test next Tuesday. Her second paper in her sociology class was due on Thursday, but she was nearly finished with that. She pulled out a pad and paper, trying to calculate how much time she could spend studying for her test between now and Tuesday morning. Magnolia, Teddy's oldest, had offered to watch Linnie for a few hours Saturday afternoon, and Teddy was taking all four kids Sunday morning. She would have a couple of hours after Linnie went to bed—at least until she got too tired to focus. Although not Saturday night.

She put down her pen. Saturday she had her date with Rick. As she thought about him, she realized she was equally excited and nervous about going out with him. Some of it was her lack of a romantic life for the past year, and some of it was how… genuine he was. Plus the whole thinking she glowed.

Before she could revel in that memory, she heard the front door slam against the doorstop and the sound of her name being called. Linnie's voice was the loudest as she raced into the house.

"Mommy! Mommy! Where are you?"

Jana grinned as she hurried to the front of the house. Linnie spotted her and ran toward her. At the last second, she launched herself. Jana caught her and spun her around.

"You're back!" she said as she set down her daughter. "How was it?"

"I had the bestest time." Her daughter danced with excitement. "We ate dim sum, which I didn't think I'd had before, but it was very good." She paused, her green eyes widening with the thrill of it all. "You eat it with your hands and there's dips and we made a mess but Dex didn't care."

Jana sank onto the floor and pulled her daughter into her lap as Teddy's three swarmed around her. Each of them talked over the other, telling her about the dinner, the movie and the games they'd played in Dex's spacious house.

The man of the hour wandered in before leaning against the wall, watching her with the kids. Despite having just spent several hours babysitting all four of them, he looked as relaxed and comfortable as always.

"How do you do it?" she asked. "You're never frazzled."

"It's a state of being," he said with a familiar grin. "One of my many gifts."

"Thanks for taking Linnie."

One shoulder rose and lowered. "Three kids, four kids—what does it matter?" He winked at Magnolia, Teddy's oldest. "Besides, I had that one to keep everyone in line."

"Magnolia's bossy," middle child and only boy Atlas announced loudly.

Magnolia glared at him. "Am not. I'm the oldest, so I know things, and it's my job to tell you younger kids what to do."

"A job you take a little too seriously," Jana said, careful to keep her voice teasing and gentle.

The truth was, the twelve-year-old had stepped into the role of surrogate mother after her own mom had died. Something Jana and her brother talked about a lot. They did their best to keep Magnolia from feeling there were expectations, but before they realized what was happening, she would slip back into "I'm the leader" mode.

"All right, everyone," Jana said, coming to her feet and drawing Linnie up with her. "Is our homework finished?"

Orchid, the baby of Teddy's family, sidled up to Dex and gave him a sweet smile. "I don't have homework."

"I know." He ruffled her hair. "Lucky you."

"I only had reading." Atlas started for the family room. "I finished it at Dex's."

"I'm done, too," Magnolia added.

Linnie tugged on Jana's hand. "I want homework."

"Soon. When you're in school." She paused. "Okay, maybe not in kindergarten or first grade."

"But that's so long to wait." Linnie's full mouth twisted. "It's hard being the youngest."

"I know, sweetie. But you're growing up so fast. I wish you'd slow down."

Linnie giggled and followed her cousins into the family room, walking with exaggeratedly measured movements. Jana watched her go, for the millionth time wondering about her daughter's bright red hair. Where on earth had it come from? Not that she had an answer to the question.

Dex pushed off the wall. "You okay?"

"I'm great. Tired. Overwhelmed, but that's not unusual." She walked toward him. "I know you said it was nothing, but I really appreciate you including Linnie. She was thrilled to finally be joining her cousins."

"She was great. If she wants to keep coming along, she's welcome."

"Thank you."

He studied her, frowning slightly—the movement of his brows only adding to his spectacular good looks. "You hear from UCLA?"

"Not yet." She held up crossed fingers. "Hopefully soon and with good news."

"You'll get in."

"Maybe. I want to." UCLA's School of Nursing was her first choice. "Assuming it's a yes, I'll also be hearing about the financial aid package, and—"

She stopped talking when she saw Dex's expression change.

"No," she said sharply. "Just no."

"I want to help."

"You do. You're a wonderful friend and member of this family, but you're not paying for nursing school. Dex, come on. We had this fight already when I started community college. I want to do this on my own. I'm not taking money from Teddy, and I'm not taking it from you."

"I can afford it."

"Yes. You could also buy Rhode Island. So what? It's not relevant. I already feel bad about living with my brother."

The frown returned. "Why? He likes you here. When Valonia died, having you move in was about all that kept him together."

Jana remembered how rough things had been back then.

Teddy's wife's death had been a shock to everyone. One second she'd been fine and the next, she'd been gone.

"You helped him hang on, too," she said. Dex had been a rock for all of them. He'd been the one to handle the funeral arrangements and had kept their lives running while they all grieved.

"We still miss her," she added. "But the kids are doing great, and Teddy's figuring out life without her."

"It's been over four years, and your brother won't even talk about dating. I'd say he has a ways to go until we can say he's figuring out life." He pointed at her. "Speaking of which, isn't it time you started having a social life?"

Her reply was automatic. "Given what happened last time I had a boyfriend, no."

"It wasn't your fault."

Her heart knew he was telling the truth, but her head and her gut still thought she'd been an idiot. The problem was she couldn't figure out what she could have done differently.

She'd been so careful, taking things slow with Paul. She'd liked how he'd been involved with his kids and had shared custody with his ex-wife. It had taken her a few months to notice how "involved" really meant controlling.

"I was dating a guy who practically turned into a stalker and then slapped my kid," she said flatly. "Hardly a testament to my good taste in men."

"He wasn't who you thought."

"An understatement for sure." She shook her head. "There were warning signs, and I ignored them. I won't do that again. If I decide to date someone, I'm going to be sure about his character."

"An excellent plan," he said, his smile easy. "But before you can put it into action, you have to start dating. The next time a guy asks you out, say yes. It'll be good for you."

Her eyes widened as she suddenly remembered she'd done just that. "Too late. I already did."

"You met someone?" He sounded more curious than concerned. "Spill."

She quickly explained about Rick, the unexpectedly sweet and skilled surgeon.

"He was just so nice. Really genuine, you know." She bit her lower lip. "I want to say he's different from Paul and that I'll be safe this time. I like him enough to take a chance, but in the back of my mind, I can't help wondering if there's something wrong with him I can't see. Which is my past talking, right?"

"Of course it is. Don't go looking for trouble. It's one date. He's taking you to dinner, right?"

She nodded.

"At worst, you'll get a good meal out of it. At best, maybe he's the one."

"You know I don't believe in the one, at least not for me." Teddy was different. She'd seen how he had loved Valonia. Theirs had been a true grand passion. "I don't have the Mr. Right genes or whatever," she added. "But maybe a nice guy hanging around wouldn't be so bad."

He stepped toward her, gave her a brief hug, then kissed the top of her head. "You go, girl."

Beth poured herself coffee and looked out the kitchen window. It was still dark with only the faintest hint of light coming from the eastern sky. For reasons not clear to her, she'd had a restless night and was up way too early. On the bright side, that circumstance meant there was plenty of time for a second cup of coffee when she finished her first one.

She'd barely settled at the table when her aunt breezed in and smiled at her.

"Good morning, darling. How are you today?"

"Good. And you?"

"Excellent."

Agatha was about Beth's height with the same dark hair both

Beth and Rick shared, although hers was shoulder-length and a pretty combination of curly and wavy.

"No Hunter this morning?" Beth asked when her aunt sat across from her.

"We're no longer together."

"Why? I thought you liked him."

Agatha stirred in milk, then added sugar before tasting her coffee. "He was getting a little too comfortable with how things were. I'd made it clear I wasn't looking for anything serious." Her gaze met Beth's. "I loved your uncle for thirty-five years, and when he died, I was devastated. I know what a good marriage can be. Some people want to repeat that, but I'm interested in trying something different. I want to play the field."

Beth was both amused and impressed. "You wanted sex and Hunter wanted to cuddle?"

Her aunt chuckled. "Something like that. It's for the best. He was talking about us moving in together, which is not happening. Worse, he said something about checking out a few retirement communities." She shuddered. "I'm far too young for that." She gave a little sigh. "But I will miss the sex."

"You'll find someone else soon enough," Beth told her. "Maybe a younger man would be more interesting."

Agatha's brown eyes danced with amusement. "I do like the looks of the guy who takes care of the yard. I wonder if he's seeing anyone."

"I have no idea," Beth murmured, hoping her aunt wasn't serious. No way their lawn guy was over twenty-five.

Agatha drew in a breath. "How are you doing? Better today? Or does the Ian situation still bother you?"

"I don't care that he's getting married, and while the billboard isn't my style, hopefully Patti was thrilled by it."

"It defines tacky," her aunt said, wrinkling her nose. "Asking someone to spend the rest of her life with you should be a private moment, not plastered up on a billboard, half a block from Costco." She paused. "Not that I don't love a big-box store."

Beth grinned. "We all do."

Her aunt nodded. "Now back to my question. How are you feeling?"

"Lost," she said without thinking. "Confused. It's been a year since the divorce, and I haven't done anything to have a personal life."

Agatha touched her hand. "You're lonely. I'm here for you always, but you need more than that. Friends your own age, a man or two."

Despite the emotions swirling inside of her, Beth smiled. "Definitely not two men. Unlike you, I'm not interested in playing the field."

Her aunt raised her eyebrows. "So you'd like to be in a relationship. Intriguing. Last time we talked about your love life, you weren't interested."

"Last time I hadn't scrolled through Ian's Instagram account and been slapped by the realization that I'm drifting through my days rather than being proactive. I want to do things and travel. I didn't just lose Ian in the divorce. I lost myself. I don't regret the end of our marriage, but what about me? Why have I let it be okay to not take care of myself emotionally?"

"When you knew better, you did better," Agatha told her.

"One of my favorite quotes."

"I know. I'm glad you're starting to think about what you want. It's important. I was devastated when I lost your uncle, but after a few months, I realized I had a choice to make. I could get lost in grief, or I could get on with my life. It wasn't easy to move forward, but I'm proud of the progress I've made."

She picked up her coffee. "You're a wonderful, caring woman, Beth. I hate how much the divorce surprised and hurt you, but I'm not sure Ian was ever the right man for you. He was content to do the same thing over and over again. That's not you.

You're always one to try something different. You could have taken the money from your half of the house and put it into your retirement account. That would have been the safer bet. But you didn't. You grew the business, and now it's more successful than ever. If I had to guess, I would say Ian would never have approved of that."

"You're right. He wouldn't have approved at all." She looked at her aunt. "I was in love with him, and he didn't want to be married to me anymore. Sometimes that's hard to process."

"I know. It's not fair. It never was." Her aunt studied her. "Do you think you still have feelings for him?"

"No." Beth didn't have to think about that one. "Like I said, I don't want him back. But I do want something more than what I have. I want friends."

"You've mentioned meeting someone at the food bank."

"Jana. I think we could get closer. She's busy, but we get along, and I admire her."

"An excellent start. Are you also going to look for a man?"

A more complicated question. "Maybe. I haven't dated in years. I wouldn't know where to start. It's not like there's a store I can go to and window shop."

"It's called a dating app, my dear. There are several to choose from."

Beth tried not to wince. "I'm not the online dating type."

"You don't actually know that. Maybe give it a try before saying it's not for you."

"I'd rather have a root canal."

Agatha laughed. "All right. Be that way. But if you won't go online, then you need to start looking for single men in your regular life. The next time a cute guy walks into the sandwich shop, flirt with him. Even if a relationship doesn't happen, maybe you can use him for hot, incredible sex. Wouldn't it be nice to have a sizzling affair to clear your mind and give you perspective?"

The outrageous suggestion made Beth laugh. "I wish, but I don't think I'm the sizzling affair type."

"I don't think you know if you are or not. You spent your early twenties helping your brother financially as he got through medical school and residency. Then you dated for a couple of years before finding Ian. To the best of my knowledge, you haven't ever had a relationship that was totally based on sex. Why not try it now?"

Was Agatha serious? "I wouldn't know how. Plus, you have to be, I don't know, exotic or outgoing to do that."

"Says who? Where are these rules coming from? You're still young, Beth. Live a little. Take a chance." Her aunt smiled. "Dance around the fire."

She knew the urging came from love and concern, but the words were a little too close to what her mother used to tell her, Beth thought uneasily. Agatha's younger sister had wanted to experience all there was, and the more precarious the situation, the better. She believed in risking it all, and had told her kids to be more like her. She wanted them to run toward danger and go out in a blaze of glory. What she'd failed to notice was that the collateral damage of her lifestyle had frequently been her two children.

"I'm not interested in any kind of flames," Beth said flatly. "Real or metaphorical."

"If you say so, my dear, but when it comes to a fiery affair, you're missing out." She softened her words with a pat on Beth's hand. "Trust me on that."

"Changing the subject," Beth said, "I'm going to have dinner with Rick tonight. Want to join me?"

"Are you having dinner with him or cooking for him and stocking his refrigerator?"

Beth tried to ignore the instant flash of guilt. Rick was one of the few things she and her aunt disagreed on. Oh, Agatha loved her nephew, but she thought Beth spent too much time taking care of him.

"I'm not stocking his refrigerator," she said, trying to smile. "I'm taking over chili. That's all."

"You do know he's perfectly capable of taking care of himself, don't you?"

"He's busy."

"So are you."

"He's busy saving lives. I own a sandwich shop."

"Your life is no less valuable." Agatha stopped herself and held up her hand. "Sorry. I'm starting to push, and I said I wouldn't. Sometimes I worry Rick takes advantage of you."

"What? No. We take care of each other." Agatha couldn't be more wrong. "I like helping him out. I'm the older sister. It's a thing. Besides, I worry about him. I wish he could find somebody and fall in love. He needs that in his life." She sighed. "He's just had such a string of romantic disasters. Remember that art major in college who nearly convinced him to give her his scholarship money? Or the woman from a couple of years ago who told him she was having his baby when she wasn't even pregnant?"

Poor Rick. He just couldn't seem to find anyone nice and normal to date.

"He's lucky he has you to be there for him," Agatha said lightly. "Have a wonderful time tonight and say hi from me."

"I will."

Kai carried the full Crock-Pot from the sandwich shop
kitchen to Beth's small SUV. She opened the passenger door, and
he placed the pot on the floor.

"Be careful going around corners," he told her. "No hot rod-
ding like you usually do."

Beth laughed. "Right. That's me. Taking the curves at ninety."
She glanced in the back seat and confirmed she had everything
she wanted to take to her brother's. She did her best to have dinner with Rick at least once a month, his schedule permitting.

She smiled at Kai. "I left you some chili in the refrigerator."

His dark eyes brightened. "For real? Sweet! Thanks, Beth. You
know I love me some chili, especially yours." He glanced at the
Crock-Pot. "If it's not too much work to make, we could offer

chili here at the shop. Maybe make it a special on Wednesdays or something."

"We're a sandwich shop. That's our sweet spot." She wrinkled her nose. "Besides, my chili isn't that special."

"You're wrong, Boss. Don't doubt yourself. You have mad skills. Your chili is delicious. Besides, people like variety. What if we got those small sourdough loaves and put the chili in there? I know the surfers would totally be into something that filling."

Chili? She wasn't sure, although he was doing a good job at selling her. "I'm still not sure my chili is good enough, but I get your point." Expanding the menu was always a risk, but once it was made, the chili wouldn't be labor-intensive to serve. If they offered a vegetarian option, that would certainly please their demographic.

"Let me run some numbers. If they work out, we could do some taste tests."

"All right." He held up his hand for a high five. "When the right wave comes, you gotta take it and ride it to the end or you risk being pulled under."

"Or you can ignore it and take the next one."

He grinned. "Naw. Take the wave. The right one doesn't come around all that often."

As she drove to Rick's, she mulled over Kai's advice. To be honest, she wasn't a "take the wave" kind of person. She was more cautious and thoughtful—mostly because of her mother. Growing up, she'd watched their mom, Caryn, take all kinds of risks. One time they'd driven out to the desert to go on a hot-air balloon. The winds had come up as a storm threatened, causing the operator to want to postpone the trip. But Caryn had pleaded with the man, lying that it was Rick's birthday and that he'd been begging for the trip. In truth, both she and Rick had been terrified, but their fear had never stopped their mom from doing anything.

Five minutes into the horrifying journey, a gust of wind had sent them off course, and they'd nearly collided with power lines. The operator had tried to get them down safely, but they'd ended up crashing onto the interstate and causing a three-car pileup. The operator had been charged, and their mom had barely talked her way out of also spending some time in jail. Only her sobs about being a single mother had saved her.

Agatha was so normal in comparison, Beth thought as she waited at a light. So where had her mother's brand of thrill-seeker come from? Regardless, Caryn's constant search for dangerous excitement was one of the reasons Beth preferred stable and calm. Oh, and predictable. She wasn't interested in fire or waves or taking chances. She never had been.

She pulled into visitor parking at her brother's ocean view condo. The building sat right on the beach, which meant it had been pricey, but oh, so worth it. Impulsively, she pulled her phone from her bag, stepped out and snapped a picture. She texted it to Jana with a text saying, Current view!

Three dots appeared. Then she saw the return text was a motivational poster of a surfer, pointing at her. Underneath it said, Seize the day...but wear sunblock.

Beth laughed before dropping her phone back into her bag and setting her tote on her shoulder. Then she picked up the hefty Crock-Pot. After Rick buzzed her in, she managed to maneuver her way through the heavy glass door and walked to the elevator. When she got to his unit, the front door was partially open. She pushed her way inside and saw her brother on his cell phone.

"Hi," she said quietly.

He smiled before crossing to give her a one-armed hug and a kiss on the top of the head before retreating to his bedroom, where he shut the door.

Beth set the Crock-Pot on the kitchen counter and dropped the tote next to it before glancing toward the shut door. No doubt he was on with his medical office, the hospital or a patient. Her brother worked too hard, but that was because he was dedicated to his patients. She could only hope that nothing bad was happening with any of them.

She unpacked the fixings for the salad she would assemble to go with their chili, then put the three casseroles she'd made into the fridge. She'd just plugged in the Crock-Pot to keep the chili warm when her brother walked back into the living room.

"Hey," he said with a smile as he crossed to her and gave her another hug. "Sorry about that. I was on with the hospital. One of my patients isn't doing well, and we were discussing possible treatments."

"I'm sorry," she said sympathetically. "Will you have to go back to the hospital?"

"I don't know yet. If things don't get better, I will."

"One of these days you're going to tell me you're on the phone with a woman."

He grinned. "I want that, too." He pointed at the Crock-Pot. "What's for dinner?"

"Chili. I made extra. I thought we'd freeze the leftovers. You should get at least four more meals from the batch. There are three casseroles in the fridge. You know what to do with those."

He studied her for a second. "You always take care of me."

"Of course." She shrugged. "You're my baby brother. What else would I do?"

"I'm less of a baby now."

She had to agree. He was nearly six inches taller than her, with broad shoulders and plenty of muscle. But the need to protect, to be responsible for him, had never gone away.

He grabbed a couple of bottles of iced tea from the refrigerator, and together they walked to the living room to catch up before dinner. He didn't offer her a cocktail or wine. Rick never drank when he was on call.

They took their familiar places—her on the sofa, him in one of the oversize chairs. The space was open, with high ceilings and a view of the Pacific Ocean. The condo had been expensive—certainly more than she could ever afford—but when she'd seen the listing, she'd known it would be perfect for him. He'd protested spending so much, but she'd talked him into it. Rick worked so hard. He deserved a great place.

She liked to think that she had, in her own small way, been a piece of his success. When Rick had gotten into medical school, they'd both been daunted by the cost. Yes, he could easily take out loans, but they would have left him a hundred thousand dollars in debt. Her Uncle Dale, Agatha's late husband, had offered an alternative. If Beth would buy the sandwich shop, then Dale would give Rick fifty thousand dollars.

She'd been saving for culinary school—it had been her dream since she and her brother had come to live with their aunt and uncle. While she'd enjoyed working in the sandwich shop, she'd never thought about staying...until Dale had made his offer.

She'd barely taken two days to decide to buy the business. After all, she would only have been a chef at the end of her training, and the world hardly needed more of those. Her brother was going to save lives. Now, all these years later, she knew she'd made the right decision. She loved her business and couldn't imagine doing anything different. Just as important, Rick was exactly where he was supposed to be.

"What are you thinking?" he asked.

"I was just remembering when you got into medical school. We were all so proud."

He gave her an easy smile. "I was mostly terrified. What if I wasn't the smartest one in class anymore?"

"Plus the cost."

His expression turned momentarily quizzical. "Right. That. Uncle Dale came through for me. And then I got a grant to pay for the rest of it."

"A lucky break." In the end, Rick had graduated without any debt. She sipped her iced tea. "I just wish you'd find someone."

"There's a change in subject."

"Not really. I was thinking about how great the condo is and how you're happy at work. All that's left is a personal life. You need to start putting yourself out there. You're a great guy with a lot to offer."

"You're my sister. You have to say that." He shifted in his chair. "It's not that easy for me. I never know what to say."

"Start with hi."

He raised his eyebrows. "You haven't been on a date since you and Ian split. I'm not sure you're the one I should be taking dating advice from."

"Fine," she said with a groan. "But take advice from someone. I need nieces and nephews in my life."

Her phone buzzed. She pulled it out of her pocket and glanced at the screen, then frowned at the text.

Just saying hi and letting you know we're still interested in having you join our mentor program. Could we get lunch?

"What?" her brother asked. "Something with Agatha?"

"No." She waved her phone. "A few weeks ago, I went to a meeting for women small business owners—just to network and maybe learn a few things. While I was there, a woman approached me and asked me about being a mentor."

He stared at her in surprise. "Who would you mentor?" Before she could protest the question, he nodded. "Oh, wait. Right. Other small business owners. Makes sense that you all network. You should do it."

"I don't know that I have much to offer."

"Don't say that. You're doing good, Beth. I was worried when you bought the business. I thought it might be too much for you, but you're thriving."

"Thanks," she murmured, wondering what he'd been worried about before. She might not be college material, but she was a successful small business owner. Although when she'd first bought the business, she'd mostly been scared, so maybe he had a point.

She rose. "Come on. You can set the table while I make the salad."

They walked into the kitchen, then took turns washing their hands. While Rick dried his, Beth reached out and lightly touched the small scar on his cheek. It had faded with time and was barely noticeable, but she still remembered how raw and jagged it had been the night he'd gotten cut.

She'd been thirteen, and he'd only been ten and small for his age. Their mother's boyfriend at the time had been home alone with them. He'd gotten drunk and had come into Beth's small room, talking about how pretty she was and how there were things he was going to teach her. She hadn't known exactly what the guy had been talking about, but she'd been scared in a way she'd never been before.

He'd reached for her, shoving her up against the wall as he pressed his hands between her legs. She'd struggled to get away, screaming for him to stop. Rick had come running.

Her small, bookish brother had gone after the guy, trying to pull him away from Beth. The boyfriend had turned on Rick, which had been terrifying enough, but then he'd pulled out a knife and had cut him on the face. Blood had spurted everywhere. Beth's and her brother's screams had caused the neighbors to start pounding on their apartment door. The boyfriend had fled. Someone had taken them to the ER, where Rick had been stitched up and she'd been questioned by a very kind social worker.

"You're the best brother ever," she said quietly.

"You're the best sister."

They'd always been there for each other, she thought. Theirs was a bond that could never be broken.

Jana refused to let herself change more than twice before her date with Rick, but she really didn't know what to wear. She took a quick selfie and texted it to Beth.

Does this look like I'm trying too hard?

Beth answered immediately. What does that mean? Are we not supposed to try? Why do we put so much pressure on ourselves? I doubt he's sweating what he's wearing. I know it's a girl thing and I'm sorry you're dealing with it. Oh, and no, BTW. You look amazing. That's the one.

Rant much? Jana sent a smiling emoji so Beth would know she was kidding.

You're right. That was a tear, huh? Wear the dress. You look fab.

Thanks. What are you up to tonight?

Three dots appeared followed by a picture of a white crocheted bikini top with a happy face on each triangle.

Jana frowned. That's very random.

My aunt makes custom crocheted bikinis, which are apparently a thing. I didn't know. She has a date, so I said I'd wait for her customer.

She inserted the sigh emoji.

I absolutely have to get a life.

What's on the bottom?

Not much.

Another picture came through—this one of an unlined crocheted thong bikini bottom.

Jana winced. Not for me.

Me, either. LMK how it goes tonight.

Promise.

Jana dropped her phone on the bed and looked at herself in the mirror. She was wearing this dress and that was the end of it. She would accept being nervous, but there was no way she was going to slip into obsessing about her wardrobe. After all, they were going out for the first time. Odds were nothing would come of it.

Thirty minutes before they were to meet, she kissed Linnie goodbye, told her brother she wouldn't be late and left. Rick had offered to pick her up, but she'd wanted to drive to the restaurant herself. Having him at the house would require more explanations than she was willing to make, what with the whole "it's only a first date" thing. She didn't want a lot of speculation or conversation until she knew a little bit more than he was a sweet man who thought she glowed.

The drive to the restaurant wasn't too bad, considering it was a Saturday night and she was heading for Moonshadows, one of the most popular restaurants in Malibu. She felt grown-up and sophisticated, in a slightly nervous, I-hope-I'm-not-wrong-about-this-guy kind of way. After all, tonight was a far cry from her usual weekend nights spent with her daughter, brother and his kids where they ordered takeout and watched cartoons. Even if the date was a bust, she was going to have some delicious seafood and possibly a glass of white wine.

She handed over her keys to the valet and walked into the restaurant. It was right on the water, and the view was incredible. The ocean stretched on to the horizon, reflecting all the pinks and yellows from the nearly set sun. She paused to enjoy the show, thinking how beautiful the world could be and how lucky she was to get to experience it.

"Jana!"

She turned and saw Rick walking toward her. His smile was happy as he stopped in front of her.

"You're here."

"I am. The sunset is so beautiful."

"So are you."

She laughed. "Thank you. And you look nice, as well."

He wore one of his suits—a bit fancy for the Malibu beach vibe, but it worked for him. Rick didn't strike her as a casual kind of person.

"Our table's ready," he said, "if you'd like to be seated."

"I would. I'm impressed you were able to get a reservation here on such short notice."

He winked at her. "I know a guy. Actually, I know the brother of a guy. A former patient."

"Ah, so you're calling in favors."

"For you? Absolutely."

They looked at each other for a second. She was pleased to feel a little tingle when he put his hand on the small of her back to guide her toward the hostess. For all his talk about being the smartest guy in the room and not having social skills, Rick was charmingly smooth. She'd been nervous about having to carry the evening, but hopefully she was wrong about that.

"I'm looking forward to our dinner," she told him.

"Excellent. That's something else we have in common."

They walked over to the hostess, and Rick gave his name. They were led to a corner table by the windows with a perfect view of the setting sun.

"This is nice," she said. "I can't remember when I last had dinner out in a restaurant this fancy."

"You said you don't date much. I find that hard to believe."

She laughed. "Believe it. I'm kind of busy with my life, and I don't, as a rule, meet many single men." Although her reasons for not dating had a lot more to do with her previous relationship disaster than a lack of opportunity.

"I'm glad you met me," he told her.

"Me, too. And you were very kind to buy my coffee for me."

He brushed her comment away. "Anyone would have done it."

She doubted that.

He leaned toward her. "I want to really get to know you, Jana. I know you work in a medical office. Tell me more."

"Okay, I go to community college." She paused, thinking she didn't want to mention she was studying to be a registered nurse. Although she'd picked her path while she was pregnant with Linnie, Rick might think her choice had something to do with him.

"Right now I'm taking a calculus class that is so much harder than I expected. I guess I'm not a math person. I thought the sciences would be the problem, but I did great in chemistry and loved biology."

"Let me know if I can help." He flashed her a quick smile. "You'll be shocked to know I did well in school."

"Thanks for the offer," she said. "I might take you up on it. Although I'm proud to say I'm maintaining a B+ average."

"Smart *and* beautiful. Lucky me."

Their server appeared and asked if they wanted something to drink.

Jana ordered a glass of white wine. Rick did the same. When their server had left, he shrugged. "I'm not on call this weekend. I don't drink when I'm on call."

Something she hadn't thought of. He was a surgeon—of course he would have times when he had to be available for emergencies.

"Do you have to deal with the unexpected very often?" she asked.

"Usually just a weekend a month, although if I have a patient in critical condition, I make myself available regardless of my schedule." He looked at her. "Does it bother you?"

"That you'd have to go deal with a health emergency? No. I think it's admirable."

"Good." He smiled. "Some women don't like that I can't always party on demand."

"First, I'm not a party-on-demand kind of person. Second, when you get called in, lives are on the line. Your patients trust you to be sober."

"I knew you'd get it." He placed his hand on hers. "What else should I know about you?"

"I have a daughter. Her name is Linnie, and she's four."

Rick brightened. "A kid? That's great. I bet she's really sweet."

"Actually, she's both precious and precocious. My brother has three kids who are all older than her, so Linnie is forever trying to keep up with them. She wants to grow up, and I want her to never change." She laughed. "It's an argument she's winning."

"Your face lights up when you talk about her."

"She's my world," she said simply.

"You see your brother a lot?"

"I live with him." For the first time that evening, Jana felt awkward. "It's, ah, not a traditional arrangement, but it works for us."

Rick listened attentively without speaking, leaving her to wonder what he was thinking. Did she sound weird? Pathetic? She told herself she had nothing to be ashamed of and yet found herself adding, "He lost his wife unexpectedly shortly after I found out I was pregnant. Moving in to help him with his kids made the most sense for both of us. When Linnie was born, he helped."

Honestly, she couldn't have survived those first few months without him. Visiting her brother and Valonia a few times a year, hanging out with their children, hadn't prepared her for having a newborn.

"Family matters," Rick told her. "I have a sister, so I get it. We've always been there for each other. Our dad took off when we were really young, and our mom wasn't exactly maternal.

Most of the time, it was just us. You never have to apologize for loving your family."

She relaxed. "Thank you."

Their server returned with their wine and asked about their orders.

"We haven't looked at the menu yet," Rick said. "Can you give us a minute?"

When they were alone, he raised his glass. "To the best first date ever."

She laughed. "That's a lot of faith. Our evening has barely started."

His gaze locked with hers. "Sometimes you know."

Deep in her chest, her heart gave a little sigh. Wow. Just wow.

He set down his glass. "What about Linnie's dad? Where does he fit in all this?"

The inevitable question, Jana thought, momentarily wondering if she should lie and... No, she told herself. She was who she was, and if Rick couldn't deal with her past, then better to find out now. She'd made mistakes, and she'd learned from them. She wasn't exactly proud of what she'd done, but she wasn't ashamed, either. She was simply human.

"He doesn't," she said quietly. "Actually, I don't know who he is. I spent a couple of weeks in Cancun nine months before Linnie was born. There was some partying and different guys. I have no idea which one is her father." She also didn't know any of their last names or how to get in touch with them. It had been spring break, and she'd been out to have a good time.

She forced herself to meet Rick's gaze, prepared for disapproval or worse. But the man shocked the crap out of her by reaching for her hand again and saying, "You're so brave."

"Excuse me?"

"Look at what you've done, all on your own. You're raising your daughter, going to college, holding down a job. Doing all that can't be easy." He released her hand and smiled at her.

She stared at him, not sure what to say. "Some days it isn't," she murmured. "But finding out I was pregnant turned out to be a really good thing. Until then I'd been pretty directionless. Learning about Linnie gave me purpose. I moved back to LA and started getting my life together. A couple of months later, Teddy's wife died. You know the rest of the story."

"What did you do before you had Linnie?"

"I worked for a few nonprofits." She picked up her wine. "I didn't go to college. In high school, my teachers kept telling me to apply, but I wasn't interested, and my parents were fine with that. I started out at AmeriCorps and went from there."

His expression was blank. "I don't know what that is."

"It's like the Peace Corps, but based here in the States. I joined out of high school, helping out communities with disaster preparedness and response. From there I went to work for a nonprofit that helped rebuild housing for farm workers. A few years later I was an aide in a charity hospital in Texas when the whole Cancun thing happened."

"As a volunteer?"

She laughed. "No, I got paid. Not much, but enough to survive. Housing was usually provided. Mostly bunkhouses or tents, but there was shelter."

"Why?"

He sounded so confused that she laughed. "Why did I do the work, or why was I okay sleeping in a tent?"

"Both."

"The tent came with the job. As to why I would choose that as my path, it was what I wanted to do, probably because that's how I was raised. My parents are very focused on service and giving. As we speak, they're building schools and churches in Africa."

"For real?"

"I swear. Volunteering and giving back is kind of in my blood. Right now I'm not doing as much as I would like, but I work a shift every week at a food bank. It's nice. The work keeps me grounded."

His expression sharpened. "You work in a food bank?"

"Uh-huh. Right here in Malibu." She picked up her menu. "We should probably decide on dinner."

Once they'd chosen their meals, he said, "Tell me about your brother."

She shook her head. "No way. We've only been talking about me. I want to know more about you, Rick."

"There's not much to tell. I was in school a long time, and now I'm not."

She grinned. "Yes, I know about the gifted surgeon thing. Have you ever been married?"

"Not yet, but I'd like to be. I want the usual stuff. Kids, a dog, a life partner." He leaned toward her. "Should I entertain you with a couple of jokes now?"

She smiled. "I would love that so much."

Jana arrived home a little after eleven. She and Rick had talked all through dinner and then had lingered over dessert and decaf coffee. The more time she'd spent with him, the more she'd liked him, and when they'd walked to the valet and he'd asked her if he could see her again, she'd happily said yes.

Now, as she pulled into the garage, she told herself she was going to enjoy the fluttery feelings for as long as possible. She was due a little romantic good luck because it had been forever since she'd had any. More important, she couldn't remember the last time a man had made her feel so...*certain* about who he was. Rick wasn't a controlling man masquerading as a concerned dad who had refused to accept when she said she was done with him. He wasn't scary or mean or distant. He was exactly who he seemed to be.

She walked into the house and was surprised to find there were still lights on. Her moment of confusion was followed by a rush of affection. She stepped out of her heels and left them by the door, then walked barefoot into the family room where her brother sat on the oversize sofa, watching TV. He muted the show and smiled at her.

"How was it?"

"Good." She walked over to the sofa and took a seat. "You didn't have to wait up. I drove myself, so I was perfectly safe. If anything bad had happened, I would have called."

"I wanted to," Teddy said easily.

"You look out for me."

"We look out for each other."

That was true, she thought. Even as kids, they'd been close. Physically they didn't look that much alike. Jana shared her mother's blond hair and slight build, but Teddy took after some distant relative no one knew about. He was tall and well-muscled, with broad shoulders. His daily practice of yoga and his devotion to all things healthy meant he always looked fit. Something Jana could admire on her good days. On the days when she struggled with her schedule, her homework and the fact that going to college at eighteen would have been a whole lot easier, she occasionally thought about force-feeding her brother Cheetos, just to even up things.

Okay, not really, she thought with a smile. Teddy was her rock. When she didn't know what to do with Linnie, he was the one she turned to.

"So, tell me about the guy. Rick, was it?"

"Uh-huh. He was great. Sweet and funny. I like him." She angled toward her brother. "I told him about Linnie's dad." She wrinkled her nose. "The not knowing part, and he was fine about it. He didn't judge."

"There's nothing to judge," Teddy said firmly. "You didn't do anything wrong. The test of your character was what you did after you decided to have Linnie. You did it all, Jana. You're a great mom."

She let the praise wash over her. "Thanks. In my head I know you're right, but sometimes I can't get the rest of me to believe. It's embarrassing to admit I was so irresponsible. It's not my fault my birth control failed, but did there have to be that many nameless guys?"

She sagged back against the sofa. "When I tell the story, I'm never the hero. I'm that slutty girl who got pregnant."

"No trash-talking. You're my sister who's a wonderful mom to a great kid."

"Yeah? Name three other women you know who partied like I did and got pregnant."

"You're not a lemming."

She laughed at the unexpected statement. "That's true. I'm not even sure I know what a lemming looks like."

"They're small and furry."

"That's hardly a specific description."

He flashed her a grin. "It's the best I can do." The smile faded. "So you like him?"

She nodded. "He was funny and attentive. He didn't just talk about himself. There was definite sparkage, but we probably shouldn't talk about that."

Teddy grinned. "Probably not. I'm glad the date went well. I assume you're going to see him again."

"That's the plan."

Teddy stood and stretched. "Then I'm happy for you. Bring him around so I can meet him."

She rose. "I think I want a second or maybe third date first."

They hugged. "I'll get the lights," she told him. "See you in the morning."

"Night."

Teddy headed for his part of the house while she turned off lamps before heading to hers. She quietly checked on Linnie, who was sound asleep in a sea of stuffed animals, before retreating to her own room. She'd just finished washing off her makeup when her phone chimed with an incoming text. She glanced at the phone, then smiled.

I know I should wait a couple of days before reaching out, but I can't stop thinking about you. When can I see you again?

Hope stirred. After being so careful, after the disaster that was Paul, after trying to do right by her daughter every minute of every day, it seemed she just might have met one of the good guys.

Beth watched as her friend devoured half a sandwich, moaning slightly between bites.

"How do you do it?" Jana asked as she picked up the second half. "I thought the sandwich last week was the best one ever, and this one is just as good." She set down the sandwich and lifted the top slice of bread. "And what is that flavoring? It's spicy but sweet at the same time."

Beth chuckled. "I know I make a good sandwich, but I can't help thinking you'd find them less amazing if you didn't go without lunch every Thursday."

"If you're saying I like them more because I'm starving, you're wrong. So, what is this one?"

"A fried chicken BLT with jalapeño honey."

"It's heaven," Jana said.

Beth waved at the food. "Then finish it up. I know you're still hungry."

Jana dug into the second half while Beth sipped her flavored water and breathed in the scent of the ocean only a couple of miles away. It was warm again—with a light breeze. The sky was that perfect shade of blue that looked so idyllic in pictures. Whatever might be wrong in her life, she could always distract herself by remembering how fortunate she was to live where she did. Just that morning on the news, the weatherperson had mentioned an early spring snowstorm in Minnesota.

Jana swallowed the last bite of her sandwich and sighed. "That was wonderful. I wonder if I could make something like that at home. The grocery store deli has pretty decent fried chicken. Do you make the jalapeño honey yourself or do you buy it?"

"We buy it, and yes, you could make the sandwiches yourself. They're pretty easy. You'd probably want to test out the jalapeño honey first, though, and see if Linnie likes it. Kids don't always like spicy things."

"You're right, although she's pretty adventurous when it comes to food. I think it's because her cousins are older and are into trying things."

Beth ignored the minor twinge she felt as Jana talked about her daughter. She'd always assumed she was going to have kids, but now she was less sure. Unlike her friend, she didn't know if she had what it took to be a single mom. As for having a child with a partner, well, even though she was intrigued by the "I'm going to start dating and fall in love" concept, she wasn't sure where to begin looking for a guy.

"Why did you decide to start dating?" she asked before she could stop herself. She shook her head. "That came out more abrupt than I'd intended. It's just I know you're busy, and you said you had a bad experience before. What made you decide it was okay to put yourself out there right now?" She laughed. "Asking for a friend, of course."

Jana laughed, too. "Interesting. Just last week you were a firm no on dating. We're making progress. Good for you."

"I've moved to the maybe column. So why now?"

"I didn't decide," Jana admitted. "I was actively opposed to getting involved, but then he said I glowed, and I couldn't say no."

"Oh, right. The glow thing." A second twinge of envy poked her hard. "I have to say, when it comes to unexpected compliments, that one's a winner. So, how was the date?"

Jana's mouth curved up into a happy smile. "Good. Really good. He was great. Nice, attentive, funny. I'm hopeful." She wrinkled her nose. "Hopeful and cautious."

"I get you have a lot at stake what with Linnie and all."

"Not to mention my ex. He was an extreme version of the bad boyfriend." She sighed. "Did you ever try to do everything right and still screw up?"

Beth lifted her can of flavored water toward her friend. "Oh, yes. I know that one for sure. You're in a good place, and a guy could mess that up. I totally get that." She paused. "And yet we as a species seem unable to resist hope."

"Yes." Jana nodded vigorously. "I tell myself not to, but then I'm tempted. Am I making the right decision? Is he a good guy? It's a lot to navigate."

"And we're doing it without GPS," Beth said with a laugh. "What's up with that?"

Jana grinned. "I know, right? But I had a good time, and I'm going to be careful. While the timing isn't ideal, he's not the kind of guy who's going to be single forever. In fact, I'm kind of surprised he's single now."

"You're doing all the things," Beth told her. "Trust yourself. You're not talking about running off after one date, so yay you."

"I'm not a love-at-first-sight person."

"Me, either." Beth couldn't imagine such a thing.

Jana opened her bag of chips. "My brother is, though. He believes in a lightning strike. That when you meet someone, you just know."

"But it takes time to learn who a person really is." To just know after a brief meeting? How was that possible?

"That's what I say, but he disagrees. When he met his wife, he knew within minutes that she was the one, and they were happy together until the day she died." Jana's tone turned doubtful. "I guess that requires more faith than I have."

"For me, too." Love at first sight had always sounded reckless and too risky. Oh, sure, it played well in the movies, but otherwise? No. Just no.

"How did you and Ian meet?" Jana asked, pulling out several chips.

"It was my day off, and I stopped to buy a hot dog at his stand. We got to talking, and I mentioned I owned Surf Sandwiches. A few days later, he came in and asked me out. Things happened from there. But over time."

"See! A perfectly normal courtship. That makes more sense to me. You mentioned you hadn't dated much since the divorce. Is that by choice or by circumstance?"

"Both," Beth admitted, then shook her head. "No, I take that back. I can't say if I would have gone out with someone who asked, but honestly, no one has since the divorce. Not that I've put myself out there. It's not like some guy's going to walk into Surf Sandwiches and ask me out."

"Ian did," Jana reminded her. "Except I guess you'd already met him. Do you flirt with your customers?"

"What? No. That's not professional."

Jana's mouth twitched. "I didn't realize there was a sandwich shop code of conduct. So, flirting is frowned on?"

Beth laughed. "I get your point. I don't see myself as flirty. At work I'm focused on my customers and making them happy."

"I'm not suggesting you flash your boobs or anything, but if someone seems cute, a little forward behavior might be fun."

"You have way more faith in my abilities than they deserve." Flirt with a stranger? She wasn't sure she remembered how. "My aunt suggested a dating app, but it seems so impersonal. She also thinks I should find a man for sex, but that seems even more terrifying than dating."

She'd always thought sex was fine, but wasn't sure it was good enough to be the reason she was with someone.

"I'm with you on the sex-only relationship," Jana admitted. "I spent my early twenties doing a lot of that, and I want to be finished with it. Next time I do the naked thing, I want it to mean something."

Beth didn't know what to say to that. She'd never had the confidence to be a "sex-only" kind of person.

"You know, not everyone has to be involved," Jana pointed out. "Some people are happier alone."

While Beth knew her friend was trying to be supportive, the statement was jarring. She wasn't comfortable thinking of herself as being happy alone.

"Maybe the bigger problem is I'm not sure I have much to offer anyone," she blurted, surprising Jana and possibly herself.

"How can you say that?" Jana sounded outraged. "No. I don't accept that at all. You're funny, you're a good person, you're smart, successful and you're so pretty."

"That's not me," Beth told her. "I like to think of myself as a kind person, but the rest of it…" She honestly didn't know what to say.

"You don't think you're successful?" Jana laughed. "What about the sandwich shop? You've grown it to what? Double the size since you bought it? How is that not successful?"

"I never went to college."

"And you're an entrepreneur anyway. That says a lot about how smart and determined you are." She rattled her can of sparkling water. "You're feeding me on a regular basis, so we know you're a giving person who is thoughtful and a good friend. As for the pretty part, let's just be honest and admit you are. Your long dark hair, your big eyes. Beth, you're a catch."

She couldn't reconcile her friend's words with how she felt about herself. A part of her wanted to protest while the rest of her thought maybe she should sit with the information for a little while before making judgments.

"Thank you," she murmured. "You're a good friend."

"And an honest one."

Beth laughed. "If you say so." Her humor faded. "Maybe I

was more beat up by my divorce than I thought. I wonder if maybe I'm not over the fact that I failed at something so big." She held up her hand. "Not failed. That's the wrong word. I guess it's more I'm not where I thought I would be, and maybe I'm a little scared to try again."

"You don't have to decide anything today. Although I will give you my best Dex advice and say get out of your head and out of your house."

"Dex is Teddy's friend, right?"

"He is, and he has a lot of surprisingly intuitive views on things."

Her life was too insular, Beth thought, and she was the one person who could change that.

"Kai, one of my employees, invited me to watch him compete in a local surf competition. It's right here in Malibu, Saturday morning. I'm going to go."

Jana raised her eyebrows. "Kai, huh? Interesting."

"No." Beth grimaced. "He's twenty-two and way more of a kid brother. But he's a sweetie and so good in the store. Anyway, I'm going to go hang out. To, as your friend Dex says, get out of my house and my head." She paused, then added, "Would you and Linnie like to join me?"

Jana looked at her. "Yes! That sounds like fun. I've never been to a surf competition before, and Linnie loves the beach. You said it's Saturday morning?"

"It is," Beth said, pleased she'd said yes.

"We'll be there."

Beth was surprised when Rick showed up Friday, a little after one. He waited in line, then ordered one of their ham, pear and Brie paninis. She stopped him from going to the cash register.

"What are you doing here?" she asked happily as she collected a bottle of iced tea from the cold case. "Shouldn't you be scrubbing up or something?"

"No surgery on Fridays unless it's an emergency," he told her. "The office shuts down early, and I thought I'd swing by and say hi."

A nice surprise, she thought, trying to remember the last time Rick had stopped by the store. He hadn't been able to make it to the grand reopening, so not since before then.

They went into the break room. Rick devoured half his sandwich in four quick bites.

"Delicious," he told her. "The place looks great, by the way. I like the new paint job. You're doing good, Beth. That makes me happy."

"Me, too. Business is up. My employees are happy. It's all good."

"How's your work at the food bank going?" he asked, picking up the other half of his sandwich.

"There's an odd question. It's fine. Why?"

He shrugged. "It's the first time you've volunteered like that. I wondered if you liked it and if the people you work with are nice. Didn't you say you're making friends?"

Because he worried about her, she thought contentedly. Just like she worried about him. "It's going great. I like the work. I'm guessing people everywhere else assume if you live in Malibu, you're rich, but we have our share of people struggling. It's good to be able to help feed a few of them. And yes, I have a new friend. Her name is Jana, and she's an inspiration."

Rick frowned. "Why do you say that?"

"A bunch of reasons. I admire how she lives her life. She's determined and has goals. She works hard. I like her company."

"I met someone, too," he told her, not quite meeting her gaze. "I mean, I went on a date."

Surprise and possibly a little envy filled her. "You're kidding. When?"

"Last Saturday." He gave her a proud smile. "I didn't want to say anything in case it went badly. I know I don't have the best luck when it comes to women, but we had a really good time, and I'm going to see her again."

"That's wonderful. I'm happy for you."

Which was true. She wanted her brother to find someone and settle down. He needed more connections in his life. But knowing that might be happening made her feel a little left behind.

"Tell me about her," she said, as much to express interest as to distract herself.

"She's a receptionist. Really pretty and nice. We met by chance. She was getting coffee at the stand in the lobby and forgot her wallet."

Beth's interest in hearing more took a turn for the WTF. "She forgot her wallet, just like Mom used to?" she asked in dismay, remembering all the times their mother had pretended to not have money to get a man to pay for everything from clothes for her children to her groceries. As a kid, Beth hadn't understood the scam, but as she'd gotten older, she'd been humiliated by her mother's actions. Her mother had scolded her for caring and had reminded her that it was important to take what you could get.

"It wasn't like that," Rick said easily. "I mean it, Beth. She carried around ten dollars for over a week until she saw me again. She paid me back." His expression softened. "She's great. A single mom to a little boy."

Beth's older sister senses went on hyper alert. "Someone with a child? Are you sure you want to deal with that?"

He looked confused. "Why would that matter?"

"Because being a stepparent isn't easy. You're involved with the child but have no say. Sometimes the other parent can be difficult."

"You mean her ex?" His expression relaxed. "Oh, you don't have to worry about that. She doesn't know who the father is."

"What?" Beth's voice was a yelp. "You're dating someone who has a child and doesn't remember who she slept with to get pregnant?"

"She wasn't trying to get pregnant. She was in Cancun. There were a lot of guys."

Too many to remember, Beth thought grimly. Why did her brother always pick the absolute worst women? The last woman he'd been involved with had asked to borrow his car, then had driven it drunk and totaled it. Now Rick was dating a slutty single mom. The situation had disaster written all over it.

"You have to be careful," she told him. "You're a successful surgeon. For someone in that position, you're probably the best thing that ever happened to her."

"She's not like that, Beth. She's not." He patted her hand reassuringly. "She's sweet. She's the kind of woman you just want to take care of, you know?" He smiled. "If it gets serious, she would be a great stay-at-home mom. It's not like she has a career she cares about."

"She said that?"

"She said it's just something she does to get by. I get that."

Which was just like her brother, she thought grimly. This was so much worse than she'd thought. "Remember the girl you dated your freshman year of college? The one who tried to get you to write a couple of papers, then stole your credit card and maxed it out in two days?"

He shifted uncomfortably on his chair. "That was a long time ago."

"And the girlfriend just before you started your fellowship, the one who claimed she was having your baby and demanded you marry her?"

He sighed. "She wasn't pregnant."

"No, she wasn't. Rick, you're an amazing guy, but you don't always see people for who they are. Some women will want to take advantage of you."

"They're not all like Mom," he said defensively. "There are good people, too."

"Yes, but you don't seem to find them. Does this new one know what you do?"

"Of course. I don't keep it a secret."

"And it never occurred to you she might be in it for a life-style change? Being a single mom is hard. One of my friends is in the same position, and she's constantly scrambling."

The difference was, Jana had integrity. She was working, putting herself through college and volunteering. Unlike Rick's money-grubbing bitch.

Rick smiled at her. "I know you're trying to protect me, but I'm okay. I know what I'm doing."

She wanted to point out that based on his past, he in fact had no clue what he was doing, but she didn't want to hurt his feelings. He was her brother, and while she saw him for exactly who he was, she knew his view of himself was slightly more idealized.

"I want to meet her," Beth said. "If I can get to know her, I'll feel better about the whole thing."

Amusement brightened his eyes. "Sis, it was one date. You don't think we should see if we get to two or three before I introduce her to you?"

"Oh. Good point."

Maybe things wouldn't work out, which would be the best solution for him. She wanted Rick to find someone—just not somebody looking for a sugar daddy so she could quit her job and leech off him for the rest of her life. Plus the whole kid thing.

"But if you keep seeing her, I want to meet her."

"I'll want that, too." His expression softened. "You always look out for me."

"Someone has to."

"You wait. You're gonna love her."

She doubted that, but didn't say it. Now that she knew what was happening, she would stay on alert, ready to step in if her brother started talking nonsense. And in the meantime...

"Don't sign anything," she said. "Don't loan her money or buy her a car."

Rick grinned. "You really don't trust me, do you? Beth, I know what I'm doing."

If only that were true, she thought wearily. But it wasn't, and she was all that stood between her sweet, foolish brother and disaster.

"Is Beth nice?" Linnie asked as she skipped along at Jana's side. They'd arrived early enough Saturday morning that there was plenty of parking. It was still ridiculously expensive, but it was available.

"She's very nice. You'll like her."

"But she doesn't have any kids, right? That's sad."

Jana held in a smile. "It is very sad."

Linnie's latest thing was a belief everyone's life would be improved by the addition of children. Just yesterday she'd asked their mail carrier if he had a family and had been delighted to learn he had four sons.

"Sometimes people don't like to talk about sad things," Jana added. "So let's not talk about Beth not having children, okay?"

Her friend had invited her and her daughter out to watch a

surfing competition and enjoy a beautiful Saturday morning. Jana doubted Beth was prepared to be grilled on her child-free state by a four-year-old.

"I won't say anything," Linnie told her. She pointed to the water. "Look, Mommy. They're already surfing."

Sure enough, there were at least a dozen surfers out beyond the breakers. Most were just sitting on their boards, but a couple paddled toward shore, then caught the wave, stood and rode it in.

"Wow! Could I do that?" Linnie asked.

"I have no idea. I've never tried to surf. Teddy and Dex used to when they were teenagers. Let's ask them about it when we get home."

They walked across the sand toward the lifeguard station, where Beth had said she would be waiting. The early morning was cool, and the fog hadn't quite burned off yet. Despite the low cloud cover, Jana had slathered both herself and Linnie with sunscreen. Burns happened fast on the beach.

She spotted the red umbrella Beth had told her to look for. Just then her friend saw them, stood and started waving.

"Is that her?" Linnie asked eagerly. "Is that your new friend?"

"It is."

They quickened their pace and reached Beth. Her daughter smiled broadly.

"I'm Linnie and I'm four. Next year I get to go to kindergarten and then I'll be in first grade and I'll have homework. I can't wait. Oh, and it's okay that you don't have any kids of your own. If you get lonely, you can borrow me."

Jana did her best not to groan at Linnie's unfiltered introduction. "Hi," she said as she shrugged off her backpack. "So this is Linnie, who says exactly what she's thinking."

Beth laughed. "Hello, Linnie. Thank you for your very generous offer. I appreciate it. So, homework, huh?"

"Magnolia and Atlas already have it." Linnie settled on the blanket Beth had unrolled under the umbrella. "Orchid doesn't."

"Orchid?" Beth glanced at Jana. "Interesting names."

"My sister-in-law was in finance. She said she spent her whole day making sense with numbers. She wanted the rest of her life to be unconventional."

"Orchid was the baby of the family," Linnie added. "Then I came along."

"I know you were a wonderful addition," Beth said.

Linnie beamed.

Jana unpacked a small plastic bucket, a shovel and a couple of towels in case her daughter decided to go into the water. She'd also brought water and juice, along with a cut-up apple.

Beth's tote had been just as filled, but her offerings were more pedestrian—things like sunscreen and hats rather than toys.

Linnie smiled at her. "I have a friend, too. Her name is Cinnamon and she's new at preschool so I sat next to her. It's hard to be new, 'specially if no one will talk to you. I wouldn't like that, so I said we could be friends." She paused. "Her name is very hard to spell. The teacher wrote it on the board and I couldn't remember all the letters. My name is easy, like Mommy's."

She quietly mouthed something. "Your name is easy, too. I think those names are the best. When we get home I'll ask Teddy to write your name down so I can learn it. We practice our letters when we get home from preschool."

Beth glanced at Jana. "Okay, I'm confused. I thought Teddy was your brother."

"He is. He gets Linnie on the days I'm in class. It's a big help."

"He works from home?" Beth grinned. "Let me guess. He has one of those fancy high-tech jobs he can do from anywhere."

"Not even close. He has a studio out back. He's an acupuncturist and a massage therapist."

Beth laughed. "That's a very Malibu career path."

Several more surfers paddled out beyond the breakwater. A few of them rode back in. Somewhere down the beach, someone started playing a Beach Boys song over a speaker.

Beth pointed to a surfer heading in to catch a wave. "That's Kai." She smiled at Linnie. "He works for me in my sandwich shop."

Linnie sprang to her feet and watched him easily make his way to shore. She clapped and bounced in place.

"Yay, Kai!"

Kai spotted them and waved. He grabbed a towel before walking over and sticking his board in the sand next to them.

"Hey."

Beth smiled at him. "You looked great, Kai."

He gave her a happy smile. "Thanks. It's a good morning. The best waves were a couple of hours ago, but no one wants to come out to watch at six or seven in the morning."

"This is my friend Jana," Beth said. "And her daughter, Linnie."

Kai nodded at Jana, then crouched in front of Linnie. "Hi, there. Do you like the ocean?"

"It's very beautiful but big and I'm supposed to be careful because I'm small and I don't want a wave to take me away. Mommy says there aren't mermaids around here because mermaids need rocks to sit on to comb their hair and we don't have the big rocks. She says one day we'll go to Northern California where there are lots of rocks on the shore, so maybe we'll see a mermaid."

Her voice turned doubtful. "Only it's not very warm there and if I were a mermaid I'd want to be in warm water, so I don't know."

"Want to hear about the time I saw a mermaid?" Kai asked, his tone serious.

Linnie's eyes widened. "You did?"

He nodded, then stood and held out his hand. "Come on. I'll walk you down to the water so I can point to where I was." He looked at Jana. "We'll stay in sight. I mean, if it's okay with you."

Jana nodded. "My daughter loves a good mermaid story, so have at it." When they were out of earshot, she added, "You never mentioned Kai was so good with kids."

Beth stared after him. "I didn't know." She smiled at her friend. "Don't worry. Later I'll grill him on the mermaid details and share all when I next see you."

Jana laughed. "Good, because wondering could keep me up nights."

She got comfortable on the blanket, all the while keeping Linnie in sight. This was nice, she thought. Usually she was running and doing. If she wasn't working, she was heading to class or home to see Linnie. There was always homework to be done, or laundry or one of a thousand things. Taking a few minutes to just relax was practically unheard-of in her life. Later that afternoon, she would return to her frantic pace, but for right now, she was going to savor the moment and breathe.

"What's new with you?" she asked casually, not expecting an answer. Only Beth grimaced and her shoulders got tight.

Uh-oh. "Something happened?"

"Not really." Beth looked at her, then back at the surfers. "My brother told me he's dating someone."

Jana processed the information. "Is that bad? I thought you wanted him involved. Or am I remembering wrong?"

"You're not. I want him happy, with a family. He needs that—the connection. He works hard, and he's a great guy with a lot to offer." She paused. "The woman scares me."

Jana wasn't sure what that meant. "How?"

"I'm afraid she's in it for what she can get." Beth sighed. "She's a single mom, which is no big deal. Not everyone needs a partner. I get that, but I look at you, at how much you have going on. You have a job. You're going to college. You're a responsible, hardworking, caring person. The woman he's seeing has told him she's working to get by. I'm afraid that translates into waiting to find a man to take care of her. My mom was like that, so maybe I'm being irrational, but I'm afraid for him. What if she doesn't actually care about him but instead sees him as a successful guy she can trap?"

Jana totally got the whole "worrying about a sibling" issue. "Have you met her?"

"Not yet." Beth held up a hand. "I know, I know. I need to meet her first and make up my mind based on who she is rather than who my brother tells me she is. It's just he's clueless when it comes to reading people. He's been burned by women being in it for the money before. I'm hoping she'll be great, but I have such a bad feeling."

"You have to meet her," Jana said quietly. "You're right. You don't have enough information yet, and speculating doesn't help. She might be terrific, or she might be exactly what you fear. But if you still have a bad feeling after you get to know her, you need to pay attention to that."

Beth looked surprised. "Why would you say that?"

Jana motioned to where Kai and Linnie were playing in the very shallow part of the waves. "You have great instincts when it comes to people. You've talked about how all your employees have been with you for several years. That means you hire the right ones. Like I said, trust your gut."

Beth visibly relaxed. "Thanks, Jana. You're right. I've already told him that if they keep going out, I want to meet her. Once I do that, I'll have more information. You give good advice."

Jana grinned. "I'm glad you think so, because my people skills are sadly lacking."

"I doubt that."

"No doubting. My last boyfriend? Paul? I was so careful with him. I was worried about having a toddler and getting involved with a man, so I waited five months before I slept with him. I thought I knew him, but I was wrong."

Beth's expression turned sympathetic. "Your tone says whatever it was, it was bad. Married?"

"No, a single dad. He belittled me, insisted Linnie abide by his very strict rules, and when she pushed back, he slapped her."

Beth's gasp was audible. "He hit her? What did you do?"

"I grabbed her and walked out. Later, when he tried to talk to me, I told him it was over and that I never wanted to see him again. He didn't take it well."

She shuddered, remembering how scared she'd been for both herself and her daughter. And then how angry. Of course, once the anger had faded, she'd been left with humiliation and shame.

"I thought dating a single dad was a good thing," she continued. "I thought Paul would get it and we could help each other the way Teddy and I do. But I was wrong about him. I dated a guy who hit my kid. I can never forgive myself for that."

"Did you ever see him hit his children?" Beth asked quietly.

"No. He was stern, but there was never any physical contact like that."

"So you didn't know, and when you found out, you left."

Jana nodded, knowing the words were meant to make her feel better, only they didn't help at all. She'd messed up, and knowing she'd put Linnie at risk haunted her.

She glanced toward her daughter, who was laughing with Kai, then looked back at Beth. "I'd been so careful. After something like that, it's really hard to trust my judgment. I still feel like the worst mother ever."

Beth touched her arm. "It wasn't your fault. You didn't do anything wrong."

"I tell myself that, but sometimes it's hard to believe the words. You would have figured out Paul was a bad guy. Trust your gut."

"I think you're giving me too much credit, but I will pay attention when I meet the new girlfriend."

Sunday morning a week later, Jana glanced around the big dining room table and let the happy wash over her. The four kids were talking and laughing over pancakes that Teddy had made. Her brother was reading the Sunday edition of the *Los Angeles Times*, as he did every weekend. The morning was already clear and warm, with the promise of a beautiful day, and she'd had a very good week.

She'd gotten an A– on her first calculus test, she and Rick had enjoyed a quick dinner Wednesday night, and Linnie continued to be her bright, adorable self. She was in a good place and grateful for it.

"Seeing the boyfriend today?" Teddy asked.

"He's on call this weekend, so no."

"He's not Mommy's boyfriend," Linnie informed her uncle. "He's a friend who's a man and they have dinner sometimes. It's not serious." She frowned. "I don't know what *serious* means."

"It means they're keeping things casual," Magnolia told her. "When they get serious, we'll meet him. It's the mature way to handle dating when one of the parties has children."

Jana stared at her niece, then looked at Teddy, who seemed equally stunned by Magnolia's words.

Magnolia offered them a smug smile. "I hear things."

"Obviously," Teddy muttered. "May I ask where these things are heard?"

"At school, mostly. A lot of my friends have divorced parents. It's a thing." She picked up a strawberry and took a bite. "I don't understand dating at all. Why would you want to go out with just one person when you could go out with a group of friends? That's a lot more fun."

"You're twelve," Jana said, more to remind herself than tell anyone else. "Dating won't be on your radar for a while."

"I'm thinking maybe at twenty-five," Teddy said.

Magnolia rolled her eyes. "Dad, you can't stunt my growth like that. It's not right."

"I think a little stunting would be fine."

Dex wandered into the dining room. He looked tired enough that Jana couldn't help grinning.

"Rough night?" she asked, keeping her tone innocent.

"It's not what you think."

"Uh-huh. You don't know what I'm thinking." She looked at Teddy. "Do we know her name?"

Her brother shook his head. "He swears he's done with short-term relationships, but I have my doubts."

Dex ignored them both, took a chair and held out his arms. All four kids swarmed over him, each wanting his attention and plenty of hugs.

"So, what's the plan for today?" he asked.

"I want to go back to the beach with Beth," Linnie announced.

Dex looked at Jana. "Who's Beth?"

"My friend from the food bank. I've talked about her. Linnie and I met her at the beach last Saturday, where we watched a surfing competition for a couple of hours. It was fun."

"I liked her very much," Linnie added. "And her friend Kai."

"A surfer who works for her. Beth owns Surf Sandwiches. We do a Thursday afternoon shift together at the food bank. When it's done, Beth and I hang out. She brings me the most amazing sandwiches."

"I know the place," Teddy said. "I haven't been there in years."

"You should go. Based on what she brings me, the food is delicious."

Dex pulled Linnie onto his lap. "All right. So today. What are we doing?"

"I need a couple of hours to study," Jana said. "Then I'm free."

"We'll do puzzles, then go play outside," Magnolia announced. "By the time we want to come in, you should be done studying."

Dex touched Magnolia's nose. "Do I get a say?"

"Of course. If you have a better plan, we can do that." Her tone indicated doubt that a better plan was possible.

Jana held in a smile as Dex pretended to consider his options.

"I think we should do puzzles for a while, then go play outside."

Everyone laughed.

He stood. "All right, everyone grab a plate and take it into the kitchen. Then back to the family room for puzzles."

When the kids were gone, Jana told herself to finish clearing, then she had to get started on her homework. Not that she was overly inspired, but it had to be done, and delaying only wasted time.

She'd reached for the bowl of strawberries when she caught sight of her brother's concerned expression.

"What?" she asked.

He nodded toward the doorway. "Magnolia's taking on too much again. She's the oldest, and it's a natural thing for her, but it's not healthy. She shouldn't have the responsibility."

Jana knew her brother was right. "She makes it so easy. Every time there's a decision to be made, she takes charge. She can't help herself, and it's difficult for us to stay on alert all the time."

"I'm failing her."

Jana stared at her brother. "Really? Is that where you're going to go? Isn't it a little early in the day for that much drama?"

She figured her brother would either sheepishly agree with her or get pissed. Teddy, being Teddy, grinned.

"Okay, maybe, but you get my point."

"I do, and it's a good reminder that we have to be more vigilant about not letting her run things. She needs to be a kid. She's always been a responsible person, but it's up to us to keep her from taking that trait too far. I'll pay more attention, and I know you'll do the same." She softened her voice. "You know she's doing good, right? She's happy. Her grades are great. She has friends and goals and dreams."

"I'm a natural born worrier. She's my daughter."

"You're a good dad."

"If I am, it's because I learned from the best."

She knew he meant their parents, and she agreed. Theirs hadn't been a conventional upbringing, but they'd learned the most important lessons.

Once she and Teddy had cleared the table, she retreated to her desk to finish up her homework. She'd just booted up her laptop when her phone buzzed with a text.

Is this an okay time to talk?

Her mouth curved into a smile as she typed a quick **Yes**. Seconds later her phone rang.

"I didn't know if you were having family time," Rick said. "I didn't want to interrupt."

Because he was always so thoughtful. "Breakfast is done. I'm about to start studying."

"Let me know if you ever need help with one of your subjects." He gave a little chuckle. "I sort of did well in all of them."

"Not a surprise, Mr. Straight A Student. I'm dating a nerd."

"How do you feel about that?"

She smiled. "Really, really good."

"I'm glad. So, I have something to ask you."

"What is it?"

"I'd like you to meet my sister. I was thinking dinner."

Jana nearly dropped the phone. "What? I couldn't. Rick, it's way too soon for us to be meeting each other's family."

They'd been on all of three dates. Yes, each of them had been great, but they were still getting to know each other. Meeting family, even a sibling, implied a level of commitment they weren't close to.

"I've made you uncomfortable," he said quietly. "I'm sorry."

"It's okay. I just… It's too soon," she repeated.

"I know we're not there with each other. In our relationship." He paused as if trying to figure out what to say. "It's just, she's my Teddy. She's a big part of my life, and I'm hoping, well, I'm hoping that's where you and I are going. I'm not suggesting I meet Linnie. That's completely different. She's a child, and this isn't about that."

While his argument was a little convoluted, she got what he was trying to say. He felt about his sister the way she felt about Teddy. In a way, he was being really sweet. Most guys would rather face a shark than admit they saw a relationship going somewhere, especially this early. But Rick didn't play games. He put it all out there and dealt with the consequences. Plus she appreciated that he was being careful about her daughter.

"This is important to you," she said.

"Yes."

"Okay, we can have dinner with your sister."

"For real?"

The delight in his voice made her smile. "Yes, for real."

"Thanks, Jana. I'll get something set up and get back to you. You're the best."

Beth tried to interest herself in dinner. Agatha was out with friends, so she was alone. Eating by herself had never been her favorite, yet she found herself doing it more and more. One of the good parts of being married had been having someone sitting across the table from her every night. She missed that. In fact, there were several things she missed about being in a relationship, so she should get serious about meeting someone.

In the past couple of weeks, she'd been trying to pay attention to her customers and figure out who was age-appropriate and single. While she could assess age fairly well, the whole "not involved with someone else" part was more of a challenge. If only people wore color-coded badges, she thought humorously. Forest green ones could indicate something like "single, straight and looking." That would help her a lot.

She closed the refrigerator door and walked over to the drawer where Agatha kept the battered takeout menus. She could have something delivered, although lately she felt she had more of a relationship with the Uber Eats driver than was healthy. She knew the problem wasn't actually about food as much as it was about her not having a personal life.

Beth stared at the menu, then shut the drawer. She wanted more, she admitted. She wanted connection. Even her brother was dating, although from the sound of it, the woman in his life was a promiscuous single mom searching for a life of ease. Which was very judgy but might not be inaccurate.

"Not the point," she murmured as she walked into the dining room, where she eyed several headless mannequins wearing very skimpy crocheted bikinis. One of the tiny, nearly nonexistent scraps was done in fluorescent orange. As all Agatha's work was custom and made to order, one of her clients obviously had a thing for the color.

"Better her than me," she murmured, fingering the slender strap holding up the barely there top.

She returned her attention to her lack of dating problem. If she wanted someone to care about, then she needed to figure out how to start meeting people. As it was, she worked, she went to the food bank once a week and she was here. Where exactly was she supposed to meet a man or even make friends? Thank goodness she and Jana had started hanging out—she appreciated having a new friend in her life, but Jana didn't solve the relationship problem.

Beth honestly had no idea what to do about that. She figured in a city the size of Los Angeles, there had to be ways for single people to meet, but wondered if, in the land of stars and beautiful people, she was too ordinary. There was a depressing thought. Should she—

Fortunately, just then, someone knocked on the front door. She headed over eagerly, happy for the distraction, only to find her brother standing on the front porch.

"Did I know you were coming by?" she asked, stepping back to let him in.

"No. I was heading home from the hospital and thought I'd

stop by here first." He smiled at her. "I knew you'd be here. You always come straight home after the store closes."

She knew he was simply stating what he saw as a fact, but there was something in his words. Something...pathetic, she thought grimly. Because she did keep to a schedule, which made her what? Predictable? Boring? Neither of which was the point of Rick's visit.

"Here I am," she said lightly, leading the way to the family room, only to stop. "Wait, did you get dinner? Should I fix you something? Or we could order in."

"I'm good." He sat on the sofa and waited until she was seated in a club chair before adding, "I want to talk to you about the woman I'm dating."

Ugh. Did they have to? That question was immediately followed by worry. "Did something happen? Does she want to borrow money?"

He frowned. "Beth, it's nothing like that. She's great, and you're going to love her."

Unlikely, Beth thought. In a perfect world, she would have nothing to do with the other woman, and Rick would end things in a few weeks.

"I want you to meet her," he said, his tone earnest. "I want to bring her here for dinner."

"What? Already? I thought you just met. How long have you been dating?"

"Only a few weeks." His expression turned happy. "I really like her. You're my family. I want you two to get to know each other."

Of course he did, she thought grimly. Because that was who he was. "If you think it's time, then let's do it."

"Yeah?" He sounded delighted. "Great."

She held in a sigh. "I know you're excited to be in a relationship, but you have to be careful. People aren't always who they seem."

"She's exactly who I think she is," he told her. "You don't have to worry."

"Worry comes with the job title."

"Then you *need* to meet her. If she's not who I think, you'll figure that out, and you can warn me away."

She liked the sound of that. "You promise you'll listen?"

He chuckled. "Yes. I won't promise I'll act on what you say, but I'll hear you out." His humor faded. "I know you look out for me, but this time, you don't have to. I swear."

Beth hoped he was right, but she had her doubts. She supposed she should be grateful he wanted her to meet the new woman so quickly. If there was a problem, he might listen to her now rather than in, say, two or three months, when he was more emotionally involved.

He rose and walked toward her. She stood, and he hugged her.

"You're the best," he told her. "I don't want you to go to any trouble for dinner. We can pick up something to go on the way."

She shook her head. "I can figure something out." The meal was the least of her concerns. The bigger problem was figuring out if the woman really cared about her brother or if she was only in it for what she could get.

Jana changed three times for her dinner with Rick's sister. She couldn't decide if she should wear a dress or jeans or what. The evening was supposed to be casual—just a meal at someone's house—and yet there were emotional consequences that made her feel that she should dress up. Unfortunately her office-student-single-mom wardrobe leaned toward the basics, which didn't leave her with a lot of choices. In the end she went with dark wash jeans, a lightweight sweater and cute flats she'd bought on sale at an outlet store.

She thought briefly about texting Beth to get her opinion on the outfit, then told herself she would put on her big-girl panties and figure it out herself.

She checked her makeup one more time before walking to the front of the house to wait for Rick. She'd agreed he could pick her up at home—a first for them—but he wouldn't be meeting any of her family. Teddy and Dex had taken all the kids out for dinner. Otherwise, she would have met Rick at his place. He might be ready for her to meet his sister, but she wasn't going to have him meet her daughter. Not for a while. Linnie would ask too many questions, and Jana didn't think she had any answers. At least not yet.

Rick showed up right on time. She let him in, aware of the familiar flutter in her belly. The man was appealing. Only this time the usual butterflies had a slightly anxious quality to them. She liked Rick a lot, and she was starting to trust him. Was this the most convenient time to have a relationship? Probably not, but men like him were rare. She wanted things to work out, and she wanted to keep moving forward, which meant meeting his sister had a high level of significance for her.

"You look so beautiful," he said by way of greeting, then lightly kissed her. "I'm the luckiest guy ever."

She laughed. "Thank you."

He studied her for a second. "You're nervous about tonight. Don't be. You and my sister are going to get along great." Something flashed in his eyes, then disappeared. "I promise tonight will be epic."

Not a promise he could keep, she thought.

He looked around. "This is a great house."

"It is. Teddy bought it for Valonia when they found out she was pregnant."

"Teddy bought it? I thought he did massage."

"He does," she said lightly, not wanting to get into the details of her brother's interesting financial situation. "This place has worked out well for our big blended family." She pointed toward the family room. "Linnie and I have our own wing. It's nice to be a part of things and to also have our private space."

He studied her. "I'm glad you're happy here. I look forward

to meeting Linnie. When you think it's time," he added hastily. "You're the mom."

He was saying all the right things, but what really got her was the slightly wistful tone to his voice. As if he envied her having a daughter.

She wanted to confirm that he liked kids and maybe wanted a couple of his own, only she didn't know how to ask without sounding like one of those scary women overeager to commit.

They walked to his car, where he held open the passenger door for her. Once she was settled, all her nerves came rushing back, and she had to remind herself to keep breathing.

"Tell me about your sister," she said. "You mentioned the two of you are close."

He drove out of the neighborhood. "We were always tight. Growing up, it was just us and our mom, and she wasn't someone we could depend on. But my sister was always there for me."

He glanced at her before returning his attention to the road. "I was always the weird kid. I was too smart, and for a long time, I was small for my age. I got picked on, but she was always right there, ready to defend me. I helped her with her homework. Once I decided to become a doctor, she was my biggest fan and did everything she could to help. When I graduated, she was cheering the loudest."

Which all sounded nice, she thought, telling herself the evening would be fine. Rick and his sister were tight, the same way she and Teddy were there for each other. It was what family was supposed to be.

"I think I'm going to like your sister a lot," she said firmly, as much to herself as to him.

"You already do."

Jana had no idea what to say to that. How could she like someone she hadn't met? But before she could ask, he was entering a small cul-de-sac.

"This is going to be fun," he said as he pulled into a driveway.

Jana stared at the ordinary house and told herself whatever happened, she would get through the evening. There was no reason to be apprehensive. Only she knew she was lying, and by the time they reached the front door, she was nearly hyperventilating.

Rick knocked once, then opened the door, calling out, "It's me."

Jana had a brief impression of a comfortable living room before Rick's sister stepped into view. Only it wasn't Rick's sister at all. It was her friend Beth, and how on earth could that be possible?

Beth stared at the woman next to Rick. No, not the woman. Jana. Someone she knew, someone she liked rather than some stranger she'd been terrified was going to be interested in her brother only for his earning potential.

"I don't understand," she said, looking from an obviously pleased Rick to Jana, who looked as confused as she felt. Rick was dating Jana? But he couldn't be. The person he'd described was nothing like her friend.

"Surprise!" her brother said happily. "Isn't this funny? When I figured out you two knew each other, I decided we all had to meet."

Jana looked at him. "What do you mean? How did you…" She shook her head. "I don't even know what to say."

Rick pointed at Beth. "You were talking about the food bank and how you made friends with your mentor there." He turned to Jana. "You mentioned the food bank one night at dinner. I put it together." He sounded pleased with himself. "This is great." He put his arm around Jana. "See, I told you that you already liked her."

Beth did her best to reconcile how her brother had described the woman he was dating with the friend she already knew. The friend who had joked about marrying money, she thought, then told herself Jana had been kidding. Of course she had been.

"You said she had a son," she blurted, remembering that detail.

Rick chuckled. "I didn't want you to guess. I knew you'd enjoy the surprise."

Beth didn't bother pointing out he was wrong about that. She was unsettled and confused, and Jana looked equally unhappy. They stared at each other.

"I, ah…" Beth drew in a breath. "Okay, let's just admit this is awkward and move on."

Jana's relief was visible. "Thank you. I'd like that as well." She offered a faint smile. "I can't believe you're Rick's sister."

"I can't believe you're dating him." She paused, remembering what her brother had said. "I thought you were in medical billing."

Jana frowned. "I am. At the derm office. Why?"

Beth shook her head. "That's what I thought." She looked at Rick. "You said she was a receptionist."

Now it was Rick's turn to look confused. "She is." He looked at Jana. "You're in medical billing?"

"Yes, but it really doesn't matter, does it?"

Beth heard the faintly desperate edge to Jana's voice and knew both of them were uncomfortable, while Rick seemed perfectly fine. She held in a sigh. Her brother had grown and changed over the past decade, but underneath the occasionally smooth exterior was the weird little kid he'd always been. The one who didn't always get the emotional nuances that occurred between people. She knew if she pointed out how he'd made both her and Jana uncomfortable, he would feel terrible. Better to just go along and make the best of the evening.

"All right. We've been standing on the porch long enough," she said, faking a cheerful tone. "Let's go sit down."

She led the way into the family room, where she'd set out cheese and crackers along with dip, chips and cut-up fresh vegetables.

"What would you like to drink?" she asked Jana. "I have wine, or I can make cocktails."

"White wine?"

Beth nodded, then looked at her brother, who was already eating the appetizers. "Are you on call?"

"No, but I'm driving. Iced tea, please."

She nodded and started for the kitchen. After a second, Jana joined her. They stared at each other.

"This is so awkward." Jana twisted her hands together. "He never said your name. I've been replaying all the times he talked about you, and he never said your name. I didn't get that until just now."

"He never said yours, either."

Beth felt like this should be a bonding moment for the two of them, yet she couldn't get past all the things Rick had said about her. Only was any of it true? He'd said Jana had a son instead of a daughter, and there was the whole medical-billing-slash-receptionist thing. Except her brother wasn't a liar, and how well did she know Jana?

"He said you don't know who Linnie's father is," she blurted, then felt instant guilt when Jana flushed.

"Oh." Jana swallowed. "I don't know who… It was a different time in my life, and I wasn't as careful as I could have been." She raised her chin slightly. "I'm not proud of what happened, but I don't regret my daughter."

Beth thought about the sweet little girl she'd spent the morning with a couple of weeks before. "I wouldn't, either," she said. "Linnie's wonderful, and you're lucky to have her." She put her hands on the island. "This is just so strange. I'm fine with you dating Rick." Sort of. "It's just the way he described the woman he was dating." She paused, not sure how much to say. "I never thought it was you."

"I get that." Jana grimaced. "I have the feeling I need to defend myself, yet I haven't done anything wrong."

"You haven't," Beth said quickly. "Rick should have told us when he figured out we knew each other."

Jana nodded. "I really do like him. He's a good man, and he's sweet to me. I'd never do anything, you know, wrong or mean. That's not who I am."

"I know that."

The words were automatic, but Beth had to admit to herself she wasn't sure what she believed anymore. But there was an evening to get through, so she smiled and pulled a bottle of white wine and a pitcher of iced tea out of the refrigerator.

Once the drinks were poured, she and Jana returned to the family room. The three of them made polite conversation, but Beth kept feeling like there was something big and unspoken lurking just out of sight. Their chitchat about the weather and Rick's work schedule was punctuated by awkward pauses. Finally Beth escaped to the kitchen to get dinner on the table.

This time Jana didn't join and her, and she was grateful. When everything was ready, she called in the other two.

She had hoped once they were seated, conversation would flow more easily. Unfortunately the "This is delicious" and "Do you want more wine?" was punctuated by a lot of silence. Beth tried to figure out some safe topic of conversation.

"Is your brother watching Linnie tonight?" she asked, thinking family was a topic they could agree on.

Jana nodded. "He and his friend Dex took the kids out." She smiled. "Their favorite place isn't anyone's idea of fine dining, but with four kids, it's more about making sure everyone has something they like and no one starts throwing food."

Beth felt herself relax and offered her first genuine smile of the evening. "Speaking as someone who owns a food establishment, we frown on food throwing. It really makes a mess." She cut off a piece of chicken. "It's nice you and Teddy can share responsibilities with the kids. Otherwise it would be tough when one of you wants to go out and have adult fun."

"Teddy doesn't date," Jana said. "But yes, it is good we're there for each other. When I had Linnie, I was so scared. I'd never been around an infant before. I'd visited Teddy and Valonia, of course, but that wasn't the same as being responsible for a newborn. But Teddy'd had three of his own, so he was a great resource. He kept me calm."

Beth glanced at Rick to see if he wanted to say something, but he only smiled at her, as if he was comfortable letting the two women talk. She had no idea what he was thinking, but then, she'd never expected him to keep Jana's identity from her. While she could admire her brother's brilliance, his emotional intelligence needed a little work.

"It's nice to have someone to support you," she said, thinking that without her brother, Jana would have been all on her own. What with not knowing who the father was.

The reality of that statement was something she was going to have to deal with later. Thinking about it now was too unsettling, especially considering that if her friend Jana had admitted to that reality, Beth wouldn't have judged her at all. But as the woman her brother was dating, well, that made everything different.

If only Rick didn't have a string of really awful relationships in his past, this would be easier, she thought grimly. She would believe what Jana said without wondering. But given the women he generally picked, well, her trust had to be earned.

"You mentioned Teddy's an acupuncturist," she began, only to have Rick interrupt.

"No, he's not. He's a massage therapist."

Beth's senses immediately went on alert as her sisterly need to protect flared. Jana set down her fork.

"Teddy studied acupuncture in China," she said softly, with only the slightest edge of defensiveness in her tone. "When he came back to LA, he also trained in massage. He has a private practice now that focuses on integrative healing."

Rick frowned. "Huh. I didn't get that."

Beth told herself not to go to the bad place in any of this. She knew Jana—liked her. Jana had goals, was in college, adored her daughter. The woman Rick talked about didn't seem to have any of that, which had made her wonder if she was only in the relationship for the lifestyle. And Jana wasn't like that at all.

Her head hurt from all the uncertainty. She was confused and uncomfortable. She wasn't sure how to get the information she needed to answer all her questions, but one thing she was sure of—Rick wouldn't be able to navigate a dating relationship with someone who might or might not be who she claimed. It was going to be up to Beth to make sure he didn't get hurt or used again.

For Jana, the awkward meal couldn't end fast enough. Although conversation got a little easier with time, it seemed no matter what she said, it was the wrong thing. Beth was pleasant enough, but Jana couldn't escape the feeling that she was being judged for things she hadn't done.

As Rick backed out of his sister's driveway, she tried to tell herself that it wasn't his fault the evening had been such a disaster. He'd only been doing what he thought was the right thing. For reasons she genuinely couldn't understand, he thought she and Beth would find the whole "oh, *you're* the one dating my brother" thing funny. She told herself this was simply one of those situations that didn't feel very good in the moment but would be all right later. Amusing even. At least that was the hope.

"That was great," he said as he drove out of Beth's neighborhood. "I had a good time tonight. Wasn't it funny how you and my sister had no idea who the other one was?"

"I'm not sure *funny* is the right word," she muttered.

He glanced at her. "What do you mean?" His voice sharpened with concern. "Jana, are you upset?"

"No," she said automatically, only to add, "Not exactly."

His hands tightened on the steering wheel. He put on his signal, then turned into a strip mall parking lot. Once he'd driven into a space, he turned off the car and angled toward her.

"I did something wrong, didn't I?" he asked. "I made you uncomfortable. I thought you'd both think it was a good joke. Was I wrong?"

He was so damned earnest, she thought grimly. So concerned. How could she tell him that yes, she'd felt awful about what he'd done, and that the evening had been a disaster? For all she knew, Beth was so freaked out, she wouldn't want to be friends anymore.

"I'm not mad," she said quietly. "More embarrassed."

His confusion seemed genuine. "Why? You're so beautiful and sweet. Beth already likes you."

Or she had, Jana thought. "Maybe it's a girl thing," she began. "I'm not sure. It's just how some things sounded. Like you saying I'm a receptionist when I told Beth I'm in medical billing."

He frowned. "I thought you were a receptionist. You're always on the phone when I visit."

"Rick, I'm in the back office. Wouldn't a receptionist need to be up front to greet people?"

"Oh, you're right. I didn't think of that. But why does it matter?"

She wanted to point out that it would be nice if the guy she was seeing actually understood her very basic job, but knew saying that wouldn't help. "The inconsistencies could make her worry that I'm lying to either her or you. Or that I'm only dating you because you're a successful surgeon." She sighed. "Like I'm looking for a man to take care of me."

"But you'd never do that. You almost didn't go out with me."

"Yes, that's what happened, but there are other interpretations. Beth could think I was playing hard to get to entice you into wanting to go out with me more."

The frown returned. "That's not who you are, Jana. You're wonderful. Beth knows that."

Jana hoped he was right, because the voice in her head told her that *wonderful* hadn't been one of the words on Beth's mind.

He stared at her for a second. "Did you think she was different with you tonight from the way she is when it's just the two of you?"

"Very. She and I never have the three thousand awkward silences we had tonight."

He hung his head. "So I was wrong about not telling you about her and vice versa."

She wanted to shriek that yes, yes, he had been the wrongest, but she didn't want to hurt his feelings.

"I don't want to create more misunderstandings," she offered instead.

He nodded slowly. "You're right. I messed up. I should have thought it through. I just wanted to make you happy. I really did think the situation was funny, but I was wrong. I'm sorry I hurt you."

"Thank you," she said, believing he'd meant well. He was so sweet and earnest and adorable. She found everything about him appealing. Well, not the attempt at humor, but everything else.

He reached for her hand. "My sister is protective of me. There have been women in the past, a couple." He paused and looked away. "They took advantage of me financially."

Jana's already upset stomach sank as she held in a shriek. "You mean like they asked you for money?"

He drew back. "It was worse than that. One of them stole my credit cards and maxed them out. That kind of thing. I should have remembered how upset she was and how she would be worried now. I'm sorry." He shook his head. "Like I said, I should have thought this through. Now I've made things worse."

She held in a groan. Great, so Beth had history with women

wanting Rick for what he could give them, and now she was going to put Jana firmly in the same category.

"How mad are you?" he asked softly.

"I'm not mad, Rick. I'm just worried. I need Beth to stay my friend." And what were the odds of that happening now?

"What can I do to help?"

"Nothing," she told him, thinking his "help" would only make things worse. "Don't worry about it." She forced a smile. "It's not that big a deal."

"You sure?"

"Yes," she said firmly.

He gazed into her eyes. "Are we okay?"

She knew there was no point in continuing the conversation. Rick was unlikely to get the subtleties of how she felt, and trying to explain the situation would only make him feel worse. He'd screwed up because he was clueless, not because he was a jerk. Later, when she wasn't so upset about Beth, she would think that he'd been sweet to try to pull off what he thought was a joke.

"We are."

He offered her that hopeful, happy smile of his and started the car. When they reached her house, he walked her to the door and kissed her. She lingered with him on the doorstep for a few minutes, more because she wanted to make him feel better than because she was feeling romantic. Finally he stepped back and promised to text her in the morning. She nodded and ducked into the house, oh so grateful the evening was over.

After kicking off her shoes and dropping her bag on the floor, she walked barefoot into the family room, where she found her brother reading. He looked up and smiled.

"You're home earlier than I thought. How was dinner with the sister?"

She flopped onto the sofa opposite and leaned back, closing her eyes against all the awful memories. "It was a disaster."

"Did you dis her cooking?"

She looked at him. "Very funny, and no. Of course not. His sister is Beth."

Teddy's momentary look of confusion cleared. "Rick's sister is your friend from the food bank?"

"Yes. He figured it out, which is probably why he arranged for us to meet. Neither of us had a clue, and let me tell you, it wasn't a happy reveal."

She thought about the shock on her friend's face when they'd seen each other. She was sure she'd looked just as startled.

"Apparently he described me as a money-grubbing bitch or something equally unflattering. Plus all the things I said before." She held in a whimper. "It was just the stupid stuff friends say together." She twisted her hands together. "I told her the guy who'd asked me out was successful, and we joked about marrying money."

Teddy dismissed the comment with a flick of his wrist. "That's not who you are."

"You know that, but she doesn't. I didn't mean it. We were being funny. But it's a lot less amusing when the guy in question is her brother. Worse, apparently Rick has a history of dating women who take advantage of him, so of course Beth's going to go on alert to protect him. Combine that with what I said and me not knowing who Linnie's dad is and him saying I was a receptionist when I'd said I was in medical billing."

"Which you are. He should know that."

"He does now, but having it come up makes it sound like I've been lying to one of them. Conversation at dinner was stilted, and that's the good part. I felt stupid and small, and I know she's upset, which means what? She doesn't want me dating her brother?"

Teddy looked at her. "You have to breathe."

"I'm breathing. If I wasn't breathing, I couldn't be talking."

He held in a smile. "I meant breathe intentionally."

"This is not a good time for one of your woo-woo lectures about the forces of the universe and how we're all one."

He flashed her a grin. "Thank you for clarifying how you feel about my work."

"Shut up."

"You shut up."

Despite her angst, she managed a smile. "You're saying I need to step back from the situation and be a little more rational? I get that. But I also feel really crappy about the whole evening."

"Do you like Rick?"

"What? Of course I do. He's a really great guy, and the chemistry's a plus. I'm being careful because hey, disaster relationship last time, but yes, I like him." She groaned. "He's so unaware. He actually thought we all had a perfectly good time tonight. Like he didn't feel the tension at all."

"Do you believe him?"

"Yes." Rick was many things, but emotionally insightful wasn't one of them. "I don't believe he would want to hurt me or his sister. Not on purpose. But wow, was that a dumb thing to do."

"This is the same guy who entertains you with dad jokes?"

Oh right, she thought. He was, and in that context, wouldn't he think the surprise reveal would be fun for all?

"Good point."

"I have more. Beth's your friend. Trust your relationship and trust her. From what you've said, she was just as shocked as you were. Getting over something like that takes time. But you have a connection, and you need to respect that and give her a chance to come through."

He was making sense, she thought. "You're saying I'm jumping to conclusions."

"I'm saying you don't have enough information. Maybe it wasn't as bad as you thought."

"Maybe it was worse."

He grinned. "Gotta love the optimism."

8

"Oh, dear. You waited up. This can't be good."

Beth wanted to protest her aunt's assessment of the situation, but there was no point. She'd already tried going to bed and found there was no way she could relax enough to sleep. After thirty minutes of tossing and turning, she'd pulled on yoga pants and a T-shirt and had settled in the family room until Agatha's return.

"Come with me," her aunt said, leading the way to the kitchen. She pulled a bottle of brandy out of the liquor cupboard and poured them each a small amount in a snifter, then moved toward the back door. Beth followed her, pausing only to grab a hoodie from a hook.

They settled on the patio. The night was still and just a little cool. She put her glass on the small table between them and pulled on her hoodie before zipping it and collapsing into the chair.

Even in a residential area of Malibu, they were too close to city lights to see any stars. Planes flew overhead, zipping to LAX from all over the globe. Beth remembered how when she was a little girl, she thought the moving lights were shooting stars and used to wish on them. Mostly her wishes had been about their mom changing so she would want to keep them safe—a dream that never came true.

"Tell me," Agatha said before sipping her brandy.

"Rick's new girlfriend is Jana from the food bank."

She quickly explained about how Rick had figured out she and Jana knew each other, then the unexpected encounter on the front porch.

"I guess he thought it would be funny to spring it on us, but it wasn't. I felt..." She paused. "I don't know how I felt."

"Betrayed?" Agatha offered. "Used?"

"I want to say no, but maybe. Which doesn't make sense. Jana was as shocked as I was, and she didn't think the situation was the least bit amusing. I was upset and confused."

She glanced at her aunt. "Rick is such a dweeb when it comes to relationships. I get that. I just wish he hadn't thought this would be great fun for all."

Agatha's mouth drew together in a line. "You're giving him too much credit." She frowned. "Or maybe not enough."

"What do you mean?"

"Your brother is far more aware than you think, although I agree that he didn't think the situation through from anyone's perspective but his own."

Beth knew that hadn't been what she'd said. "You're blaming him?"

"I don't think blame is called for, and I have no idea why he did what he did, but Rick is a grown man who has experienced a lot of life. He's not the shy, overly intelligent child you remember."

"He hasn't changed that much. Jana's the first woman he's gone out with in what? A year?"

"Oh, I suspect there have been other women. He just chooses not to tell you about them."

Beth shook her head. "You're wrong. Rick tells me everything."

"No one tells their sibling everything. You have secrets."

"No good ones," she grumbled, then turned her attention back to the actual problem. "I was prepared to hate her. The girlfriend. The way Rick described her, the things he said." She sipped her brandy. "Only I like Jana." In fact, having Jana in her life had become much more important ever since the billboard incident. "Except I can't reconcile who I know with who he described. Only one of us is telling the truth."

She set down her glass and shifted in her seat. "I don't mean that how it sounded. I don't think Jana's lied to me, and we both know Rick tends to say the wrong thing. I guess it was just a misunderstanding."

"What's your concern?" Agatha asked. "That Jana's secretly only dating your brother for the money and potential lifestyle?"

Beth didn't want to admit that, but knew her silence was its own answer.

"It's happened a bunch of times in the past," she said instead. "And then there's what Mom did with men."

Her mother had always been looking for a man to take care of her. Caryn would seduce them with talk of the adventures they would have together. While she always came through on being game for anything, she also insisted on expensive gifts or help paying the bills in return.

"Jana isn't your mother, and she's not the women from Rick's past. Maybe you should consider judging her for what she has and hasn't done instead of by your brother's history."

"You're right."

Agatha sighed. "But?"

"I need to take care of him," she admitted. "Rick doesn't see the world as it is."

"Oh, he's very clear on the world, but again, we'll agree to disagree. Jana's your friend."

"Rick's my brother." The words were automatic and defensive. And while she was desperate to have a friend in her life, family came first.

"So you've made up your mind. You're Team Rick."

"I've always been Team Rick."

"You have, and your loyalty is admirable. I just hope you'll consider that this time around, you might want to think about being Team Jana, as well. To be blunt, my dear, she didn't do anything wrong."

"Unless she's dating Rick because he's a surgeon and she doesn't care about him at all."

"Quite the leap."

Beth thought about Jana recalling Rick asking her out. He'd said she glowed. Jana had been starry-eyed and hopeful and genuine.

"I don't know what to believe," she admitted.

"I hope that's true. Because making up your mind before you have all the facts may cost you a friendship, and that's something you would regret for a very long time."

Beth almost didn't show up for her shift at the food bank. She'd also debated bringing sandwiches, as was their thing now. She both wanted and didn't want to see Jana. While part of her missed hanging out with her friend, part of her couldn't get past the voice that whispered she was only interested in Rick because of what she could get from him. Awful and judgy, but also the truth.

In the end, she packed the picnic basket and arrived right

on time. When she saw Jana, she smiled and waved, then went back to work. But as the time grew closer to six, she found herself fighting nerves and wishing for a reason to simply duck out without speaking to her friend.

At the end of their shift, she collected the basket from her car and went out to the tables behind the food bank. There were a few clouds in the sky, and the temperature was cooler than usual. Beth slipped on her jean jacket and waited for Jana to appear. A minute or so later, her friend walked out. They stared at each other without speaking, as if they were waiting for the other one to speak first.

"Are we okay?" Jana asked, her voice tentative.

Emotions rose inside Beth. A simple enough question and one for which she didn't seem to have an answer. Except she found herself wanting to move close to hug Jana and swear that yes, they were fine.

"I don't know," she admitted. "That evening was so strange and confusing."

Jana's chin came up. "It was the same for me. I can't believe you never said his name."

Beth blinked. "Excuse me?"

"You never said Rick's name. You said 'my brother' but never 'Rick.' I know you didn't do it on purpose, but it was so shocking when I realized you were his sister. If you'd called him by name, we might have put all this together."

There was a perspective, Beth thought in surprise, because one of her complaints was that Jana never called Rick by name, either. She thought back to their conversations and couldn't remember what she'd done. It was definitely possible that she'd never actually said the R word at all.

"That makes me feel foolish," she admitted, relaxing a little. "How could we both have avoided actual names?"

Jana managed a faint smile. "Not just us, but your brother as well."

Beth nodded, remembering Jana mentioning that the night of the very awkward, totally uncomfortable dinner. She knew she had a decision to make. Either she trusted her friend or she didn't. The bottom line was she wanted Jana in her life. Their relationship was important to her, and she didn't want to mess it up.

"How about from now on we name everything?" Beth suggested. "People mostly, because while I happen to know this table likes to be called George, admitting it would get weird."

She waited to see what Jana would do. She figured the other woman could easily dismiss her and walk away. Thankfully Jana grinned and walked toward the table.

"George? He told me he liked to be called Stan."

Beth laughed, and they both sat down.

"What a mess," she said as she opened the basket. "All of it. I'm sorry things were unsettled. It's hard to reconcile who you are with how my brother described you." She handed over a chicken Waldorf salad sandwich and a to-go container of the store's popular broccoli salad.

She looked up. "He only said good things. It's just how he phrased them. You know how he is."

Jana hesitated. "He can see the world in a different way."

"Absolutely. Plus I'm protective. He and I look out for each other, so I went on alert, which I wouldn't have done if I'd known you were the woman in his life."

"I get that," Jana said quietly. "When he took me home, Rick talked about the other women he's dated. The ones who were in it for what they could get. You're worried I'm one of them. Or just as bad, that I've played you."

Beth did her best not to shift on her seat. While that had been her first reaction, she knew it wasn't a rational one. "How exactly were you going to play me? Our meeting was totally random. It's not as if you were waiting for me to apply to be a volunteer here so you could become my mentor and then secretly date my brother."

Jana picked up her sandwich. "If I had that much power, I'd use it to win the lottery."

"So would I."

Jana drew in a breath. "I don't care that Rick's a doctor. I mean, it's who he is, but it's not why I'm going out with him."

"I know."

"I really didn't know you were his sister," Jana added.

Beth nodded. "I believe you. I didn't know, either." She smiled. "Actually, I *did* know I'm his sister, but you know what I mean."

Jana grinned. "I do. You said you and Rick were always tight when you were kids. Where were your parents?"

Beth paused with a bite of salad on her fork. "We never knew our dad. He might have been around when I was a baby, but I don't remember. For all I know, we have different fathers. Our mom wasn't exactly into commitments or anything conventional. Her idea of fun was living on the edge. The more dangerous something was, the more she wanted to do it. 'Go out in blaze of glory,'" Beth added, using air quotes. "Although in her case it wasn't an expression. She meant actual fire."

"That's scary, especially for a little kid. Linnie is always up for an adventure, but in a safe way."

"Mom didn't believe in safe. I knew I was all that stood between Rick and the world, and I made sure I was there."

Jana's expression softened. "I get that. Magnolia, Teddy's oldest, keeps taking on too much responsibility with the other kids. It started when she lost her mom. I'm sorry you had to deal with that. Growing up is hard enough without that added pressure. I know Rick's grateful for all you did."

"Thanks. We knew we always had each other." Beth thought about that time in her life. "The guys Mom dated didn't much like my brother. Looking back, I wonder if his intelligence intimidated them. Some of them took on the task of making a man of him, which usually involved a lot of physical activities that Rick failed at. Some of them thought they could beat the smart out of him."

Beth was used to the memories, but Jana flinched. "I'm so sorry. That's awful."

"It was, but it never got him down. He would just wait out the guy, because Mom always moved on." She hesitated, then decided not to mention how Caryn had used men to get what she could from them. No way Jana would see that as just information and not as a comparison.

Memories surfaced—the ugly ones she mostly tried to forget.

"When I was thirteen, one of my mom's boyfriends attacked me." She kept the story short and left out most of the details. Even so, Jana put down her sandwich and touched her belly as if the food there had just turned.

"He saved you," she breathed. "I've noticed the scar, of course, but I didn't have any idea where it came from."

"He could have been killed," Beth said quietly. "He could have died protecting me. I know he's okay, but sometimes I let myself think about all the ways that night could have gone wrong. It's only one of a thousand reasons why I'm so protective of him. He's my family, and I would do anything for him."

"Of course you would. That's a good thing."

"I worry about him," she admitted. "The whole dating thing is complicated because honestly, in the past he's had the worst taste in women. If he had better skills, maybe I could let it go. It's why I go to the bad place. I don't mean to. I keep hoping he'll meet a nice surgeon or maybe a radiologist. Someone who understands his world and isn't in it for what they can get."

Jana's warm expression froze. "Are you saying that's why I'm dating him?"

Beth stiffened, instantly aware that she'd said the wrong thing. "No. Of course not. You're my friend. I get where you're coming from. You're not like the woman I thought he was seeing."

"A single mom who works as a receptionist?" Jana's voice was cool. "Because I'm not all that far from that, am I? I'm just the slut who doesn't know who my daughter's father is, so you're probably right to be worried."

She put down her sandwich. "That's what you think of me, isn't it?"

"No! Jana, please. I wasn't trying to insult you or imply anything awful about you. I'm sorry. Please, I didn't mean to hurt you."

"You just said you start from the bad place, so I think you do mean to insult me. I think your reaction the other night was honest. I'm not a doctor. I'm studying to be a nurse, but that wasn't on your list of approved professions. Apparently I'm good enough to hang out with but not good enough for Rick to date."

She pointed at her half-eaten meal. "Thanks for dinner, but I need to get home."

Beth watched her go. It was only after Jana had walked back into the building that she realized she should have stopped her. Except there had been a fair amount of truth in what Jana had said. It wasn't pretty, but it was real. Beth *had* judged her in all the ways she'd implied. While she was willing to trust the friend she knew, deep down inside, wasn't she worried that Jana was— as she'd said—not good enough for Rick?

Which made her a bitch and a bit of a hater. It also meant she might very well have lost her friend.

Jana was practically frothing by the time she got home. With her brother still working and the kids with Dex, the house was silent, but for once she didn't find the quiet comforting. As she couldn't settle, she spent the next hour pacing rather than using the time to study. She was so pissed, but she knew that under the energy was a lot of hurt she didn't want to face.

Dex arrived home with the kids around seven. After the usual wild and loud greeting, everyone got settled in the family room for a little wind-down time. But instead of leaving, Dex sat down with the battered copy of *The Lion, the Witch and the Wardrobe* and picked up where Teddy had left off. Jana told herself to use the time to get a few things done, but found herself pulled into the story, drawn by Dex's perfect "radio voice" and the adventures of the four siblings.

She dropped onto the sofa next to Linnie and pulled her daughter close. Linnie snuggled in and whispered, "I love this story."

"Me, too."

Ninety minutes later, the younger kids were in bed and the two oldest were in their rooms. Dex followed Jana back into the family room before asking, "Want to talk about it?"

"I'm fine."

He flashed her his famous smile. "You are such a bad liar. I'm not saying that isn't a good thing, but I could see the second I walked in that something had happened." He sat on the sofa and patted the cushion next to him. "Tell Uncle Dex what's going on."

She drew in a breath, then eased into an overstuffed chair opposite the sectional. "Things blew up with Beth tonight."

"What happened?"

"I don't know. She was talking about Rick and how she worries about him and that she's always been afraid he would get involved with the wrong sort of woman."

"She doesn't trust his judgment?"

"No, and just between us, I wouldn't trust his judgment, and we're just dating. Plus it turns out there were other women in his past who took advantage of him, so she has reason to be cautious."

"Sounds reasonable. So what's the problem?"

She glared at him. "You know what the problem is."

"She thinks you're not good enough for her brother."

The blunt words made her wince. "That's so harsh."

"Am I wrong?"

"No. She wasn't directly talking about me, but when she described the woman she always hoped Rick would fall for, it definitely wasn't anyone like me." She slid to the front of the seat and stared at him. "I get I have a checkered past. I've screwed up big-time. I'm flawed. But I would never go out with a guy because he was rich or successful. I care about the person."

"Does Beth believe that?"

"I don't know, and that's where it all went wrong. The way she acted the other night…" She sucked in a breath. "If you could have seen her face when she realized I was the one dating her brother. She was upset and disapproving. Part of me understands that she's protective, but she knows me. Or she should. I'm a good person."

"So what happened tonight?"

"She was going on about the perfect woman, and I realized I would never be what she wanted for him. I told her I was obviously good enough to hang out with but not good enough for her brother to date. Then I stomped out."

The smile returned. "You always did have style."

"Thanks, but this time style isn't enough." She glared at him. "She should be a better friend."

"I agree."

"And she's wrong about me."

"Yes, she is. So what are you going to do?"

Jana frowned. "There isn't anything *to* do."

"I meant are you and Beth still going to be friends or is that done? And if the friendship is over, what about dating Rick? If things get serious, then Beth is going to be a part of your life, kid. You said they're tight which means there's no escaping her. If you want the relationship to work with him, you're going to have to find a way to get along with his sister."

She knew the truth of his words, but she didn't like it. "I'm not the problem. She is."

"I've always admired how mature you are."

She stuck her tongue out at him, then flopped back against the chair. Dex was right about all of it. If she wanted to keep seeing Rick then she had to solve "the Beth problem." And although she knew she'd been in the right, there was also a slight possibility she hadn't helped by walking out of their dinner.

"How did this get so twisted so fast?" she muttered.

"Rick screwed up. He should have told you both when he figured out you knew each other."

"He thought it was going to be a great surprise."

Something flashed in Dex's eyes, but he didn't speak.

"What?" she demanded. "You're thinking something."

"I hope his motivation is that pure."

"What does that mean?"

Dex paused before speaking. "I don't know the guy, so I could be completely wrong."

"But?"

"What if he's better at all this than everyone thinks? He's figured out what works for him, and that's acting like the hapless nerd. What if he knows exactly what he's doing?"

Jana tried to consider Dex's point, but honestly she couldn't reconcile a secretly smooth romantic player with the guy she knew.

"I can't see it," she admitted. "He's too awkward. Too honest."

Dex held up a hand. "Like I said, you're the one who knows him. Not me. It was just a thought."

"I know you're looking out for me, and I appreciate it, but Rick's a good guy."

He rose and walked over to the chair, then pulled her to her feet and hugged her.

"That's what I want for you," he told her. "A good guy. If you're happy, I'm happy."

He kissed the top of her head. "I'm going home. See you soon."

She walked him to the front door, then closed and locked it behind him. Teddy had clients until nine and would let himself in the back door.

She checked on Atlas and Magnolia. The former was already in bed, asleep, and the latter smiled at her, looking up from the book she was reading.

"You'll turn your light out at nine thirty?" Jana asked.

Magnolia sighed. "I'm very responsible. You don't have to worry about me."

"I can't help it. I love you. Worry comes with the package. Night."

After a quick peek at a sleeping Linnie, then Orchid, Jana made her way to her own room and shut the door. Her mind was swirling with thoughts from her conversation with Dex.

She appreciated his ability to get to the heart of the problem. If she wanted to keep seeing Rick, she had to deal with Beth. Just as important, excluding Rick, she'd liked having the other woman as a friend. Which meant she had to find a solution, although what it might be eluded her.

Her phone buzzed. She glanced at the screen and saw Rick had texted, asking if he could call her. Instead of answering in kind, she pushed the button to dial his number.

"I know the cool kids don't want to actually talk on the phone," he said with a chuckle. "I can't help it. I like the sound of your voice."

And just like that, all her upset faded. "I like the sound of your voice, too."

"Yeah? That makes me happy. So, I was wondering if I could cook you dinner. I only know how to make one thing, but it's pretty good."

She heard the smile in his voice and couldn't help laughing. "You sound sure of yourself."

"When I got my first place, I made it every weekend for six months. You know, to get it right."

A simple confession that touched her in ways he could never understand. Dex was wrong about Rick—the man was exactly who he said. He was sweet and caring, and he tried so hard to do the right thing.

"I'd love to have you cook me dinner," she told him.

"For sure? That's great. I can't wait, Jana."

They settled on a date and time, then talked for a few more minutes before hanging up. When she'd set her phone on her nightstand, she headed for the bathroom to get ready for bed. Whatever Beth thought of her didn't matter, she told herself. She liked Rick a lot, and she was going to continue to see him. Because men like him didn't come around very often, and there was no way Jana was going to lose him—not without a fight.

9

Beth sat on the beach, watching the surfers ride the waves. It was early—barely dawn—and cold. The air was salty and damp, and the sand had yet to absorb any warmth from the not-yet-seen sun. Despite the sweatshirt she'd pulled on, she was shivering slightly.

She hadn't been able to sleep much and sometime around four had given up trying. All night long she'd replayed her conversation with Jana, wondering how much of the problem was what she'd said and how much of it was Jana being too sensitive. Only there didn't seem to be much way for her to blame the other woman, which meant the majority of the responsibility lay with her.

One of the surfers paddled into shore, then got out of the water. He anchored his board in the sand, then unzipped his wetsuit and began toweling off. When he'd pulled on a thick hoodie, he started toward her.

"You're up early, B," Kai said, settling beside her. "Couldn't sleep?"

"How'd you guess?"

"A lot of people have that problem. Coming here clears the mind. It's something about the rhythm of the waves, plus it's the beach, so there's no bad there." He glanced at her. "What's up?"

She was going to tell him she was fine, that it had simply been one of those nights. Instead she found herself blurting out, "I messed up with Rick's new girlfriend."

Kai frowned at her. "You said she was your friend Jana. How could you mess up?"

"In a thousand ways."

She told him about their conversation after working at the food bank. "I went on and on about how I hoped Rick would find a nice surgeon or a radiologist." She groaned. "Seriously, who talks about wanting their brother to date a radiologist? I sounded awful. I know she thought I was judging her and being mean."

"You sounded like you're worried about keeping Rick safe." He flashed her a smile. "I wouldn't mind dating a radiologist."

"I'll ask around." She sighed. "I really do like Jana. Why can't I talk to her like a normal person? Why is this such a big deal?"

"Because you think she's not good enough."

His blunt statement made her wince. "That's not true. Like you said, we're friends. I like her a lot."

"For you, yes. For Rick, not so much. You're assigning value to how you feel, and you've decided some of what you're dealing with is bad. You can't pick your emotions, Boss, but you can control how you act despite them. Last night you weren't in as much control as you would like. You hurt someone you care about, and that's not who you are."

He was right, she thought. About all of it. She was ashamed

of what she'd said, and at the same time, she couldn't shake the need to protect her brother.

"What do I do?" she asked, trying not to think about the fact that she was seeking life advice from a kid in his twenties. Only Kai had an old soul, and she trusted him.

"Have a little faith. Rick's a grown man with a successful career. He can take care of himself."

If only. "He has a terrible track record with women."

Kai shot her a knowing look. "Maybe, but even if he has, that's not your rock. You get too involved. Remember last year when he was buying his condo? You were all up in his business."

She felt herself flush. "That's not true. I was helping. He'd never bought a place before. He didn't know how the whole process was going to go."

Plus he'd been so busy with his new practice. She'd been happy to go look at different condos, sorting through them so he only had to go see the top contenders.

"You take on too much with Rick because doing that allows you to hide from your own life. If you're always worrying about him, there's no time to think about you and what you want. You don't have to put yourself out there. Which sounds good, but then you end up with nothing while Rick has an ocean-front condo."

She stared at Kai, unable to take in what he'd just said. "I'm not like that," she protested. "I have a lot of things in my life. The store, my friends…" Her voice trailed off as she tried to make the list longer and realized she couldn't. Worse, she didn't have actual "friends." She'd lost them in the divorce and hadn't done anything to replace them.

Except for Jana, she thought wistfully. And look how she'd screwed up there. Worse, it seemed everyone knew what was wrong with her. Agatha, Jana and now Kai had blithely talked about her flaws as if they were completely obvious to the world. A reality that made her feel even more pathetic than usual.

"I want my brother to be happy," she said without a lot of energy, but it was the only argument she had. "That's a good thing."

Kai nodded. "You're a great sister. I wish you were mine and always looking out for me the way you look out for him. Believe me. But it's more than that, B. You say you want Rick to have someone in his life and be happy. From what you've told me, he sounds happy with Jana, yet you're still worried. Is this all about Jana, or would you be upset about anyone Rick was dating?"

"I wouldn't be," she began, only to stop. While she wanted to say Kai was being ridiculous, she thought maybe she didn't know if he was. Was he right? Was she specifically upset about Jana, or was she upset about the change in the status quo? Because if Rick fell in love, everything between them would be different. He wouldn't need her the way he did now. He would have someone else to take care of the details of his life, and she would be left behind. Alone.

"I don't know," she whispered. "Am I the problem?"

"We're all the problem, B. That's what makes life so interesting."

Jana took in the perfect ocean view, the champagne on ice and the sweet, funny, handsome man standing in front of her.

"Wow," she said with a smile. "This is very fancy."

"I wanted the evening to be special." Rick paused. "You okay?"

Really? He chose this moment to be perceptive? "I'm a little stressed, but I'll be fine."

He nodded. "I'm reading a book on antigravity. It's impossible to put down."

She stared at him for a second, not understanding what he was talking—

The pieces fell into place as she got the joke and immediately relaxed. "Good one."

"I like the science ones the best," he admitted. "So, I've planned the evening. I'm making chicken piccata with angel hair pasta.

And a salad." He flashed her a grin. "Dessert is a surprise—but a good one this time. I swear."

"Sounds wonderful. Dinner is the famous 'I've practiced the recipe for six months' chicken piccata?"

"It is."

She'd driven over in a state of worry, thinking about Beth and telling herself that what the other woman thought of her wasn't her business. She'd nearly turned around twice, but had decided she wanted to see Rick because she liked him and because being around him made her feel good. If his stupid sister couldn't understand that, then shame on her.

"I can't wait," she told him, setting her bag on the table by the door and moving closer. "Your condo is amazing."

His smile grew. "You like it? The view is good. Sometimes, if I've had a tough day in surgery, I sit outside and listen to the ocean. It relaxes me."

He walked over to the champagne bottle and drew it out of the ice bucket. "Would you like a glass?"

"Thank you, yes."

He opened the bottle expertly, removing the cork without making a sound or spilling a drop, then poured them each a glass.

"You're not supposed to pop the cork," he told her. "When you do that, you waste the carbonation, and that changes the experience." His smile returned. "I watched a couple of videos online a few years ago to learn how to do it right. When I was a kid, we weren't a champagne kind of family."

"Us, either," she told him. Plus he'd grown up without a dad. There hadn't been anyone to teach him guy stuff. But he'd filled in the blanks on his own. She admired that. And him.

She tried to remember the last time a man had made her dinner. Teddy and Dex both cooked, but as far as anyone like a boyfriend? It had never happened.

Rick held out her glass. She reached for it, but instead of keeping it, she put it down on the table and stepped closer.

"You are a wonderful man," she told him, staring into his brown eyes. "I'm really glad you asked me out and that I said yes."

"You almost didn't," he teased.

She laughed. "You're right, and that would have been a huge loss."

"For both of us," he murmured right before he kissed her.

She wrapped her arms around his neck and leaned into him, enjoying the moment and the feel of his mouth on hers. This was right, she thought happily. He made her feel good and safe, and it had been a very long time since that had happened.

The kiss lingered, then deepened. She felt the beginning of those wonderful tingles that signaled she was all in for whatever he wanted. Not that they were going to do anything, but it was nice to feel desire and know she'd recovered from the trauma of her last relationship.

Rick closed the distance between them and pressed his body to hers. She felt the telltale ridge of his arousal against her belly and felt an answering spark inside. But before she could decide what she wanted to do, he broke the kiss and stepped back.

"Sorry," he mumbled, turning away from her. "I didn't mean for that to, ah…" He cleared his throat. "It's just being with you makes it difficult to…" Another throat clear. "I'm sorry."

He was apologizing for getting an erection from kissing her? She wanted to melt, and not just from the thought of them having sex.

"It's okay," she told him, smiling. "It's kind of a compliment."

He faced her, relief visible. "I appreciate that. Sexual arousal is often involuntary." His eyes brightened with humor. "It's the result of stimulus."

"Any stimulus?" she asked, her voice teasing.

"The good kind. In this case, it's being close to and kissing a very beautiful woman I happen to like a lot."

"Then why would I be mad?" It wasn't as if he expected anything. She knew he would never push her. "I might be feeling a little stimulus reaction myself."

He gave her a slow, sexy smile. "That's very convenient."

"Isn't it?"

She walked toward him and took his hands in hers, then placed them on her breasts.

"Did you want to touch these?" she asked softly as she stared into his eyes.

"Very much."

"Me, too."

He pulled her close and kissed her again. This time his hands roamed her back and slid down to her hips. She had a thought that they were about to cross the line of no return and wondered if she was ready. Then she decided it didn't much matter because when it came to this man, she was all in.

The second the deed was done, Jana knew she'd made a huge mistake. Not that the sex hadn't been great, but it was too soon. They needed to get to know each other better. Only before she could work up a real sense of dread, Rick sat up.

"We had sex!" he announced, beaming at her. "You had an orgasm."

There was no arguing with that, she thought, still remembering how he'd gone down on her with a skill and enthusiasm that had left her unable to do anything but speed toward her very satisfying release. Did he have his ability in bed because he paid attention to details, or had those anatomy classes taught him something special?

"I had an excellent orgasm," she told him, speaking the truth.

"Me, too." He picked up her hand and kissed her knuckles. "Best date ever. Now I'm going to make you dinner."

He dressed quickly and headed for the kitchen, leaving Jana alone in his large bed. Okay, so much for the postcoital cuddle, she thought humorously, but it was a small flaw to worry about.

And in about thirty minutes, the man was going to feed her chicken piccata. Where was the bad?

Several hours later, she let herself into her house. Despite the late hour, she wasn't sleepy at all. Dinner had been great, with Rick being his normal chatty self. They'd talked about how the Dodgers were off to a slow start and had compared fantasy travel destinations. He'd been attentive, kind and hadn't tried to get her back into bed—something for which she was grateful. She needed time to think.

She walked into the living room and found Teddy waiting up for her. He glanced up from his e-reader.

"Have a good time?"

"I did, and this is ridiculous. I'm an adult. You can go to bed, you know. If something bad happens, I promise I'll call and wake you up."

"I was reading."

"Normally you read in your room."

"I needed a change of scene." He studied her for a second, then raised his eyebrows. "Interesting."

She felt herself flush and knew he'd guessed what had happened. She didn't know how he did it, but Teddy had a sense about things like that.

"I know, I know." She sank onto the sofa and shook her head. "It was too soon. I can't even tell you how it happened."

"You've had a child, Jana. You have to know how it happens."

She glared at him. "Ha ha. You know what I mean. I wasn't planning on sleeping with him, but suddenly there we were."

"Do you like him?"

"Yes. Otherwise there wouldn't have been the sex."

"Things are moving fast. Should I be worried?"

"About Rick? No. He's a good guy."

"I'd actually be worried about you."

"I'm fine."

She was. Mostly. There were complications with dating Rick—

complications in the form of her friend Beth. Why oh why did she have to be his sister?

"I want to meet him," Teddy said firmly.

She groaned. "No. You can't. You're making this more than it is."

He looked at her without speaking, but she could hear his voice in her head—the one pointing out that if things were moving too quickly, whose fault was that? She'd agreed to meet Rick's sister. It was only fair Teddy got to meet Rick as well.

"Could you just look him up online?" she asked, trying to keep the whine out of her voice.

"Already did. He seems legit. Now I want to look him in the eye. Man to man." He paused, then smiled. "And the sister."

"Teddy, no. Come on. It's too much. It'll be like a parade or something."

"I was thinking more like dinner. We'll keep it casual. Invite them over here. I'll cook. Dex can take the kids." He gentled his voice. "You like this guy. That's great. I want you to be happy, but you have to remember that there's always family lurking, and family doesn't go away. To make this work with him, you have to make it work with Beth. Maybe I can help smooth things over with her."

While she appreciated his concern, she wasn't six anymore, crying because some bully stole her lunch money. "I can fight my own battles."

"You can, but you don't always have to. I got your back, kid. Always."

Beth spent the week trying to figure out why she'd acted so badly with Jana. She knew some of the problem was how Rick had described the other woman. Not on purpose—he would never deliberately mislead her about something important, but he didn't always get the details right. Beth was also willing to admit she might have been a little too quick to assume the worst instead of waiting for more information. But the real issue, the very heart of the problem, seemed to lie more in what Kai had so bluntly told her. That no one would ever be good enough for her brother.

And while that was pretty bad, Beth was fairly sure that there was an even uglier truth lurking underneath. That in her heart of hearts, she didn't want her brother to find anyone because if he did, she would be alone.

Not that they hung out all the time now, but knowing he wasn't able to find someone and settle down meant maybe her problems weren't her fault. Maybe they were both just damaged, and if they were, then she had less responsibility to fix herself. The cowardly and lazy way out.

She wasn't sure how long she'd been hiding that feeling. While she would guess it had always been there, the divorce might have given it a little more power. She'd focused on her brother because he was a distraction, and it was easier to worry about him than try to fix herself.

The week of soul searching had been mentally exhausting, but Beth liked to think she'd grown from the experience. She wasn't healed, but she felt she had a lot more clarity. With that had come the realization that she'd been a horrible friend. She liked Jana very much, admired her, even, and yet had treated her badly. When she thought about what she'd said and how she'd acted, she was embarrassed and ashamed.

She got to the food bank a few minutes early and went right to work. Part of her wondered if Jana would show up. She didn't doubt her friend would still volunteer, but maybe she'd arranged to change her day. An hour into her shift, she caught sight of Jana helping someone in produce. For a second their eyes locked, but neither of them said anything. Jana returned her attention to her customer.

Beth spent much of her time with a grocery cart filled with frozen turkeys. The unexpected donation had filled the freezer, so Beth was asked to make personal appeals to see if they could move the turkeys even though it was early April rather than a more traditional time of year.

She approached customers one at a time, offering a free turkey to anyone who would take one. By the end of her shift, she'd gotten rid of all but two, leaving much-needed freezer space open for the next donation.

She signed out, went to her car for the small picnic basket she'd used to pack the dinner she'd brought, then made her way to the rear of the building. She and Jana hadn't spoken, and she didn't know if they were having dinner together or not. If Jana didn't show up, Beth planned to text her an apology, but she was hoping to deliver it in person.

The seconds crawled by. Finally at a few minutes after six, Jana walked out onto the patio and looked at her. Beth was instantly on her feet.

"I'm sorry," she said quickly. "I was such a horrible person. I said things and thought things and acted awful. I hurt you. I embarrassed myself. I'm still not sure why, but I'm wondering if maybe my actions were more about me and Rick than you at all. Maybe I was feeling that if Rick found someone and was happy, I would have to face the fact that I'm in such a stagnant place since my divorce. I thought I was doing well, but now I wonder if that's not true, and somehow you got caught up in that. I'm sorry," she repeated.

Jana smiled. "You have to breathe."

"I am. I feel stupid and sad."

"I didn't help the situation," Jana said as she walked to the table. "I joked about dating a guy with money. I know it's just a thing women do and we don't mean it, but the thought got planted in your brain. Plus the confusion between what Rick said about me and what you know and his past with other women."

She paused, and the smile widened. "Don't take this wrong, but your brother isn't very good with details."

"Right? You'd think he would be, given his work is *all* about details."

Some of her tension faded, and the icky feeling she'd been carrying around seemed to ease a little.

"I really am sorry," she whispered.

"Me, too."

"I want to start over. Our friendship is important to me."

Jana smiled. "Same here. So let's do that."

Beth impulsively reached for her friend. Jana stepped close, and they hugged. When they stepped back, Beth added, "I brought dinner."

"I can be bribed with your delicious food."

They sat down, and Beth passed out sandwiches, salad and sparkling water.

"Tell me everything," Jana said. "What have I missed?"

Beth resisted the need to roll her eyes. "My life is very boring. I have nothing new to report, except I think my Aunt Agatha might be dating a new guy, which both impresses and depresses me. I admire her willingness to put herself out there, and yet I find myself intimidated by my sixtysomething aunt's love life."

"Go, Agatha. Are you serious about wanting to date someone?"

"Yes, I think so. But I haven't dated since the divorce. I worry that I've forgotten what few skills I might have had before I got married." She paused, then grinned. "I should ask Rick if he knows any single guys. Then we could both be dating doctors."

Jana laughed. "We could form a club."

Beth picked up her sandwich, relieved conversation was flowing easily. Maybe her mistakes weren't unrecoverable.

"How's Linnie?"

"Growing every day. She's so mature for her age. I know that's from being the youngest, but I'm terrified I'll blink and she'll want to be borrowing the car."

Beth thought about how she'd enjoyed her day with the four-year-old. "She's at a great age."

As she spoke, she heard the wistfulness in her voice. Where were the children in her own life? she wondered. She was only a few years shy of forty, and kids had somehow never been on her radar. She'd meant to have them, had assumed she would. But what if she didn't?

Unexpected sadness gripped her. Was she going to die child-less? Somehow that seemed worse than simply being alone.

"So, I have a weird question," Jana said, drawing Beth away from her uncomfortable thoughts. "I guess it's more of a state-ment."

Beth nodded, encouraging her friend to continue.

"Teddy would like to meet you and Rick. You've already met me, and he's feeling a little left out."

Teddy her brother. The massage-therapist-slash-acupuncturist who was a widower with three children. Before her mind could go in dark directions and start making assumptions, she reminded herself how badly that had worked out last time. She was going to meet Jana's brother with an open mind and only see the good in the situation.

"It's way too soon for that," she said with a smile. "But you're right. I've already met you, which sounds strange, but I get what you're saying. Sure. Let's do it. Then we will all have met."

Jana relaxed in her chair. "I know this is all a little unusual, but thanks for agreeing. Once it's done, we can return to our regular lives."

"I can't remember if you told me how long ago Teddy's wife died."

Jana thought for a second. "It's been nearly five years." She frowned. "I didn't realize it had been that long. But I was preg-nant with Linnie when she passed. Time goes so quickly. Any-way, it'll just be the four of us. Dex will take the kids." She laughed. "They're all terrific, but having them join us means we won't get a second to just talk. They can be a handful and very loud."

Four was a lot, Beth thought. Growing up it had just been her and Rick, and her brother had been more interested in reading or being on his computer than interacting with anyone.

"I've checked with Rick," Jana added. "He can do this Saturday if that works for you. Or is it too soon?"

Beth's gut response was that she wanted more time, but even as she thought that, she wondered why. It wasn't as if she had a pressing social calendar. Better to get the meeting behind her so she could undo all her Jana mistakes and start fresh on her... on her...

Once again she was forced to acknowledge that she genuinely had nothing to look forward to—not in a personal way. No date, no concert, no summer weekend away with friends. Wow, did she need to figure out how to find a life.

"Saturday is perfect," she told Jana. "I can't wait."

A true statement. And come Sunday morning, she was going to have a serious talk with herself and figure out a way to have more in her small world. She was capable and knew how to be successful. She had Jana back as her friend, and that was an excellent start.

10

"Is this a date?" Magnolia asked as she arranged radish quarters on a small platter. She spoke without looking up from what she was doing, as if the answer didn't matter.

Jana reached for another washed radish and quartered it. "No, sweetie. It's just adults getting together. Beth is my friend from the food bank. I know her brother Rick, so they're coming over for dinner. Your dad has never met Beth before. It's not a date."

Because Teddy hadn't been out with anyone since Valonia's death—something Jana had been thinking about since realizing it had been nearly five years.

As if reading her mind, Magnolia said, "He's been alone a long time. That's not good. He needs someone."

"Have you been listening in on conversations again?" Jana asked, her voice teasing.

Magnolia flashed her a grin. "Some, but I remember when we went to the child psychologist after Mommy died. I remember what she said about moving on emotionally. She said healthy people fall in love again and that someday our dad might want that. She said Mommy would always be our forever mom but it would be good for us to have another woman in our lives. That role models were advantageous."

Jana gave a little prayer of thanks that her brother had been together enough to get his kids into therapy after the tragic loss. They'd all been in shock and not dealing with the emptiness.

"*Advantageous* is a pretty big word," she said. "I'm impressed."

"I'm an impressive sort of girl." Magnolia's smile faded. "I have friends whose parents are divorced, and they date. Sometimes it's good and sometimes it's not."

"I think you can trust your dad to find one of the good ones, should that ever happen."

"I know, but I'm wondering if it's ever going to happen. I remember Mommy the most. Atlas remembers some, but Orchid doesn't at all. She was too young when Mommy died. She needs an older woman to look up to and learn from. You and I can only do so much."

Jana had moved on to slicing peeled cucumber for the veggie tray they were having as an appetizer. Now she set down her knife and hugged her niece.

"I love you so much," she said, thinking Magnolia was one amazing kid.

"I love you, too. I know you said Rick is a friend, but he's really your boyfriend, isn't he?"

Jana groaned. "More listening in when you shouldn't?"

Magnolia laughed. "Maybe a little. I won't say anything to Linnie. She's still pretty young. I know you want to be sure before you introduce him to her and us." She wrinkled her nose. "I don't think I'm going to like having a boyfriend. I don't get the point."

"Sometimes boys are nice to hang out with."

Magnolia looked doubtful. "Why? Atlas can be really annoying, and we like different stuff."

"A brother is very different from a boyfriend. Plus, when you get older, you'll find you have more in common with boys than you do now."

"My friend Alicia has two moms. They're lesbians. So it's only girls in the house. Even their cats are girls." She sounded intrigued by the concept. "That could be nice."

Jana felt the weight of the topic and wasn't sure what to say. "Being a lesbian is a little bit more than having a female-only household, but it's nothing you have to decide right now." She pointed at the tray. "Do you think we have enough appetizers?"

Magnolia considered the question. "You've got the veggies and crab dip and deviled eggs. You're going to have dinner right after. I don't think you need anything more."

"Thanks for your help."

Jana eyed the colorful array of cut vegetables and thought about the rest of menu. With luck everything would turn out. She felt oddly nervous about the evening and hoped everyone would get along.

Magnolia glanced at the clock on the wall. "Dex will be here soon. I'm going to get everyone ready." She pointed at Jana. "I'm gonna want a full report when I get home."

Jana grinned. "Yes, ma'am. I'll share the deets for sure."

As Beth approached her destination, she found herself driving slower and slower. She wasn't just nervous about the upcoming dinner. She was embarrassed by the reason it was happening in the first place. Because she could tell herself it was all in the name of fairness—she'd met the woman Rick was dating, so Teddy wanted to meet her—but she had a rock in her belly that said it was a whole lot more about her bad behavior. Humiliating but true.

"It's one dinner. You'll survive," she murmured aloud as she turned onto what she thought was the right street. Faster than she would have liked, she was pulling into a wide driveway in front of a large, sprawling single-story house.

The neighborhood was nice. Older, with oversize lots and established landscaping. She was a couple of miles inland—still in the "good weather" zone of the beach but far enough away that land was at slightly less of a premium, although it was still Malibu and nothing was cheap.

She parked and looked around. She didn't see Rick's car, so he wasn't here yet. Hmm, what to do? Sitting outside waiting for him seemed weird, but going in by herself was also not something she wanted to do. Why had she come on time? If she'd been a few minutes late, Rick probably would have beaten her here.

She wrestled with indecision for about twenty seconds, then grabbed the floral arrangement she'd stopped to get and walked toward the front of the house. Apprehension and nausea churned, and she nearly turned around twice. As soon as she reached the door, she pushed the bell so she wouldn't change her mind and bolt.

"You made it," Jana said with a warm smile. "Come on in."

Seeing her friend allowed Beth to relax a little. "I did. Great house. I love the neighborhood. It's like where I live, although a bit more fancy."

Jana laughed. "Wait until you see the beams and vaulted ceiling in the living room. The 1970s are alive and well in this house."

Beth handed her the flowers. The tightly arranged, elegant flowers were in a square glass vase. Orchids nestled with baby roses.

"Thanks for having me," Beth said.

Jana touched one of the petals. "They're beautiful. Thank you." She grinned. "Now that you've brought me flowers, I'm going to invite you over more often."

Beth followed her into the house. It was big and spacious, done in warm colors. As promised, the living room had a distinctive seventies vibe, but that suited the house.

"Let me put the flowers on the table," Jana said. "Then we can sit and talk until Rick gets here."

Just as she left the room, a tall man entered through a different door. Beth automatically smiled and took a step in his direction, only to come to a stop when her eyes met his.

He. Was. Gorgeous. Tall with broad shoulders, chiseled features and piercing blue eyes. His hair was dark, and he moved with an easy grace that took her breath away. She went cold, then hot, and her lungs stopped working. No doubt she was gaping at him like a fish, but she couldn't help it. Her brain had shut down along with the rest of her organs. She was probably close to passing out, but none of that mattered. Honest to God, she didn't care if the world stopped turning.

The intense visceral response stunned her nearly as much as the amazing man in front of her. Sure, she'd thought men were attractive before, and she vaguely remembered having a man crush or two in her life, but nothing like this.

Time seemed to slow as he approached, then held out his hand. She was caught up in his gaze, in her need to be near him, to hear the sound of his voice, to breathe in the scent of his body. She wanted him, wanted *them* in whatever form that took.

"Hi, Beth. I'm Teddy."

She fumbled her way through a quick handshake, ignoring the heat and tingles that danced through her body when their palms lightly brushed. She thought maybe she'd managed a faint "hello" back, although she couldn't be sure. Not with him staring at her.

She wanted to believe he felt whatever it was the same as she did, but knew his attention was probably because she was coming off as some clueless, socially inept person who until eight seconds ago had been living her life in a cave. Why couldn't she be younger or taller or prettier or French? Anything other than the boring, flawed person she was?

She forced herself to breathe and tried to mentally shake off her never-felt-before chemical reaction so she could form sentences.

"Your house is great," she managed.

He smiled. "Thanks."

Oh, no. The smile made everything worse. He had little lines by his eyes and a dimple in his left cheek. The smile was sexy and warm and promising. She nearly took a step toward him, only able to stop herself at the last second.

Thankfully the doorbell sounded just then, and Jana came back with the flowers. Relief poured through Beth—Rick had arrived and now there would be a distraction. She would focus on her brother and try to ignore Teddy as best she could.

The next few minutes were filled with greetings. Beth hurried up to Rick, wishing there was a way to get him alone long enough for her to beg for his help. Only she didn't know how to do that without Jana and Teddy wondering what was wrong with her.

"Hey, sis," he said, smiling at her.

"Hi, yourself." She hugged him and started to step back, only to pause when she caught a faint but unfamiliar fragrance. "Did you change fabric softeners?"

He frowned at her. "I don't know. I use what I use. Why?"

Saying he smelled different would sound too strange, so she simply smiled and shrugged. "Just asking."

Thankfully Teddy suggested they all go outside. They walked through a large family room and through open sliding doors into a big backyard. There were several seating areas in shade and out in the sun. At the far end of the yard was a gate that, she would guess, led to Teddy's workspace. A half-dozen Adirondack chairs circled a fire pit in the far corner, but what most caught her eye were all the toys scattered around. There was a swing set with a slide, several balls, two scooters and a sandbox.

"That's right," she said aloud. "You have children."

The killer smile returned. "Three. They're with a friend for the evening, along with Jana's daughter. We thought it would be easier for us to talk without them around. They tend to dominate any conversation."

"Children do that."

They settled in the shade. A platter of appetizers and a pitcher of sangria were already there, along with plates and glasses. Jana poured them drinks. Beth took hers and sipped, then set down her glass and tried not to look at Teddy.

But it was like being too close to the sun—the man was impossible to ignore. She wanted to study him and learn every plane of his face. She wanted to touch his hands, his chest, and stare deeply into his eyes. She was also terrified of saying something stupid, which made it difficult to have a normal conversation.

She turned to her brother, thinking he could do the talking, but saw that somehow Rick and Jana were seated a little bit away from her and Teddy. As if they were separate couples. Not that she and Teddy were a couple or anything other than strangers who—

Stop! she commanded herself. She had to get a grip and act normal.

She opened her mouth and blurted, "Jana tells me you're a massage therapist."

One eyebrow rose. "Massage is part of my practice, but most of my patients come to see me for acupuncture."

Oh, right. "That sounds interesting. How long have you been doing that?"

"I went to China to study when I was sixteen."

"You didn't finish high school first?"

He smiled. "I graduated early. I had tutors, which helped."

Tutors because... Not that she was going to ask. She couldn't be trusted to guide a conversation. Better to just say the next obvious thing.

"Sixteen seems really young to travel halfway around the world. Did one of your parents go with you?"

"They stayed home with Jana. We had family friends over there. I lived with them the first couple of years, then got a place on my own. Once I'd completed my studies, I moved back here. I was a little young to open my own practice, so I worked with someone."

"I can't imagine leaving everything I know to go all that way. Certainly not when I was sixteen," she admitted. "Did you speak the language?"

He chuckled. "Very badly. My instructors spoke English well enough, and I picked up as much Mandarin as I could." He winked at her. "I'm good to have around in an authentic Chinese restaurant because I can read the menu."

She laughed and felt some of her tension ease. Not her attraction—that was still at unheard-of levels—but she was going to do her best to ignore it.

"Jana mentioned you own Surf Sandwiches," he said.

"I do, although what I do isn't anywhere near as exciting as moving to China."

"I know that place. Great sandwiches."

While the words were kind, she doubted he'd ever been in her store. Given her reaction to him tonight, she definitely would have remembered seeing him.

She allowed herself a brief, vivid fantasy of him walking in to order something only to have their eyes meet over the selection of condiments. The background music would swell, they would smile at each other, and then he would suggest they run away to a tropical island for the next six or eight months.

"Are you married?" he asked.

"Divorced."

"Any kids?"

She shook her head. "But you have three."

He waved toward the array of toys scattered around. "How

did you guess? They're great. Magnolia is twelve but sometimes acts like she's forty. She likes to take charge, something that kicked into overdrive after she lost her mom. Jana and I constantly have to remind ourselves not to let her take on too much responsibility. She needs to be my daughter, not my protector."

"That's got to be hard for you. They were so young when your wife died. I'm sorry."

"Thanks. It came out of nowhere. Valonia was happy and healthy. One second she was on a conference call at work, and then she was dead from a pulmonary embolism. There was no warning."

His gaze looked past her, as if he was reliving the day. "She was the vice president at a large brokerage company. She had so many dreams and plans for us and the kids. When her assistant called to tell me she'd collapsed, I thought it was a mistake."

Her heart ached for him and his children—for what they'd lost and all they'd gone through.

"I can't imagine," she admitted. "They were so young."

"Orchid was only eighteen months. She and Atlas, the middle one, couldn't understand where Mommy was." He looked at her, the pain visible in his eyes. "Jana got us through. She moved in and took charge. I was a wreck. Valonia and I were supposed to have the rest of our lives together. I kept waiting for her to call and say she was on her way home."

He drew in a breath. "She'd always had the high-powered career. We'd met through friends." The smile returned. "On paper we had nothing in common, and I wasn't that interested in meeting her, but I didn't know how to get out of it. She was a rising star in the corporate world. I was a too-serious vegetarian, alternative medicine practitioner who didn't own much more than I could fit into a backpack. But we clicked, you know? I took one look at her and knew she was the one."

She could feel his pain, along with the bittersweetness of his memories. Beth sat there, not sure what to do. Running seemed to be the most sensible choice, only she was committed to having dinner with Jana and Teddy. But staying seemed impossible. She tried to tell herself the irony of the situation was actually kind of funny—if only it didn't sting so much.

All her life she'd done her best to avoid strong emotions. She'd tried to be sensible and thoughtful about any decisions she made. Living like her mother—racing toward the fire to burn as hot as possible—was an anathema to her. Yet here she was—wildly attracted to a man she barely knew, wishing he felt the same, and desperate to have him notice her as a woman. For the first time ever she was willing to risk it all, to be impulsive and damn the consequences. At the same time, the man in question was clearly and deeply still in love with his late wife. And wasn't that a kick in the gut?

Rick helped Jana clear the table. Beth had already left, claiming an early morning, and Jana had shooed Teddy back to his side of the house.

"Tonight was great," Rick said happily, carrying in two wineglasses and setting them on the counter. "Thanks for suggesting this. I liked getting to know Teddy."

"He felt the same about you," she said, relieved everything had gone so well. Her brother had spent the first hour or so talking to Beth. Then the four of them had chatted easily over dinner.

Rick drew her close and lightly kissed her. "So we're good? Everyone is friends?"

She saw the faint line of worry between his eyebrows and touched his cheek. "We are all excellent," she told him. "I'm glad we did this."

"Me, too."

She gave him a quick smile, then stepped out of his embrace before glancing at the clock on the wall. He followed her gaze.

"Do you need me to leave? I was going to help with the

cleanup, but if you're worried about Linnie coming home, I get it."

"I appreciate that, Rick. You're right. Dex will be bringing the kids back and, well, it's still soon for you to meet any of the kids."

She looked at him, wondering if he would get upset. Instead he moved close again and hugged her.

"Of course. You need to worry about her, and that's a good thing." His mouth brushed hers. "But I want to see you again. I'm on call this weekend, but after that, okay?"

"Absolutely."

Because the more she was with Rick, the more she was willing to believe he might be exactly who she'd been waiting for.

Beth spent the drive home trying not to think about the evening or Teddy or the twisting, hungry wanting swirling through her belly. She was uncomfortable in ways she couldn't explain and restless to the point of barely being able to focus on her driving. Once she was in the house, she walked directly to the liquor cabinet and pulled out the bottle of brandy.

"Oh, dear. That can't be good."

She turned and saw Agatha walking into the kitchen.

"Dinner not go well?" her aunt asked sympathetically. "Do we not like the brother?"

"The brother is fine." Beth took out two glasses and poured, then handed her aunt one. She walked to the kitchen table and sat down.

Agatha settled across from her, but didn't speak, as if willing to let Beth lead the conversation.

"He was very nice. He does acupuncture. Or practices it." She frowned. "I don't know the correct verb. He's successful at what he does, although I'm pretty sure any money comes from his late wife. She was in finance. She died very suddenly about five years ago. He has three kids, and Jana has Linnie. They're a beautiful blended family."

Agatha pressed her lips together. "While that all sounds lovely, there's something in your voice. Was it Rick?"

"What? No. He was fine. He adores Jana, by the way. And she's great." Beth looked at her aunt. "I was attracted to Teddy."

"The brother?"

She nodded. "I can't explain it. I've never felt like that before. One second I was perfectly normal, living my life, breathing. You know, all the regular stuff. Then he walked into the room and everything changed." She clutched her glass. "I was humiliated."

Her aunt smiled at her. "Unless you started taking your clothes off, there's no humiliation required."

"I stayed dressed, thankfully. But I couldn't think. I don't get it. Yes, he's attractive, but so are millions of other people. I've had movie stars in my store. I don't care—that's not my thing. I don't gush or overreact. But being around him." She shook her head. "I can't explain it, and I sure don't like it."

"Well, I do. Bravo."

Beth glared at her aunt. "This isn't a good thing. I don't want to be irrational or out of control. I refuse to be my mother."

"Darling, there's an entire Grand Canyon between what you're describing and acting like your mother. You met a nice man who turns you on. That's exciting."

"He's still in love with his late wife. He talked about her. Nothing overly gushy, but his voice." She winced at the memory. "I was jealous of a dead woman. I'm attracted to a dead woman's husband."

"There's a cheerful perspective." Agatha sipped her drink. "You're looking at this all wrong. Tonight was a revelation. You discovered you have the ability to throw yourself into the moment. You've been moping around here for weeks, ever since you saw that very tacky billboard of Ian proposing." She flicked her wrist. "Now you know you're well and truly ready to move on."

Beth wasn't sure she wanted to hear what her aunt had to say but still cautiously asked, "In what way?"

"Now you can find your passion. You said you'd never been so attracted to a man before. That means you have unexplored depths. So explore them now. What else excites you? A new hobby? Travel? You used to talk about horseback riding. What about that? Or maybe get yourself out there and start dating. If Teddy could inspire you, there must be other men who can do the same."

While her aunt's words made sense, Beth wasn't so sure her hidden depths should be brought to life. As for finding someone else who made her feel the way Teddy did—um, no.

"I don't like being out of control," she said. "It's too risky and uncomfortable."

"It's exciting."

"Now you sound like Mom."

"We both know that's not true. Your mother had an extreme view of chasing danger. You don't want to be like her, but sometimes I worry you've gone too far in the other direction. What is it you young people talk about? FOMO? You need a little more of that in your life."

Beth grinned. "How do you know about fear of missing out?"

"I'm very in tune with young people today," Agatha said with a laugh. "They adore me."

"We all adore you."

She thought about what her aunt had said. Yes, avoiding her mother's path of destruction had always seemed wise, but she supposed a case could be made for being *too* cautious. And while she hated to admit to moping, seeing the billboard and all the pictures on Ian's Instagram account had rattled her. Her business was thriving, but that was only one part of her life. She needed more than just the success of her sandwich shop. Just as important, she wanted more. Connections, a man who cared about her, and yes, maybe a couple of hobbies. Kids.

The latter seemed the least likely. She was thirty-eight and single. She wasn't the type to go out and find a sperm donor, which meant getting pregnant the old-fashioned way or accepting it simply wasn't going to happen for her.

"About your young man," Agatha began.

"He's not mine. I told you, he's still in love with his late wife."

"You don't know that."

"You weren't there." Teddy had looked so stricken as he'd talked about Valonia. "They were in love when she died. There was no time to prepare. She was just gone."

"Which is tragic, but even the most shattered heart heals. You should call him."

Beth looked at her aunt and started laughing. "Because that's so who I am? Call him and say what? 'Hi. We just met, and I'm pretty sure you're in love with someone else, but did you want to come over for sex?' I don't think so."

"I was thinking more along the lines of dinner, but if you want to jump right to dessert, then that's another option."

Beth rose and set her half-finished brandy on the counter by the sink, then returned to the table and kissed her aunt on the cheek.

"I love you, and I appreciate how you worry about me. I'm going to take my Teddy obsession and carefully lock it away where it won't hurt anyone. Especially me." She smiled. "But I promise to think about the passion thing. Maybe there's a slightly safer way to channel my wild side into something a little more productive than an unrequited crush."

"That sounds like an excellent plan."

11

Beth did her best to put the irresistible and unobtainable
Teddy out of her mind. Monday at the shop, she focused solely
on work and her employees, doing her best to act completely
normal. As no one seemed to be whispering about her behind
her back, she thought maybe she was doing all right. Sure, she
was still thinking about him every forty seconds, but that was
okay. By this time next week, she would bet she could go a
whole ninety seconds without him crossing her mind.

The lunch crowd poured in, and the line of waiting customers stretched out the door. Beth stepped up to the counter, completing sandwiches and upselling the sides, while Kai and Albert
expertly manned the cash registers. The small printer on the
counter spit out phone orders one after the other.

By one thirty the crowd had thinned to something more

manageable. Beth stayed up front until everyone had taken a
break. She was about to retreat to her office when the front door
opened and Teddy stepped inside the store.

In less than a nanosecond, the air went from normal to elec-
trically charged. Her chest got tight, and she couldn't catch her
breath. His gaze scanned the space before settling on her face,
and while it was very unlikely, she would swear she heard the
upswell of a movie score at that point where the hero returns
to claim his woman.

He was just as gorgeous as she remembered with deep blue
eyes and dark hair. He had on jeans and a long-sleeved shirt—
normal attire for the average American male, yet on him, it took
on supermodel importance. She was instantly aware of her bright
yellow apron over her Surf Sandwiches T-shirt and that she was
wearing a hairnet and no makeup. Frustration joined the heat
in her belly. Just once, couldn't she dazzle?

He stepped toward her and smiled. Fortunately she'd thought
to grab onto the counter so she didn't fall over.

"Hi," he said.

"Hi."

"I came by earlier. You were slammed."

"Lunch is like that around here."

Wait, what? He'd come by earlier? To see her? No, that couldn't
be right. He must want a sandwich, and she sold sandwiches.
Things were working out already.

"Can I, um, get you something?"

The smile returned, inspiring more heat and a nearly buzz-
ing tingle in all her girl places.

"I thought maybe we could take a walk."

He didn't want a sandwich? Now she was totally confused,
which must have shown, because Kai moved close and gave her
a little push toward the back.

"Go ahead," he told her. "Albert and I have this." He turned
to Teddy. "I'm Kai."

"Teddy."

Kai's gaze was steady. "You're a friend of Beth's?"

"He's Jana's brother," she said before retreating to the break room, where she ripped off the hairnet and apron and wondered what else she should do before taking a walk with Teddy. She had on shoes, so that was good, and she was familiar with the outdoors.

"Get a grip," she whispered to herself as she pressed a hand to her belly. "He's just a guy, and you're acting weird." Being overly cautious was one thing, but slipping into madness wasn't okay.

It was just that being around him did something to her. Something she'd never experienced before and didn't know how to deal with. She glanced at the small mirror by the lockers, brushed back a few stray hairs and headed to the front, where Teddy and Kai were talking. They both looked at her when she appeared, but she could only see Teddy.

She'd never considered looks especially important, but there was something about that man, she thought dreamily. Something that made her feel weak and strong at the same time. She was oh so grateful to be a single, age-appropriate woman in his presence. Not that he would be interested in her that way, she reminded herself. After all, they weren't in the same league at all. Plus the whole "in love with his late wife" thing. So why was he here? Not that she would ask. She would simply enjoy the moment and overanalyze it later.

They walked outside. Teddy pointed back at the store. "I was reading the menu. Peanut butter and pickles almost make sense, but peanut butter and cold cereal?" He shuddered. "That sounds like something my kids would ask for."

She smiled at him. "And you'd say no?"

He grinned. "I don't know. They don't get a lot of processed breakfast cereal, so I might say yes. It's fortified, and the peanut butter would mitigate the sugar. But it's not anything I'd want to eat."

"You should try it before you judge," she teased. "All the PB sandwiches are very popular with the high school crowd. Hey, wait a minute. The other night you ate chicken."

He looked confused. "Asking or telling?"

"Pointing out that you ate chicken."

"We all did. I barbecued it special for our meal." His expression turned concerned. "Is that a problem?"

"You said you and Valonia had nothing in common and that you were a vegetarian."

"I'm less committed these days," he said with a smile. "We have meat-free days every week, but with the kids around and trying to get the right nutrients into them, I caved." He studied her. "Do you think less of me now?"

"Of course not." She couldn't believe she'd blurted out the chicken thing. What did it matter? Why couldn't she act normal?

They started walking along the sidewalk. Across the street was a huge public parking lot, and beyond that were the beach and the ocean. The sound of the surf was barely audible over the cry of the gulls and the traffic rushing by, but the scent of salt air carried to them. The afternoon was warm, the breeze light.

"How long have you owned Surf Sandwiches?" he asked.

"About fourteen years. I bought it from my aunt and uncle." She didn't mention the deal she'd made that they would help pay for Rick's medical school tuition in return. "My mom died when Rick and I were young—I was barely a teenager. We went into foster care for about eighteen months. My mom and aunt were estranged, so Agatha didn't know anything about her death. As Rick and I hadn't seen her since we were maybe six and three, I never thought to have anyone try to find her."

She told herself to stop talking, that he couldn't possibly want to know all this, but somehow the words kept coming. "One day Agatha tried to find her sister, only to learn she'd died. She immediately started looking for us and then took us in. We were so grateful. Foster care was tough. Rick never talks about his time, but when we were back together, he was different. More withdrawn. I don't know exactly. But the point is, Agatha saved us."

"That was generous of her."

She nodded. "She's such a sweet and giving person. She and her husband never really wanted kids, and they had no idea how to be parents, but they made sure Rick and I knew they would be there for us, no matter what. I started working in the sandwich shop right away."

"Did you like it?" he asked. "Was it meaningful or just a job?"

An interesting question. "I wanted to earn money as a way to keep me and Rick safe. You know, in case something bad happened again." Because being ripped out of their home, separated and sent to live with strangers, had been terrifying.

"But aside from that, I did enjoy working in the shop. I liked the certainty of it, if that makes sense."

He stopped and faced her. "You were what? Fifteen? Sixteen? How could you save enough money to keep your brother safe?"

"I couldn't," she admitted. "But I had to try. He needed me. Rick's younger by three years, but it's more than that. He was so smart. The other kids couldn't handle it and picked on him. Sometimes the teachers didn't know what to do with him."

"You protected him."

She nodded.

"I get that," he told her. "I have a strong need to protect Jana." One corner of his mouth turned up. "Although she would tell you that she can take care of herself."

Beth laughed. "I hear that, too, but once the oldest, always the oldest. It's a thing."

They were looking at each other, eyes locked. She felt floaty and happy and couldn't help wishing he would kiss her. Right there, in front of God and everyone. She wanted a kiss and so much more.

The need, the attraction were unfamiliar. Like being back in high school but without the cute clothes.

"I told you my wife's been gone nearly five years," he said.

Her stomach sank. Great. He'd figured out she was interested in him and was trying to let her down gently. The butterflies died, leaving only faint nausea and a need to run away to somewhere small and dark.

"I have three kids and a house that's mostly in chaos," he continued, his gaze intense. "I haven't dated since I lost her. I didn't want to. It wasn't about being ready to move on so much as there not being a reason. I didn't see the point. Until now."

If she'd been a cartoon character, her eyes would have bugged out as someone in the Foley department made some comical sound in the background.

No, she told herself. He hadn't said what she thought he'd said. He was him, and she was not what he was looking for.

"Would you have dinner with me?" he asked.

Her mind went blank. It totally emptied, and she could only stare at him.

"Why?" she squeaked, then cleared her throat. "I mean, why?"

He smiled. "I want to get to know you better. You intrigue me."

That was good, right? Wasn't it? She'd never intrigued anyone before. "But I was so awkward the other night. I was like a gecko trying to learn to crochet."

He laughed. "That's a very specific visual. You weren't awkward, you were lovely. So, dinner?"

"Yes." Of course. They could go to Paris if he wanted. Not that she knew where her passport was, but she could find it, and they could go right now. Or dinner would be good, too.

"I'm nervous," he admitted. "But excited."

"Me, too."

"Is Friday too soon?"

If it were up to her, they would start their date now. But saying that might mean giving him second thoughts. "Friday's perfect."

He pulled out his phone. "Let me get your number."

★ ★ ★

Jana had never taken dance as a child. Her mom had suggested it a few times, but Jana had been more of an outdoor kid than an indoor one. She would rather be running around and playing than in a dance studio somewhere, learning foundational steps and practicing them over and over.

Now, as she got out of her car and raced toward the house, she thought maybe she could do a grand jeté or two right there on the porch. Of course, if she was wrong, she would pull something or fall on her face, but did that really matter? Sometimes the happiness inside needed to be expressed in dance—even without professional training.

She leaped onto the porch, stumbled a little, then started laughing. She spun once and flung open the front door.

"Where are you?" she shouted into the house. She'd seen Dex's SUV parked in front and knew he was somewhere inside.

"Family room. What's up?"

She ran toward his voice, and when she saw him, she flung herself at him.

"I got in! I got in! I start in the fall and they sent me a financial aid package and I got in!"

Dex caught her and spun her around. "Good for you. That's fantastic."

The kids gathered around, cheering and jumping. Linnie hugged her.

"Mommy, you're going to be a nurse."

"I am." Jana picked up her daughter and held her tight. "It's going to mean more studying, but I'm ready."

The other three wanted their hugs as well. Once they'd all collapsed on the sofa, Jana waved her phone. "I have to fill out the financial aid paperwork and get it back to them. But I'm pretty sure my tuition will be covered, and most of my books."

That would mean she was only responsible for her labs and the normal fees that came with being in college.

"You worked hard," Dex told her. "I'm proud of you."

"Me, too. UCLA nursing school." She squealed. "I got in and I got financial aid."

A muscle in Dex's cheek flexed. She pointed at him. "No! You're not going to tell me you could have paid for school. We talked about this. I need to do it on my own."

Linnie and Orchid looked at each other, as if they didn't understand.

"Are you fighting?" Linnie asked, her voice concerned.

"Never." Jana pulled her daughter onto her lap. "Dex is just as happy for me as you are." She glanced at him, waiting for him to confirm.

He nodded. "Nursing school is great. I'm proud of your mom and impressed by how hard she's working. But sometimes she can be stubborn."

Magnolia looked at the two younger kids. "That's when someone won't change their mind, even when there's a good reason why they should."

"I'm not being stubborn," Jana told her. "I'm being determined. I want to pay for college myself. It was my decision not to go when I graduated from high school. Back then it would have been easier. But I decided to go a different way."

At the time she'd been so sure. Now, ten-plus years later, she was a single mom with minimal skills and no real way to support her daughter, and she wished she'd been a little more conventional. But there was no changing the past.

Linnie nodded slowly. "Now you have to figure something out."

"Exactly. And that means paying for college myself. I don't have the money sitting around, so I applied for financial aid, and I got it." Wonderful news considering how much more expensive UCLA was going to be when compared with community college.

"Will I need financial aid?" Linnie asked, sounding worried.

Jana smiled at her. "I'll have a good job by then, and I will have put money aside. You'll be fine."

"What about me?" Orchid asked.

"Dad has a college fund for each of us," Magnolia told her. "We're covered."

Linnie hugged her. "I'm glad you got financial aid, Mommy. You're going to be the best nurse ever."

"Thank you, sweetie. I hope you're right."

Jana hovered in the hallway, trying not to look like a stalker. She was going to give Rick five more minutes, and if he didn't show up by then, she would head downstairs to the derm office and start her day.

She supposed it would have made more sense to simply text him her good news, but she'd wanted to tell him in person. Rick was the kind of guy who would get how excited she was and want to celebrate with her.

She walked back and forth in front of the doors to his medical suite, stepping out of the way as patients arrived. She was just about to head to the elevator when he rounded the corner.

"Hi," she said brightly, hurrying toward him.

He came to a stop and stared at her. There was no welcoming smile, no eager greeting. Instead he looked at her as if he barely knew who she was and wished she wasn't there. She stumbled to a stop.

"You're at my office," he said, his tone more cool than friendly.

"I wanted to, uh, is everything all right?"

"I wasn't expecting to see you here."

Nor did he want to. That much was clear.

The man standing in front of her was so different from the normally warm, friendly, affectionate guy she knew that it was almost like meeting a stranger.

All her happy feelings faded away. Suddenly her good news

didn't seem important, which meant she'd been standing in the hallway, waiting for him, for no reason at all.

"Did you want something?" he asked.

She hesitated. "I wanted to tell you I got into the UCLA School of Nursing. They notified me yesterday. It was my first choice because it's such a great school."

He stared at her blankly. "Why would you be going to nursing school?"

"To get my RN. We talked about this. Rick, what's going on? You're acting really strange."

He glanced at his watch. "I have patients waiting. Can we discuss this later?"

"Of course."

She stepped around him and walked to the elevator. When it arrived, she pushed the button for her floor. As the doors closed, she tried to figure out what had just happened. It was like the man she knew didn't exist and a stranger had taken his place. Not just a stranger, she amended. Someone cold and distant who didn't much like her.

She retreated to her small office, where she forced herself to focus on work. The frustrations of dealing with the various insurance companies and their ever-changing rules took up her morning and helped to distract her from what had happened earlier. At little before noon, someone knocked on her half-open door.

She glanced up and was surprised to see Rick standing there, a bouquet of flowers in his hand.

"I'm sorry," he said by way of greeting. "About before. How I acted. Seeing you was a surprise. You've never just shown up at my office."

She ignored the flowers. "You don't have to worry. It won't happen again."

His shoulders slumped a little. "I hurt you. I didn't mean to." He set the bouquet on her desk and shoved his hands into his trouser front pockets. "I keep my work and my personal life separate. I compartmentalize because sometimes what I do is difficult. When I'm operating on someone, I need to be fully focused on that. When I leave the surgery center, I try to disconnect from what was happening there. I avoid overlap."

She felt a little of her anger fade. "You're saying I was out of context?"

"Yes. I had a patient first thing." He glanced away. "I had to tell him something he didn't want to hear. When I saw you, I was trying to figure out the best way to do that. Like I said, you surprised me, and I couldn't unfocus on work."

He sank down on the chair opposite. "I didn't mean to hurt you, Jana. I'm sorry."

The last of her mad faded, and she realized that what she did in a day and what Rick did in a day had nothing in common. The man was busy saving lives. When things didn't go well for him, it was a lot more than simply having to tell someone their mole removal was going to cost an extra fifty dollars.

"Oh, Rick." She came to her feet and circled the desk. He rose and pulled her close.

"I'd never hurt you on purpose," he murmured.

"I know. I promise not to surprise you like that. You're right—you have to stay in your head for your patients. I can't be a distraction."

He drew back and smiled at her. "Tell me about nursing school. You got in. That's exciting. I know how hard you've worked."

She clutched his upper arms. "I also got financial aid, which is the best."

"We have to celebrate."

And here he was, she thought happily. The sweet, supportive guy she knew. "That would be nice. Thank you."

"Not just dinner," he told her. "Let's go away for the weekend." He hesitated. "Unless you think I'm rushing things."

Her heart melted. "Going away sounds perfect. I'd need to

talk to Teddy about keeping Linnie, but I don't think that would be a problem. What about your schedule?"

"I could get a weekend off." He brushed his mouth against hers. "Let me look at my calendar and get back to you. Then I'll plan the whole weekend. It'll be special for sure. For you, Jana."

"Thank you."

He kissed her again. "As much as I'd like to stay, I have patients, and you have to get to class. Can we talk later?"

"Yes, please."

He left. She logged off her computer, then collected her backpack and the flowers. The sweet scent and perfect petals made her smile. After the disaster that was her last relationship, she was probably due for a little good luck in the romance department, but with Rick, she'd really hit the jackpot. Now that he'd explained himself, she understood what had gone wrong and vowed it would never happen again. Everyone had quirks, and his made perfect sense to her.

Still smiling, she walked toward her car. In a few weeks, she and Rick would go away for the weekend. She couldn't wait. And between now and then, she should probably think about introducing him to Linnie. Because if it was up to her, Rick was going to be in her life for a very long time.

12

Beth carefully stored the celebration cupcakes she'd bought in the food bank's storeroom refrigerator until after her shift. She'd ordered them as soon as she'd received Jana's text about making it into nursing school. They were two parts "yay for my friend" and one part "holy crap—how do I tell her about Teddy?" Which made them celebration and *guilt* cupcakes, she supposed. Not that she had anything to be guilty about, she told herself as she transferred pints of blueberries from the big crates onto the display in the produce section. She was a single adult. Teddy was a single adult. They could go out if they wanted to.

Which sounded fine, but with Jana dating Rick, it was all so...twisted. Okay, not twisted exactly, but strange. And she'd been such a cow about Jana dating Rick. What if Jana wanted payback for that? Beth tried telling herself Jana wasn't that kind of person, but wasn't sure she deserved her friend's grace.

There was also the possibility that Teddy had already told Jana about asking her out to dinner and Jana was fine with it, but why be rational when there was so much worrying she could do instead?

Finally her shift ended. She collected the cupcakes and the sandwiches she'd brought and went to their usual table out back. Jana was already there and smiled at her.

"Next time I bring the food. Seriously, you have to let me. You're doing all the work."

Beth laughed. "This is where I remind you that I have a sandwich shop. Pulling together whatever's left over for our dinner is easy."

"Not the point. Next time I'm taking over."

"If you insist. But first, there's these." Beth set the small bakery box on the table. "Ta-da and congratulations on getting into nursing school. I never doubted you, but it's nice the admissions department agreed with me."

Jana pressed a hand to her chest. "Thank you." She opened the box and grinned at the two cupcakes, each overly frosted, then topped with a little plastic sign reading, "Congratulations, Superstar."

"I wanted them to put on a little stethoscope, but they didn't have any."

"I love them just as they are. This is so thoughtful."

They hugged, then sat down.

"Are you excited and nervous or just excited?" Beth asked as she passed out sandwiches and salad.

"Both," Jana admitted. "I'm terrified I won't be able to get through the curriculum. It's going to be daunting for sure."

"You'll do great. You've practically gotten straight A's at community college."

"That's different. I'll be moving right into more advanced

science subjects, along with things like anatomy. Plus I'll be taking a full load rather than going part-time like I have been."

"That will be a change." Beth hadn't been to college, but she would guess that three or four science classes a quarter would be challenging. "So you won't be working?"

"Not once I start there. I've been saving as much as I can to cover my expenses. Teddy agrees this is the best way for me to be successful in the program. He's going to help where he can. And Dex will pitch in, too."

"Dex is Teddy's friend, right?" she asked without thinking, then wished she could call back the question. A week ago, it would have been as innocent as it seemed. In a few minutes, when she confessed all, it would sound like she was fishing for information. "As in Dex Thursdays for the kids."

"That's him." Jana rolled her eyes. "He's annoyed with me for applying for financial aid. He offered to pay for college when I started back, but I want to get through it on my own. Maybe it sounds silly to him, but I have something to prove to myself. I need to be capable and handle it."

Another admirable quality, Jana thought, trying to remember why she'd been so upset at the thought of Jana dating her brother. And speaking of which, she needed to just say it.

"You're doing it all," she told her friend. "I admire that."

Jana laughed. "Don't give me too much credit. I struggle, but I'm in a good place right now." Her expression turned shy. "Rick was really happy for me. He mentioned something about us going away for the weekend."

Beth waited for the jolt of apprehension, but there wasn't any. A relief for sure. She could say with all honesty she was totally and completely on board with their relationship.

"That will be fun. You're both working so hard—a break would be really good, and it's always fun to go away with a guy."

"The thought of it makes me nervous," Jana admitted. "Which

is weird because I really like him. I guess going away makes things seem more real. But I'm excited."

Beth cleared her throat. "So, I have some news. Teddy stopped by the store."

Jana looked at her, as if waiting for more, because saying her brother had come into Surf Sandwiches wasn't exactly earth-shattering.

"We went for a walk," she added, trying to sound calm instead of excited. "He, ah, he asked me out." She looked at Jana. "On a date."

Her friend's eyes widened as she set down her sandwich. Beth held her breath, waiting for more of a response. Was Jana going to be okay with it, or was she—

"OMG! Teddy likes you!" Jana laughed. "He asked you out. That's so great. He's been on his own since we lost Valonia, and I've been worried about him. He needs more in his life. I've told him that, but he said he wasn't ready or wasn't interested. He picked you."

Beth sagged in her seat. "I thought you might be mad."

"Why? You're my friend. Why wouldn't I want someone like you for my brother?"

The kind words made her feel worse. "Because I was so terrible before and said things and made a mess and hurt your feelings."

Jana waved that away. "It's done. I get what happened and why, and you were sorry. We've moved on. Back to Teddy. Interesting that he never said anything to me about seeing you." She grinned. "Believe me, he's going to suffer for that."

Beth felt herself relax. "I'm glad you're okay with us going out. I mean, it's probably not going anywhere, but I was worried."

"Don't be." Jana picked up her sandwich. "Just to be clear, Teddy really hasn't dated since his wife died. I mean, no one. So I'm asking you as my friend—don't break his heart."

Beth stared at her, wondering if Jana was making another joke, but the other woman seemed serious.

"I'm hardly the heartbreaking type."

"I'm not so sure. Just be careful with him, okay?"

"I promise."

Beth felt like a character in an old 1990s sitcom. She'd pretty much emptied her closet looking for something to wear to dinner with Teddy. She'd tried on dresses, capris, dressy jeans and everything else she owned and hadn't been happy with anything. As he was due to arrive in twenty minutes, ordering something online wasn't going to work.

"It's just dinner," she told herself. She'd eaten the meal her entire life. It was no big deal. As for the date aspect of the evening, she could date. She used to date. Yes, it had been a long time, but Teddy wasn't exactly a player. He was a single dad of three kids. So neither of them were experts—they could figure it out together.

That realization calmed her for about seven seconds, until she realized he would be arriving in fifteen minutes and she was still standing in her bra and bikini briefs.

She shrieked once, then grabbed the navy sleeveless dress she'd tried on first. Whether or not she loved it, the dress was going to have to work. She was out of time and options.

She zipped it up, then carefully fluffed her hair before spraying it. She'd curled it earlier and had applied a little makeup. Anything to compensate for the fact that Teddy had seen her in her work uniform and, yes, a hairnet.

She grabbed the small cross-body bag she'd dug out of her closet. She'd already transferred her essentials to it and would leave her utilitarian everyday backpack bag at home. As she hurried to the front of the house, Agatha fell into step with her.

"Nervous?" her aunt asked.

"Petrified. I may vomit."

Agatha laughed. "You'll be fine. Dating is like riding a bike. The skills will come back to you."

"What if I never had skills?"

Her aunt's expression turned speculative. "You like this man, don't you?"

"I don't know him well enough to say how I feel. I'm reacting to some strange chemical attraction that I can't seem to get under control." She pressed a hand to her belly and wished the faint nausea would go away. Or that the evening was behind her and she could finally relax.

"There's something about him," she added. "He's like a drug."

Agatha hugged her. "That makes me so happy."

"That I'm obsessing about someone I don't know and who may be a serial killer?"

"I doubt he's killed even one person. Besides, he's Jana's brother, so he comes with excellent references."

Her aunt was making sense. Unfortunately, all the sense in the world was no match for her quivering, hopeful, terrified state of mind.

"I think I need therapy," she said, then forced herself to suck in a breath. "Calm. I need to be calm."

Before she had time to practice finding her zen state, the doorbell rang. She flinched at the sound.

"I can't do this," she whispered.

"Open the door? Nonsense. You've done it hundreds of times."

Beth gave her a sharp "you're not helping" glare before walking to the small foyer and opening the door.

"Hi," she said, then nearly fainted at the sight of him.

He looked amazing. All tall and handsome, wearing a button-down shirt with dark trousers. He was lean and muscled, with those movie-star chiseled features. And his mouth—the one smiling at her. If only he would kiss her, she could die happy.

"Hi," he said, his voice low and sexy. "You look beautiful."

She blinked. Sure he was being polite, but she was fairly certain no one had ever used that particular *B* word to describe her before. Ian had always said she was cute. Beautiful was much, much better.

"Come in," she said, stepping back. "This is my aunt. Agatha, Teddy Mead."

They shook hands.

"Beth tells me you practice Chinese medicine. That's so interesting."

He gave her an easy smile. "Nothing so grand. I specialize in acupuncture."

"Oh." Agatha took a step back. "Needles. I'm not a fan."

"They don't hurt, if that's your concern."

Agatha didn't look convinced. "Needles hurt. It's one of the laws of physics. The seventh, I believe. Or maybe the eighth."

"I'm sure you're right," he said politely, but Beth thought she saw a hint of a smile in his straight mouth.

"Shall we?" Beth said, then turned to her aunt. "I'll see you later."

"Text if you're going to stay out all night," Agatha told Beth.

"Very funny."

Beth and Teddy walked outside. He motioned to his large SUV parked in the driveway, then opened the passenger door for her.

She slid onto the seat and tried to regulate her breathing. Everything about this moment felt surreal. That she was on a date, that she was with Teddy. A week ago she hadn't even met him, and now she felt as if her life had been changed forever.

Teddy went around to his side and got in beside her.

"I'm nervous," he said as he started the engine.

She stared at him. "You are?"

He smiled at her. "Of course. I've been on edge all day."

"Me, too."

But her being anxious about their date made sense, while him being unsettled seemed odd. He was amazing, and she was just plain normal. Even so, his admission gave her comfort.

"Who has the kids tonight?" she asked.

"My friend Dex is over and hanging with Jana and Linnie."

"Jana appreciates that Dex takes Linnie on Thursdays when she has her food bank shift. He sounds like a great guy."

"He is. He's seen me through some rough times."

"He doesn't have children of his own?" she asked.

"No. I'm sure he wants them, but Dex hasn't found the right woman."

Something Beth could relate to. She'd yet to find the right man. Obviously it hadn't been Ian.

They talked about their respective days as he navigated the usual Malibu traffic. She was just about to ask him where they were going when he pulled in front of a low, one-story building with a valet sign out front. Her breath caught as she took in the elegant arched entry and the lush landscaping of the exclusive, upscale restaurant.

"We're eating here?" she asked. "But how? It takes months to get a reservation."

Teddy gave her a modest shrug. "I know the owner and made a call."

"Impressive connections."

The valet opened her door and held out his hand to assist her out of the vehicle. She stepped down and told herself that if any famous people were dining inside, she wouldn't gawk at them. She was a seasoned Malibu resident. Celebrity sightings were a part of life. Then Teddy moved close and put his hand on the small of her back. Her body went on instant high alert as she instinctively moved closer to him. The good news was that as long as Teddy was nearby, she doubted she would notice if they were seated next to one of the Hemsworth brothers.

They were shown to a quiet corner table with a view of the ocean. Their server poured water and left them with menus.

Teddy put his down without glancing at it. Instead his attention was on her.

"I'm still nervous," he told her, "but happy to be with you."

"I feel the same."

"So we'll figure this out together." He leaned toward her. "Jana mentioned you were divorced."

"Yes, for over a year now. You said you hadn't dated since your wife died. I haven't dated since my divorce." She picked up the menu, then put it down. "I needed to heal and think things through. I never thought I'd get a divorce. I thought we'd be together forever, so when we weren't, it was an adjustment."

She offered a rueful smile. "Ian wanted to keep the house, and I had no interest in it, so he bought me out. I took the money and invested in Surf Sandwiches. It turns out expanding my business was a great distraction."

"Also a smart decision. The place is busy. You made the right move."

"I think so."

"I'm having dinner with a successful entrepreneur," he teased. "I should have dressed better."

"You're dressed just fine."

He brushed the front of his shirt. "And no spit-up stains. It's nice to have all three kids past that stage."

"Not a baby person?"

"I learned to be. I think I was like every other guy. I wanted to be a father, but I didn't think through the whole logistics of raising kids until Valonia got pregnant."

"An unexpected baby?" she asked.

He chuckled. "It was more we didn't do anything to prevent it from happening."

"You mentioned you were introduced by friends and clicked right away. So no drama in the relationship?"

"None. I figured out I wanted to marry her within two days."

The smile returned. "She took a day or two longer, but we both sensed a connection right away."

"I can't imagine what that would be like," she admitted. "The instant knowing."

"You don't believe in that?"

"It's more I haven't experienced it. I seem to be a more slow and steady kind of person."

At least, that was how it had been with Ian, she thought. Their first few dates had been a little awkward, but they'd both hung in there and had eventually figured out what worked for them. Until it hadn't.

"I don't know what that's like," he admitted

"There's an element of caution that's probably both good and bad." She hesitated, then added, "My mother was very much a 'just go for it' kind of person. She wanted to experience everything, and if it was dangerous, all the better. But when I was little, that kind of attitude frightened me. I wanted security and safety more than adventure."

"Of course you did." His voice was gentle. "Kids need to feel secure most of all. Once they know they're taken care of, they can be comfortable exploring."

She appreciated that he understood what she was trying to say. "My philosophy hasn't changed all that much. I tend to think things through and act sensibly."

"You say that like it's a bad thing."

"It's not exactly exciting."

Their server returned to take their drink orders and explain about the specials. Beth ordered a glass of white wine, and Teddy did the same.

When they were alone, she said, "Did you and Valonia always plan on having a big family?"

"After Atlas was born, we debated whether or not to have a third kid. Then she got pregnant. The decision was made for us. I don't know if we would have kept having children. Three seems like plenty."

"But you love them."

"Every second of every day. They get me through." He looked at her. "You and Ian didn't want children?"

"We did." She paused and tried to remember the conversations she and her ex had had about starting a family. "At least at first. But we wanted to wait a couple of years, and then somehow the idea got lost."

Their server returned with their drinks and left. Beth picked up her wine and took a sip.

"I think we drifted apart. Toward the end, we seemed to be living separate lives. One day he said he thought our marriage was in trouble. The words shocked me, but I knew he wasn't wrong."

She explained about how they'd made the decision to work on their marriage. "We started counseling and doing all the things. After a couple of months, we had an assessment meeting with our counselor." She drew in a breath and braced herself for the telling.

"I was so happy. I talked about how close we'd gotten and how in love with Ian I was. I said that having things fall apart had ended up making them so much better."

Teddy's expression turned sympathetic. "Ian didn't agree."

"No. He said while he appreciated that we'd both tried, he wasn't in love with me anymore, and he wanted a divorce. Then he walked out of our session, and that was it."

"I'm sorry."

"Thanks. Once I got over the shock and we split up, it didn't take me long to realize we really hadn't had a very good marriage. I healed and moved on. Ian is engaged, by the way, and I only wish him the best."

She realized she meant the words, which was a nice testament to her character. The shock of finding out had both faded and given her the nudge she'd needed to start looking around for a life of her own.

"You're still friends?"

"What? We're not. I found out about the engagement..." She paused, suddenly embarrassed for Ian. Strange but true. "He proposed on a billboard, and I happened to see it."

Teddy looked surprised. "People do that?"

"I guess. Agatha talks about how tacky that was."

Teddy's lips twitched. "I have to agree with your aunt."

They looked at the menus and then ordered their meals. Conversation flowed easily, and Beth found herself relaxing a little. By the time they agreed to split the dessert special, she was able to see past Teddy's very attractive outside enough to admire the man he was on the inside.

There was a brief tussle over the check. She tried to pay, but he wouldn't let her. As they walked to the valet station, she wished there was a way to extend the evening. She wasn't ready to say good-night but couldn't think of anything for them to do. She wasn't the type to want to hang out at a bar, and inviting him in for coffee seemed too suggestive.

He pulled out of the parking lot, but instead of turning toward her house, he went in the opposite direction. Five minutes later, he drove onto a lookout point where tourists frequently stopped to get pictures of the Southern California coastline.

The sun had long since set, so there wasn't much of a view beyond lights twinkling in the distance, and there were no other cars there. Despite that, Teddy parked, then turned off the engine, although he left the radio on its easy listening channel. Before she could ask what they were doing here, he got out of the SUV and walked around to her side. After opening the door, he held out his hand to her.

"Dance with me?"

Three simple words that shouldn't have meant anything sent

awareness skittering through her. Deep in her belly, muscles clenched, and she felt a faint prickling slipping down her spine.

"Of course," she whispered, stepping down and moving close. As if on cue, the current song ended, and "At Last" began to play. Teddy settled one hand on her waist, took her fingers in the other and began to move.

She'd never been much of a dancer but found him easy to follow. The night was still with the sound of the surf below blending with the rush of cars driving by. There was no moon, but overhead, airplanes headed either to or from LAX, their lights reminding her of falling stars.

She closed her eyes and let herself only feel the moment. Their bodies weren't touching, which was probably for the best. Being this close to him was heady enough. If there was too much contact, she might lose herself forever and never find her way back.

This man, she thought hazily. What was it about him that captured her attention so thoroughly? She'd never felt this way before—not even in high school, where crushes had been a regular part of her teenaged life.

"Beth?"

She opened her eyes and looked at him. He was watching her intently.

"I enjoyed tonight very much," he told her.

"Me, too."

"I want to see you again."

She smiled. "If you didn't, I'd be very sad."

She expected him to respond with something funny, but instead he leaned close and brushed his mouth against hers. The unexpected kiss burned through her, igniting a need unlike anything she'd felt before. The wanting was as instant as it was intense. Every cell in her body screamed at her to close the distance between them so she could feel all of him pressing against all of her.

She must have made a sound, because he drew back and looked at her. "Are you all right?"

"No." She tried to catch her breath. "What just happened?"

"I kissed you."

Despite her confusion, she managed a laugh. "I got that part. I meant my reaction to it."

The second she said the words, she had the awful thought that maybe her attraction had been one-sided. Maybe he hadn't felt anything but regular kiss stuff.

"Not just yours," he told her, right before he kissed her again.

The need returned, along with heat and desire. She felt both lost and rescued at the same time. As the kiss went on—still chaste with their bodies held at a careful distance—she realized the restraint was self-preservation on both their parts. Because if they gave in even a little, they might not have the control to stop.

He stepped back. "When can I see you again?"

"Is tomorrow too soon?"

He grinned. "Tomorrow is perfect."

13

"You know your brother is a grown man and perfectly capable of going on a date and getting himself home without your involvement."

Dex's voice was teasing. Jana leaned over and grabbed the TV remote to pause the movie they were watching on Netflix.

"I'm not involved with my brother. I'm hanging out with a friend for the evening."

Dex raised one eyebrow. "From here it looks like you're waiting up."

"He waited up for me after my first date with Rick. It's a thing, I guess."

She kept her voice light, but she was willing to admit that on the inside, she was nervous. Teddy hadn't shown interest in anyone since he'd lost Valonia. While he'd been married, he'd been a loving and devoted husband, which meant he hadn't been on a first date in nearly fifteen years. What if he forgot how? What if Beth broke his heart? She didn't seem the type, but the world could be a scary place, and how well did she really know her friend? Besides...

"Oh, wow," she breathed. "Now I get it. This is how Beth felt about Rick dating. She was being protective because he's just not that sophisticated."

"What are you talking about?"

"That I'm worried about Teddy the way she was worried about Rick. Now I know why she acted the way she did."

Dex didn't look pleased at her insight. "That's one way to look at it."

"What do you mean?"

"Why is everyone assuming Rick is clueless when it comes to women? He's had plenty of opportunity to hone his skills."

She leaned over and patted his arm. "You're sweet to worry, but there's no reason. Rick's exactly who he claims to be. The next time I have him over, I'll make sure you're here so you can meet him. You'll see. It's all good."

She worried about a lot of things in her life, but Rick not being genuine wasn't one of them.

She heard the front door open and immediately sat up. "Act casual."

Dex grinned at her. "How exactly is that different from what I've been doing?"

She glared at him, but Teddy walked into the family room before she could say anything.

"Hey," she called. "How was the date?"

He stared at them. "I expected Jana to wait up, but what are you doing here?"

"Keeping her company."

"You're weird."

"Possibly."

The two men smiled at each other. Teddy glanced at Jana. "I know how to date."

"I wasn't sure you remembered." She studied him, looking for clues. "How was it?"

His entire body relaxed as he sank onto the corner of the sectional and grinned.

"Good. Really good. I like her, and we got along great. I can't wait to see her again."

"So it's a thing," she said.

"Absolutely."

Which all sounded fine, but she knew what he really meant. When it came to women, Teddy was either not interested or all in. There was no middle ground. She wanted to protest that he couldn't possibly know anything about a person after a couple of hours over dinner. That it took time and familiarity to be sure.

"I want to tell you to be careful, but I know you won't listen."

He flashed her a smile. "You're right about that."

Dex shook his head. "Congratulations, man. You deserve to be happy."

"You deserve the same."

Dex shrugged. "I do what I do."

Teddy rose and circled the sectional, then kissed the top of Jana's head. "Night, kid."

"Night."

When he'd left, Dex stood. "I'm heading out. You okay about your brother?"

Jana looked down the hall, but Teddy was already gone. "I find his attitude confusing. How can he just know? In the rest of his life he's completely pragmatic, so why is this different? Why does he believe?"

"Maybe the bigger question is, why is he right? At least, he was with Valonia. I understand attraction, but Teddy swears it's more than that."

She'd never experienced anything like that. Obviously when

she'd partied, she'd been willing to sleep with guys she barely knew, but Teddy wasn't talking about casual sex. If his relationship with Beth followed the same path as it had with Valonia, he wouldn't try to sleep with her for weeks. Her late sister-in-law had explained about an intense bonding with lots of time spent together and hours of long, meaningful conversation. For them, passion had grown but was ignored until one day it simply took over.

She had the brief thought she should warn her friend about that trajectory, then told herself to stay out of it. What Beth and Teddy had or didn't have was going to be different, and even if it wasn't, their relationship wasn't her business.

"I don't think I could believe in love at first sight," she admitted. "Nor would I want to. It feels risky."

"Don't tell Rick," Dex teased. "You'll break his heart."

"I doubt that. We're following the usual conventional path in our relationship. Something Teddy would never do. So which one of us is wrong? Me or Teddy?"

"You're overthinking the process," Dex told her. "People are different. The slow and steady kind of love is just as valid."

"In my head I know you're right, but somehow Teddy's way is more visually appealing."

Dex chuckled, then pulled her close and kissed her cheek. "Love you, kid. I'll see you soon."

"Love you, too." She walked him to the door, then locked it behind him. Standing alone in the quiet house, she thought about what Dex had said about a slow and steady kind of love. His words made a lot of sense. Not everyone could fall the way Teddy did. She, for example, had always...

Jana looked down the hall, then back at the door as the truth hit her. The reason she was so confused about what kind of love she wanted for herself was that she'd never been in love. Not romantically. Not with anyone. She didn't know what she wanted because she didn't know what that kind of love felt like. Maybe it was time for that to change.

★ ★ ★

Beth looked at the selection of organic drinks. Her cold case display space was limited, and during the peak of the lunch rush, they were too busy to keep refilling it. Adding one more product to monitor seemed foolish. Yet when she'd done the taste test with her crew and a few trusted customers, the response had been overwhelmingly positive.

She smiled at her rep. "I can't say no. Everyone loved them." She signed the tablet, confirming the order.

"Great. Your first delivery will be next Tuesday."

"Thanks."

She walked the sales guy out and was about to return to her small office to finish up some paperwork when Teddy walked into the store. It had only been a few hours since their date had ended, yet her heart still thudded hard and her breath caught.

He smiled at her, looking both happy and sheepish. "I know we have a date later, but I wanted to see you."

Warmth swept through her. "I'm glad." She glanced at the clock. It was nearly one thirty. "Have you had lunch?"

"No."

"Good."

Beth stepped behind the counter to wash her hands at the sink. Teddy watched as she set out rosemary bread and thinly sliced Brie. She added mozzarella, then put on pear slices.

"Thank you for honoring my inner vegetarian," he said with a grin.

"Of course. You should come here on Wednesday. We usually have plantains then. We make a grilled ciabatta with plantains, black beans, Havarti and avocado. It'll rock your world."

Teddy's gaze locked with hers. "I look forward to that."

While the sandwiches were in the press, she collected chips, cans of the new organic soda and a couple of cookies. Teddy pulled his wallet out of his jeans, but she shook her head.

"Lunch is on me."

"I didn't come here so you could feed me."

Which begged the question, why had he shown up? Only she was happy to see him, and a sandwich was certainly easy for her.

"You're still not paying," she said lightly, handing him the two sandwiches and the sodas. She tucked her hairnet into her jeans pocket, then carried the chips and cookies, and they went outside.

The tables to the north of the building were empty. She picked one in the shade and sat down. The air was warm, the sky a perfect blue, and across the street was the sound of the ocean.

Teddy settled across from her, but instead of reaching for one of the sandwiches, he smiled.

"I missed you," he said simply.

She could have teased him by pointing out that their date had been less than twenty-four hours ago, but somehow instead she murmured, "I missed you, too."

They stared at each other. She had no idea what he was feeling, but she was awash in sensations—all of them new and exciting. She was conscious of her breathing, of the way his hands were quietly resting on the table. They were in public yet the moment felt intimate. Special.

"Your store makes you happy," he said.

She smiled. "It does. Every day. I know serving sandwiches doesn't change the world, but when people are hungry, I feed them. I like that. Sometimes there are challenges, but we work through them."

He passed her one of the sandwiches and opened the wrapper of his own. "Where'd you get your business degree?"

She stared at him. "I didn't go to college." Her cheeks went hot. "I learned about running the store from my aunt and uncle. I've taken a few classes here and there, but that's all."

She told herself not everyone had to go to college and she was doing just fine without a degree, which even in her head sounded defensive. Teddy had just been asking a logical question.

He leaned toward her. "Really? You just figured it all out on your own?" He sounded impressed.

She relaxed as she realized he wasn't judging her. "Most small business owners don't have a formal education. The majority of us get into an area we're familiar with and see a way to do it better. I worked in the store when I was in high school. Like I said, Agatha and Dale taught me everything I needed to know."

"But you've made changes."

She laughed. "Of course. Some of the processes are different. I've expanded the store, and before that I changed up the menu. Food trends are just like everything else. The classics stay the same, but what's popular is always an evolution. Ten years ago no one asked about vegan options. Today about fifteen percent of my sales are vegan sandwiches. Vegetarian is a bigger chunk, of course. But in the end, meat is king."

"Did you ever think of not buying into the family business?"

She hesitated, then admitted, "Originally I wanted to go to culinary school. I was saving so that I could be in school full-time and not have to work to support myself."

His blue gaze was steady. "What changed your mind?"

"Rick got into medical school. He'd gotten through college on a scholarship, but medical school was different. I wanted to help. That's when my uncle approached me about the store. He wanted to sell it to me. In return, he would self-finance the purchase, and he would also help Rick cover half of the cost for medical school. It made the most sense."

Teddy's expression didn't change, so she had no idea what he was thinking. "You gave up a lot for him."

"He's my brother. I wanted him to achieve his dreams, and I didn't want him saddled with a lot of debt." She shrugged. "Culinary school would have been nice, but I'm happy where I am now."

"I can see that." He smiled at her. "I didn't take a traditional path, either."

"No kidding, Mr. I Went to China on My Own When I Was Sixteen."

He chuckled. "I actually think my age was an asset. I wasn't mature enough to realize what I was getting into, and it never occurred to me I could fail."

"Which you didn't."

He took a bite of his sandwich and then made a sound low in his throat. "This is incredible."

"Thanks. Our grilled cheese sandwiches with the fruit of your choice are really popular. Some of the combinations weird me out, but people want what they want."

"You knew what you wanted."

"As did you. Any regrets on not going down the quote-unquote traditional path?" she asked.

"No," he said easily. "You?"

"College? I couldn't have done it."

He frowned. "What do you mean?"

"I wouldn't have been successful." She put down her sandwich, wondering how much to admit. "I wasn't great in school. I had trouble in some of my classes. Even though Rick is three years younger, he would always step in and help me."

She sipped her drink. "In high school I briefly thought about trying community college, but Rick pointed out I was unlikely to get through on my own. Just passing the classes would be a struggle."

As soon as she spoke, she realized how bad the words sounded and quickly added, "He wasn't being mean or judging me. He wanted to help. He knew I wasn't college-smart, and he wanted to save me the pain and embarrassment of failing."

Teddy frowned. "Beth, you're plenty smart enough to go to college. I'm not saying it would be helpful now, but look at how successful you are at your business."

"That's different. It's what I do. The studying and taking

tests." She wrinkled her nose. "Those are not my thing. I'm fine with it," she added.

"You're very much better than fine. You're amazing."

She laughed. "I'm not sure you know me well enough to be saying that, but thank you."

"Anytime."

He started talking about the production it was to get all four kids out the door every morning. She appreciated the change in subject. She hadn't meant to say anything bad about her brother and had botched up the telling of how Rick had been looking out for her.

When they'd finished their lunch, Teddy sighed regretfully. "I have patients this afternoon, and you have a business to run. But I'm looking forward to our date tonight."

"Me, too."

He touched the back of her hand. "I want to get to know you and have you get to know me. I like you, and I want us to explore what feels like very powerful chemistry. And I very much want us to be lovers."

Her breath caught as her insides began to melt. She knew she was probably blushing, but she couldn't help it. He was just putting it out there. The man had courage, and she admired that...and him.

"But," he added, his gaze locked with hers. "Sex is a complication." One corner of his mouth tilted up. "And a wonderful distraction. My preference is we ignore the sparks until we're a little further along emotionally. I'm not saying it will be easy for me to resist you, because it won't be, but I think waiting is the right thing." He wound his fingers through hers. "I wanted to let you know what I was thinking and get your thoughts, because this needs to be a joint decision."

If she'd been the fainting type, she would have collapsed right there, falling off her seat and onto the grass. As it was, she had to figure out what to say in response. Not only because the turn in the conversation was unexpected but also because no man had ever been so open and honest with her.

Now to the actual discussion. She did want to have sex with him—more than anything. As for that being a distraction, well, he was right. Because as much as she wanted the man in her bed, getting to know him more first was even more appealing.

"You're saying we take it slow. Get to know each other better first."

He nodded.

"I agree."

He smiled. "Just to be clear, I don't want to wait. But I will."

"Me, too."

"Good."

He stood, took her hand and pulled her to her feet, then lightly kissed her. "I'll see you tonight."

"Can't wait."

"Sad Bunny stared at all the other woodland creatures standing outside his front door," Jana read, her voice soft. "His sad heart puffed up with love, and his sad mouth turned into a happy smile. 'We love you, Sad Bunny,' the woodland creatures shouted out together. 'Today and for always.'"

Jana looked at her daughter, who was fighting to stay awake in her bed. "Sad Bunny believed them, and he was never sad again." She closed the book. "The end."

"Sad Bunny is going to have to change his name," Linnie said with a yawn.

"I think so, too."

"I'm glad he has friends. Magnolia says a support system is very important."

"I have no idea where she gets her information, but she is right about a support system and family. I love you, baby girl. Always and forever."

Linnie's eyes closed, and she snuggled into her pillow. "I love you, too, Mommy. Forever and always."

Jana leaned down and kissed her cheek. Just like Sad Bunny, she felt her heart puff up with all the feels. Linnie had been unexpected, but she had turned out to be the best thing that had ever happened to her. Having her daughter had grounded her and sent her into a different kind of future. One she was excited about.

She turned off the bedside lamp and walked over to the small bookcase, where she returned Sad Bunny to his place, then crossed to the door. She paused to look at her now-sleeping daughter. Linnie was growing so fast, yet asleep in her bed, she seemed small and defenseless. The need to protect, to guide her through all the twists and turns life could offer, burned fiercely inside her. Not that Linnie needed extra coddling. She was smart and tough, and like Sad Bunny, she had an excellent support system. All would be well.

She stepped out into the hallway and partially closed the door before heading to the kitchen. She was going to make herself a mug of herbal tea, then get in about an hour of homework before heading to bed herself. She had an early morning.

She'd just put the mug of water into the microwave when her brother walked into the kitchen.

"Linnie in bed?" he asked.

"Yes, and already asleep." She smiled at him. "What's up?"

"I saw Beth yesterday."

"You mean last night on your second date in less than a week?" She grinned. "Yes, I know. For a guy who doesn't date, you've sure gotten back into the practice."

Teddy didn't smile in return. When she realized he wanted to talk, her stomach sank. Had something bad happened?

"Tell me," she said urgently.

"It's not Beth. She's great." His expression softened. "I can't wait to see her again."

Jana relaxed. "Counting the minutes?" she teased. "Try not to stalk her. A restraining order would put a damper on things."

The microwave dinged. She retrieved the mug, then dropped in the tea bag. They both took a seat at the island.

"So if all is well with Beth, then what's the problem?" she asked.

"There's no problem. It's more of a question." He looked at her. "What does Rick think of his sister?"

Jana hadn't known what Teddy was worried about, but that particular question came from nowhere.

"What do you mean? They're tight. From what she's told me, their mom was kind of flaky, so they looked after each other." She remembered Beth telling her about Rick trying to protect her from one of their mom's boyfriends and how he still had the scar, but wasn't sure the story was relevant.

"Did Beth say something about Rick?" she asked.

"Not in the way you mean." He drew in a breath as if considering his words. "We were talking about her store and what it takes to run it. I assumed she'd gone to college and had a business degree, but she said she doesn't. She never went to college because Rick told her she wasn't smart enough and wouldn't make it through."

Jana stared at him. "I don't believe that. He wouldn't do that. He's a really good guy."

"I know you'd only go out with someone who was respectful. That's why I asked. It didn't make sense."

She had to agree with him on that. No way Rick would say that. "We haven't actually talked about Beth that much, but he's never said anything bad, and when it was the three of us at dinner, he was great." He'd left most of the talking to the two of them, but that wasn't unusual. Men often preferred to listen rather than guide the conversation.

"Maybe she misunderstood him," Jana said slowly. "Like she was afraid and he was trying to be helpful."

She heard the question in her voice and knew her brother did, too.

"She actually said Rick told her she wasn't smart enough for college? Those words?"

"That's what she said. I don't get it," he added. "She's successful. Her employees really like her. When I went there yesterday, they were totally checking me out. After I walked her back to the store, this guy Kai—he's maybe twenty-two or twenty-three—pulled me aside and flat-out asked me my intentions." He smiled at the memory. "You've got to be the right kind of person to inspire loyalty like that."

"I agree. Kai's a sweetie and Beth's great. She's always feeding me after our shift at the food bank." Jana remembered a conversation from a few weeks ago. "She said she wasn't college material."

Teddy stared at her. "Beth?"

She nodded. "We were talking about her being single and my schedule. I can't remember exactly, but she made a point of saying she wasn't college material. I told her she was wrong."

Teddy frowned. "You know I don't care about her education. I'm more concerned about what Rick said."

Because he was already getting protective, Jana thought, wondering how he could simply know so quickly. Which wasn't the point, she told herself. The more compelling issue was whether or not Rick had dissed his sister.

"He wouldn't put her down like that," she said firmly. "He's a kindhearted, easygoing guy. My schedule is a challenge, and he never complains." Of course, he was also busy with work. One of the surgeons in his practice was on vacation, so more of the load now fell on him. They weren't going to be able to see each other for over a week.

"Then I can't explain it." Teddy shook his head. "It was just strange."

"I agree, but we'll probably never know exactly what happened. Can you let it go, or is this going to fester?"

He smiled. "No festering. I promise. You have homework."

"About an hour's worth."

"I'll leave you to it."

He walked out of the kitchen. She paused to drop her tea bag into the trash, then turned out the light and headed for her wing of the house. As she settled at her desk, she remembered Rick's surprise when she'd told him she'd gotten into nursing school. As if he hadn't been listening all the times she'd talked about her classes and how she was hoping to get in and get financial aid. He'd thought she was a receptionist and claimed to have no idea she was in medical billing. None of which mattered. He was a busy man with a lot on his mind. It wasn't personal.

She thought about how cold he'd been when she'd shown up at his office without warning. Maybe his conversation with Beth about college had been like that. He'd been thinking of other things rather than paying attention, and he'd blurted out a thoughtless remark.

Even if that was how things had gone, that didn't make him a bad person. Okay, so he could be a little self-absorbed at times. Everyone had flaws, and in his heart, Rick was a sweetie. There was nothing to worry about.

14

Three weeks into her new dating life, Beth still got fluttery every time her phone rang. Or at least anticipated getting fluttery, because the world was neatly divided into Teddy and not-Teddy. Not-Teddy calls were important but far less thrill-worthy. But when Teddy called, everything was more sparkly and wonderful.

She'd stopped telling herself to get over it, that he was just a guy, blah, blah, blah—mostly because she couldn't seem to believe herself. There was something about him that made her happy. She spent her day thinking about him, counting the minutes until she could see him, or remembering when they'd last been together.

True to his word, he hadn't tried to push her into bed, and thus far, their kissing had been on the chaste side. Although she wanted to take things to the next level, a part of her appreciated the slow build. They were getting to know each other—making sure they had their emotional relationship solid before taking the next step. The only downside was how she spent every waking moment in a state of low-key arousal. She was starting to think she should have gotten a more powerful shower massager.

She left the sandwich shop right on time to go get ready for their date. He was coming over and she was cooking. Although she'd invited Agatha to join them, her aunt had said she would make other plans so the two of them could have a nice evening alone. Sweet, but unnecessary, Beth thought as she drove home. At some point she did want Teddy and Agatha to hang out so they could get to know each other. She was also toying with the idea of a double date with Rick and Jana. She smiled as she pulled into the driveway. Funny how suddenly there were so many possibilities.

She had just shut off her engine when her phone rang. She glanced at the screen and enjoyed a rush of giddiness when she saw Teddy's name.

"Hi," she said, wondering if she sounded breathless. "I was just thinking about you."

"Beth, I'm sorry," he began, his voice thick with tension and regret. "I can't make it tonight."

Disappointment flooded her. "Oh. Okay."

"Orchid fell off her bike. We're just back from urgent care. She's banged up, but nothing's broken. She needed a couple of stitches on her chin and has a few scrapes and bruises. She's going to be fine, but I'm not comfortable leaving her tonight."

"Of course you're not," she said automatically. Orchid was just a little girl. She was in pain and needed her dad. Beth could be mature about the situation and ignore the crushing disappointment of missing time with Teddy. "I understand. It's totally fine. We'll reschedule."

"I want to see you," he said. "Would you be open to coming

by later so we could hang out for a couple of hours? I know it's not exactly a fun date, but—"

"You're talking about me showing up after the kids are in bed," she clarified.

"Yes."

"I'll be there." She didn't need a fancy evening or dinner out. Just seeing him for a little while would be enough to get her Teddy fix.

"Good." Relief filled his voice. "My days don't seem right if I don't see you."

She mentally hugged those heart-stealing words. "Mine, either."

"Nine okay?"

"It's perfect." She paused to steel herself to say the understanding thing. "And if the kids won't settle, just text me and I won't come over."

"Thanks, but I really need to see you. I'll get them settled. Jana's at a study group, so she won't be around, in case you were wondering. See you in a few hours."

"You will."

They hung up. Beth went into the house, where she found Agatha in the kitchen.

"I'll be out of your way in no time," her aunt said cheerfully. "Unless you want my help with the cooking before I duck out."

"No ducking required." She explained about Orchid's accident.

"That sounds painful," Agatha said. "I'm glad she's all right." She raised her eyebrows. "Disappointed he's not coming over?"

"Yes, but I appreciate he has responsibilities."

"Orchid is an unusual name. Pretty, though, and there won't be three in her class." She wrinkled her nose. "There were no Agathas in my class, which I would have liked, because I always thought mine was an old lady name." She smiled. "I was named after my maternal grandmother. By the time *your* mother was born, our parents seemed to have forgotten about our paternal grandmother, and she got to be called Caryn with a *C*. Back then it was very exotic."

"Just like Mom," Beth said lightly, thinking she didn't want to start a mental spiral about her mother. "Teddy's other kids are Magnolia and Atlas. His late wife was Valonia, so unique names might have been a thing with her." She glanced at the wall clock.

"Counting the minutes until you can go over?" Agatha asked, her voice teasing.

Beth nodded. "I can't help it. I want to see him." She laughed. "It's like he's in my head and I can't get him out. Not that I want to."

"You're obsessed," her aunt teased. "It's nice to see. Passion matters. It makes us feel alive and rearranges our priorities. I always knew you had it in you."

"I didn't. I've never felt like this. It's all happening so fast." She thought about the time she spent with Teddy. "It's like we connect on a deeper level. I know what he means when he talks. I'm starting to understand how he thinks. We're sharing who we are in a deliberate way that should terrify me, but doesn't. I want him to know everything, and I want to know the same about him."

She drew in a breath. "I'm both scared and excited, and I don't know why it has to take so long to be nine o'clock."

Her aunt laughed, then hugged her. "Passion," she repeated. "I'm so happy for you. This is what it's like to be alive. Savor every moment."

"I'd rather time went more quickly."

"It's already speeding by. All right. I'm off. Enjoy your clandestine meeting with your young man. I won't wait up."

"Nothing's going to happen. Not with his kids in the house." Plus she and Teddy were waiting—a decision that frustrated her body but gave her mental clarity. He'd been right by saying sex would complicate things. Oh, she wanted him with a desperation that was nearly crippling, but this was better. She liked that they were thoughtful and deliberate. It meant they mattered.

She drove to Teddy's house, arriving five minutes after nine. Rather than knocking, she texted to say she'd arrived. Seconds later the front door opened, and he stepped out onto the porch. They looked at each other before rushing together. The second his arms came around her, she relaxed into his embrace, welcoming the sense of homecoming.

"Now I can breathe," he murmured, his body pressing against hers.

"You must have been so scared."

"Down to my bones. Orchid's tough, but when I saw her lying on the sidewalk, I knew it was going to be bad. I've never been so glad to be wrong."

Teddy kept his arm around her as he led her into the house.

"But she's okay now," she said as she dropped her bag onto the entry table and faced him.

He nodded. "She's banged up. Like I said, there are a couple of stitches." He grimaced. "She was trying to pop the curb like she's seen Atlas do."

She must have looked confused, because he added, "You ride fast toward the curb and pull up on the front handlebars right before you hit it."

"Or you could use the driveway," she said.

He grinned at her. "There's nothing cool about that." The smile faded. "She and I are going to have a talk later, though. At least she was wearing her helmet, or it could have been worse." He drew in a breath. "I want them to be kids, you know? Have fun, take risks, but there's always a downside."

"Risk," she said lightly. It was something she'd avoided her whole life. She'd always been a "take the driveway" kind of person. Until now—with Teddy. He was the biggest chance she'd ever taken.

"Do you have pictures of Valonia?" she asked. "I've never

seen her." She paused at his look of surprise. "Should I not have asked that? She's a part of your life, Teddy. If she hadn't died, you'd still be together."

Something she'd thought about back before she realized he was attracted to her. She'd tried to talk herself out of her crush by pointing out that Teddy hadn't broken up with his late wife. Their marriage hadn't fallen apart and ended on its own. It had been severed by cruel fate.

He took her hand. "We'll have to be quiet," he said. "The pictures are in the hallway by the bedrooms."

He led the way, flipping on an overhead light as they went. She saw a set of double doors and an archway at the far end of the hall. In between were dozens of framed pictures.

She released his hand and walked to the large wedding portrait of Teddy with a petite, dark-haired woman. They were both smiling at the camera, looking happy and very much in love. The woman was lovely—curvy and pretty, with a bright smile and a hint of mischief in her eyes.

There were pictures of them on vacation, then a side shot of her showing off her pregnancy belly. Beth walked down the hallway, taking in pictures of Christmases and birthdays, the swaddled newborn shot of each of the kids. Halfway to the main bedroom, the pictures changed from a family of five to a family of four. There were still the birthday parties, the family by the tree, but the heart of them all was gone.

She felt the pain almost as if it was her own. She wondered how lost the children must have felt to suddenly not have their mother. How had they all survived? She looked at Teddy, knowing he would have felt it most of all. His life's partner ripped away with no warning.

Unexpected tears filled her eyes. She did her best to blink them away, but he saw them and quickly pulled her back to the front of the house.

"What's wrong?" he asked quietly. "You're upset."

"I'm not. It's fine." She brushed away the moisture. "Obviously I never knew Valonia, but looking at those pictures, I felt so sad. As if I could touch the grief." She grimaced. "Sorry. I'm not making sense."

Instead of answering, he drew her close again. "Thank you," he murmured.

"I didn't do anything."

"You understood." He drew back enough to look at her, his gazing locking with hers. "I want you to know how much you mean to me."

His voice was fierce, his expression intense. She got what he was saying—something had happened between them. Not just tonight, but from the moment they'd met. She didn't understand it, wasn't willing to name it just yet, but it was real and alive and she never wanted it to end.

"You matter to me, too."

Because he did, and while he was completely unexpected, she was so grateful to have found both him and them.

"This is silly," Beth said as they slid into a booth at the small café in the busy shopping center.

"It's not silly." Jana put her hands on the table and leaned toward her friend. "It's long overdue. You've been feeding me for weeks. The least I can do is return the favor once in a while. Besides, we're celebrating my calculus test. I got another B and I'm thrilled."

"Good for you!" Beth smiled at her. "You're such a Brainiac. I couldn't ever pass a basic college-level math class, let alone calculus. But you've worked hard, and you're getting a B!"

The casual self-put-down reminded Jana of the conversation she'd had with Teddy about Beth's thoughts on college and what Rick might or might not have said. She thought about mentioning her concern, then decided this wasn't the time. She wanted to have a fun dinner with her friend, not get into something about Rick. Besides, he was just so great, she couldn't imagine him telling his sister she was too dumb to go to college.

"One of the things I like about the class," Jana said, "assuming I can like anything about calculus, is how the professor structured the quarter. Instead of a midterm and final, we have bi-weekly tests, with the final simply being the last of them. No one test has more value than the others. It takes off some of the pressure." She shimmied in her seat. "If I could end up with a B in the class, I would be thrilled."

"You should be. We'll get you a plaque to hang on the wall."

Jana laughed. "I'd like that."

"Have you decided about graduation?"

Jana grimaced. "No. It's silly. It's just community college."

"The key word being *college*," Beth told her. "Come on. You have to do it. I want to go and cheer you on as you get your diploma."

The deadline for signing up to participate in graduation was fast approaching. Jana was torn. Teddy wanted her to do it, and Jana was kind of excited about the idea, only every now and then she thought it was silly. She wasn't some twenty-year-old like most of the other students. She was nearly thirty, and it wasn't that big a deal.

"I'll think about it," she murmured.

"You'd better. It's important. Not just for you but for Linnie. She needs to see the payoff of all your hard work."

Something Jana hadn't thought of. "Good point. Thank you."

"You're welcome. So, after finals, you have the summer off. Nursing school doesn't start until September, right?"

"Yes. Once the semester is over, I'll start working more hours to save as much as I can. I want to cover my and Linnie's expenses as much as possible."

Beth's expression softened. "You know Teddy would be happy to help. He's proud of you and what you've accomplished."

"Is this your way of telling me the two of you talk about me behind my back?" Jana asked, her voice teasing.

"Only a little, and we always say good things." Beth looked at her. "He would do anything for you."

"He's a good brother, and I love him right back."

They picked up menus and made their selections. Jana was in the mood for a big, juicy burger and fries. Not the healthiest choice, but this was a special meal.

"How's Orchid doing?" Beth asked after they'd placed their order. "Teddy mentioned her bike accident."

"It turns out his youngest has a flare for drama. Last night at dinner, she did a reenactment of the fall, complete with moans of pain and what I assume was her fainting." Jana grinned. "So I'm going to say she's doing fine."

"I'm glad. It has to be terrifying to be a parent. The worry about something awful happening and then when it does, the terror and concern. I don't know how you do it."

"I try not to think about the bad stuff. It's easier now that Linnie can tell me what's wrong. The baby part was really tough. Fortunately Teddy had had his three, so he was a big help." He'd spent more than one night reassuring her that whatever had Linnie crying would pass.

"It's so much responsibility."

"It is, but it's worth it."

Their server arrived with their drinks. Jana added sweetener to her iced tea.

"So things are going good with Teddy," she said.

Beth smiled at her. "Asking or telling?"

They both laughed.

"My brother's pretty happy," Jana admitted.

"I'm glad. I am, too. How about you and Rick?" She frowned. "I just realized I haven't seen him in a while. He mentioned one of his partners was on vacation."

"I know. He's been so busy. He's barely had time to text. We haven't seen each other in nearly two weeks. I miss him."

"I'm sure he misses you."

Jana appreciated the comment. She was also happy that Beth had gotten over her initial concerns. She wanted them to be friends, and while dating each other's brothers could be a complication, for them it was working out.

"I'm thinking of introducing him to Linnie," she said. "What do you think?"

Beth leaned forward. "You're the one who has to decide. She's your little girl. For what it's worth, I think Rick will be great with her." She paused. "It's a thing, though, right? Introducing your kid to the person you're seeing. It says something. Like I said—a lot of responsibility."

"Especially when he turns out to be a jerk, like the last guy I dated. But I think I'm ready for Rick to meet her. I'm thinking something casual. Teddy and I talked briefly about a barbecue. Nothing specific, and I'm not speaking on his behalf here, but what if it was all of us?"

Beth stared, her eyes widening. "What does that mean? All of us as in me?"

"Sure. Me, Linnie, Rick, Teddy, his kids and Dex." She frowned. "I can't remember if Dex is seeing anyone, but if he is, then her." She shrugged. "The kids are used to meeting Dex's many girlfriends, so that won't faze them."

She had more to say, but Beth had gone completely still.

"What?" she asked. "Are you all right?"

"No, I'm not. You're suggesting I meet Teddy's kids? We've barely been seeing each other a month. We haven't even slept together."

She immediately slapped her hand over her mouth. "Oh, God. I didn't say that. Pretend you didn't hear that. I mean, it doesn't make a difference, right? I like him so much, but children are a whole other thing. They make it real. Plus there are so many of them. Three. That's like a lot. What if I can't keep their names straight? What if they hate me? I just don't know. I screwed up with you about Rick and nearly lost our friendship. The potential for damage is huge!"

Jana reached across the table and touched her hand. "Breathe. It's okay."

"It's not. This is a bad idea. I don't want to disappoint him, and this seems like a place that I would."

Jana hadn't ever had doubts about Teddy dating Beth, but watching her friend freak out warmed her heart. It was obvious that Beth cared about Teddy and their relationship to the point that she was hyperventilating. She wouldn't have thought such a successful, together person could be vulnerable, but she could see Beth was actually shaking.

"You'll do fine," she told her friend. "For what it's worth, I think having all of us together at one time would be easier. The kids will have a lot of places to put their attention so you won't be in the spotlight."

Beth didn't look convinced. "I'll be the first woman their dad has brought home since their mom died. I'm pretty sure they're going to notice."

Orchid and Atlas would be fine with it, Jana thought, but Magnolia might have a few things to say. She was the one who remembered their mom the most.

"Does it bother you he has the kids?"

Beth frowned. "I don't understand the question. If you're asking if I wish he didn't, the answer is no. His family is everything to Teddy. He wouldn't be who he is without them. Being a father is what he was destined for. I'm the weak link in all of this, not him or the kids."

A good answer, Jana thought.

"That doesn't mean I'm prepared to meet them," Beth added as she pressed a hand to her belly. "Now I feel sick."

Jana couldn't help laughing. "You're making this more than it is."

"Easy for you to say. I'm the one who has to measure up."

"No, you don't. You can be yourself. That's plenty."

"If only that were true."

"I heard about your freak-out," Teddy said over the phone, his voice filled with amusement.

Beth sank onto her bed. She'd only been home from dinner with Jana for a couple of hours. Word traveled fast in the Mead household.

"Is that what we're calling it?" she asked, careful to keep her voice light. "I was thinking more of a natural and understandable concern. I don't have a lot of kids in my life. It's not like I'm the director of a daycare center. My main interactions these days are at the store, where I ask them if they want apple slices with their sandwich and point out the animal cracker selections."

Hardly real encounters where conversation and play were expected. Although under other circumstances, Beth knew she would be perfectly fine. Maybe a little quiet or awkward, but nothing overly noteworthy. The problem was, these were Teddy's kids, so the pressure was on. She wanted their relationship to work out, and that meant dealing with more than just the hunky guy who haunted her dreams. The children added a challenging element—one that terrified her.

"Hey, are you okay?" he asked softly.

"Of course."

"Why do I know that's not true? Beth, you have nothing to be worried about. You're amazing, and my kids are going to see that." He paused. "I'd like you to meet them, but if it's too soon for you, we'll put it off a few more weeks."

She felt a rush of gratitude, followed by a sense of indecision. On the one hand, she would prefer to wait. On the other hand, him wanting to introduce her to his children meant something.

It was a sign that he was just as interested in her as she was in him. Plus Jana was ready for Linnie to meet Rick. Her friend had been right—having a big family barbecue would add a level of casualness to the event. Better that than something more formal like dinner out.

"Let's see what Rick wants to do," she said. "If he's comfortable meeting Linnie, then I'll meet your kids. It'll be more natural that way."

"You sure?"

No. A thousand times no. But instead of admitting that, she did her best to sound happy and confident as she said, "Of course. It'll be great."

They talked for a few more minutes, then hung up. When she'd tossed her phone on the bed, she went in search of her aunt. Agatha was in her small home studio, carefully fitting a bikini top on one of her mannequins. She smiled at Beth.

"I'm thinking of working with yak yarn. It's going to be a thing, and I like to stay ahead of the trends. Do you—" Agatha studied her for a second. "Oh, dear. Something's happened."

Beth sank onto the love seat opposite the desk. "I'm fine. Nothing's wrong. Not exactly. It's just…" Ack, how to explain? Probably the simple truth would work best. "Teddy wants me to meet his kids. It's only been a month, so it feels too soon, but things are moving fast and we're both interested in each other, so is it too soon or am I reacting to the whole kid thing?"

Agatha nodded in understanding. "You're concerned about being a stepmother. It would be a challenge."

Beth nearly came out of her seat. "A what? Don't say the *S* word. No. Teddy and I are barely dating. There's no stepmother talk."

She'd never thought of herself that way, probably because she'd never dated a guy with kids before. Stepmother. She couldn't.

"I haven't even met the kids. I've seen pictures, but I don't know anything about them." Teddy had shared a few things, but it wasn't like getting to know them.

"Nothing is going to happen today," Agatha told her. "You don't have to do anything or solve anything."

True, Beth thought, trying to do as Jana had suggested earlier and breathe. Even if she was going to meet them, it wouldn't be for a little while.

"I have a serious lack of kid experience," she said. "I've never been around them. I didn't babysit in middle school. Ian and I talked about having children, but neither of us seemed overly enthused. What if I'm not a kid person?"

Agatha smiled at her. "You have a very giving heart, my dear. That's what matters most. As for the rest of it, you'll learn as you go. That's what I did with you and your brother."

"I know you and Uncle Dale never wanted children, but you were totally there for us." Beth remembered when her aunt had rescued Rick and her from their respective foster care situations. It had been about eighteen months after they'd lost their mom.

"Dale didn't, and I wasn't sure I wanted to push things. By the time I realized I felt an emptiness in my life, I was well into my thirties." She smiled sadly. "He agreed we could try, but I never got pregnant. Eventually I accepted it would just be the two of us."

Beth thought maybe Agatha had been her age when she'd realized she would never have children. Not that Beth was looking to be a single mother, but times had changed, and if she decided to have a baby, she still could.

"I was at a low point about the decision when I decided to reach out to your mother. We hadn't spoken in at least five years."

Beth knew about the family drama—how her mother had always been difficult—getting into trouble, running away, hanging out with the "bad" kids. She and Agatha had never been

close, never gotten along, something Beth had trouble understanding. Agatha had such a warm, gentle, giving spirit.

"You found out she'd died," Beth murmured.

Agatha nodded slowly. "I felt so terrible for not insisting we
stay in touch. My guilt for what happened to you and Rick has
haunted me for years."

"We've talked about this," Beth told her. "There was no way
you could have known what happened."

She and Rick never remembered meeting Agatha and her
husband, although they must have at least a couple of times, and
their mother had never talked about her sister, so when she'd
died, neither of them had thought to mention a not-so-distant
relative. Instead they'd been split up and sent to separate foster homes. Beth remembered how frantic she'd felt, knowing
that Rick was alone. He'd always needed her to get through
life. He was too smart, too quiet and awkward to navigate the
world easily.

"Besides," she added, smiling at her aunt. "The second you
found out Mom had died, you rushed to find us."

Beth remembered the shock of being called out of class to
meet her aunt and uncle. When she'd seen them, there'd been
no sense of recognition, and she'd been more than a little nervous about going home with strangers. Then Agatha had mentioned they were going to get Rick as well and they would be
living together. That was all Beth had needed to hear to happily
collect her things and join them. After nearly eighteen months
apart, she and Rick had been reunited, and they'd started new
lives with Agatha and Dale.

Agatha had done all she could to make the two frightened
children comfortable. She'd been caring and warm, while Dale
had been a quiet and stern man. He'd made the rules clear. Although he'd never completely warmed to having her and Rick
around, he'd appreciated her eagerness to work in the store.
While her friends had spent their job money on pretty clothes

or makeup, she'd saved so she would know she could always take care of herself and her brother—should disaster strike.

Over time that need had eased, but had never gone away. It was why to this day, she looked out for her brother, and he looked out for her. Sure, they were capable of taking care of themselves, no matter the circumstances, but some lessons could never be unlearned.

Still, the four of them had become a family, and losing Dale had been devastating for all of them.

"You rescued us," she told her aunt. "I would be stepping in to replace a beloved mother. It's different."

"You wouldn't be replacing her. No one can do that. And didn't you say the younger two barely remember her? They wouldn't judge."

That was something Beth hadn't thought of. With them, there wouldn't be any comparisons. Magnolia was older, though, and she would have all the memories and with them, expectations.

"I wouldn't want to mess up," she said, then added, "I'm not a naturally warm person."

Her aunt smiled. "You are very loving and giving. Don't worry about that. Just meet them and see how it goes. If it turns out there's a problem, we can work to fix it. But what if—and here's an unexpected thought—what if it goes well? What if they like you and everything is fine?"

Something Beth hadn't considered. "My luck isn't that good."

"Are you sure? It seems to me that since meeting Teddy, your luck has taken a turn for the very good."

15

Jana sat on Rick's leather sofa wearing his oversize plush bathrobe and nothing else. Several open cartons of Chinese food were on the coffee table in front of them. The evening was cool and a little foggy, so the gas fireplace was on, and soft jazz played from hidden speakers.

She used her chopsticks to pick up a piece of General Tso's chicken and thought to herself how she could get used to living like this. A great condo with a view of the water, sex with a very nice man who was intent on pleasing her in and out of bed, and delicious food.

Rick had pulled on jeans and a T-shirt after they'd made love and ordered in dinner. Now he smiled at her.

"You're so beautiful."

She laughed. "Thanks. I'm a little mussed, but I feel good."

She raised her eyebrows. "I'm trying to decide if your skill in bed is about your doctor training or it was just something you were born with."

He ducked his head a little. "I like making you happy."

"You do a good job of it."

He leaned forward and lightly kissed her. "I'm sorry work's been so busy. I've missed seeing you. I also want to get our weekend away planned. I just need a few more days to pull together my schedule."

"Of course." While she wanted to go away with him, she was willing to wait until the time was right. Now that she'd gotten into nursing school, she was feeling very mellow about everything.

As they chatted, she thought about how much she liked him. She wasn't in love with him—unlike her brother, she needed more than fifteen minutes to feel she'd found "the one"—but she thought maybe she and Rick had possibilities. She wanted to keep seeing him for sure, and if things worked out...

"Do you want to meet Linnie?" she blurted.

Rick looked at her in surprise. "Your daughter? Of course." He brightened. "Are you ready for that? I wouldn't want to rush either of you."

"I've been thinking about it," she admitted.

"I like kids. I don't have a lot to do with them, but I'd like to get to know her."

"I'm glad. Teddy and I were talking about maybe a family get-together. Something low-key. A barbecue one afternoon."

"I'm in."

"Good. So it would be you, me and Linnie, Teddy and his three, Beth, Dex and whomever Dex is currently seeing. How does that sound?"

He set down his plate and chopsticks. "Why would Beth be there?"

Jana stared at him in confusion. "Because they're dating."

"Teddy and Beth?" He stared at her, obviously clueless about their status. "What are you talking about? They're not dating. They can't be."

Now it was her turn to not know what was going on. "She didn't tell you? They've been going out for a few weeks now."

He rose and crossed to the window. His shoulders were tense, and a knot of worry formed in her stomach.

How could he not have known? Beth had mentioned she hadn't talked to him in a while, but surely she would have mentioned the new man in her life. Although looking at Rick now, she would guess Beth hadn't mentioned anything.

"Rick?"

His body relaxed, and he turned to face her, then walked back to the sofa.

"Sorry," he said, then shrugged. "I've been so busy with work, Beth and I haven't talked much. Or I guess at all." He looked away, then back at her. "I was, ah, I was hurt that she hadn't said anything. I didn't think she'd seen anyone since Ian, so this is a big deal, right?"

Her heart melted. "I'm sorry. I didn't mean to upset you."

"It's okay. We're both busy. And it's not like I told her about dating you right away." He reached for his plate. "Teddy, huh? I didn't see that coming."

"You remember when they met, right? At his place when you two came over?"

He nodded. "I figured that was it. I didn't notice anything between them." He gave a self-deprecating smile. "Not that I would see that sort of thing." He looked at her. "So we'll have a big family barbecue. I finally get to meet Linnie. I can't wait, Jana."

"I'm excited, too."

About four in the afternoon, Rick walked into Surf Sandwiches. Beth was helping out with the post–high school rush.

She started to smile at her brother only to realize from his stark expression that something was seriously wrong.

She immediately stripped off her gloves and motioned for him to follow her into the break room, where she closed the door before asking, "What's going on? Are you okay?"

He glared at her. "What the hell, Beth? You're dating Jana's brother?"

The words were so unexpected, she had to take a second for them to sink in. Once they did, she didn't understand his attitude any more than she had before.

"We've been going out for a few weeks now. Are you upset about that?"

"Upset?" He offered a cold laugh. "Pissed is more like it. You didn't think to say anything?"

"We haven't talked. You've been busy with work. I don't understand. Why are you mad? You've never cared about who I dated before."

"You don't date," he said, his voice loud. "And it's Jana's brother. That's information I should have."

"Why? How does my dating Teddy affect you? Rick, what's going on? You're acting strange. Who I go out with shouldn't matter to you."

He turned away. "It does this time, and a little advanced notice would have been helpful. I still don't know how it happened."

"Us dating? He asked me out."

He spun back to her. "Why? What did you do?"

Now *she* was starting to get annoyed. "Thanks for the compliment. You were there when we met. We talked, we liked each other and he asked me out."

"Just like that? There's nothing else going on?"

She threw up her hands. "What else would there be? Are you asking if I drugged him with a love potion because there's no other way he'd want to date me? I mean it, Rick. What's wrong with you?"

Her brother ignored the question. "You can't keep seeing him. I'm with Jana. We were together first. You have no right to do this."

"Because he's her brother?"

"It's a complication I don't need."

He'd moved from annoying to taking an apartment in stubborn town, she thought grimly. "You're not making any sense."

He glared at her. "If it doesn't work out with Jana, you'll still be seeing her brother. That will be impossible for me."

She wasn't sure when he'd become a stranger, but honest to God, she didn't know the man standing in front of her. Worse, she didn't like him at all. Anger gave her strength and courage. She didn't usually stand up to her brother, but maybe it was time for that to change.

"No," she said loudly. "You don't get a say in my personal life. Who I date doesn't affect you, and while I used to care about your opinion, right now I don't. I'll see Teddy for as long as we both want that. You can keep dating Jana or not. That's on you. I have no idea what's going on with you, but it's something."

She squared her shoulders. "This is where I work, Rick. Next time you want to act like a jerk, don't do it during business hours." She pointed at the door. "Unless you want to apologize for whatever this was, it's time for you to leave."

He glared at her with a coldness that chilled her to her bones. "Whatever," he muttered before stalking out of the break room.

She stayed where she was for a few seconds so she could catch her breath and urge her heart to slow down. Tension tightened every muscle, and her breathing was rapid. She felt like she'd been in a car accident or some other kind of trauma. She had no idea what Rick had been thinking to attack her like that.

Still confused, she hurried back to the front of the store. There were customers to serve. She washed her hands and got behind the counter, where she smiled brightly and began adding condiments onto sandwiches.

A half hour later, the crowd cleared. Kai cornered her by the drinks and asked in a low voice, "You okay?"

"I'm fine." Her bright tone was faked, but she didn't want him to know what had happened. "Rick just, ah, had a question."

Kai stared at her. "It was a whole lot more than that."

She flushed. "You heard?"

"Bits and pieces."

Note to self, she thought grimly. There were to be no personal conversations in the break room unless the store was empty.

She looked around to make sure no one was nearby, then quietly said, "I don't get it. He's mad because I'm dating Teddy."

Kai shook his head. "He's mad because you're dating Jana's brother. There's a difference."

"How?"

"I don't know, but that's what he kept saying. Jana's brother. He never called him Teddy."

She hadn't noticed. "I'm not sure that matters, but he was so strange."

He held up both hands. "I have no idea what's going on with him, B. I just know he's worried about something."

Beth arrived at Teddy's house for the infamous barbecue with no clearer understanding about Rick's problem. He hadn't reached out to her, and she couldn't bring herself to text him. She was annoyed, hurt and more than a little confused. She couldn't remember him ever talking to her like that before, and she hadn't liked it.

Despite her apprehension, she'd agreed to the Saturday late-afternoon date Teddy had suggested. She would arrive at four, the barbecue would be at five thirty, and she would be home by eight. She would host him for dinner on Sunday night when it would just be the two of them. Something he'd brought up at least sixteen times. His eagerness to be alone with her was gratifying as she found herself needing Teddy time for sure.

She parked in the driveway as she had the first time she'd been to the house. Back then she'd been just as nervous, but for different reasons. As before, Rick hadn't arrived yet, and she was grateful. She would rather get in and be settled before he showed up. She had no idea if he was going to say anything mean or rude. It wasn't like him, but since his unexpected visit to the store, she wasn't sure about anything when it came to her brother.

Teddy pulled open the front door before she could knock. He took the large bakery box from her, set it on the table by the door, then drew her into his arms and kissed her with a thoroughness that stole her breath away.

"I've missed you," he murmured against her mouth. "It's been too long."

She laughed. "Three days?"

"Nearly a lifetime."

He kissed her again, more slowly this time. She leaned into him, savoring the feel of his hard body against hers. Wanting grew—delicious and a tiny bit frustrating. Because they still weren't lovers, and there was no way that status was going to change today.

She drew back and stared into his dark blue eyes. "Hi."

He smiled. "Hi, yourself. Ready for this?"

Her smile faded as she remembered why she was here. "Oh, God. Your children. Did you mean to have three?"

He laughed. "You'll do great."

She pointed to the large pink box. "Are they going to judge me because I didn't bake?"

"This is a judgment-free zone."

"You have no idea how much I wish that was true." She picked up the box. "I'm bribing them with a bear cake. Is it wrong? Probably, but I'll take the stain on my soul."

"Bear cake. What do you mean?"

They went into the kitchen. She carefully unfastened the box and let the sides fall away. Inside was a tall round cake covered in rich brown rosettes. She turned the cake so he could see the big black eyes, the long lashes and the bulbous nose. Large bear ears sat on top of the cake with a two-inch marzipan bee by one of them. The animal's expression was friendly, and the bee had a tiny smile.

"It's all edible," she said. "The decorations are mostly sugar. Actually the whole thing is mostly sugar. But it's cute, and I thought they might like it." And by association, her.

She twisted her hands together as she looked from the cake to him. "Too much?"

He put his arm around her. "It's perfect. They're going to love it."

"I hope so."

Jana walked into the kitchen. "Hi. I thought I heard voices. How are you—" She caught sight of the cake and clapped her hands together. "Oh, look! It's a bear. So adorable. Where did you find that?"

Beth felt some of her tension ease. "There's a bakery I know. They do whimsical cakes, and I thought the kids might like this one."

"They're going to love it."

"Hey, it's me," a male voice called.

"In the kitchen." Jana turned back to her. "You haven't met Dex yet, have you?"

Beth shook her head and quickly rubbed her hands against her jeans. A day of reckoning, she thought frantically. The children *and* the best friend. *Oh, please, oh, please let it go well.*

A man walked into the kitchen and smiled. Beth glanced at him, prepared to walk over and hold out her hand for an introduction. Instead she found she couldn't move.

She was staring at a surprisingly familiar face—one she'd seen hundreds of times up on the big screen, or in her living room when she'd streamed a movie. She'd seen him as a Special Forces leader who saved the village and got the girl. He'd been a spaceship pilot, a firefighter and a spy whose sense of humor and ability to get out of tight situations had rivaled the old James Bond movies.

"Shit," Teddy said, his voice coming from behind her. "We didn't tell her."

Jana moved next to Beth. "I'm sorry. I forgot. I'm a terrible friend."

Beth looked at her, trying to understand the words, but she couldn't. The moment was too surreal. Yes, this was Malibu, and famous people were part of everyday life. Just not Dex Sanders in Teddy's kitchen.

"You're the best friend," Beth managed.

Dex smiled at her. "For what? More than twenty years. We met on the set of *That Last Year*. He's tried to shake me a few times, but I'm like a tick. I don't let go."

That Last Year? That Last Year? Her already spinning brain struggled to remember the old sitcom. It had been about a working-class family living in the Midwest, but the real stars had been the two brothers. If Dex had been one of them...

She turned to look at Teddy. He was older and he'd changed, of course, but somehow she now saw he looked exactly like—

"You're Theo Mead, who played Sammy?"

Teddy shifted uncomfortably. "Yeah. Sorry. I probably should have said something. If people recognize me, I'll talk about it, but that's not part of my everyday life, and when you didn't mention it, I kind of forgot."

He'd forgotten that he'd been part of one of the most popular television shows in the country? She still remembered watching the last episode and crying with her friends when Sammy finally got the girl of his dreams to go out with him. Dex had parlayed his stardom into a successful action career, but Teddy had dropped out of sight. He'd...

"You left acting and went to China," she said more to herself than to him. "You studied acupuncture."

He crossed to her and put his hands on her shoulders. "I should have said something before. I'm sorry. I swear I just didn't think about it. That was all a long time ago."

Dex grinned. "And yet the residuals live forever."

Teddy chuckled. "He's right about that."

Residuals? From the show. Of course, she thought, still trying to take it all in. *That Last Year* was still popular, gaining a new audience every three or four years as teenagers discovered it. She'd seen it mentioned as one of the most successful reruns ever. She looked around at the large, sprawling house. Maybe they hadn't used Valonia's money to purchase it after all. Maybe it was all Teddy.

Beth knew she had to pull it together. Yes, Dex was a surprise, but he was still Teddy's best friend, and that was the context she was going to focus on.

"Hi," she said, holding out her hand. "I'm Beth. Nice to meet you."

They shook. Dex winked at her. "You're taking it really well. I appreciate you not getting weird."

"You were a surprise," she told him. "But honestly, compared with meeting the kids, you're just a blip. A famous blip, but still."

"A blip?" he asked with a chuckle, then turned to Teddy. "I like this one. You should keep her."

"That's the plan." Teddy put his arm around her. "Ready to go out back?"

To where she would guess the children were playing. No. Not now, not ever. But getting it over with made the most sense.

"I can't wait," she lied cheerfully.

They all went out the sliding glass doors.

Beth remembered the backyard from her first visit to the house, but somehow with four kids running around and playing, it seemed much smaller. In the second it took for them to notice the adults had joined them, Beth had a chance to study Teddy's three. They all had dark hair and brown eyes—a legacy

from their mother, she thought. Linnie was very much not like
the others with her bright red hair.

"Dex!" Teddy's youngest shrieked and started toward them.
Then she spotted Beth and came to a stop.

Teddy's other two joined her. The older girl took Orchid's
hand, and they all approached. Linnie grinned at Beth and hurried over.

"You came!" the four-year-old said enthusiastically. "Everyone, this is my friend Beth. She took me to the beach and we
made sandcastles and I met Kai who bought me an ice cream!"

Dex leaned close. "How are the rest of us supposed to compete with that?"

Linnie rushed forward. Beth crouched down and hugged her.

"It's good to see you again," she said. "Want to introduce me
to your family?"

Linnie looked delighted to be handed such an important task.
She pointed to Teddy's three. "That's Magnolia. She's the oldest
and she can be bossy, but it's because she knows things. Atlas is
the only boy. That's hard for him, but he's okay with it. Orchid
was the baby until I came along and now I'm the baby." She
sighed heavily. "I want to be oldest, but Mommy says that can't
happen, so I'm stuck. Which were you?"

Beth stood and smiled at Teddy's kids, hoping Linnie's enthusiasm bought her a few points.

"I'm the oldest," she said, glancing at Magnolia. "My brother
Rick is the youngest. It was just the two of us, so no middle
sibling."

"You'll meet Rick in a bit," Jana said easily. "He had to work
some this morning, but he'll be here soon."

Magnolia looked between Beth and her father. "Dad says
you're dating."

"We are," Teddy said easily, moving close to Beth. "That's
why I wanted you to meet her."

"And Jana is dating your brother, Rick?"

Beth nodded. "That's kind of fun, isn't it? Your mom and I met volunteering at the food bank. Rick met Jana because their offices are in the same building."

"Mommy said Rick's a doctor," Linnie said importantly. Then her smile faded. "I don't want him to give me a shot."

Jana laughed. "He's not that kind of doctor."

Dex swept up the four-year-old. "I'll protect you if he tries." He spun her around, and she squealed. When he set her down, he pointed to the swing set. "Race you."

Linnie and Dex took off. Atlas and Orchid followed, with Magnolia trailing them. Beth drew in a breath, grateful Teddy's friend had offered a distraction.

"You doing all right?" Teddy asked, resting his hand on her waist. "I know it's a lot."

"I'm okay," she said, watching the kids jump around Dex. He quickly sorted them into two teams and sent them up the slide.

Jana pulled her phone out of her back pocket and smiled at the screen. "Rick's here. I'll go get him."

She disappeared into the house. Beth watched her go, not sure what was going to happen with her brother. He'd been so angry with her when he'd shown up at her store.

A shriek of laughter distracted her. Orchid was coming down the slide, laughing so hard she nearly rolled off. Linnie begged to be next. Atlas was running around to get on again, while Magnolia was watching Beth and her father.

Was the preteen worried? Apprehensive? Given the circumstances, Magnolia was probably feeling all kinds of emotions.

Jana and Rick stepped outside. Linnie caught sight of her mom and started toward her, only to stop. She looked from her mom to Rick and back, then rushed to Beth's side and grabbed her hand. The other kids joined Linnie, crowding close. Dex came up behind them.

"This is a crowd," Rick said, sounding faintly nervous. Then he spotted her and smiled. "I know you." He moved close and lightly kissed her cheek. "Hey, sis."

His voice was full of affection, his posture relaxed. He didn't look anything like the angry man who'd confronted her only a few days before.

"Everyone," Jana said happily. "This is Rick, Beth's brother."

"Are you really a doctor?" Orchid asked.

"I am. I'm a surgeon."

Linnie and Orchid seemed confused, but Atlas immediately stepped toward him.

"For real? You cut people open and stuff?" He sounded intrigued.

Rick leaned close. "I touch guts every day."

"Sweet!"

Magnolia made a face. "That's gross. I'm Magnolia." She pointed. "He's Atlas. Orchid is the youngest of us three. Linnie is Jana's daughter and our cousin."

Rick immediately looked at Linnie and smiled. "Hi. You're cute."

Linnie dimpled. "Thank you. I don't want you to give me a shot."

"Then I won't. I promise."

Dex strolled up and held out his hand. Jana made the introductions. Beth watched her brother, but either he was better at concealing his surprise than she had been or he had no idea who Dex was. Knowing Rick as she did, she would guess it was the latter.

There were a few minutes of getting everyone drinks. The younger kids and Dex returned to their play while the adults and Teddy's oldest settled in the shade. Somehow Beth found herself sitting next to Magnolia.

"I have questions," Magnolia announced. "Is this a good time?"

Dread settled like a rock in Beth's stomach. She glanced around frantically, hoping for Teddy or Jana to rescue her, but they were busy talking to Rick, leaving her alone with her inquisitor.

"This is a very good time," she lied. "What would you like to know?"

Magnolia pulled a piece of paper out of her shorts front pocket and scanned it. She looked at Beth. "Have you been married before?"

"Yes. Once. We got a divorce a little over a year ago."

"Do you have children?"

"No."

Magnolia looked surprised. "Why not?"

"I'm not sure," she admitted. "I wanted to have kids, but I don't think the man I married did. We should have talked about it more before getting serious. That was a mistake. But I like children."

Magnolia's neutral expression didn't change. "Do you consider yourself a fair person?"

"Yes."

"Do you have a job?"

Teddy glanced over, as if just realizing what was happening. He hurried in their direction and grabbed the paper from Magnolia.

"What are you doing?"

"Asking questions. Beth said I could. I checked with her first, Dad. I wasn't rude."

He pulled a chair close and sat down. "No grilling our guests."

Magnolia raised her eyebrows. "You're dating, and we have the right to know what kind of person she is. What if you fall in love? We're a family, Dad. We have a dynamic, and you're bringing in someone who could change that. It's not right to tell us to simply accept that. This is important."

Beth's heart ached for the girl. She was so strong and yet so scared at the same time. As the oldest, she would be the one most likely to step into her mother's role. Teddy had talked about how he had to consciously keep from letting her take over. As an oldest herself, Beth got the need to protect. It was biological.

"I'm okay with the questions," she said gently. She smiled at Magnolia. "Yes, I do have a job. I own a sandwich shop called Surf Sandwiches."

Magnolia's expression relaxed a little. "For real? That's you?"

"Well, me and about fifteen employees, but yes. The store was originally owned by my aunt and uncle. When Rick and I lost our mom, we went to live with them, and I started working in the store. Eventually I bought them out, and now I own the place."

Magnolia stared at her. "Your mom died when you were little?"

For the first time since the questioning began, Beth felt she was on solid ground. "I was a couple of years older than you when it happened. She died in an accident, so it was a shock."

Magnolia's gaze lowered. "My mom died of an embolism. She was just gone."

"That makes it so hard, because neither of us got to say goodbye."

Teddy touched his daughter's arm. "You okay?"

Magnolia nodded, then looked at Beth. "You understand. A lot of people don't." She drew in a breath. "And I'm really glad you have your own source of income."

Teddy groaned. "Seriously, kid? You went there?"

"It's stuff you gotta know, Dad. I did some reading online. You have assets, and sometimes people get into relationships because there's money. I'm looking out for you."

The moment of bonding seemed to be over, leaving Beth both impressed and a little terrified. Magnolia was way too mature for her age, but what a thoughtful and caring kid.

"I have a successful business, my own 401(k) and savings," she said. "So no, I'm not here for the money. I just like your dad."

The preteen relaxed a little. "Okay. That's good. Thank you for answering my questions. You didn't have to."

Beth nodded. "I know this is difficult and strange. Like you said, there's a family dynamic, and if your dad's dating me, that could change. I've never dated anyone with kids before, so this is new for me, too. Maybe we could kind of help each other out."

Magnolia studied her for a second before smiling. "I'd like that."

"Good. Me, too. By the way, I brought cake to try to make you like me."

Magnolia laughed. "Good call."

16

Dex walked over with a glass of wine. "How you holding up?" he asked as he took the chair next to her.

Beth accepted the wine. So far she'd only carried hers around. She'd wanted a clear head through the dinner. But as they were nearly done with the meal and she would be leaving soon, she figured she would indulge in three sips and call it a night.

"Good," she said, looking around at the post-dinner crowd. The kids were huddled around their dad, talking and laughing. Linnie was on Rick's lap, smiling at him. An evening that could have been a disaster had gone surprisingly well. She'd gotten through the meal just fine. She'd talked to each of Teddy's children and had, she thought, managed to avoid messing up.

"I'm the best friend," Dex said casually. "So we should probably get to know each other."

Beth looked at him and grinned. "If you're the best friend, don't you already know too much about me?"

He chuckled. "Less than you'd think. Teddy's still at the stage where he wants to keep you to himself."

She wasn't sure how Dex had meant the statement, but to her it was everything she wanted to hear. It made her feel precious and important.

"You didn't know about his past," he said.

"The child acting?" She shook her head. "He never said anything. I mean, this is LA, and a lot of people have been a part of the business, but no, I didn't have a clue. About either of you. I didn't put the name thing together." She looked across the table to where Teddy was laughing with his kids. "Now that I know, of course I can see the resemblance, but until I found out, I wouldn't have guessed."

"What do you think about the fact that he didn't stay in acting?"

"I'm not surprised. He loves what he does. His patients are important to him." Interesting that her brother and the man she was falling for both healed others. In different ways, of course, but the core mission was similar.

"You don't want to be with someone famous?" he asked, his voice teasing.

"Not really my thing. I'm not a limelight kind of person." She studied Dex. "You gave it up, though. And not because you had to. You walked away."

Dex glanced at Teddy. "It's his fault."

"How?"

"I was best man at his wedding to Valonia. Watching them, seeing what they had, made me realize I wanted the same for myself. There was no way that was going to happen while I was living in a fishbowl. I had plenty of money, and I'd done what I set out to do, so I walked away."

"How's normal life?" she asked, wondering if he ever regretted his decision. She didn't know Dex at all, but if she had to guess, she would say the answer was no.

"It's good."

"And Mrs. Right?"

He chuckled. "She's out there. Of that I am sure."

"I hope you find her soon."

"Thanks. Me, too."

The evening slowly wound down. Jana had to rescue Rick, who'd gotten roped into pushing both Orchid and Linnie on the swings.

"I'm fine," he said with a laugh as she told both girls to leave him be. "It's a good upper-body workout."

"You have surgery on Monday. You can't have sore arms because these two wouldn't take no for an answer." She looked at the girls. "Did you thank Rick for pushing you?"

Orchid and Linnie both grinned.

"Thank you, Rick," they said together, then ran off.

"It wasn't that bad," he told her, pulling her close. "I like their company."

"I'm glad."

She stared into his eyes and thought that she'd gotten very lucky that first day they'd met. He was so sweet, and she liked being with him. Even better, he'd been great with all the kids. No snapping or over-monitoring. No hint that he was secretly a jerk like Paul.

"I've missed you," he told her. "I'm sorry work's been so difficult."

"I've missed you, too. As for work—it's important. And with only a couple more weeks in my quarter, I'm plenty busy myself."

"But you still want to go away with me," he clarified. "I'm going to start looking at hotels."

"I can't wait," she told him. A weekend away sounded perfect, she thought. Just the two of them alone. No responsibilities, nowhere to be.

"Good. We'll get something on the calendar in the next week or so."

"Perfect."

He released her and turned to where Orchid and Linnie were running around the table.

"She sure has a lot of energy," he said.

"I think it's all the excitement. Normally she's a little quieter. She'll crash soon, and I'll put her to bed."

"Does she ask about her father?"

The question was unexpected. She shook her head. "Not really. She knows she doesn't have a father but nothing beyond that. Sometimes I wonder if she assumes he died. After all, her cousins don't have a mother. But eventually she's going to want to know more."

"What are you going to tell her?"

Although his voice was gentle and she sensed Rick was only asking the obvious, she couldn't help feeling judged. Or maybe she was doing it to herself. She'd been the one to party in Cancun and end up pregnant.

"Some version of the truth. I haven't figured out exactly what that is yet, but I'll get there." She wanted to be honest, but didn't want to give her daughter more information than she could handle.

He put his arm around her. "She loves you, and she'll understand."

Jana hoped he was right.

"How long did you and Dex go out?" he asked.

She stepped back and spun to face him. She was sure she looked like a cartoon character with big eyes and her mouth hanging open, but she couldn't help it.

"What are you talking about? Dex and I never dated."

Rick stared at her intently. "You sure?"

"I think I'd know if I dated someone. Dex and I are friends. I've known him most of my life. We're family." Was Rick worried about Dex? "There's nothing between us, I swear. There never has been."

Rick didn't look convinced. "He has a thing for you."

"Not possible." Dex into her? Hardly. "I know he has the whole former star thing going on, and that can be intimidating, but you don't have to worry. Dex is like another brother." She moved close. "He's not the one I'm interested in."

She waited for Rick to relax and smile at her, only when he did, she couldn't help thinking he was pretending rather than believing, which made her sad. Of all the things he could be worried about, Dex was absolutely not ever going to be a problem. There'd never been a hint of anything between them, and there never would be.

Beth hummed happily as she sliced mozzarella for the caprese salad she was preparing in her kitchen. Her good mood had lasted a full three days and showed no signs of ending. The weekend dinner with Teddy and his kids had gone really well. She'd gotten through the afternoon and evening without saying the wrong thing, the kids had been friendly, and she'd enjoyed meeting and hanging out with Dex.

Teddy had been just as pleased. He'd told her fifty times at their private evening the next night, and he'd been texting her regularly since, telling her how happy he was and how the kids wanted to know when they were going to see her again. While she was excited to hang out with them more, she was more excited about tonight—it was the makeup dinner for the one she and Teddy had missed when Orchid had been in her bike accident. Agatha was out with friends, Beth had a nice bottle of white wine chilling and she was more than ready for a little Teddy time.

She was happy, she thought as she continued her food prep.

More than happy. She felt good and liked the changes in her life. Funny how they'd all started when she and Jana had become friends. Or rather, when she'd first signed up to work at the food bank. Taking a single step out of her comfort zone had brought her so many rewards. A wonderful friendship with a woman she admired and a new man who made her tingle in all the right places.

Teddy arrived ten minutes early and was looking a little sheepish when she opened the door.

"I couldn't wait," he admitted as he stepped into the house. "I've missed you."

"I've missed you, too," she breathed, looking into his eyes and feeling all the happy bubbling inside of her. Neither of them mentioned they'd spent the day together less than forty-eight hours ago. It felt so much longer.

He pulled her close and lightly kissed her. Passion joined the happy bubbles, but she was used to the very insistent wanting that plagued her whenever he was near, so she stepped back, prepared to describe that evening's menu. Only instead of retreating, he moved closer and kissed her again.

Rather than the carefully controlled brush of his mouth against hers, this kiss was intense and determined. He wrapped his arms around her, pulling her tight against his body. She felt the hard planes of his muscles and the thick ridge of his erection. Need exploded inside of her, making her want to rub against him, to plead that they stop playing and make love for real.

He pulled back just enough to lean his forehead against hers.

"I know what I said," he whispered, his voice thick with passion. "About us waiting and how it was important for us to get to know each other. It's just that I want you so much. I can't sleep. I'm not eating. I think about you all the time." He looked into her eyes. "I need you, Beth. Is that all right?"

Oh. My. God! The man sounded desperate. He was practically pleading. Even if she hadn't already been on fire for him, she would have been instantly ready after hearing his words. And yet—despite his obvious arousal, he was still waiting for her to voice her opinion. Because this would be a joint decision.

"Agatha's gone, I'm on the Pill and I have condoms," she said, meeting his gaze directly. Knowing how much he wanted her made her brave, and she reveled in the feeling. "And I'm more than ready to make love with you."

His breath caught. Then he laughed. "I'll let you lead the way."

Thirty minutes later, Beth struggled to catch her breath. She wasn't sure how to describe what she'd just experienced. She'd had orgasms before—lots of them. It was a biological reaction to physical intimacy. No big deal. At least, that was what she'd thought before. But with Teddy, everything was different. *She* was different. Instead of a slow build to a satisfying conclusion, she'd found herself rushing toward an impossible goal. She'd panted, she'd begged, she'd gotten lost in the sensations that had swept through her until she'd had no choice but to lose herself in the glory of a release that had shaken her to her very core.

Even as her pulse slowed and she could inhale normally, she had the strangest urge to burst into tears. Teddy returned from the bathroom, where he'd disposed of the condom, and climbed back into bed with her. He rolled onto his side so he was facing her and played his hand across her belly.

"Thank you," he murmured, brushing a kiss against her still-sensitive nipple. "I knew making love with you would be special, but I wasn't expecting..." He paused, then smiled. "That much chemistry."

"Is that what we're calling it?" she asked, staring at him. "Because I don't know what that was. How did you do that to me? Is it your fancy acupuncture training? The massage stuff? A deal with the devil?"

She pulled the sheet to her shoulders and sat up. "I've never felt anything like that before. I'm not kidding. It's like I was doing it all wrong before."

He sat up, facing her. "No deal with the devil. I promise. That was us, Beth. That's how bright we burn together."

"Was it different for you?" she asked, then shook her head. "Sorry. I'm not asking for a comparison. I guess I don't know what I want to know."

Which was only partially true. She supposed the real question was, had he felt it too, or was she in this alone? As she'd already used up her quota of bravery for the day, she wasn't going to mention that.

He cupped her face and kissed her. "Yes, it was different. It was us connecting. It was perfect."

The best sex ever? Which was another question she couldn't or wouldn't ask.

Until this moment, she hadn't been troubled by his previous marriage. She understood how much he'd loved his wife and how devastated he'd been by the loss. Or at least, she'd thought she got it. Now she was less sure. Because her worldview was forever altered. Or maybe just shattered.

"I should start dinner," she said, turning to slip out of bed. But Teddy touched her arm.

"Don't," he murmured, drawing her back to him. "Not yet. There's so much more I want to do."

As if to prove his point, he took her hand and brought it to his erect penis. Her eyes widened.

"Already?"

His smile turned knowing. "What did you think would happen?"

Before she could answer, he started kissing his way down her body. Her legs parted involuntarily, and her breath caught as he flicked his tongue against the very heart of her. It was very possible that him bringing her to orgasm this way would kill her, but what a way to go.

★ ★ ★

"Solvang?" Jana asked, staring at the picture on Rick's tablet. "I've never been."

"It's fun," he said. "Agatha and Dale took us one summer. It's touristy, but in a good way. But we'd stay in the Santa Ynez Valley."

He took the tablet from her and typed for a second, then handed it back to her. She looked at the picture of the Garden Suite at the Hotel Ynez.

The room was glorious. Big with a living room. She flipped through the pictures, then looked at Rick.

"There's a fire pit and a soaking tub?"

He winked. "A private soaking tub. See? There's a fence all around. No one can see us. I thought we'd go wine tasting and just hang out. If we leave Friday morning, we'll be in Solvang by lunch. We can spend the rest of the day there, then go check in to our hotel. I could set up the wine tasting for Saturday. Sunday we'd have a leisurely brunch, then head home."

He paused, suddenly looking anxious. "Is it too much? Did you want to make changes to the plan?"

His obvious worry and concern touched her. "Everything is perfect," she told him. "I love the plan. It sounds like fun, and the hotel looks amazing."

"Yeah?" He smiled. "Okay, good. When I talked to them this morning, they had a cancellation, so the room's available in two weeks. I can get the Friday off work. What about you?"

Two weeks from now? She wouldn't be done with finals, but she was doing well in both her classes and didn't need extra time to study, which meant she could make that part of it work. Teddy had already said he would watch Linnie, so she didn't have to worry about that. She liked Rick and wanted to spend time with him.

"Let's do it," she said.

Rick grabbed her and kissed her. "We're really doing this. You're going away with me!"

"You sound happy," she teased.

"I am." His smiled faded. "I mean that, Jana. I got the best girl ever." He grinned. "Ah, woman. I mean woman."

She laughed. "I know in that context, saying *girl* is just an expression. You're not in trouble."

His smile faded a little. "You've never been mad at me. Why is that?"

"You've never messed up."

"I think about you a lot. I want to make you happy."

"I want you to be happy, too."

He smiled at her. "Of course I am. I'm with you."

17

Beth sat on the beach, watching the surfers. It was early and her day off, but she'd been unable to sleep. The last couple of nights, all she'd done was toss and turn as her mind refused to quiet and let her rest.

The morning clouds weren't very thick and promised to burn off early, leaving the day bright and sunny. Overhead seagulls circled, calling out to each other. The air smelled damp and salty, and the sand was cold, but she'd dressed in layers and was physically comfortable sitting there. Mentally she was in a very strange place.

She couldn't stop thinking about her evening with Teddy. Not just the sex, although that had been incredible all three times, but what it had meant to her. She'd never had an experience that came close to what she'd felt with him. It was as if there were parts of herself she'd never known that had finally been uncovered. The act of making love with him had been transformative. Which sounded amazing but honestly just scared her.

Worse, it had caused her to wonder about his relationship with his late wife. Because if he had been equally transformed by loving Valonia, then how much worse the loss would have been for him. It hadn't just been ordinary grief, because theirs would have been an extraordinary love.

She was also confused about the kid thing. Specifically his children. She'd enjoyed spending time with them and could see herself getting emotionally involved. A week ago she would have been determined to avoid the S word, but now...maybe...the thought of being a stepmother was something she could imagine.

A realization she would keep to herself, because hey, was it too soon? And yet thinking about his kids made her happy. If only the night with Teddy hadn't left her so off-balance.

One of the surfers rode his board to shore, then walked out of the surf. She recognized Kai and waved to him. He planted his board in the sand, grabbed a towel and walked toward her.

"Are you making a habit of showing up here?" he asked with a smile.

"Maybe. I find being near the morning ocean restful. Plus watching all of you out there being so athletic is inspiring." She looked at him. "Not that I have any plans to exercise."

"Surfing isn't exercise," he told her. "It's a spiritual experience."

"And a great way to get women."

He flashed her a grin. "I don't usually have trouble with that, but yes. Surfing is sexy."

They sat in silence for a few minutes. Beth told herself to stop thinking about Teddy and to let her mind empty. She was mentally and physically exhausted, and she had to find a way to relax. Maybe she should download a meditation app or something.

"You either had sex, or one of you said I love you," Kai said unexpectedly.

Beth blinked. "What are you talking about?"

"Something's wrong. That's why you're here. But it's not a crisis, because if there'd been an accident, you'd be dealing with that. Not sitting here thinking. You're in a new relationship, so I figured it's that. You're not crying, so it's not over. That leaves sex or love."

She sighed. "Couldn't you just for once act your age and be self-absorbed and clueless? You must have the oldest soul ever."

"Uh-huh. You're not answering the question, B, which means it's sex, because you'd be comfortable talking about love."

She opened her mouth, then closed it. How could someone so young be so insightful? "Fine, it was sex. Amazing sex."

"You're not saying it was too good, are you? Because that's not possible."

She managed a faint laugh. "That's not exactly what I'm saying. It was different. Better than, you know, with Ian."

"Not a surprise, but why is it a problem?"

"He's a widower. He was very much in love with his wife, and she died unexpectedly. She wasn't sick or anything. That was nearly five years ago. Now it's just him and his three kids. There hasn't been anyone else. I'm the first woman he's dated since her death."

"Are you feeling the pressure of that?"

"Yes!" She practically shouted the word, then drew in a breath and murmured, "Sorry."

"Don't be. It's a thing, and you're going to have to deal."

"It's less the dealing than the why. Why did he pick me? Why do we have this amazing chemistry? How much does he still think about her? Is it just him and me, or are there three of us in the relationship? And if sex with her was anything like what we just experienced, then how on earth can he ever let go of what he had long enough to want something else?"

The "something," of course, was really "someone," namely her, but why state the obvious?

She paused to breathe. In that second when she inhaled, she had the thought she could either start laughing hysterically or burst into tears. As she wasn't comfortable with either, she settled for more breathing.

"That's a lot," Kai said quietly. "Plus the kids."

She nodded. "You're right. His kids. I liked them."

"You're also scared of them."

"I'm not afraid exactly."

"You're dealing with a lot. Do you want kids of your own?"

"I don't know. Sometimes."

"Would his be enough?"

Would they? she wondered, turning the question over in her mind. "Maybe," she said slowly. "I'm nearly forty. If I was desperate to have a baby, I would have done it by now."

"Do you think Teddy's caught up in the past?" he asked.

A reasonable question, so she considered her answer. "There's a line between being honest and forthcoming, and being obsessed. I would give him the benefit of the doubt on that one. He's told me about Valonia and their marriage, but he doesn't dwell on it, and I don't feel he talks about her too much. It's not that. If anything it's how deeply he loved her. Like they were on a different emotional plane. Thinking about that, knowing what they had, changes things."

"No, it doesn't." Kai looked at her. "It scares you."

She wanted to say he was wrong, that of course she wasn't afraid, only she knew she was—big-time.

"My mom was all about the flame," she said. *"Burn hot and bright. Burn yourself out. If you're not afraid, you're not living."*

"Not a restful way to grow up."

"Exactly. I was afraid all the time, but not the way she meant. I worried what would happen to us, who she would bring home, whether or not she'd remember to feed us. There was no emotional room for regular 'kid' concerns. I tried to be there for Rick so he could focus on himself, but he rescued me more than once."

"You rescued each other. Do you think the problem with Teddy is you're afraid you can't love him as deeply as he loves you?"

The question surprised her. "I don't know. I hadn't thought of it that way, but maybe. I sure didn't love Ian the way Teddy loved Valonia. Maybe I'm emotionally stunted."

"That's a leap. You're cautious because you didn't get to be a kid the way you should have. The ability to give it all comes from knowing you'll always be safe. Now you've met a man who embodies self-confidence in the emotional sense, and you're not sure where you fit in."

He was right about all of it, she thought, barely surprised. Kai had depths. "Plus the kids. They're great, and as Teddy and I continue to see each other, I'm going to have to deal with them." She paused. "No, I want to deal with them. I just hope I can do a good job."

Kai stared at her. "You're worried about not being a good mom?" His voice was thick with disbelief. "I'll accept the other stuff, but not that. B, you're the most nurturing person I know."

Now it was her turn to stare. "What are you talking about? That can't be true."

Her, nurturing? Sure, she tried to be nice and thoughtful, but didn't everyone?

"When I had that big fight with my folks," he said, "and they threw me out because I'd rather surf than go to college, you let me crash on your sofa for two weeks while I figured it out."

She waved the comment away. "Anyone would have helped out. That was no big deal."

"It was a big deal to me. Mr. Kazinsky comes in, what? Three times a week, but always on different days. Still, every morning you make up that special sauce he likes so it's ready whenever he shows up. Every day, when the store closes, you have the team make up sandwiches using all the food that's going to go bad, and we take them to the shelter."

He shifted on the sand so he was facing her. "You gave up culinary school and your savings so your brother could go to medical school. B, you give and you give. You're always thinking of other people. If you and Teddy want to take things to the next level, those kids are going to get a great stepmom. They'll be lucky to have you."

She stared at him. Was this really how he saw her? Even more startling were the tears she saw in his eyes—a testament to his sincerity.

"You've touched my heart," she whispered.

"You touch mine all the time."

She leaned in and hugged him, only to realize his wet suit was damp and cold, and pressing against it soaked her shirt. She started to laugh.

"You must be freezing."

"Naw. I'm used to it."

They looked at each other. Kai was like a much, much younger brother, she thought. He was sweet and kind, and she enjoyed his company. Not to mention the fact that he gave killer advice.

"I feel better," she admitted. "Thank you for listening and telling me what to do."

Kai grimaced. "I didn't tell you what to do. I don't do that."

"I know. I was messing with you." She sighed. "It's up to me to be brave. Part of what makes Teddy special is how he's different from anyone I know. Hearts are made to be given. He's learned that lesson, and now it's time I do, too. If I don't put myself out there, I'm going to regret it always. He's an amazing man, and I don't want to lose him."

"You're gonna be scared," Kai told her.

"Probably every day. But that's where the growth happens,

right? Because if this relationship turns out to be real, then he'll be the best thing that ever happened to me."

He stood and brushed off the sand. "I'm heading back in. See you at work tomorrow."

"You will. Thanks, Kai."

"Anytime."

He jogged back to his surfboard. After dropping the towel, he headed into the water. Beth stood and collected her things. She still had a lot to think about, but most of the fear was gone. Yes, she was in a relationship that was unlike any she'd ever had, but so far it was going great. She liked Teddy a lot and wanted to keep seeing him. She would figure out the kid thing as they went. As for the sex being the best ever in the history of the universe, well, wasn't that the kind of problem every woman wanted to have?

Beth went home to collect her list of errands. She had a lot to get through on her day off. Talking to Kai had made her feel better, and when Teddy texted her a quick **Good morning**, she immediately felt all fluttery inside.

They made arrangements to meet in a couple of days, and for the fourteenth time, he reminded her about a seminar where he would be teaching. While it was local, he would be working fourteen-hour days, which meant no getting together.

I don't want you to worry I'm running out on you.

She stared at the message, feeling the warmth in her belly. He wanted her to be comfortable, to know what was happening in his life. That he wasn't hiding anything.

I trust you, Teddy.

Good, because I can't stop thinking about you and having you dump me would really suck.

She smiled. *Not gonna happen.*

She slipped her phone into her bag, grabbed her list and headed out. She needed shampoo and conditioner from the ridiculously expensive salon in Santa Monica. She'd tried other brands, but somehow they were the only ones that really worked for her hair, so every few months she made the trek and whimpered as she handed over her credit card.

From there she made a quick stop at the very urban farmer's market that brought in fresh fruit directly from Hawaii. She and Agatha had been craving papaya and pineapple—ripe from the source. She hit the bookstore for her favorite author's new release, then decided to treat herself to a latte and a croissant from that little place by Rick's condo. Their coffee was pretty average, but the croissants were a religious experience and worth the extra fifteen-minute drive.

She found parking right out front—a miracle on its own—and went inside. After placing her order, she went to wait for it. The store was plenty crowded—a good thing, she thought absently. Small businesses could be a challenge, and she always wanted her fellow owners to do well.

She glanced around at the well-dressed customers. There were women in expensive workout clothes, office people on break, a mom with two toddlers in a double stroller, and—

Her entire body stiffened as her head involuntarily swung back. Her gaze locked on a man and woman sitting together on two stools. His arm was around her, their heads were close together, and their legs were tangled together in that casually intimate way of long-time couples.

As she watched, the man kissed the woman on the mouth. There was an ease about the act, a familiarity. As if he'd kissed her a thousand times before. Only he couldn't have. Rick was dating Jana, not this other woman.

Her stomach lurched and her body went cold as she tried desperately to understand what she was seeing. Her brother with another woman? He couldn't be. Rick was with Jana. He adored Jana. And he wouldn't ever cheat on someone.

"Beth? Your order's up."

It took her a second to realize that they meant her. She collected the latte and the croissant, then stood in the center of the coffee place, trying to figure out what on earth happened now. Did she leave? Did she walk up to her brother and confront him? Did she simply throw up? Because that was starting to feel like the easiest option.

After what felt like a lifetime but was probably only a second or two, she walked to where her brother sat with a thin, leggy redhead who *definitely* wasn't Jana.

"Rick?"

He raised his head and saw her. For one single heartbeat, he stared at her as if he didn't know her. His blankness was so convincing, she almost wondered if she'd mistaken a stranger for her brother. Then he straightened and gave her a happy smile.

"Beth! What are you doing here?" he asked, coming to his feet. "You're not in your neighborhood."

"I was in the area." She waved her coffee and croissant. "You're not working?"

"I have the day off."

The woman watched them as they spoke. She looked relaxed, if mildly curious. Up close, Beth could see she was exceptionally beautiful—probably in her late twenties. And she was with Rick—a fact Beth couldn't fully grasp.

"Galaxy, this is my sister, Beth."

Galaxy? Who named their kid that? But before she could react, the other woman immediately brightened. "Finally! I've been dying to meet you. Oh, wow! Rick's sister. You're the best."

Galaxy stood—and it turned out she was very tall—and folded Beth in a close hug that surrounded her with a familiar scent. One she'd experienced before, although she couldn't place where.

"Join us," Galaxy said happily. "I've been wanting to talk to you. This is great. Do you live nearby? I know you have that sandwich shop, right? Surf Sandwiches. It's so cute." She beamed with happiness, even as she took Rick's hand in hers.

Too much was happening too fast, Beth thought. Any second now the room was going to start spinning, and once that started, she was terrified it would never stop. She felt sick to her stomach, confused and more scared than she'd ever been in her life. Because however she tried to explain away what she was seeing, there was no way around the fact that Rick was cheating on Jana. No, Rick was cheating on her *friend*. A concept she couldn't grasp—probably because she didn't want any of this to be happening.

"I need to get back," she said, aware her voice sounded stilted. "I have to…" She couldn't think of a lie, so stopped trying.

"Oh, that's too bad." Galaxy sounded genuinely distressed. "It was so great to finally meet you. We need to get together."

Beth ignored that and stared at her brother, who was watching her without speaking, his expression completely unreadable. She had no idea what he was thinking, but shouldn't he be upset or guilty or horrified or something? Only he wasn't any of those things—at least not on the surface—and in some ways that was the scariest thing of all.

She nodded at both of them and quickly left. Once out of the store, she dumped her coffee and croissant in the trash and hurried to her car. She started the engine and quickly drove away. It was only when she was back in her familiar neighborhood that she allowed herself to think about what had just happened.

She'd seen Rick with another woman. Rick was cheating on Jana, and from the looks of things, he'd been doing so for a while. She remembered the quick burst of scent when Galaxy had hugged her and suddenly recalled smelling it on her brother. But when… She pulled in to her driveway and parked, then closed her eyes. He'd hugged her, she thought, focusing on the feel of that so she could—

"Oh, God!" It had been the night she'd met Teddy. She'd
arrived first, and when Rick had shown up, she'd asked if he'd
changed fabric softeners. But it hadn't been that at all. He'd
smelled of Galaxy's perfume!

She pulled her phone out of her bag and texted her brother.

Call me!!!!!

They had to talk. They needed a plan. No, not a plan. First
she had to figure out what on earth was happening. How could
Rick be cheating? He barely knew how to date. He was socially
awkward and just so eager to be with Jana. He talked about her
like she was his princess or something. And yet there was another woman in his life.

Her brother was cheating on Jana. He was risking his relationship with her. He was putting her own wonderful friendship at risk. Worse, he was cheating on Teddy's sister, and Beth
was caught in the middle of something so big and calamitous
that she couldn't figure out what to do or think or say. All she
knew for sure was it was going to be really, really bad.

Beth spent the next twenty-four hours trying to catch her
breath. She was still reeling from the revelation and waiting for
her brother to get in touch with her. But no matter how many
times she texted and called, Rick stayed silent. She alternated
between fury and fear. No wonder he'd been upset when he'd
discovered she was seeing Teddy. At the time his reaction hadn't
made any sense, but now she totally got why he'd been pissed.
Her dating Teddy was one more connection—one more vari-
able in what she would guess was the juggling job that was his
dating life.

She spent a restless night and a crappy morning trying to shake
a headache that clung tenaciously, no doubt a combination of
exhaustion and worry. A low sense of dread followed her ev-

erywhere, and she alternated between telling herself she had to come clean with Jana and mentally running in the opposite direction. Worst of all, for the very first time in her adult life, she didn't want to go into the store. She didn't want to see anyone or talk to anyone. She was terrified that Rick would show up to talk and afraid he wouldn't. Having Teddy stroll in would be a complete nightmare, because what was she supposed to say to him? "Hey, I just found out my brother's cheating on your sister, but you and I are still okay, right?"

Fortunately her work ethic was strong, and right on time she parked her car behind Surf Sandwiches. She got through the morning without anyone asking if she was all right, even though she checked her phone every fifteen seconds to see if she'd heard from Rick.

The lunch crowd was especially busy—something for which she was grateful. Hustling to get everyone's sandwiches made quickly and correctly distracted her from her sense of dread. She started to feel like she could breathe again and her headache seemed to fade, right up until the shop door opened and Dex stepped inside, all four kids with him.

Beth's first thought was to bolt. She could hide out in back until they were gone. *Like they wouldn't notice?* she asked herself. At least Teddy wasn't with them, she thought gratefully. Dex and the kids she could handle. Sort of. If she ignored how guilty she felt.

She stepped out of the work line and went to greet them. Linnie rushed toward her, Orchid at her heels. Magnolia and Atlas both smiled at her, as did Dex. She hugged the children.

"This is a surprise," she said cheerfully. "You're here! I hope everyone is hungry."

"It was early release day for Teddy's kids," Dex said easily. "We were talking about where to go for lunch when Magnolia suggested we come see you." He ruffled Linnie's hair. "I knew this one would have a cow if she wasn't included, so here we are. You okay with the invasion?"

"I'm delighted," she said, knowing her only reason for lying was the "Rick issue." If she hadn't known about Galaxy, she really would have been genuinely happy to see Dex and the kids. "The lunch rush is slowing, so if you want to get sandwiches and eat either in here or outside, there's going to be plenty of room."

"Outside!" Orchid jumped in place. "Like a picnic! Please, Dex. Please!"

"I'd like to eat outside, too," Magnolia said. "It's pretty here with the ocean across the street."

"Outside it is," Dex said. "All right. Let's go pick sandwiches." He winked at Beth. "I hear you have a famous collection of PB&J choices."

Beth pointed to the board. "You're right. We do. One of my favorites is peanut butter with breakfast cereal. You get to pick the kind. Or we can do a grilled PB&J." She saw Dex grimace and grinned at him. "I could suggest something else for you. Maybe a fried chicken BLT with jalapeño honey."

"I could go for that," he admitted.

She went through the line with the kids and helped them place their orders. There was a long and serious discussion of the various drink options. All four children insisted she join them, so she quickly made herself a sandwich, and they walked outside to the tables in the shade. She and Dex pushed two together to give them room. Linnie and Orchid wanted to sit on either side of her, while Magnolia planted herself opposite.

"This is nice," Beth said. "Thank you for visiting me today."

"Great view," Dex said, motioning to the ocean. "You must get a good breeze later in the afternoon."

"We do. And the fog in the morning. Gotta love the beach."

She took a bite of her sandwich and realized she was actually hungry. She hadn't eaten dinner the night before or breakfast this morning. Hopefully her sandwich would sit all right in her tummy.

Atlas pointed at the water. "They surf here in the morning, don't they? This is a surfer beach." There was a wistfulness in his tone.

"You like surfing?" she asked.

"He loves it," Orchid announced in a tone of long suffering. "He talks about it all the time."

Magnolia nodded. "He wants lessons, but Dad says he's too young. He has to wait until next summer."

"Are you working on your swimming?" Beth asked. "You need to be a strong swimmer so you can fight the tide."

"Dad takes me to the park pool sometimes," Atlas grumbled. "And I swim at Dex's, but Dad won't put a pool in at home."

"We live in shame because of that," Dex said, his expression deadpan.

She tried not to laugh. "A pool's a really big project."

"Plus we have to worry about Orchid and Linnie," Magnolia pointed out. "Because even with a fence around it, they could fall in."

"We're older now." Linnie smiled up at Beth. "I'm four. Next year I get to go to kindergarten and then the first grade and then I get homework."

Beth smiled at her. "I remember. You're very excited about it."

"I am."

Everyone talked as they ate their lunch. Beth managed to relax enough to enjoy the jokes and laughter, and the ease of just hanging out. She'd deliberately left her phone in her desk drawer so she wouldn't be tempted to check it every fifteen seconds as she waited to hear back from Rick. While she was desperate to talk to him, she also dreaded the conversation.

When lunch was finished, Dex suggested they cross the street and walk along the beach before heading home. Beth begged off, saying she had to get back to work. Magnolia surprised her by asking if they could talk for a second.

Dex nodded slightly, as if he knew what the conversation was going to be about, then ushered the other kids away.

Beth sat back down at the table. "Are you okay?" she asked.

Magnolia sighed before looking at her. "Daddy was mad about the list."

It took Beth a second to realize she meant the list of questions she'd been asking.

"He said the questions were intrusive and rude and that he was disappointed in me." Tears filled her eyes. "So I wanted to say I'm sorry."

Beth felt so bad for her. "I'm sorry about that. I was fine with the questions, and I respected you for taking the time to think them through."

She paused, not wanting to get between Teddy and his daughter or undermine his authority. Suddenly a simple conversation felt like a minefield.

"I'm going to talk to your dad about this," she said slowly. "I'm going to explain I was okay with the questions and that you apologized. I appreciate that."

Magnolia watched her without speaking.

"This is hard," Beth said with a faint smile. "For both of us. I know when your mom was alive, she was the heart of the family. I know you loved her so much. As the oldest, you knew her the best, and in a way, you're the keeper of the memories."

Magnolia brushed away tears. "Orchid doesn't remember her at all."

"That has to make you sad. Nothing about losing her is right or fair, and you've been doing such a good job taking care of your family." She leaned closer. "I'm guessing you do more than you should."

"Dad tells me to be a kid and that I'm not in charge, but I see things that need to be done."

Her heart ached for the preteen. "I get that. Like I told you before, I'm the oldest, too. When my brother was little, I had to look out for him. It's a lot of responsibility."

Magnolia nodded.

"So here's the thing." Beth offered a smile. "I think we should just take it really slow. I'm dating your dad, and that's weird for you three. I get that. It's different for me, too. I mean, come on, three kids? Doesn't that seem like a lot?"

The corners of Magnolia's mouth turned up. "Four would be more."

"Four would send me screaming into the night," Beth joked. She let her smile fade. "Whatever happens between me and your dad won't change how much he and your mom were in love. That will always be true. She will always be in your heart and your memories. She will always be in the stories you tell. That's a good thing. As for your dad and me, I don't know what's going to happen, but I do like him a lot."

More than a lot, she thought fiercely, knowing that all she had with Teddy was being threatened by her brother's actions. Not that she would discuss that with Magnolia.

"I'll never be your mom. No one can be her. She was unique and lovely, and it's sad she's gone."

"It is," Magnolia whispered.

"However it works out with me and your dad, I'm hoping you and Atlas and Orchid and I can be friends."

"I think we could."

"Thank you." Beth pointed at the building. "Want to pick out some cookies to take home for a snack later?"

Magnolia grinned. "Are you kidding? We love cookies."

18

It took another twenty-four hours for Rick to finally reach out. Beth lost count of the number of texts she'd sent and messages she'd left. She'd been about to stake out his condo when he finally answered. Although staring at his brief text, she thought maybe not hearing from him had been better.

Where's the fire?

She stared at the three words, feeling her temper rise. "Where's the fire?" she asked out loud. "Where's the fire? You created it, Rick. You piled on the kindling and lit the match."

She angrily stabbed out a reply.

Where do you think? I saw you with someone who isn't Jana.

That's a big deal. We need to talk about what happened. I need
to understand.

Over a minute passed before she saw the three dots that indicated he was typing his response.

I'll be at your place about seven.

His assumption that she would simply be home, waiting,
rankled, but she told herself that was the least of it. Finally she
was going to get some answers. Only as she paced the living
room while she waited, she found she wasn't sure she wanted
to know anything about his relationship with Galaxy. Whatever he said, it was going to be bad. Worse, once she knew the
facts, she had decisions to make. Did she tell Jana? And assuming she did, then what? No one was going to be happy. For all
she knew, Jana would blame her or assume she'd known from
the beginning. And where Jana went, Teddy would follow, she
thought grimly. She could lose both of them over this, and she
hadn't been the one screwing around.

She stopped in the middle of the living room and told herself to get a grip. Rick was on his way over, and they would
talk. Once she understood the problem, they could work together to solve it.

She thought briefly of texting her aunt to ask her to come
home from her dinner out with friends, but then decided against
it. Rick and Agatha didn't always get along, plus she could get
her aunt's advice later. Okay, first she would have to explain
what she'd seen, because so far she hadn't said a word to anyone. She hadn't wanted to try to describe what she'd witnessed.

It had to be a mistake, she told herself as she resumed pacing. Maybe she'd misunderstood. Although they'd been so *intimate* and Galaxy had said something about "finally meeting
her" or however she'd phrased it. That implied she and Rick

had known each other a while. Plus the kissing. And the perfume she'd smelled.

After what felt like forever, she heard his car in the driveway
and hurried to the front door. She had it open before he reached
the porch stairs.

"I'm sorry," he said as he walked inside and stopped in front
of her. "I'm really sorry."

Good words, but honestly they weren't nearly enough.

"No," she snapped. "Just no. You don't get to be sorry. What
the hell are you doing? You're cheating on Jana?"

He sat on the sofa and dropped his head. "I know."

"You know. You *know*? I don't get it. How could you do that?
When did you learn to do that? You're in a great relationship. You
like Jana. You act happy when you're with her. But all this time,
you're cheating on her with someone else? You've always been
such a good guy. When did you become the asshole brother?"

"Yeah, I know. It's bad." He looked at her with regret in his
eyes. "Beth, I'm sorry. I messed up."

"Yes, you did." She glared at him. "Jana's my friend. A good
friend. I care about her, and I don't want her to get hurt. At the
same time, I'm dating her brother. We are all connected in this,
and I just found out that you've got some chickie on the side.
Ignoring how that's tacky, I'm dealing with a little disappointment about my brother's character, not to mention the complete
cluster-you-know-what this could make of my life."

She put her hands on her hips. "I'm trapped in the middle.
Do I tell? Do I not tell?"

She absolutely didn't want to say anything to anyone. Because
when this hit the fan—and it was sure going to—her relationship with Jana could very well be on the line.

"What about what happens to me?" she asked, continuing that
line of thought. "Do you think Jana is going to believe me when
I tell her I knew nothing about Galaxy?" She stomped away, then
swung back to face him. "Galaxy? What kind of name is that?"

"Her father's an astrophysicist at Caltech."

She wanted to scream. "I don't need to know that, and it's so not the point."

He frowned. "But you asked."

"It doesn't matter. You're cheating on Jana. I don't get it. I thought your relationship with her was important to you."

She knew she was ranting and starting to repeat herself, but she didn't know how to get through to him. Nothing about this situation made sense.

"It's like I don't even know you," she said quietly, then sank into one of the chairs.

He looked at her, his face stricken. "You're right," he said, his voice thick with emotion. "I messed up so bad. I made a huge mistake, and I don't know how to fix it."

The fear and contrition combined with the helpless, worried expression in his eyes eased some of her concern.

"I wasn't thinking," he admitted, staring helplessly at her. "I'm not an asshole."

"You sure about that?"

He shook his head. "No, but I don't want to be."

She slid to the edge of her seat. "Tell me what happened."

"I don't know."

She glared at him. "Don't play me, Rick. This is serious. Other people's lives are involved."

He ducked his head in shame. "You're right. When I said I didn't know what happened, I wasn't being flippant. I'm not sure when it all changed."

He looked at her. "You know Jana. She's wonderful and so beautiful. I can't believe she's going out with me. I like being with her, and I like Linnie a lot." He hesitated. "I have feelings for Jana."

Which, she was pretty sure, translated to he was falling in love with her.

"Galaxy works at the urgent care place in the same building

as our Santa Monica location. That's where we met. We'd just say hi, but she started asking me about my day and stuff." He shifted uncomfortably as he spoke.

"You're saying she was flirting with you."

Rick nodded. "She's so pretty and outgoing. I was surprised she even noticed me."

He'd been in over his head, she thought. Charmed by the attention of a beautiful woman. She could see it happening. Rick didn't have the experience to see what he was doing was wrong. After a lifetime of being the guy women overlooked, suddenly he was sought-after. That would be heady stuff.

He sighed heavily. "At first we were just talking. You know, like friends. But then one thing led to another, and suddenly we were seeing each other."

"Seeing as in..." She stared at him. "Holy crap, are you sleeping with both of them?"

Rick nodded slowly.

Beth stood and walked the length of the living room. Her heart was pounding, her head hurt and she was barely able to breathe. Rick was having sex with two different women? No, it was so much worse than that. He was having sex with her friend/her boyfriend's sister and with another woman.

"This can't be happening," she whispered. "It can't. After all the shit I've been through, I finally have everything I want. A friendship that matters and a wonderful man. I'm going to lose both of them because my brother suddenly decided to get an ego and act like a dick?"

She spun to face him. "You're going to ruin this for me, aren't you? My friendship with Jana is on the line and I'm falling for Teddy, and you're going to make it all go away."

"I'm not, Beth. I swear. I wouldn't do that to you. And I'm not a bad person." He drew in a breath. "It just happened."

"Then it has to unhappen. Jana is my friend. I can't not tell her what you're doing. The guy she's excited to go away with is sleeping with someone else. That's not okay." She crossed to him and glared at him. "Ignoring the whole moral 'this is wrong' aspect of what you're doing, you in no way have the emotional experience to be juggling two women. You were bound to get caught and have it blow up in your face. The question is, what do you do now?"

He stared at her blankly. "What do you mean?"

"You can't keep seeing them both. Your actions are wrong, and you're hurting people by what you're doing. Just as bad, you're hurting yourself. Either you tell Jana or I will." The third alternative was that he broke up with Galaxy and they never spoke of this again, but Beth wasn't sure she wanted to be responsible for keeping that kind of secret.

Rick stared at her for several seconds, then nodded as he came to his feet.

"You're right. I got caught in something, which isn't an excuse, Beth. I was wrong. I've hurt Jana, but I've also hurt you, and I never wanted to do that. I'm going to break up with Galaxy. Jana's the one I want to be with. She's the miracle."

Beth felt tension ease inside of her. "You swear?"

He made an X over his heart. "I want Jana to be the one." He pressed his lips together. "Are you going to tell her?"

Beth's stomach sank as she realized what he was asking. Was she going to tell her friend what she'd seen? Was she going to tell her boyfriend that his sister was dating someone who'd cheated on her? Didn't she owe them the truth?

She stared at her brother. Rick stood there, watching her, not saying anything. He seemed ready to accept whatever punishment she demanded, even if it meant losing Jana, because that was what would happen. Jana would dump him and Teddy would dump Beth and everyone would be hurt and nothing would be right again.

She thought about how when Rick had been a scrawny kid, she'd been the one to take on the bullies who tormented him.

How on the nights when their mother was gone and they were alone and scared, he climbed into bed with her and hung on while she promised she would protect him forever. She thought about how she'd brought him food when he'd been cramming to pass classes in medical school. How when she walked into his tiny apartment, he would be so lost in his homework that he would stare at her blankly for a second, then give her the smile she knew so well. She thought of how proud she'd been when he'd graduated from medical school.

He was her brother, and she'd always been there for him. He was her responsibility. They were family, and she loved him more than anyone in the world. She always had. Her gaze settled on the faint scar on his cheek. The reminder that when he'd been only ten years old, he'd risked his life to save her.

"Give me your word you'll break up with Galaxy," she murmured.

"You have my word. I'm doing it today."

She drew in a breath. "Then I won't say anything."

He rushed toward her and hugged her tight. "Thank you, Beth. Thank you. I'm sorry for what I did. It was wrong. So wrong. I'll never do anything like that again. I swear."

She hugged him back, already regretting her decision. Because although Rick wasn't a natural born cheater, she wasn't someone who lied comfortably. She also knew that in some deep, dark place in her soul, she'd made the most expedient decision rather than the moral one. If she kept quiet, Jana stayed her friend and Teddy remained in her life. But at what price? And what would happen if the truth ever came out?

While Beth had been dreading Teddy's weeklong health seminar, she had to admit that it couldn't have come at a better time. His long hours speaking and his drive in from the Valley every day meant they couldn't see each other, and their daily conversations were limited to quick late-night check-in calls. Although even those had been perilous—at least from her end. She was constantly worried that he would hear something in her voice and want to know if she was okay. Answering that would mean lying yet again, because she was about as far from okay as it was possible to be.

She felt awful. Guilty, confused, angry. Yes, Rick had been remorseful and had broken things off with Galaxy. In fact, he'd texted her that it was done the morning after he'd come over. But somehow that wasn't enough. She was still having trouble reconciling the man she knew with the player who'd been sleeping with two women at the same time. Ignoring the ick factor, when had he learned how to do that? It required a certain confidence, not to mention logistical planning. The brother she knew could barely keep food in his refrigerator.

She remembered Agatha telling her that Rick was far more capable than she was willing to see. Back then she'd brushed off the comment, but now, lying in her bed and waiting for Teddy's latenight call, she wondered if she should have listened to her aunt.

Her phone rang. In the second before she answered, she pressed a hand to her chest, assessing her own emotions. She was two parts excited and one part racked with guilt about speaking to Teddy.

"Hi," she said. "How exhausted are you?"

He gave a low chuckle that sent waves of desire rippling through her. "I'm barely hanging on, but just one more day and I'm done. Next time I'm asked to teach at one of these events, please remind me to say no."

"Too many people wanting too much of your time and emotional energy?" she asked.

"Yeah, I'm not like you. I don't like big groups. I do better one-on-one."

"I'm not a big group person."

"You're way more of an extrovert than I am."

Was that how he saw her? She considered herself quiet and

a little shy. But she did enjoy spending time with people. Her staff and customers were the best part of her day at Surf Sandwiches. She could never be comfortable spending hours by herself, working in solitude.

"Are you in bed?"

The unexpected question made her smile. "I'm not sure you have the energy for that kind of phone call."

"You're right. I was trying to picture you, not make a play for phone sex."

She heard the smile in his voice. "Yes, I'm in bed."

"Good. Me, too. I'd rather be in your bed, though. Just give me a couple of days to get through this."

"How are the kids doing?" she asked. "I know they're missing you."

"They're good. Dex has stepped in to help, just like always. We've got to find that guy someone. He's been alone for too long."

"I'm surprised he isn't fighting off women everywhere he goes. He's Dex Sanders." He wasn't for her, but she could sure get the appeal.

"He used to be into volume, but not anymore. Now he's waiting for the right person. Have any single friends who might be interested?"

"No, and even if I did, I wouldn't be comfortable setting up anyone. It's too much responsibility."

Which was exactly the wrong thing to say, she thought grimly as she remembered what Rick had done and how she was keeping secrets from both Teddy and Jana. She searched frantically for a different topic.

"Oh, I didn't tell you that when Dex brought the kids by for lunch the other day, Magnolia apologized for asking me all those questions at the barbecue." She lowered her voice. "I didn't mind at all. She wasn't intrusive, she was worried. I'm new, and you're her dad. It's okay for her to ask."

"She grilled you."

"In a sweet and funny way. I was fine with it, but regardless, she apologized. I wanted you to know."

"Thanks. She's a good kid."

"She is. They all are. We discussed three was too many, but we couldn't decide who to let go."

"That would be a tough one," he agreed with a chuckle, then yawned. "Sorry."

"No, you're exhausted. We're going to hang up now, and you're going to get some sleep."

"You sure?"

"I am. Only a couple more days and then you can have your regular life back."

"And my girl," he said, his voice sleepy. "I can't wait. Talk to you soon. Night."

"Night, Teddy."

She ended the call and put the phone on the nightstand. Guilt gnawed at her, making her question her decision to keep Rick's tawdry secret. Damn him for not being able to keep his dick in his pants in the first place—something she still couldn't reconcile with the man she knew. He didn't seem the type, although apparently he was.

She flopped back on her pillow and stared at the ceiling. Talking to Teddy was one thing, but facing Jana was going to be another. How was she supposed to sit across from her friend and pretend everything was fine between them?

She clicked on the lamp by her bed, then grabbed her phone. She quickly sent a note to the volunteer coordinator saying she wouldn't be able to make it in for her shift tomorrow. Her guilt multiplied, but she ignored it. In the morning, she would text Jana and make up a reason for not being at the food bank. Then she would spend her day trying to do good for others to make up for the crappy way she was living her life.

★ ★ ★

Jana finished the simple addition, then crossed both fingers and hit the solve button on her calculus online program. Instantly the screen filled with the correct way to reach the solution. She compared her handwritten answer and gave a loud "Yes!" when she saw she'd gotten the answer right. Twice she'd been tripped up not by the complicated math necessary to work the issue, but by the adding and subtracting at the end. Not the end of the world as she would get partial credit by showing her work, but still. It was gratifying to nail it.

She still had time until her last test, but with her weekend away with Rick coming up, she wanted to make sure she stayed on track with her study schedule.

She tossed down her pencil so she could stand and stretch. According to her instructor, if she got an A on the final, she would be able to earn an A in the class. She'd turned in all the homework assignments to get the extra points, and they might be enough to push her over the top. When class had started, her goal had been to get a B, but knowing she was close to an A made her want to try harder.

She'd come a long way, she thought happily. Not just with calculus but with her life. Five years ago she'd been pregnant and scared and living with the shame of not knowing who had fathered Linnie. That combination of unsettling emotions and a grim reality had forced her to take a look at her life. She'd been determined to do better, to grow as a person so she could raise a happy and healthy child.

Now she was completing her AA degree, and in the fall she would start nursing school. She had a plan and she was making it happen. Linnie was thriving. Just as exciting, her daughter was watching her figure out her goals and then work hard to make them happen. A priceless lesson she would always remember.

There was also the little matter of finally finding a good guy. Rick was so sweet and caring. He was sending her funny little countdown messages about their trip. He'd moved from days to hours. She was pretty sure he would start counting in seconds as the date got closer.

The front door opened. "It's me," Teddy called.

"In the kitchen."

He walked in. "Hey. How's the calculus homework going?"

She smiled. "Pretty good. I think there's a decent chance I'm a genius."

He laughed. "Good for you."

She glanced at him. He looked exhausted, thin and pale, with dark circles under his eyes.

"Have you eaten?" she asked, heading for the refrigerator.

"I'd rather just go to bed."

"No, you're going to eat first. How many more days?"

"Saturday's the end of the seminar. Unfortunately it's the day everything is open to the public."

Meaning he would be scrambling with even bigger crowds. Teddy might not like being a celebrated speaker, but he was good at giving talks on acupuncture and alternative medicine. He had an easy and engaging style, no doubt because of his years of acting.

"All the more reason you need to eat. Dex took the kids out for Italian and ordered extra for both of us." She smiled at him. "The lasagna is excellent, by the way. You'll want some of that."

"Thanks." He sank onto a stool at the big island, then turned to her and frowned. "Didn't you have dinner with Beth tonight? It's your food bank day."

"She couldn't make her shift." She held up a hand as her brother immediately came to his feet, ready to do battle over whatever was wrong.

"She's fine," she added. "She's having a bad period. It's a girl thing and it happens. She just needs time."

"What makes a period bad?"

"Usually cramping. Sometimes it hurts and sometimes it hurts a lot."

"Should I go see her?"

Jana thought of her own occasional bouts with a difficult "time of the month." Ibuprofen and a heating pad were how she got through.

"Let her deal with this on her own," she advised. "She's not feeling her best, and the last thing she wants to do is worry about grossing you out."

"I was there when all three of the kids were born. I can't be grossed out."

"Yeah, you saying that and her feeling it are two different things. Like I said, just let her be."

He sat back down on the stool. "You're the expert on the topic."

"I am." She slid lasagna and the rest of the chicken parmesan onto a plate and put it in the microwave. While it heated, she put the leftover salad into a bowl and added dressing.

Teddy got himself a beer from the fridge then held up an open bottle of white wine. She nodded, and he poured her a glass.

"So, you're ready for your calculus final?" he asked.

"So ready that I'm thinking I should switch and become a math major."

He grinned. "Good for you. I'm proud of you, kid. You work hard and you get results."

"I'm feeling a little smug myself."

She was in a good place with so much of her life, she thought happily.

The microwave beeped. She got out the plate and put it in front of Teddy. "Eat."

"Thanks."

For a minute or two there was only silence as he dug into his dinner. She wondered if he bothered to feed himself during his long days and figured the answer to that was no. When he was out of his regular routine, he went into caretaker mode, and at a big event, there were far too many people who desperately wanted his time and attention.

Only a couple more days, she told herself. Then he would be home, and Beth could work her magic on him. The kids were going to want to hang out with their dad for sure, but Jana was confident he would make time for both.

"Why are you smiling?" he asked.

"I'm thinking funny thoughts," she told him. "I'm good at entertaining myself that way."

"It's a gift." He studied her. "You okay about me and Beth?"

"Yes. I was just thinking she's good for you. Why would you worry?"

"She's your friend. I'm your brother. You're dating *her* brother. It's complicated."

"It's very LA, and yes, it's all good. I've been waiting for you to be healed enough to find someone to care about. I'm happy that's where you are."

"You never set her up with Dex," he said.

"Why would I do that?"

"He's single. She's single. It seems like a natural fit."

"Beth and Dex?" She shook her head. "I don't see it at all." She smiled. "Besides, now she's taken."

"That she is, and tell Dex not to forget it."

"I'm pretty sure he already knows."

19

"Jana told me about your period being bad," Teddy said, his voice warm with concern. "She says I should just let you be and see you on Sunday like we planned, only I happen to be a skilled practitioner when it comes to acupuncture, and that can help."

Beth felt her eyes start to burn. She wasn't much of a crier, but lately her emotions had been right at the surface. While she desperately wanted to see Teddy, she was terrified to actually be face-to-face with him. How could they be in the same room without her blurting out what she'd seen and what Rick had done? She hated knowing she had to lie. It was her nature to be honest, but her brother had made that impossible.

No, she thought grimly. Not Rick. The decision to keep quiet had been hers. If he hadn't agreed to stop seeing Galaxy, she would have come clean, but once he'd admitted what he was doing was wrong, she'd felt obligated to protect him.

There was probably a bit of self-interest in there, too, she admitted, if only to herself. Because spilling the truth put her relationship with Teddy at risk.

"I appreciate the offer," she said, her voice low. "But I'm going to pass. Give me a day or two and I'll be fine."

She silently winced as she lied, knowing one reason she couldn't see Teddy was the fact that she didn't have her period. Being around him was a huge temptation, and if she gave in, he would quickly figure out she'd lied.

Yet another reason she preferred to live her life in a straightforward manner. It was so much easier.

"I'll do whatever you want," he said. "But I miss you."

"I miss you, too. So much." She needed to see him and hold him. Being around him would make her world right itself.

"Sunday for sure," he told herself. "I'll be tired, but I need to see you."

"I need to see you, too."

"Good. Then next weekend, we're all hanging out while Jana takes off with Rick."

Beth clutched her phone. He was right—next weekend was the big getaway. Her stomach churned as she thought of all the things that could go wrong. What if Rick blurted out the truth? What if Jana guessed? What if…

She cleared her throat. "I'm a little nervous about all the kid time, but you've promised to help me through it." Because she was going to spend much of the weekend with Teddy and the four kids. Not the night—neither of them was ready for that. But Friday evening and all day Saturday and Sunday. Teddy had promised Dex would be with them for much of it, so she was pretty sure she would be all right. If nothing else, it would be an interesting test for their relationship.

"I will," he said. "And now I'm going to let you get some
sleep. Talk soon?"

"Yes. Night, Teddy."

They hung up. She put the phone on her nightstand. It was
still relatively early in the evening. She should do something
with her time. Maybe laundry, or she could clean her bathroom.
Anything to take her mind off the lies she'd told the man she
was falling for.

Only none of those options sounded right, and before she
could realize what was happening, tears filled her eyes. They
seemed to come from nowhere, and suddenly she was crying
and she couldn't seem to stop. She covered her face with her
hands and gave in to all the undefined emotions swirling inside
of her. She was lost and anxious and angry and so afraid, and the
worst part was, none of it was her fault. At least, it hadn't been
until she'd decided to keep Rick's secret.

"Whatever it is, we'll handle it together," Agatha said, walking into her room and sitting next to her on the bed. She put her
arm around Beth and hung on. "Just let go. Crying can be ca-
thartic. We'll deal with the swollen eyes and running nose later."

The unexpected comment made her laugh, which turned into
a hiccup. Her aunt pressed tissues into her hand.

"Wipe your face. Then let's go to the living room and talk."
She paused. "I know you didn't go to the food bank today. Are
you sick? Should I make chicken soup? Or do you want herbal
tea to settle your stomach?"

Beth looked at the woman who had welcomed her into her
home with all the love in her heart. "Maybe something stronger."

"I have that, too."

When they were seated across from each other, a small brandy
beside each of them and a tissue box carefully within reach of
Beth's chair, Agatha leaned toward her.

"Just blurt it out. Whatever you have to say is fine. I know a good lawyer, and a friend of your uncle's used to be a detective. The airport is less than thirty minutes away. We can have you on a flight to Mexico by midnight."

"I appreciate the attempt at humor," Beth told her. "I'm fine."

"I wasn't being funny. Surprisingly, Alaska Airlines has the best flight to Cabo. You wouldn't guess it from their name."

Beth knew her aunt was trying to ease the tension and make her feel comfortable talking about whatever the problem was. That was Agatha's way.

"It's not me," she said. "I'm not sick or anything. It's Rick. He's been cheating on Jana."

Agatha's wide-eyed stare was more than a little gratifying. "Your brother is cheating on his new girlfriend?"

"I couldn't believe it, either." Beth explained about how she'd seen them and how Galaxy had known who she was and had been excited to meet her.

"I was horrified and stunned," Beth admitted. "Not just because that isn't who he is but because of how it affects my relationship with Jana. She's my friend. I need her in my life."

Agatha went white. "You're right. She matters to you. Oh, dear. What about Teddy?"

"I know. I'm terrified either of them will find out." Beth clutched her brandy. "Everything is so messed up."

"And entwined, and now Rick has blown up the whole thing."

A mixed metaphor but an accurate description.

"What happened when you confronted him?" Agatha asked. "Did he try to deny it?"

"He couldn't. He knew I'd seen him. He sort of fell apart. He really got what he'd been doing was wrong and felt awful about the mistakes he'd made."

Agatha picked up her drink. "Somehow I doubt that."

"No, he was remorseful. He said he was breaking things off with Galaxy."

"That name."

"He said her father works at Caltech."

"I don't care if he works on Mars, it's a ridiculous name, but not the point. So Rick is going to stay with Jana, dump Galaxy and all is well? I don't think it's going to be that easy."

"It's not." Beth thought of all she'd been wrestling with. "I know Rick is sorry."

"You sure about that?"

"He's texted me about fifteen times, telling me how wrong he was." She looked at her aunt. "I don't think he really meant to cheat. He said Galaxy was flirting and things just happened. A beautiful woman coming on to him would be a big deal for him."

"You're saying he was flattered?" Agatha didn't sound convinced. "Or that it was an accident?"

"Not exactly, but he doesn't have much experience when it comes to women, and until Jana, he's always chosen so badly."

"He has a lot more experience than you know. The man carried on an affair for who knows how long, and if you hadn't caught him in the act, you wouldn't have known. No one gets it that right the first time."

Beth didn't want to think about that. "He's sorry he messed up, and he's stopped seeing her. So everything is fine."

"If it was fine, you wouldn't have been crying in your bedroom earlier. You're scared, and you don't like that you have to cover for his lie."

Beth ducked her head. "Something like that." She drew in a breath. "Part of me thinks I need to tell the truth, but if I do…"

"Everything could fall apart. Jana would be hurt. You could lose Teddy."

"I just found them," Beth said, her voice pleading. "Things are so good right now. Jana's a wonderful friend, and Teddy is… he's perfect." He was amazing, and she loved how she felt when she was around him. "We're just getting to the good part."

"Plus Rick's your brother," Agatha said flatly. "If it were any-one else, you wouldn't feel torn, but it's Rick, and you've always taken care of him."

"What would you do if you were me?"

"Kick Rick to the curb." Agatha held up her hand. "I didn't mean that, exactly. I understand the dilemma. If he's no longer seeing Galaxy and he's committed to Jana, then I guess you just move forward. It was wrong of your brother to put you in this position, though. I knew he was more than we all guessed, but I never would have thought he was a player."

"He's not."

"You saw him, my dear. You have physical proof. It might be time to accept your brother isn't exactly who you thought."

Not possible. Rick was who he'd always been. Maybe a little older and slightly more together, but not anyone who was ca-pable of real deception. Not in the long term. What had hap-pened with Galaxy was...a mistake. He'd said so.

Only as she did her best to convince herself, there was a tiny part of her that wasn't so willing to believe. That same part wor-ried that if any of this came out, it would be so much worse at a future date than it would be now. More would be on the line—more feelings, more hearts, more lives.

But to tell was to betray her brother. Her whole life she'd taken care of him—there was no way she could stop doing that now. Not for anything.

Jana ran her hand along the smooth, soft leather of the pas-senger seat. Every time she got into Rick's sleek sports car, she was transported to a different world. There was nothing practi-cal about the vehicle. It was low, it was fast and it was beautiful. Totally unrealistic for a single mom or just about anyone. Plus she was sure it had cost more than she made in a year. However, it was nice, and she liked the way it still smelled new.

"I'm excited about our weekend away," Rick told her as he

headed north on the 101 freeway. "You've been working hard with your classes and your job. Getting away will be good for you."

"I've been counting the days," she admitted, watching him drive. His attention was fully on the road, and she knew he was paying attention to traffic. Rick was all about the details.

"Getting ready for finals is always exhausting," she added. "This time more so because I wanted to be able to take the weekend off without worrying about school. But it will be worth it."

He gave her a quick, warm glance. "I hope so."

"I'm not worried at all."

"Once finals are done, you're taking the summer off?" he asked.

"I'm working, but I'll be done with school. Technically I'll have my associate's degree." She thought about the emails she'd been receiving from the college. "There's a graduation, but I don't know how I feel about going to it. I signed up to go, but I might change my mind. I kind of think I want to wait and just go to the one at UCLA." She wrinkled her nose. "Teddy wants me to walk in the community college one. What do you think?"

"It's just community college. I'm surprised they even have a graduation ceremony."

His answer startled her. "For a lot of people, an associate's degree is a big deal. There are many programs that don't require a four-year degree, so for them, this is the only graduation they're going to have. It's a rite of passage, and—"

Some of her energy dissipated as she realized he was smiling. "What?" she asked.

"You have a lot to say on the topic. Maybe that's your answer."

She laughed. "Okay, so you said what you did to get a reaction out of me. I get it. And I hadn't thought of it that way. Maybe I do care more than I thought. Plus it will be something Linnie will remember. That's important."

"A kid's memories are forever." He glanced at her, then back at the road. "Can I come?"

Deep in her chest, something fluttered. "To my graduation? Do you want to?"

"Yeah, I do. I think it would be cool to be a part of that."

She smiled. "I'd like that."

"So, decision made."

She leaned back in the comfy seat. "How many graduations have you had? Twenty-seven?"

He chuckled. "Just two. College and medical school. There wasn't anything after my fellowships." His expression turned self-deprecating. "Except, you know, job offers."

"Better than a certificate."

"I thought so."

"Medical school must have been expensive. I'm sweating nursing school and I have financial aid. You had what? A grant, plus the money Beth gave you and the money your uncle paid?"

"I had a scholarship for my bachelor's. A mentor helped me get the money for medical school."

"I thought Beth gave you her culinary school money."

"She did. It was a few thousand and Uncle Dale gave me close to fifty thousand, but the rest came from a mentor."

He sounded casual about the whole thing—especially Beth's contribution. "But that money was all she had, and she gave up her dream of cooking school for you."

Rick shook his head. "No, no, that's not what I meant. I wasn't dismissing what she did. It was great. I was saying it costs a lot of money to get through. I had help, and I'm grateful."

Which sounded better, she thought. Sometimes Rick really didn't say it right, but his heart seemed to be in a good place.

"She has the sandwich shop now," she said. "It's such a great business."

"She's happy there, and that's what matters." He looked at her. "You make me happy."

"I'm glad."

"I hope you like the hotel and the plans I made. If you want to change anything, we can. I just want you to have a good time."

He sounded so sincere, and he'd gone to a lot of trouble to get it all right, she thought. "I'm sure everything will be perfect."

He laughed. "Nobody's perfect, Jana. You come close, but the rest of us just struggle to get by."

"I'm as flawed as everyone else."

"I don't believe that, but if it's true, you hide it well."

The first time Beth had seen the media room at Teddy's house, she'd thought it was plenty big. The sectional was huge, with lots of cushions and areas to stretch out. Saturday night, caught in a pile of kids that had Orchid on one side of her and Linnie on the other, she had to admit there was a whole lot less room than she would have thought. It didn't help that Teddy and Dex were both big guys who liked to sprawl.

But she wasn't really complaining, she thought as Linnie snuggled closer. Hanging out with the kids was really fun. She appreciated how they'd accepted her as Teddy's girlfriend. Even Magnolia had stopped asking questions and was now comfortable simply treating her like an adult friend.

Every now and then she glanced over at Teddy, unable to believe such an amazing man was in her life. Every time she saw him, she was drawn in just a little more, as if her heart was expanding to contain all her feelings. It was way too soon for her to be thinking the *L* word, but she knew she was well on her way to falling hard. He was everything she'd ever wanted and more.

And she'd come so close to losing him.

Her chest tightened at the thought, and she forced herself away from the disaster that was her brother's cheating. Guilt still plagued her, making her want to squirm in her seat. Instead she focused on the adventures of Riley and her band of emotions in *Inside Out 2*. Humorously, she could totally relate to the upset of the established emotions when new ones appeared. She would never have guessed that she could feel disgust for her brother. He'd been such a fool.

She glanced at Teddy, who caught her eye and smiled at her. Heat instantly flared. She pushed it away and returned her attention to the movie.

Given the choice between her friend and the man she was falling for and her brother, she'd never actually had a choice to make. She just hoped he never put her in that position again. If he'd learned his lesson, they could move on, and all would be well.

Beth's phone buzzed. Magnolia immediately paused the movie while everyone looked at Beth expectantly. Jana had been texting regularly, sending pictures of her day. Her new text showed a picture of a huge slice of chocolate cake with shavings on the side and what looked like scrollwork done in some yummy frosting.

"I'm jealous for sure," Beth said, passing her phone around. "That looks delicious."

"I want one," Linnie said, a faint whine in her voice.

Dex touched her nose. "We have brownies and ice cream. I think that's better than cake."

"It is," Magnolia said, handing the phone to her dad. "Sometimes chocolate cake can be dry."

"Good point." Teddy passed the phone back. "You should tell her we're worried the cake won't be good."

"I will."

Beth texted their concern, adding she hoped they were having a good time. Jana sent back heart emojis.

"Speaking of brownies," Teddy said. "How about we have dessert now before it gets too late?"

There were loud shrieks of agreement as the kids raced from the media room to the kitchen. Beth and Dex followed more slowly.

"How are you holding up?" he asked. "It's been an intense day and a half."

She'd arrived about three the previous afternoon and had stayed until the kids were in bed, then had returned early that morning.

"There is an element of being thrown in the deep end," she admitted. "But I'm having fun."

"You're good with them. You don't try too hard. You're just yourself."

She flushed at the unexpected compliment. "Thank you. I like all four of them. Their personalities are so distinct, which is fun. You're a wonderful uncle. Teddy and Jana would be lost without you."

"They're family. Where else would I be?"

"You and Jana were never an item?"

Dex offered a faint smile. "No."

"Not your type?"

"Something like that."

They walked into the kitchen to find Teddy expertly cutting up the tray of brownies that Beth and the kids had made that afternoon. Magnolia had already collected dishes while Atlas got the ice cream out of the freezer.

The next few minutes were a cacophony of "she got more" and "I want whipped cream" until everyone settled down with their dessert.

Beth enjoyed sitting at the large kitchen table and being a part of the evening. Her growing up had never been like this. When her mom had been alive, more often than not it had just been her and Rick, with their mom off on some adventure that didn't include them. After she'd died, Beth and Rick had been in different foster care homes. There had been plenty of children around, but Beth had never felt as if she belonged. No, that wasn't right, she mentally amended. She'd never felt safe.

This was different. Not only was she an adult and able to take care of herself, but Teddy and his kids and Jana and Linnie and Dex were a family. It would always be safe here.

"You haven't seen my room," Orchid said, pointing at her.

"Mine, either." Linnie pushed her empty bowl onto the table and stood. "Come see!" She paused, then grinned and added, "Please."

"Rooms it is." Teddy came to his feet. "Youngest to oldest."

He moved close and added in a low voice, "Any interest in seeing mine?"

She knew he was teasing—they'd already agreed she wouldn't be spending the night. But his words made her insides quiver in anticipation. She was ready for a little one-on-one time with the man. The things he did to her still left her gasping and bone-less and wondering how she'd been doing it so very wrong for all those years.

They all trooped down the hall to Linnie's room. It was big and bright, done in shades of lavender. Circular shelves in the corner provided storage for her stuffed animal collection.

"Dex made these for me," Linnie said, running to the shelves and tossing several toys onto the floor so Beth could see. "They fit right into the corner and everything."

Beth smiled at him. "Impressive."

"I have skills."

Teddy surprised her by stepping between them and putting his arm around her. "Yeah, yeah, no talking to the handsome actor."

She knew he was teasing and hoped that was all it was. There weren't words to describe how little interest she had in Dex.

After looking at the desk where Linnie planned to do her future homework, they all went to the other end of the house.

"We made some modifications after we lost Valonia," Teddy said. "It's not really a traditional floor plan anymore."

"We all got a say," Magnolia added. "We stayed with Dex while the work was done, and then we moved back home."

Beth wasn't sure what to expect. They walked past Teddy's bedroom, and she was careful not to look in. Instead she focused on the arched doorway that led to a big, open flex space.

There were three desks and a couple of sofas. Bookshelves were overflowing with books and board games. The carpeting was plush—the kind that invited sprawling and play.

Orchid grabbed her hand. "Start with my room!"

They went into the door on the left. The big bedroom had high ceilings and a large window with a window seat. The walls were yellow, the bedding a bright green. Through the far door was a sink, and beyond that was the shared tub-shower combo with a toilet. They kept going to another sink, then a room exactly like Orchid's, but this one was done in blues. Beth guessed from the sports-themed bedspread and the football mural that this was Atlas's room. From there they walked through another shared bathroom and into Magnolia's room done in all shades of pink.

Beth returned to the flex space and realized each room was connected with the others and the family room they all shared. There was privacy, yet no one had to be alone.

"It's a brilliant design," she said.

"It works for us," Teddy told her. "Planning it, figuring out what we wanted, helped get us through. We had to add on a little and mess up the roof line, but it was worth it."

She looked at the kids, then at Teddy. As she'd thought before, they were a unit. They'd found their way through a dark time, and now they were healed. There were still the scars—those would always be there—but the kids were whole and thriving.

"We have pictures," Orchid said, pulling her to one of the sofas. "Of all of us. Come see!"

Teddy stopped her from running over to the bookcase. "Beth doesn't need to see the photo albums right now."

"Why not?" Orchid asked.

Beth smiled at him. "I'm fine with it. I love a good photo album journey."

Orchid cheered, then pulled one off the shelf and hurried to the sofa. She set it on Beth's lap.

"This is the story of me!"

There were pictures of a very pregnant Valonia, then Orchid as a newborn. Beth wanted to linger over the former, but Orchid flipped the pages before she could do much more than glance at the images. There were photos of all the usual events. Atlas went next, then Magnolia. Each album was a little longer than the one before. Dex helped Linnie get the album from her room so Beth could see the story of her life. When she saw a very pregnant and scared Jana, her heart went out to her friend. She'd been so alone back then. Teddy and Valonia had been her only lifeline, and then she'd lost her sister-in-law.

"One more," Orchid said when Beth had finished.

She took the album, but before she could open it, Teddy was hurrying toward her. "You don't have to look at that."

She saw the two names etched on the front and immediately knew this one had nothing to do with the kids and everything to do with Teddy and Valonia's love story.

"It's our mom," Orchid told her.

Magnolia sat next to Beth. "She was really beautiful. Everyone said so."

Beth looked at Teddy. "It's okay." She opened the album.

The pictures were stunning. A very young Valonia on what Beth would guess was an early date with Teddy. They barely looked twenty, but were probably a couple of years older. There were candid shots at the beach, a couple of ski trips, then a formal engagement portrait.

Magnolia offered a running commentary, as if she'd been at all the events, but no doubt her information came from having been told the same stories over and over again.

There were pictures of the wedding and a tropical honeymoon. There were Christmases and birthdays, pregnancies and births. Then Beth turned a page, and there was only the program from her funeral. An abrupt ending to a life cut short.

"Thank you for showing me all the pictures of your mom," she told the kids. "I feel like I know her better."

Dex pulled a couple of books out of the bookshelf. "I'm in the mood for a story. Who wants me to read?"

"Me! Me!"

The children shifted their attention from the album to where Dex was holding up different books.

"I want lots of voices," Linnie said. "Do the one about the wolf and his hat."

In less than a minute, the mood had shifted, and the four children were sitting in front of Dex while he half read, half acted out the story.

While his friend entertained, Teddy quietly put the albums away, then took a seat next to Beth. He put his arm around her, and she leaned against him, breathing in the scent of him.

Getting involved with him was complicated, she thought. All those lives intertwined, all the grief the family had dealt with. She was unequipped to deal with everything the kids were going through, but in her heart, she knew she wanted to try. Whatever was happening between her and Teddy, it created the most powerful emotions she'd ever felt.

Worry tried to creep in, but she pushed it away. Rick had done what he'd done, but he'd learned his lesson. She knew he was sorry to have come so close to losing what was most important. They were all moving forward, and everything would be fine.

She stayed through the bedtime ritual. Once all the bedroom doors were closed and Dex had left, she smiled up at Teddy.

"That was intense, but in a good way. Thanks for including me."

She had more to say. She was going to mention coming over in the morning if he wanted, and that maybe they could all go out to breakfast or something, but she got caught up by the fire burning hot and bright in his eyes.

"I know what I said," he told her, his voice thick with passion as he cupped her face in his hands. "That it was too soon for you to sleep over. I still don't want them to know, but I need you, Beth. My door has a lock. Could you stay for another hour?"

Passion swamped her, making her knees weak. He hadn't even kissed her, but she was already ready to take and be taken. She wanted his hands, his tongue. She wanted his body moving in and out of hers.

"I can stay," she whispered. "For however long you want."

20

Rick dropped Jana off in the late afternoon. She thanked him again, then grabbed her bag and walked up toward the house. She was a little tired and slightly unsettled. The former was the result of a strange bed and sharing said bed with Rick. She was used to being by herself, unless Linnie had a bad dream. The latter was less easy to explain.

She liked Rick a lot—he was a sweetie who was obviously totally into her. He'd kept her laughing with his dad jokes throughout the weekend. He'd been attentive, kind and thoughtful the entire time. She should have been floating on air, and she wasn't. Falling in love with him was the next obvious step, but instead of feeling closer to him, she felt like she needed to pull away, and she had no idea why. She was nearly thirty years old, and she'd never once been in love with a man. She'd assumed that was because of circumstances, but now she was starting to wonder if there was a bigger problem.

Her.

Was she flawed? Incapable of strong romantic emotions? Those were questions she was going to have to deal with, but maybe not right now, she thought as she stepped inside the house and called out, "I'm home!"

"Mommy, Mommy! You're back." Linnie came running and threw her arms around her. "I missed you so much."

"I missed you, too, peanut. Have you had a good weekend?"

"Uh-huh. Beth's been here every day, and we made brownies. This morning we went to the park and played. Teddy said he was trying to tire us out, but I feel fine."

The other kids joined them and led her into the family room. Dex was there, along with Beth and Teddy.

"Welcome back," her brother said. "Have a good time?"

"I did. Solvang was great. We should rent a house and all go there sometime." She looked at Beth. "Linnie says you've been here the whole time. I never meant for you to feel obligated."

Beth smiled easily. "I've been having a great time myself. I'm catching up on my kid movies. My education has been sadly lacking."

Jana spent a few minutes talking, then excused herself to go unpack. Beth went with her.

"How was the hotel?" her friend asked. "I saw the pictures you sent, and it looked wonderful."

"It was perfect. Our room was really private, and there was a fire pit out back. We sat up late Friday night and watched the stars come out." She laughed. "Real stars that we can't see around here."

Beth smiled. "Good. I'm glad you and Rick did well together. That first weekend away can be stressful."

She was saying all the right things, but there was something about her tone, Jana thought. Or maybe she was imagining things.

"Rick made the whole time easy. He had a plan and a grid with all our reservations."

Beth winced. "You were on a schedule, weren't you?"

"A little bit, but I liked having someone else take charge. All I had to do was show up."

Rick had taken care of her. She'd enjoyed hanging out with him, and the sex had been nice. So why was she questioning her feelings?

Once Jana had unpacked, she checked in with Teddy about his plans for the rest of the day. Not a surprise—he was hoping for a little one-on-one time with Beth. Jana said she would feed the kids and get them ready to start their week, so they were free to leave. Dex offered to hang out for the evening. There was chicken to barbecue, and they had ingredients for salad. She and Atlas made her easy cheddar biscuit recipe, and they sat down to dinner a little before six.

By seven thirty, they were all watching a movie together. Partway through, she excused herself to go check email. But instead of retreating to a quiet part of the house to scroll through her phone, she sat in the quiet, dark kitchen and tried to understand what she was feeling and why.

What was the restlessness about? Rick? Their relationship? Was she just reacting to spending so much time together, or was her subconscious trying to send her a message? Was it everything else in her life—getting ready for finals, waiting to start nursing school?

Dex came in and saw her. He walked over to the table.

"You okay?" he asked. "You've had something on your mind since you got home."

"I'm fine." She forced a smile. "You were great this weekend. Thanks for that."

"Don't distract me with compliments." He sat across from her. "The boyfriend less perfect than you'd hoped?"

She winced at the question. "Not exactly. It's more…" She paused. "I'm not in love with Rick."

Nothing about his expression changed. "Were you supposed to be?"

"I don't know. We just spent a great weekend together. I should be feeling the feels, right? Planning a future, and I'm not." She leaned toward him. "I've never been in love. Not romantically. Am I broken?"

"No. There's nothing wrong with you. We can't all be Teddy. For the rest of us, love takes time."

"I guess. I just can't figure out if the problem is me or if it's Rick. Sometimes when we're together, he says things that I don't understand."

"Like math equations?"

Despite her worry, she laughed. "No, I mean like, I don't know. When we were driving up on Friday, we talked about him getting into medical school and how Beth gave him all the money she had to help pay for it. It wasn't a huge amount in the overall scheme, but it was big for her. She gave up her dream of being a chef for him. He didn't seem appreciative."

She shook her head. "And even as I listen to myself talk, I'm thinking I'm not making sense at all." She looked at Dex. "I'm overreacting, right? No one is perfect. He was always the smartest kid in class. That has to leave a scar."

Dex shrugged. "I don't know about that, but the man's a surgeon. Every day he cuts open someone and fixes them. In the time it takes him to do that, they are completely at his mercy. One wrong move and he could kill them. It's an awesome responsibility that most of us don't want to deal with. Even if I could get through medical school, there's no way I want to do that. Most people don't."

"You're saying what makes him good at his job makes him a crappy human being?"

Dex flashed her a smile. "I wouldn't go that far, but doing what he does takes a certain kind of character and a lot of training. I'm not sure there's much left over for what you and I consider normal."

He had a point, she thought.

"Does he show up when he says?" Dex asked. "Does he text and stay in touch? Do you feel good when you're around him? Have you ever caught him in a lie?"

Was Rick who he said he was? That was what Dex was getting at. "He's always come through," she told him. "I trust him to show up."

"Then maybe that's your answer. Trust your gut."

"My gut liked Paul, and he turned out to be a control freak who hit my kid."

"Paul was an asshole."

"Shouldn't my gut have mentioned that?"

"You're too hard on yourself," Dex told her. "On the surface, Rick's given you no reason not to trust him. Unless your gut tells you otherwise, go with it." His tone softened. "What if you're reacting because you're scared of making another mistake? It's one thing to be cautious and a whole other to screw up a great relationship for the wrong reason."

"You mean there's a right reason to screw up a relationship?" she asked, then sighed. "I get what you're saying, and I want to believe you. It's just my entire dating life has been one big mistake. When I was younger, I never wanted to be tied down, so I never really had any serious boyfriends. Now I'm ready to have a real relationship, but I don't have the experience to make that happen. It's pathetic."

"You're distracting yourself with self-pity."

"Ouch."

He shrugged. "I call 'em like I see 'em."

"Dex, I don't know who Linnie's father is. That's how badly I did. I slept with a bunch of guys during spring break, and one of them got me pregnant. I'll never know who her father is. At some point I have to tell her that. It's not something to be proud of."

She shook her head. "Then I got involved with Paul. I don't have a good track record. You're right about Rick. I have no reason not to trust him. But honestly, every now and then, I can't shake some weird feeling inside. At the same time, I'm pretty sure it's just me being scared of messing up again. And if that's true, I'm, as you said, putting a really great relationship with a really great guy at risk, out of fear."

His gaze was steady. "Maybe it's time for therapy." One corner of his mouth twitched. "The intensive, inpatient kind."

She swatted his arm. "Very funny."

He stood and leaned over to kiss the top of her head. "Trust yourself, kid. You got this."

He walked back to the family room. Jana stayed where she was, going over what Dex had said. Maybe she was overthinking the problem. Maybe there wasn't a problem at all. But as she got up to return to the family room, that damned voice in her head whispered one last question. Would she trust Rick with her daughter? If push came to shove, would she call him to take care of Linnie?

And in that moment she knew, in her heart of hearts, the answer might be no. Honest to God, she had no idea why.

Rick opened his front door and grinned. "You don't have to keep feeding me, you know."

"You say that," Beth commented, walking in with several bags of takeout. "Yet you never tell me no when I offer to bring dinner."

He hugged her. "I like the company."

Any tension she'd had at seeing him again quickly faded as she realized she was happy to hang out with her brother.

"We're both so busy these days," she said. "I hardly get to see you."

He helped her unload the takeout. She'd stopped at a local Italian restaurant and had picked up a couple of different green salads, three kinds of pasta and the garlic knots they both loved.

"You're not complaining about being busy, are you?" he asked, his voice teasing. "You and Teddy seem pretty hot and heavy."

She did her best not to blush. "We're getting along."

"Is that what we're calling it?"

"Rick!"

He started dishing up his dinner. "I'm just saying you're spending quality time with him. You seem happy."

"So do you." She waited for him to set down his plate before taking food for herself. "You had a good weekend away?"

"It was the best. Jana's terrific, and we really got along. She's sweet and funny and beautiful. The whole package." He put down his fork. "Thank you for slapping some sense into me before. I was such a fool with that other woman." His mouth turned down. "I've been thinking about it a lot, and I know I got caught up in having an attractive woman come on to me. I reacted without thinking about what's important, and I nearly lost Jana because of it."

His gaze sharpened. "You were there for me. You told me the truth when I needed to hear it, and I want you to know I'm grateful."

She smiled at him. "Of course. I'm glad it all worked out." She was still a little weirded out that Rick had cheated in the first place—it so wasn't him. But he'd made a mistake, realized it, self-corrected and moved on. That was what mattered.

"How was it hanging out with Linnie and the other kids while Jana and I were away?" he asked.

"Good. Intense. Teddy's children are really fun. Their personalities are so distinct." She thought about all they'd done and how she'd managed to spend one-on-one time with each of them. "I freak out a little when I think about what it would mean if Teddy and I got serious."

"You'd be a good stepmom," he said casually. "You like to take care of people, and it suits your talents."

"My talents?"

"The things you're good at. You know, like making sandwiches."

Her good mood seemed to fade a little. "That sounds like you're saying making sandwiches is the best I can expect from myself. There's more to running the business than adding mayonnaise to a ciabatta roll."

He stared at her in obvious confusion. "What did I say? You're upset."

"Sometimes you act like I'm incapable of doing much of anything. I might not have gone to medical school, but I'm not dumb."

"I never said you were. You're mad. I just said you're good at taking care of people. Like with the sandwiches. You connect with your customers and do special things for them." He looked baffled. "Why is that the wrong thing to say?"

Is that what he'd meant? "It's not what you said. You made a crack about me making sandwiches. It felt like a dig."

"Beth, I genuinely have no idea what you're talking about."

"Sometimes you act like you don't respect me, Rick. You put down what I do. Yes, you're a surgeon, and that's amazing, but the rest of us have value, too."

She could see him struggling to understand. No doubt he was thinking something along the lines of "but anyone can make a sandwich," which really pissed her off. Not that her reaction was fair, because he hadn't said the words.

Wow, she was in a mood and she had no idea why. Maybe it really was being tired. Or maybe it was something else she didn't want to define. Because as Agatha had pointed out more than once, Rick never brought her takeout. He never did anything for her.

"It's what we've always done," she said aloud.

He frowned. "What is?"

"This." She waved between their plates. "We're in a pattern. I take care of you, but you don't take care of me. You're my little brother. I look out for you and do things for you. I always have. Just like you've always been the smart one, while I've struggled. Or at least I did."

Because she wasn't struggling anymore. She was, in fact, thriving. She was happy. For the first time in at least a couple of years, she knew what she wanted, and she had things to look forward to.

She looked at her brother, who was watching her cautiously, as if not sure what was going to happen next.

"You need to buy the takeout," she told him.

"Okay. Are you on Zelle?" He pulled his phone out of his pocket. "I can send you the money right now."

She held in a laugh. "No. That's not what I mean. Next time you need to be the one to stop and buy our dinner."

"Sure. I'll go wherever you want. Next time I'll text you and set up dinner, and then I'll pick it up and bring it to you."

"Thank you."

"Damn," he said as he shook his head. "Relationships are complicated."

"Sometimes."

He looked at her. "You want to have dinner with Teddy and Jana? The four of us. Like a double date?"

"That would be fun. Yes, I would."

He pulled out his phone and quickly texted. "I'm asking Jana about it right now. We can get something set up for this weekend." His good-natured smile returned. "I won't be on call."

She got up and collected her phone from her bag. "I'll ask Teddy."

Rick grinned. "See, this is good. We can be a team."

"We can."

Later, when she was home, she thought about the evening with her brother. She was glad she'd spoken up and so grateful that he'd responded as he had. She wasn't sure what had spurred her to confront him, but she knew that conversation was long overdue. Some of the problem was her accepting what had always been, and some of it was how clueless he was. And maybe, she admitted, if only to herself, Rick was a little bit lazy. She'd always looked out for him. Most people liked being taken care of. Why would he change on his own?

But he'd gotten her point, and she felt better for making it. These days she felt better about a lot of things.

She reached for her phone and read through the text exchange she'd had with Teddy. He was looking forward to their double date on Saturday. Afterwards, he was going to come home with her. Dex would stay with the kids until Jana got home. Beth was both nervous and excited about having Teddy stay the night. Agatha had promised to keep to her room, then had offered to make cinnamon rolls in the morning. Beth wasn't sure about her aunt and Teddy chit-chatting over sugar and coffee, but why not?

It was all so good, she thought happily. This time, this man. There was so much promise. She wasn't sure if she believed in "the one," but she had a feeling that of all the men in the world, he was one of the very few she could love for the rest of her life.

The customer flow at Surf Sandwiches on weekends had a different rhythm than on the weekdays. There was less of a lunch rush, and more of a steady stream of customers. Large to-go orders started piling up at about ten as families planned their days and decided to get sandwiches to take with them. This Saturday they'd had two catering jobs for backyard pre-graduation parties. Beth and Yolanda had started an hour early to get all the food prepped.

The warm, sunny day promised lots of beachgoers, which was good news for her business.

A little after one, Beth saw a familiar, tall redhead walk into the store. Galaxy spotted her and offered a warm smile and a wave. Beth froze as she watched the other woman walk toward her.

Galaxy didn't look upset or determined—not like someone here to confront her ex-boyfriend's sister. In fact, she seemed friendly as she approached.

"Hi, Beth. I was driving by and saw the sign. This is your store, isn't it?" Galaxy laughed. "I mean, you're here, so of course it is." The smile widened. "Sorry. I'm a little nervous." She glanced around. "I know it's short notice and you're probably too busy, but do you have a few minutes for us to talk?"

Her first instinct was to refuse. No good would come out of the conversation. Yet she couldn't seem to summon the words.

"I got this, Boss," Yolanda told her.

Which was true. Between Yolanda and their weekend staff, the counter was covered. Beth could take a break. Only she wasn't sure why Galaxy wanted to talk to her. Shouldn't the other woman be sad and avoiding Rick's family?

"Did you want a sandwich?" she asked.

"I'm good," Galaxy told her.

Beth eyed her trim thighs and wondered if Galaxy ate more than a single meal a day. And if so, no doubt she favored something vegan or water-based.

"Then we should at least get a drink," Beth said, pointing to the display case. "They're all organic and popular with my customers."

"Thank you."

Galaxy chose a flavored seltzer with zero calories. Beth decided to do the same. Together they walked outside and found a table in the shade.

Beth wrapped her hands around her drink and told herself

that if Galaxy started yelling at her, she would simply go inside and text Rick. Dealing with her brother's angry ex wasn't her job. Except Galaxy continued to smile at her and seemed perfectly calm.

"I know I should have given you some notice," the other woman began. "But now that we've met, I thought it would be okay. I've been talking to Rick about us getting together." She gave a little laugh. "It seems like it's time, don't you think? So maybe a double date or something."

Beth stared at her blankly. A double date? What was she talking about? A double date with who?

Galaxy's perfect brows drew together. "Oh, dear. Did I say something wrong? Rick mentioned you were seeing someone. Did it not work out?"

Okay, maybe it was just her, but Galaxy wasn't making any sense. What would Teddy have to do with...

A truth she didn't want to think about, didn't want to acknowledge, smacked her on the side of the head. She was sure she flinched, but couldn't help it. Horror swept through her. Horror and disbelief and a sense of being slightly out of step with the earth's rotation. This couldn't be happening. It *wasn't* happening.

"Because you're still dating my brother," she whispered.

Galaxy's expression turned concerned. "Are you all right?" She leaned back a little, as if wanting to put distance between herself and whatever Beth was dealing with.

Not that Beth cared about her comfort level. What the hell? Rick had lied. He'd pretended to be all remorseful, and he'd lied to her. He'd looked her in the eye and had said he'd broken up with Galaxy, and it hadn't been true at all.

He'd lied. Until this second, she would have said he was incapable of being deceitful. It wasn't his way. Only it obviously was. He'd cheated on Jana and was still cheating on her. He'd betrayed his own sister because of whatever sick game he was playing. It was too much for her to take in.

Beth wanted to escape back into the store but also knew she needed to get more information. None of it was going to be good, but she had to know what was going on. She mentally searched for a reasonable excuse for her odd behavior and decided to go with the familiar.

"Oh my goodness," she said, hoping she sounded more normal than she felt. "I'm having the worst period. I took a pain pill, and I'm a little out of it. Forgive me."

Galaxy instantly relaxed as she reached out and touched Beth's hand. "I'm sorry. I get really bad cramps, too. What was God thinking when He designed our reproductive system? Can I get you something? Maybe a little food would help?"

Beth felt sick to her stomach. Bad enough that Galaxy was here. Worse that she was nice.

"Thank you. I'll be fine." She struggled to make sense of what was happening. "Rick doesn't talk about his personal life. I think it's a guy thing. I really don't know that much about you. How long have you been going out?"

Galaxy tossed her head, sending her gorgeous red hair flying over her shoulder. "Nearly nine months. I can't believe how fast time has gone." She leaned forward. "Between you and me, my mother is over the moon. I'm dating a doctor. She never thought it would happen."

Beth couldn't breathe. Her chest was tight, her mouth was dry. Nine months? No. It couldn't be. Nine months? Oh, God, she'd been so wrong. Rick hadn't been cheating with Galaxy—he was cheating with Jana. Teddy's sister was the other woman.

"I work at an urgent care clinic in Santa Monica. Rick's practice has an office in the building. That's how we met. It was kind of romantic. We literally ran into each other. He was so apologetic, and we got to talking." She glanced down, then back at Beth. "He said I glowed. No one has ever said that to me before. I couldn't resist him."

Galaxy pressed a hand to her chest. "It was kind of love at first sight for both of us." The other woman giggled. "At least, it was for me. It took Rick a tiny bit longer to admit his feelings, but now we're both in love, and it's amazing."

Beth had never been a fainter, but she thought this might be a good time to start. Everything the other woman was saying made the situation worse. Rick had more than lied—he had an entire secret life. Nothing he'd told her was true. It was as if he'd become another person—one she neither knew nor liked.

Galaxy kept talking, telling funny, charming stories about her boyfriend. The more she detailed, the more Beth got that they weren't just dating—they were serious, and they had been for a while.

"I went to Salt Lake City to visit my sister a couple of weeks ago," Galaxy said. "For a long weekend. Rick texted me constantly. He missed me so much. It was sweet."

Beth was pretty sure that had been the weekend he'd taken Jana away, so she doubted he'd missed Galaxy as much as she thought.

The other woman smiled at her. "I so want us to be friends. If you're not comfortable with a double date, let's at least get together, just the three of us."

"Of course," Beth told her. "We'll set something up."

"Good. I want you to know how much I'm in love with your brother. He's so wonderful."

"He's, ah, lucky to have found you," Beth managed.

"I'm the lucky one." She glanced at the store. "I should let you get back to work, but I appreciate you taking the time to talk to me."

"I'm glad you stopped by."

Galaxy rose, waved and then walked away. Beth stared after her, wondering how it was possible for her world to shatter so completely and yet leave no physical evidence. Cars still drove by on the road. Families played on the beach. The sun still shone down—all as if nothing had happened. But she knew differently. She knew from this moment going forward, nothing would ever be the same.

21

"B, you okay?"

Beth looked up and saw Kai standing by the table. Because he worked for a few hours on Saturday afternoons and it must be time for his shift to start.

She tried to form words, but there weren't any. Her brain couldn't seem to keep processing what she'd just learned and still do the human things required for everyday life.

Rick had lied. Worse, he'd played her and made her a part of his deception. She didn't understand what sick game he was playing, but the end result would be the loss of a wonderful friendship. She'd hurt Jana. Someone she liked and respected and admired. She'd knowingly let Jana continue to date a cheater. In part to save herself and in part because she'd trusted her brother. She'd taken a significant friendship and tossed it aside as if it meant nothing. And it wasn't just Jana she'd betrayed. There was also Teddy. Because of what had happened, she was going to lose the man she was falling in love with. No matter how she explained, she'd known her brother was cheating on Jana and she hadn't said anything. She'd been an accomplice. She understood how Teddy was going to feel, because that was what she would feel if their situations were reversed.

"B?" Kai sat across from her. "You're scaring me."

"What? Oh, sorry. No, I'm fine. It's not anything..." She was about to say it wasn't anything bad, but of course it was. It was horrible and awful and nothing she had ever been able to imagine.

"Tell me," he said quietly. "I won't say anything. I give you my word."

That nearly made her smile. Funny how she could trust the twenty-two-year-old sitting across from her. Of course she'd thought she could trust Rick. But Kai was different. She couldn't explain how, but she knew he was.

"It's Rick."

"Was he in a car accident?"

She shook her head. "He lied to me."

"People lie, B. It's kind of a thing."

"Not like this. Not over and over." She stared into Kai's kind eyes and told him about catching her brother with Galaxy.

"I couldn't believe it. I didn't think he was that kind of person." She tried to remember all he'd said. "He acted sorry and kept saying all the things you'd expect. He told me Jana was the woman he wanted to keep seeing, and he swore he would end things with Galaxy."

More memories came to her. "He was so angry when he found out I was dating Teddy. He talked about how it wasn't good for him, that if he broke up with Jana, I'd still be with Teddy, and that wasn't going to work for him."

She shook her head. "I don't remember it all, and it doesn't matter now, because everything's over."

"He's still dating Galaxy."

Kai wasn't asking a question.

"He is. They've been going out for nine months. He's not cheating on Jana, he's cheating *with* her. Galaxy's the real girlfriend. When I found out what he was doing, I kept quiet. I didn't tell Jana and I didn't tell Teddy. Rick said it was over and I believed him, so I took the easy way out."

"It doesn't sound like it's been very easy," he told her. "This isn't your fault. You're not the one who messed up."

"You sure about that?" She felt her lower lip tremble as she fought tears. "I've hurt a friend I care about very much. I've lied to Teddy—oh, not directly, but I still lied. I thought I knew my brother and I don't at all. What else is a lie? All those horrible women he told me about. I never met any of them. Were they real? Now I've created a situation that is going to damage so many people, and that's on me."

The threat of tears continued, and now she fought against nausea. "I thought I knew him. I would swear I understood his character, but I don't. He's my brother. We've been there for each other all our lives. I've always taken care of him. How didn't I know he was capable of this?" She looked at Kai. "He lied to me again and again and I had no idea."

Tears spilled over, running down her cheeks. Her breath caught in a sob. Kai shifted close and wrapped his arms around her.

"It's okay," he told her.

She appreciated the words but knew they weren't true. Nothing was okay. Worse, whatever she was feeling now was nothing compared with the emotions she would experience once the shock wore off.

"It's all gone," she whispered. "Teddy and Jana. They're never going to forgive me." She looked at him. "I wouldn't if I were them. Plus I was just getting to know Teddy's kids. Magnolia wants to be my friend. She takes care of the family, and she was willing to trust me, and I betrayed her, too."

His mouth twisted. "I'm sorry."

"Thanks."

She drew back and wiped her face. "You don't have to sit here, Kai. You can go to work. I'm going to get my things and head home."

"You all right to drive?"

"Yeah. I'm all right."

She wasn't, of course. She might never be again.

Beth spent the rest of the afternoon trying to get in touch with her brother. She left messages and voicemails and nearly went by his house. She didn't think he was on call, and she didn't think he was with Galaxy. Jana was studying for finals, so unlikely to be hanging out with him. But no matter how many times she reached out, he didn't call her back.

Her mind went to the darkest of places. Was there a third woman he was seeing? Yet another life he was going to destroy? She paced and cried and flung herself on her bed, yet nothing changed. She still had to deal with the fact that her brother had lied so fundamentally about so many things. She had no idea what was real with him and what wasn't. Was he in love with Galaxy? Did he prefer Jana? And in the end, did it matter at all?

Almost worse, she'd been a part of it. She'd enabled him. She wanted to say it had been unwillingly—that she'd been sucked into his game unknowingly. Except she *had* known about Galaxy. She'd confronted him and told him to choose. Then she'd kept his secret. She had lied for him because he was her brother.

No, she thought as she sat on the edge of her bed. That wasn't the real reason. She'd lied for him because she hadn't wanted to lose the happy life she'd finally found. She'd wanted to keep Jana as her best friend and Teddy as her lover and their kids as her family. She'd wanted them all to get closer. She'd wanted the fantasy, and she'd been willing to sacrifice what was right to get it.

Every few minutes, her brain circled back to how they'd come to this. When had Rick changed? They were supposed to be a team—they'd always been there for each other. She couldn't reconcile what she knew with who she thought he was. Just a few days ago, he'd talked about how grateful he'd been that she'd steered him in the right direction. He'd said that Jana was the one and that they were happy together. He'd never once hinted that he was still seeing Galaxy.

She glanced at her watch and realized she had to get ready for her "double date" with Jana and Teddy. That or cancel. She honestly didn't know what to do. Faking her way through the evening seemed impossible. But if she didn't go, she would need an excuse. It seemed having her period was the only lie she was good at these days, and she couldn't use that one again.

Plus if she showed up, she could drag Rick into a corner and have it out with him. Because she was done keeping his secrets. Either he told the truth or she did.

Just thinking that statement made her sick to her stomach. Jana was going to be hurt, and Teddy would protect his sister. Rick might have been the one who cheated, but Beth had known and was guilty by her sin of omission.

She sucked in a breath and crossed to her bathroom. Her hands were shaking so much, she could barely put on makeup. She gave up on eyeliner and just put on a little mascara. She had already put her hair in hot rollers, so that was easy. Once in her closet, she thought about the restaurant where they were all meeting. It was nice but casual. She slipped on a sleeveless dress and sandals, then pulled out the rollers and fluffed her curls.

As she collected her bag and her keys, she fought against the sense of dread building inside of her. Everything about the moment felt inevitable. From the second she'd seen Rick with Galaxy, she'd known she was going to pay the price, and that time was now. She wanted to be optimistic, but she couldn't see any way this night ended well.

She was the first to arrive at the restaurant. She handed her keys over to the valet and paced in the foyer while she waited, her body on edge, her mind racing. Her emotions alternated between rage and bitterness. She wanted to scream at Rick and demand he not mess up her life. She wanted to know when he'd changed and have him tell her how she hadn't noticed. She wanted her old brother back—the one who never knew what to say and who came to her to help him navigate the emotionally confusing world he existed in.

"Well, you're beautiful. Are you waiting for someone, or can a guy dream you might be single?"

She turned and saw Teddy walking in, Jana next to him. His smile was familiar, as was her body's reaction to him being near. She instinctively rushed toward him, arms outstretched. He caught her and hung on to her so tightly, she couldn't breathe.

This, she thought frantically. This moment, this man. This was what she wanted, what she needed. He was everything and more, and she was in love with him. She probably had been from that first night.

He drew back just enough to lightly kiss her. She didn't want to let him go, but reluctantly released him. His smile returned.

"That was a really good greeting," he teased. "Makes me want to go outside and come back in again."

"You can if you'd like," she told him, doing her best to act normal when she mostly wanted to beg him to run away with her. Only there was nowhere to go that the truth wouldn't follow.

She turned to Jana and hugged her. "How's the studying going?"

Jana groaned. "Good, I think. Either I'm totally prepared or I don't understand the material at all."

"I think that means you're prepared."

Teddy put his hand on the small of Beth's back. "Shall we get our table or should we wait for Rick?"

"Why don't you two get the table and I'll wait here for Rick," she said, not quite meeting his gaze. "I want to talk to him about Agatha for a second. It won't take long."

She thought they might push back or at the very least question her, but they both just nodded. Teddy gave her a quick kiss before he and his sister went to the hostess and gave their name.

Beth waited until they were led to the table to start pacing again. She anxiously watched the door, then lunged for her brother when he walked in.

"There you are. Why didn't you call me back?"

He stared at her. "What's wrong with you?"

She grabbed his arm and led him outside. "I left you messages and texts. You could have gotten back to me."

She led the way to the side of the building and glared at him. "Dammit, Rick." Tears burned. "You lied to me."

"I have no idea what you're talking about. Why are you upset? Do you have your period?"

The verbal dismissal made her want to slug him. Instead she poked him in the chest and glared at him. "You don't even have to try to be an asshole, do you? It just kind of comes naturally. Galaxy stopped by today."

Under any other circumstances, his look of surprise would have been comical. He blinked several times, then took a step back.

"Galaxy?"

"Yes. You remember her, don't you? The two of you have been going out for nine months!" She had to consciously lower her voice. "You lied about all of it. You're not cheating on Jana, you're cheating *with* her. Galaxy thinks you're in love, but that can't possibly be true, because that would require you to have a heart, and you obviously don't. You lied to everyone, including me."

"Stop saying that," he told her, then glanced over his shoulder. "Who I'm seeing shouldn't matter to you."

"What?" Her voice was practically a yelp. "Not matter? Jana's my best friend. She matters to me, and you're hurting her. Teddy's her brother. I'm dating the brother of the woman you're cheating on."

"I told you to stop seeing him," he said, his voice low and angry. "You should have listened."

She couldn't believe it. "That's it? That's all you have to say? I kept your secret because I believed your song and dance about making a mistake before. But none of it was true. You were playing me."

His glare was cold. "You make it so easy."

It was as if he'd slapped her. She inhaled sharply and stared at the man she thought she knew. But there was no familiar Rick in his angry expression—he wasn't anyone she recognized at all.

"I don't get the game," she told him, "but I'm no longer taking part in it. Either you tell Jana the truth or I do."

He grabbed her arm, his fingers biting into her skin. "The hell you will."

"Unless you plan to physically lock me up, you can't stop me. You've been cheating with Jana since the first day you asked her out. She deserves to know the truth. Man up, Rick. Or is that too much to ask?"

"Beth?"

Her body froze, but that wasn't enough to block out the horror of looking up and seeing Teddy standing there. At first he looked confused, but then his face tightened as if he were grasping what he'd overheard.

"What's going on?" he asked.

And just like that it was done, she thought sadly. All her hopes, all her dreams—they were gone. There was no recovery from what had happened or her part in it. The pain was physical, nearly stealing her breath. Still she forced herself to move toward him. No matter what, she was going to tell the truth.

"Don't," Rick commanded.

She ignored him and stopped in front of Teddy. "Rick's been seeing someone else the whole time he's been dating Jana. I didn't know until a few weeks ago when I saw them together. I confronted him, and he promised he would end things with Galaxy. He swore it was over, and I believed him. He allowed me to think that Jana was the girlfriend and Galaxy was the one he was cheating with. But it was the other way around. I found out when she came to see me today and told me everything. He and Galaxy have been going out for nine months. He never broke up with her. She says they're in love."

She saw Rick turn and walk away, then returned her attention to Teddy.

"I swear Rick told me they'd broken up, and I believed him. He said he'd made a terrible mistake and Jana was the one."

Teddy was right there in front of her, listening intently, but to her it felt like he was a million miles away. She couldn't say exactly why. It was probably something in the way he was standing or how he looked at her. But with every word, he grew more and more out of reach.

"So you didn't tell," he said quietly. "You kept it to yourself. You came into my house, played with my children, slept in my bed, and all the while you were lying to me and hurting my sister."

She felt tears on her cheeks but ignored them. "I thought it would be all right. I thought Rick cared about Jana. She's my friend. I would never do anything bad to her."

"Yes, you would. You did. Deliberately." His shoulders slumped. "I thought I knew you."

"Teddy, don't say that. You do know me. He's my brother. I

had to protect him." But even as she said them, she knew the words were foolish. Protect Rick? From what?

"I'm sorry," she whispered. "I'm so sorry. I was wrong, and if I could change what I did…" She brushed away the tears. "Only it wouldn't matter, would it? Because Rick would still have cheated, and that was the end."

"Jana's my sister. I thought she was your friend, and she did, too. Shame on us."

With that, he walked toward the restaurant, leaving her alone.

Jana stood in her room, trying to understand what had just happened. One second she'd been anticipating a fun dinner with Rick, Beth and Teddy, and the next her brother was saying they had to leave. It was only after they were in his car and had driven a few blocks that he pulled over and told her what he'd learned. She still couldn't believe it. Rick had cheated on her and Beth had known? No. That wasn't possible. She wouldn't believe it of either of them.

She was still in shock, she thought as she unzipped her dress and let it fall to the floor. She had to be. Otherwise she would be hysterical or crying or something. But she only felt numb—and possibly confused. Nothing about the situation made sense. How could it?

She changed into yoga pants and a T-shirt, then went out to check on her brother. Dex and the kids were still out to dinner, but they would be back soon.

She found Teddy in the kitchen, leaning against the island and staring at the wall.

"You okay?" she asked.

"No. You?"

"Nothing's sunk in." She pulled up a barstool and sat down. "Tell me again what she said."

"You really want to hear it?"

"I think I have to."

"Rick cheated. Beth knew and didn't tell either of us. They both lied."

As far as recaps went, it was short and brutal.

Rick had cheated. There was another woman in his life. There had been the whole time. When he'd stood there, asking her out, acting like he was scared and saying she glowed, he'd been involved with someone else.

"But he was so nice," she whispered. "Funny but awkward and unsure."

"Apparently not."

The first stab of pain caught her unaware. It went fast and deep, cutting through the happy numbness. Her breath caught.

"I can't believe it." Not of him and not of Beth. "She was my friend. Oh, no." She looked at Teddy. "What are you thinking?"

"Nothing you want to know."

"It wasn't her fault."

Even as she said the words, she wondered why she was defending the other woman. Beth had known what Rick was doing and hadn't said anything.

"I trusted her," she whispered.

"So did I." His voice was stark. "She was your friend, my lover, and she betrayed us both."

The pain grew, shattering whatever wall she'd put between it and her heart. There was no escape, no place to hide.

Teddy's phone buzzed. He glanced at the screen. "Dex is on his way back with the kids. Go wait in your room. Once they're in the house, you go with Dex."

"I don't understand."

"You need to talk to someone, and I can't be that person."

"But you're hurting, too."

"You won the coin toss." He offered her a smile that didn't reach his eyes. "I'll figure this out on my own." He was retreating— at least emotionally. He'd done the same when Valonia had died. Teddy preferred to mourn in solitude.

"I want to help," she said, unable to stop the words.

"Tomorrow, maybe."

She went to him and hugged him. "I know she cares about you. I've seen it in her eyes."

He stepped back. "Maybe we saw what we wanted to see. Maybe none of it was real. Maybe they're exactly alike."

She wanted to protest that wasn't possible. Beth was great. She adored Linnie and brought Jana food every Thursday. Only she hadn't wanted her dating Rick. At first Beth had been so against the relationship. At the time Jana had assumed Beth was judging her for her past, but what if it was something else?

Only if Beth had known about Rick's cheating at the time, then she would have been protecting Jana by acting all bitchy. And if she hadn't, then she really was a bitch.

"My head's spinning."

Her brother gently pushed her toward the back of the house. "Go wait in your room. I'll distract Linnie so you and Dex can slip out."

"He knows?"

Teddy nodded. "Not the details, but enough."

She walked to her room and sat on the bed. Her chest was a little tight, and she thought maybe she was breathing too fast. Rick had another girlfriend. Galaxy something. The whole time he'd been with her, he'd also been with Galaxy. If it wasn't so painful, it would be comical, she thought.

A few minutes later she heard the kids in the kitchen, followed by quiet. Seconds later, Dex knocked on her door, then opened it.

"Hey."

He stared at her with a combination of concern and anger. She knew the latter wasn't about her but was instead directed at the man who had hurt her. No matter what, Dex was going to be there for her. He was family, and he looked out for those he loved.

She crossed to him. He opened his arms, and she threw herself against his hard chest and hung on.

"I don't know what to think," she admitted. "I hurt everywhere and I'm so confused. None of this makes sense."

"Let's take a walk."

22

They went outside and started down the street. Despite the fact that it felt like days since she and Teddy had left the restaurant, it was only about seven thirty. The sun had set, but the sky hadn't reached that night color. Windows were open in neighboring houses with the sounds of conversation and television spilling out.

For the first block, she didn't speak, but then she started explaining about Galaxy and how she was the real girlfriend. "I was someone he was seeing on the side," she said. "I can't believe it. I'm the other woman."

"You didn't know. How could you?" Dex stopped and faced her. "Rick had a plan from the beginning. You think this is the first time he's done this?"

"What? Of course. It has to be. He's not…"

She pressed her lips together as she tried to comprehend Dex's point. Rick was good at the game. From how bashful he'd looked when they talked to telling her she glowed, to how he'd had a string of dad jokes to make her laugh. He'd been adoring, and she'd fallen for the act like the idiot she was.

"He played me," she said slowly. "We met so randomly. I didn't have my wallet with me, and he was behind me in line. He bought my coffee. The next time I saw him, I paid him back, and we started talking."

"A crime of opportunity," Dex said lightly as they continued walking.

"But why?" she asked, breathing through the pain. "Why can't one woman be enough?"

"Who knows. Power, maybe. The thrill of manipulating the women in his life. Or the knife's edge of wondering when he'll be caught."

Or it could be a thousand things they would never figure out because they didn't think the way he did.

"I just wanted someone regular," she said quietly. "A man who cared about me and could welcome Linnie in his life. He didn't have to be anything special. I never wanted to date a doctor. I didn't care about that. I thought Rick was…"

"Who he pretended to be."

She nodded. "I pick the wrong guys. I have all my life. You're going to say it's not my fault, but I'm the person all the relationships have in common. I need to be done."

He put his arm around her and pulled her close. "You're probably not in the best place to be making life decisions right now."

"It hurts."

"I know, kid. I know."

"Then there's the whole Beth mess." She didn't want to think about her friend because in some ways, what she'd done was worse. "I trusted her."

"You did."

"She lied to me." She stopped walking and faced him. "She hurt Teddy. He's devastated. He was falling for her."

"Was?"

She stared at Dex. "You're saying he's already in love with her?"

"You know how he is. When it comes to relationships, Teddy doesn't do middle ground."

She wanted to curl up in a ball so the pain couldn't find her. "None of this makes sense. I know she cares about him. I could see it in her eyes. She was practically giddy when she talked about him. Why would she risk everything? She was about to get all she'd been wishing for."

"You already know the answer."

Jana did. "Rick's her brother."

"You'd lie for Teddy."

She would do a lot more for him. She understood the whole family thing. They had a lifetime of watching each other's back. Now their lives were even more entwined with all their kids growing up together.

"I feel sick," she whispered as they turned back the way they'd come. "You know, it's strange. I was thinking the other day that I didn't know if I'd ever leave Linnie with Rick. It was just a gut feeling. But I would have left her with Beth, no problem. I've seen her with the people she works with. She's good and kind, but she let me continue to see her brother, all the while knowing Rick was sleeping with someone else."

She glanced at Dex. "Are you going to defend her?"

"Nope. She should have said something."

"She should have." Jana pressed a hand to her stomach. "This is going to get so much worse before it gets better."

"But it will get better."

"I went to his office once. I wanted to tell him I got into nursing school, to share the news." She frowned as she remembered. "He was really pissed that I showed up like that. It was so unlike him. I remember being confused by his reaction." She felt the start of tears. "Now it makes sense. He couldn't have one of his women appearing randomly like that. It was too risky."

She brushed her cheeks and tried to focus on her mad. "He was such a jerk. He came by later and apologized for snapping at me. He said he'd been thinking about a patient. I actually felt bad." She stopped and glared at him. "I think I apologized. I hate that! He manipulated me from the start. He led me along like some...some cow or something."

"Cow?"

"I don't know." She punched Dex's upper arm, then winced when her knuckles impacted solid muscle. "What do you lead? A goat?"

"What's with the farm animals?"

"I'm making a point."

"Not a very good one."

She started to laugh, then immediately began to sob. Dex pulled her close as her body shook.

"I t-thought he cared about me. I t-thought he was a good guy. I thought Beth was my friend. Why didn't I know they were lying?"

He kept his arms around her. "Because you're not a deceitful person. You lead with your heart, and that's a good thing. Don't change, Jana. You're perfect just the way you are."

She sniffed and raised her head. "I'm so stupid about men. I can't be trusted in the dating world. I need to stay single forever."

"Hey." He kissed the tip of her nose. "We talked about this. Not the time to make life-altering decisions."

She wiped her cheeks. "It's gonna hurt a whole lot more tomorrow, isn't it?"

"Yeah, it is."

"I can't believe it," Agatha said for the third time. She pressed a hand to her chest. "I can't. Oh, sweetie, this is horrible. I don't know what to say."

"There isn't anything."

Beth's tone was flat. She'd already cried, had screamed into a pillow and was now settling into a low-grade pain that wasn't going anywhere. She'd known there was a possibility for disaster. No, not a possibility, she amended. A likelihood. She just hadn't thought it would happen so fast. One minute everything had been perfect, and the next, her hopes and dreams had crumbled to dust.

"I hurt so many people," she whispered. "Not just Teddy and Jana, but the kids. I won't ever see them again. I wasn't sure about having children in my life, but now I know I like them a lot." She stared at her aunt. "He's going to have to tell them something. Teddy won't make me a monster, but he won't lie, either. We were just getting started, and now it's over."

"You don't know that. Right now the pain is fresh, but in a few days…" Her voice trailed off.

While Beth wanted that to be true, she had her doubts. "Would you forgive me?"

"Of course."

Despite everything, she managed a faint smile. "You're saying that as my aunt who loves me."

"It's how I view the world."

"You see it more clearly than me." Beth threw herself back against the sofa and closed her eyes. "You tried to warn me about Rick. You said he wasn't who I thought."

When her aunt didn't respond, Beth opened her eyes and looked at her. "What?"

"I didn't say anything."

"You were thinking it. How did you figure out he'd changed?"

"He hasn't changed, my dear. This is who he's been for a long time."

The gentle words were like a blow to the heart. "No. He's not like that. He's sweet and needy and uncomfortable in the world.

I refuse to believe he's a lying, manipulative bastard who only cares about himself."

"You love him and you've always taken care of him. But in doing that, you've somehow convinced yourself he's not capable." Agatha's tone was gentle. "Maybe that was true when he was eleven, but it hasn't been true for a long time."

Beth wanted to say her aunt was wrong, only she had proof. "I can't believe he set out to hurt me."

"I don't think he did. I don't think he was considering you at all. Everything was about what he wanted. I'm not sure how much of his relationships is about him caring and how much is about him seeing what he can get away with."

Again she wanted to protest, but couldn't. "Rick knew he was cheating when he brought Jana over to meet me. He'd already been dating Galaxy for a few months. He thought it was funny that he figured out Jana and I knew each other. He was entertained that I was upset."

She spoke her thoughts out loud—maybe in an effort to make them more real. It was as if after all this time, he'd become a stranger to her. The man she thought she knew wasn't who she'd thought he was at all. Honestly she couldn't reconcile his actions with the sweet boy who had come crying to her when one of the big kids threatened to beat him up.

"I can't wrap my mind around it," she admitted. "I don't know what to believe. Does he not know what he's doing is wrong, or doesn't he care?"

She ached everywhere. Not just because she was starting to see she'd never known Rick at all, but because of what that revelation was going to cost her.

"I've lost Jana and Teddy."

"You can't know that, my dear. As I said before, everyone needs a little time."

She shook her head. "It's not going to be that simple. If I'd just found out about his cheating, it might be okay, but I've known for a while. I kept it from my friend and I kept it from her brother. I wouldn't forgive me."

Hopelessness gripped her, squeezing her chest so tight, she couldn't catch her breath.

"I finally found exactly who I was meant to be with, and now I've lost him."

Agatha hugged her tight. "He might not be as lost as you think."

Beth didn't answer because there was no point. Agatha was hoping for the best while she knew better. She knew that Teddy might have overlooked a lot, but hurting Jana was going too far. He would risk himself but not those he loved. Not for anyone.

Jana spent the morning arguing with a health insurance company on behalf of a patient. Sixty-two minutes into the call, the representative put through the authorization required for the procedure. Jana thanked her, hung up and walked to the break room to get more coffee. She hadn't slept in two nights. Exhaustion made it feel as if she were trying to walk through thick water. Her mind was cloudy, her body ached and her heart—her poor, broken heart—seemed to stumble through every beat.

She knew she had to pull herself together. Whatever was or wasn't happening in her personal life, she had finals, and there was no way she was going to risk her GPA over some asshole. Rick wasn't worth it.

She rode her righteous indignation through the next hour of work, but as she processed claims, she found herself thinking less about the man and more about his sister.

In some ways she missed Beth so much more. As Jana worked through the stages of grief, she wanted a friend to talk to. Someone who understood the complexities of the relationship and could possibly explain Rick's actions. Only talking to Beth wasn't an option because Beth had known what Rick had been doing and hadn't said anything.

In her moments of strength, she understood. Jana would have stood by Teddy, no matter how wrong he'd been, and Beth had stood by her brother. In her weak moments, she wondered if any part of her relationships with the Nield family had been real. Had they both been playing some sick game? Had she even been a person to them?

She thought about how Beth had come to the house and hung out with Teddy and the kids, knowing Rick had cheated. Maybe he really had said it was over and maybe she'd believed him, but Beth had let her go away with him, all the while knowing about the other woman.

She was embarrassed and ashamed and angry and all kinds of other emotions she couldn't name. She felt lost and broken and used, and mostly she missed her friend.

She added creamer to her coffee, thought briefly about the box of doughnuts on the counter but decided she didn't need the inevitable blood sugar crash that was to follow, then returned to her office.

She was about to get into it with yet another insurance company when Rick strolled into her office.

"Morning," he said casually and leaned against the doorframe.

She stared at him in disbelief. How did he have the balls to show up like nothing had happened?

"No," she said firmly, coming to her feet. "Just no."

His expression immediately turned sheepish and contrite. "You're mad. I get that."

"How comforting."

"Jana, don't. I'm sorry. It's not what you think." He took a step toward her, then stopped. "I miss you so much."

"How would you have the time?" she asked sharply. "Or is Galaxy out of town, so you're lonely?"

"I deserve that," he told her. "And I'm sorry."

"About?"

He stared at her blankly.

"For what are you apologizing?" she asked, grateful for the anger burning hot and bright. It would give her strength and clarity.

"I hurt you. I would never do that on purpose. If you'll let me explain, I can—"

"No," she said again. "There's no explanation. You're dating someone else. From what I heard, it's pretty serious. It's been going on for months. At the same time you were going out with me, telling me how magical it all was and how much you cared. Everything you said is a lie. You're not at all the person you pretended to be. You're not unsure and awkward. This is some kind of sick game you play. I don't get why you feel the act is necessary, but that doesn't matter. I'm not going to be a part of it anymore."

"Jana, don't do this." His tone cajoled. "We were so good together. Remember our weekend away?"

"How did you manage that? Was she out of town?"

Something flickered in his eyes.

"She was." Jana laughed. "That's so classic. Wow, so our, quote, scheduling around your work, unquote, was just you waiting until your real girlfriend was gone. You must have been texting her the whole time. How do you keep us straight? Isn't that exhausting?"

The contrition faded, as if he'd decided to drop the act. "It's not as hard as you think," he said, his voice astonishingly casual. "So you're really going to do this? End things?"

"I am. You're a whole lot less than you think, Rick. It's not going to take me very long to get over you."

His expression turned contemptuous. "You're hoping that's true, but let's face it. You're not going to do better than me."

He started for the door, then turned back. "As for the act, it worked on you, didn't it? Women like you make it easy. If you want to blame someone, blame yourself."

With that, he was gone.

She sank into her chair and stared at the open door. She felt as if she'd just been in an emotional hit-and-run. Adrenaline joined anger, adding a faint twist of nausea to the mix. How was she supposed to reconcile what had just happened with the man she'd been dating for the past few months? While she was shocked by what he'd said, she supposed the real kicker was the almost villainous confidence. Something like that only came from a lot of success. So how many women had there been, and under what circumstances?

She thought about what Dex had said—that a person couldn't cut open bodies on a regular basis, fighting back death, and not have a different mindset. She assumed most surgeons were warm, giving people and that Rick was the exception. Or more likely, his personality had always been there. The cool job simply gave him more opportunity to be a jerk.

On the bright side, their encounter had gone a long way to helping her get over him. The only thing to mourn was how gullible she'd been. Thank goodness he hadn't been around enough for Linnie to get attached.

As she reached for her headset, she had the brief thought that there was no way Beth had seen this side of her brother. The other woman was too giving, too kind, to be comfortable with someone like that. Or did she know and look the other way because they were family? And in the end, did it really matter at all?

The lull between the lunch rush and the high school kid invasion at the store gave Beth too much time to think. She needed to stay busy enough to keep her mind occupied so she wouldn't keep going over and over what had happened Saturday night. She kept seeing the shock on Teddy's face, hearing her own voice as she pleaded, then feeling the helplessness of having him walk away.

Just as distressing was imagining what Jana must be going through. While Teddy was probably pissed, his involvement wasn't direct. Jana, on the other hand, had been betrayed both by a friend and by the man who was supposed to be falling in love with her. She'd been the innocent party but had ended up with the most pain.

Beth wanted to reach out, but wasn't sure what to say. She'd texted an apology—one without excuses. She'd acknowledged she was wrong and had expressed her regret. It wasn't much, but she didn't know what else to do. Should she try to call? Show up at her house? Only she couldn't do that because of Teddy.

Just thinking his name sent a sharp pain through her. She continued to load paper towels into the dispensers in the bathroom. She'd already filled the soap and checked the toilet paper. Next up she was going to do a quick condiment inventory because it would occupy her mind just enough to keep the worst of the regret at bay.

"B?"

She stepped out into the small hallway and saw Kai.

"It's Teddy," he told her, not quite meeting her gaze. "He wants to talk to you."

Emotions rushed through her. Hope, yearning, guilt. She must have gone pale or something because Kai took a step toward her. She shook her head.

"I'm okay. He's up front?"

"He said he'd wait outside."

She quickly put away the paper towels, wiped her hands on her apron, squared her shoulders and walked toward the front door.

When she stepped out into the bright sunlight, she saw him standing a few feet away. Her heart leaped, her breath caught and she was swamped by a longing so intense, it burned.

She'd missed him with every breath, she thought, studying him. Had dreamed about him, picked up the phone to text him a thousand times. But she'd kept her distance because she knew that was what he wanted. Now she took in the dark circles under his eyes and the stiffness in his body and realized his being here wasn't a happy thing. He had nothing good to say to her.

She walked past him to the side of the building by the tables and chairs. It was more private here, quieter. She wanted to suggest they sit down, but knew in her gut whatever he had to say wouldn't take very long.

They stared at each other. She tried to memorize his features so that years from now she could recall him clearly. Sorrow welled up inside of her. So much was lost because of a single decision, she thought sadly. For that one moment, she'd held all she wanted in the palm of her hand, and then she'd lied.

"I'm sorry," she said involuntarily.

He looked away, then back at her. "You knew your brother was cheating on my sister and you didn't say anything."

The blunt statement made her flinch. "It wasn't that simple," she said quietly. "Yes, I saw Rick with Galaxy. I was stunned and upset, and I confronted him as soon as I could. He agreed to break things off. At the time, I assumed he was cheating on Jana and that Galaxy was the new girlfriend. He was regretful, and I made the decision not to say anything."

She had more to tell him—she wanted to explain that Rick was family and that she'd always stepped in to protect him. Only Teddy already knew, and looking back, she wondered if instead of protecting, she'd been enabling. But she didn't mention how she wasn't sure she knew her brother anymore—how maybe she hadn't known him for a long time. That would sound like an excuse, or worse.

"I didn't want to hurt you or Jana," she said. "I did what I thought was best. I see now it was a huge mistake, and I'm sorry."

He looked at her. "I won't ghost you. I'll tell you in person. It's over."

Tears immediately spilled down her cheeks. She wanted to say something, to try to change his mind, only there was no point. She knew him—knew what his family meant to him. She knew how much he loved his children, his sister, and how much he'd loved Valonia. He couldn't forgive the betrayal. If she'd just hurt him, he might have gotten over it, but she'd hurt his sister.

"I don't know what I would have done," he said, still looking at her. "If it had been me. I probably would have kept Jana's secret. I don't know. Family makes it hard. I'm not sure there was a right thing to do."

Then don't go. But she only thought the words, then instead whispered, "I love you."

He stiffened. "Don't."

"I want you to know it was real for me." She sucked in a breath as she struggled to stop the tears. "All of it. I wasn't part of the game. You and the kids… Jana… It mattered. I know it doesn't mean anything, but I wanted you to know."

He turned away. "You're right, Beth. It doesn't mean anything."

23

Jana carefully squeezed limes into the shaker. She'd already measured out Cointreau and tequila. Teddy walked into the kitchen.

"Margaritas?" he asked. "Not your usual thing."

"I'm celebrating, and you're going to join me, because it would be sad to drink alone."

"What are we celebrating?"

"I saw Rick today."

Teddy raised his eyebrows. "You're getting back together?"

"God, no!"

She looked into the shaker and decided she had enough juice, then poured in the other ingredients and added ice. Once she'd put the cap on, she shook it until the metal container frosted over, then uncapped it and poured the margaritas into the waiting glasses.

She handed Teddy one of the drinks and took the other for herself, then raised it slightly.

"To me. I told off the asshole." She took a sip and sighed at the tart, delicious taste. "He came in all smarmy and smug, acting like nothing was wrong. He wanted me to forgive him."

"Dick," her brother muttered.

"Tell me about it. I told him he'd cheated and lied and that it was over." She leaned against the counter. "He turned into someone else. He basically said I couldn't do better and that it was all my fault. There's something wrong with him. That nice, 'aw shucks' thing is an act. I can't believe I didn't see it before."

She took another drink. "While I'm going to have to deal with that, he's gone and I'm relieved. I'll tell you, seeing who he is really helped me deal with the whole missing him thing. I'm done with him."

"I'm glad."

There was something in Teddy's tone. "What? Don't say you hired some guy to beat him up."

"I wouldn't do that. I'd ask Dex to take care of him."

She smiled. "Dex has the skill set." She put down her glass and faced her brother. "You're thinking of Beth."

"It's the day for dealing with the Nield family," he said with a lightness that didn't reach his eyes. "I went to see her today and ended things."

She sighed, not surprised but unexpectedly sad. "Because you wanted her to be clear. You wouldn't just let it die on its own."

She supposed it was the right thing to do, but it had to have hurt both of them. She knew how much her brother had cared about Beth. She walked to him and hugged him.

"I'm sorry."

"It's okay."

She stepped back and looked at him. "It's not. You and Beth were doing great. I feel like it's my fault you're not together."

"Hey, no." His voice was serious. "This isn't on you. Not any of it. You're the innocent party in all this. Rick is some kind of monster, and you got caught up in his twisted game."

"Maybe I'm not the only one."

Her brother stared at her. "You're okay with what Beth did? She lied, Jana. She let you date her brother, knowing what he'd done."

"I know. I'm still upset. She was wrong."

"But?"

"I don't know. Like I said before, seeing Rick for who he is kind of changed my view of everything. Beth's a good person. I miss her. And I can see she was in an impossible situation."

"Assuming she didn't know what Rick is."

There was that. "I can't believe she did."

"You don't sound convinced."

"From everything I've seen about her, she wouldn't deliberately hurt either of us."

He picked up his glass. "How about if we make a hard and fast rule? No dating brothers and sisters again."

"I can drink to that."

They touched glasses. She looked at Teddy.

"You need to talk to her."

"I already did. There's nothing else to say. I did the responsible thing and ended it in person. We're finished."

"But you're in love with her."

He flinched slightly. "I'll get over it."

"Don't not be with her for me. I don't want that responsibility."

"What happened isn't about you," he told her. "It's about what she did."

"Maybe she didn't have a choice."

"I get that, but she hurt you, and that crosses a line for me."

She glared at him, but he seemed unmoved.

"Relationships suck," she said. "I'm done. Paul was a bully, and Rick is some kind of narcissistic sociopath. I have the worst taste in men. I was obviously not meant to be in a relationship."

"That's because you're looking for love in all the wrong places."

She frowned. "Wasn't that a song?"

"Very funny." He finished his drink and set the glass on the counter. "Find someone who is always there for you. Someone you already like and trust."

"What are you talking about?"

He shook his head. "You really don't get it, do you?"

"Get what?"

"You're going to have to figure that out for yourself."

The banging on the front door was insistent. Beth hurried to pull it open, only to find her brother standing on the front porch.

He shot her a death glare before pushing past her and stalking into the house.

Usually she was happy to see him—even when he dropped by without telling her in advance—but tonight was different. She still hadn't come to terms with everything that had happened. No—that wasn't right. She hadn't come to terms with everything he'd done. Because the disasters that had followed were on him.

He paced the room, looking furious and distraught. Any other time that combination would have made her feel instantly guilty, but right now she felt zero need to apologize. She'd done nothing wrong, at least not in the way he'd meant. She'd kept the truth about him from a dear friend and from the man she loved, which was totally on her, but the root cause was all Rick.

He stopped at the far end of the living room and spun to face her. "What the hell were you thinking?" he demanded. "You ruined everything."

"I take it that means Jana wasn't willing to forgive you?"

"No, she ended things. She wouldn't even let me explain." He glared at her. "You really screwed up, Beth. You could have kept your mouth shut, but you didn't. You screwed up, and now you have to fix it."

His statement was so outrageous, she nearly laughed out loud.

"No way," she told him, determined to stand her ground. "You're the one who messed up, not me. This is all on you. I'm just collateral damage."

"You told. Why couldn't you keep the truth to yourself?"

"Why couldn't you keep it in your pants? You've been cheating on Galaxy for months. I don't get it. Why do you need them both?"

He moved closer, his fury taking up the oxygen in the room. "Because I can," he said as he glared at her. "Because it's easy and I like the game. I play and I win. Everyone likes winning."

She had no idea what he was saying. Oh, the words were all simple enough to comprehend, but strung together in a sentence— not so much.

"But you've had horrible luck with women in the past. They take advantage of you."

His expression turned pitying. "None of that happened. Those were just stories I told you to keep you on my side." He smiled. "You take care of me, Beth, and I like that."

"No," she whispered in horror. She had suspected, briefly, but as those fears were confirmed, she felt the blood drain from her face. "You're lying." He had to be. Because if he wasn't, if he really was as awful as he claimed, then she'd destroyed her life for nothing.

"You don't get it, do you?" he continued, his tone almost kind. "You think I'm still that skinny, too-intelligent baby brother you grew up with. Well, I'm not. I'm brilliant, gifted, and the rules don't apply." He pointed at the door. "Out there,

I'm a god. Women want to be with me, and they'll go out of their way to rationalize my behavior to make it happen."

Her breath caught as the ugly truth slammed into her. This was who he was—this was the real Rick. Not the sweet, bumbling man she'd always thought. She didn't want to believe it, and she sure as hell didn't like it.

Agatha had tried to warn her. Even Kai had hinted at the truth. But she hadn't wanted to listen, hadn't wanted to know. He was right—she'd heard what she'd wanted to hear, and had ignored the rest.

Even as she admitted the truth, she could feel herself starting to rationalize. He was too smart to understand how he hurt people. He was busy, so he couldn't take time for things like empathy or caring. But examples lined up like parade floats, each one flashing past her in bright neon colors.

The time he'd told her she wasn't smart enough to make it in college. The dinner they'd had a week or so before her wedding to Ian, when Rick had said he was glad she'd found someone because he'd worried she would be alone forever. The way he talked about Surf Sandwiches with borderline contempt. How after she'd spent every spare minute looking for condos for him, he'd never thanked her.

Yet despite all that, she struggled to reconcile the man in front of her with the boy she'd known.

"When did you change?" she asked softly.

He shrugged. "I don't think of it as change so much as an evolution, but if I had to pin it down, I would guess in foster care." He smiled. "Eleanor, my foster mother, was an orthopedic surgeon. She's the one who saw my potential, who explained how easily people could be manipulated."

His mouth twisted. "You were so grateful when Agatha and Dale came to get us, but I wanted to stay where I was. Only I didn't have a choice. Still, Eleanor and I kept in touch. She was my mentor in college. She's the one who helped pay for medical school." His tone sounded reverent. "She's a great, great woman."

Beth felt sick to her stomach. Was he telling the truth? Had the last twenty years been a lie?

"This Eleanor person is the reason you act the way you do with women?"

"No. I act the way I do because I like it."

"Did you ever care about Jana?"

"Sure. She's great. At some point I want to get married and have kids. She was a contender."

She felt a little sick to her stomach. "But you were never in love with her."

"Love is for suckers."

"Galaxy thinks you're in love. You've been dating her for nine months. Is she a contender, too?"

"Of course. While she's not the brightest bulb, her father is brilliant. My son could be a genius."

The calculation of his words left her mentally gasping. "I can't reconcile what you're saying with the ten-year-old boy who tried to save me."

Rick rolled his eyes. "I was a kid. What did I know?"

His casual dismissal burned. "But I'm your sister. I sacrificed for you."

"Oh, please. What did you do?"

She thought about the money she'd saved for culinary school and how she'd made the deal with her uncle to buy the business. But even as she prepared to mention those things to him, she knew there wasn't any point. As hard as it was for her to accept—the man in front of her was telling the truth about himself.

Even so, she found herself saying, "I was always there for you. When you graduated from college and then medical school, I was right there in front, clapping the loudest."

His cold gaze settled on her face. "Those who can, do. Those who can't, clap."

The blow would have been crippling, but she'd moved from feeling to numbness. All this time, she thought in disbelief, all these years. He'd never been her family. He hadn't been anyone she'd thought. She'd loved him and supported him, and somewhere along the way, he'd become a monster.

She stood and walked to the front door. She held it open. Rick stared at her for several seconds, then walked out. He didn't say anything, not even when he got in his car. She didn't wait to watch him drive away.

Later, after she'd thrown up, then cried, then thrown up again, she went into the garage and got out the big bin where she kept all the mementos from when they were kids. She looked at photos and the silly handmade birthday cards Rick had given her. For the first time, she realized he'd stopped giving her cards after he'd come back from foster care.

Around dawn, she went into the kitchen to start coffee and saw that Agatha was already up. Her aunt smiled at her, then pulled out ingredients for breakfast.

"I'm in the mood for an omelet. What would you like in yours?"

Beth looked at the kind woman who had rearranged her entire life to take in two children she barely knew. No matter what, Agatha had been there for her, loving and supporting her.

"Rick's gone," she said quietly. "He came by last night because he was mad about losing Jana." She sank onto a kitchen chair and quickly recapped what had happened. "The things he said." She looked at her aunt. "You were right about him. Why couldn't I see it?"

"Because you love him, and it's not in your nature to think the worst of anyone." Agatha settled next to her and hugged her. "I'm sorry."

"I can't feel it yet. I don't know my own brother. I haven't known him in years. I thought we were tight, but he was only using me because it was easy. I lied for him. I lost Jana and Teddy for him. He was my family, and now he's gone."

Agatha hung on tight. "You didn't do anything wrong. You believed in him, and that makes you a good person."

"It makes me a fool."

"No." Her aunt drew back and shook her head. "Don't say that. It's never wrong to give your heart. You sacrificed out of love, because that's who you are. Rick's the broken one, not you."

"But I didn't know."

"That's the point, Beth. You're the one who wouldn't go looking for the bad. You believed in him, you wanted the best for him. Those are wonderful qualities."

"Maybe, but they don't feel very good right now." She blinked back tears. "I've been thinking about this all night. You know what I realized? I've let him make me feel smaller. He's said awful things to me, and I accepted them as truth, even though they hurt. I believed him when he said I wasn't smart or capable."

A hard truth that had been as shattering as his betrayal. "How do I unlearn that? How do I make myself believe I've lost my brother?"

Agatha squeezed her hand. "Right now you don't do anything but eat something and get some sleep. You can face the rest of it later."

"While I'd like to follow that advice, it sounds a little bit like avoiding the hard truths. I think we can both agree I've already been doing that too much as it is."

Agatha looked at her. "You want a few hard truths?"

No, Beth thought frantically. She wanted to hide in a cave and lick her wounds for a couple of months. Instead she forced herself to nod. Whatever her aunt said, the words would come from a place of love.

"From the time you were little, you protected Rick," Agatha began. "Not just because he was your baby brother and you wanted to keep him safe, but because you saw him as special. Rick was the smart one, the one with potential. Somehow you learned the lesson that his life was more important than yours."

Beth inhaled sharply. "I never thought of it that way. I was always willing to sacrifice, but I didn't consider that it was because I thought he had more value than me." She poked around her heart and was shocked to find a rightness sitting there. "That *is* how I saw things."

"Then when you were barely a teenager, he saved you from that horrible man's attack, and in the process was injured. The scar was a tangible reminder of his bravery, his love and how he put himself on the line for you. That only reinforced the dynamic of him being worthy of all you were doing."

Her aunt got up and poured them each a mug of coffee. She carried them back to the table.

"I'm not saying Rick was always selfish and uncaring. I'm sure when he was younger he was a sweet, loving little boy. I believe we all have a dark side, but most of us have a moral code and possibly social pressures to keep it in check. Rick was left to explore his darker side, and over time, it took over."

"I don't want to agree, but you're right."

"So much of your relationship is about habit," Agatha said. "You like taking care of him, and he likes being taken care of. It's not a bad thing unless the relationship becomes toxic, and in your case, it did."

"He didn't see me as an equal," Beth said slowly, ignoring the pain her own words caused. "He barely saw me as a person. He dismissed me and my life. He doesn't care I lost Teddy and my friendship with Jana." She looked at her aunt and swallowed against the tightness in her chest. "I didn't lose my brother, did I? He's been gone for a long time."

"I'm sorry, my dear."

A gentle way of agreeing.

"So now what?" she asked. "What do I do?"

"What do you want to do?"

"I have no idea," Beth admitted. "Part of me says to cut him off, but why invest in the drama? What does that even mean? Do I text him and tell him to never call me again?"

Tears fell down her cheeks as she spoke. "What a waste of time," she whispered, more to herself than her aunt. "He won't care."

Agatha reached for her again and held her tight. "You do what feels right. My guess is at this minute, you don't want to do anything about Rick. I think that's wise."

Startled, Beth drew back and stared at her aunt. "You don't think that's weak?"

"Not at all. You don't need anything from him. Oh, a heartfelt apology would go a long way, but that's not going to happen. So why stress yourself? He's not important. You are. Focus on healing. In time, you'll get more clarity about your brother."

"I thought you'd tell me to cut him off."

"Never." Agatha gave her a faint smile. "I've been relatively clear on who he is all these years, but I've continued to welcome him into my life. Whatever he's done, he's still my only nephew. I'm just a little careful with my heart."

"I'd like to get to that place," Beth said, thinking about how she wasn't even through the pain yet. It was going to be a long, ugly road. "How do I get there? And please don't say therapy. I couldn't do it."

Agatha studied her for a second. "No, not therapy. Do you remember when your uncle died?"

"Of course." His heart attack had been so unexpected, and his death had shocked them all. Agatha had been devastated. She and Dale had been together for nearly forty years. She hadn't ever been an adult without Dale at her side.

"I joined a grief group—mostly because I got tired of people offering me advice on how to heal. Through that group, I met

several women in my exact situation. Their friendship helped me
so much."

Was she suggesting Beth find new friends? After what had
happened with Jana, she wasn't sure she had the skill set.

"And I journaled."

Beth stared at her blankly. "You what?"

"I journaled. Wait right here."

Agatha walked out of the kitchen, only to return less than a
minute later with two large board game–size boxes. She handed
Beth the first one.

"Journaling Kit," Beth read, hearing the doubt in her voice.
"This hasn't been opened."

"I overbought," her aunt said with a smile. "I did three of these
the first year after your uncle passed. I told our story, starting
at the beginning and working my way up to the present. Take
a look."

Beth ripped open the plastic, then spread out the supplies.
There were colored markers, pens and stickers. The journal itself was the size of a notebook, with thick, lined pages.

"You asked where it all started to change with Rick," her aunt
said. "Start at the beginning. Tell your story with your brother.
You might surprise yourself with what you find."

"I'm not a diary person," Beth said, knowing Agatha was
only trying to help, but really? A journal? Who had the time?

"Just try it. Give it a week. If you hate it or think it's not
helping, then stop." Agatha gave her a gentle smile. "If nothing
else, you can call him a big fat poopy head over and over again.
That could be satisfying."

Despite everything, Beth laughed. "I like to think I could be
a little more aggressive than that."

"I don't know. Calling someone a poopy head is kind of bad-
ass."

Beth looked at her aunt. "You're always rescuing me."

"I believe it was just the one time, but I do love you, and I would do anything for you."

"I love you, too."

And with those words, Beth realized she did still have family and a soft place to fall. Today, that was going to be enough.

24

It took several days for the shock to wear off. Unfortunately that left Beth with no buffer against the pain she felt. Discovering who and what her brother was so soon after losing both Teddy and Jana had been like a nearly mortal emotional injury—recovering would take a long time. But going through the motions of her life helped, and when it came to distractions, being at work was a big one.

Thursday, a little after one, Yolanda stuck her head in the prep kitchen.

"Mr. Kazinsky just walked in, Boss. I thought you'd want to know."

"Finally," Beth said, stripping off her disposable gloves and heading for the front of the store. "He hasn't been in this whole week. I was getting worried." She smiled at her employee. "Thanks for telling me. I appreciate it."

"I was worried, too. He's an old man. Anything could happen."

Ugh. Not something Beth wanted to think about. She couldn't take any more bad news for at least six months.

She got the container of the special horseradish cream sauce she'd prepared from the under-counter refrigerator, then collected half a sliced baguette, roast beef and Brie. After putting the sandwich together, sans cucumber, she grilled it, then added the sauce and sliced cucumber before placing it on a paper plate, along with a fruit cup. By the time Mr. Kazinsky reached the front of the line, the sandwich was ready.

"You're a fine-looking woman who takes good care of me," he told Beth as he paid. "If I was twenty years younger, I'd ask you to marry me."

She grinned at their familiar banter. "If you were twenty years younger, I'd say yes."

She collected two bottles of organic soda, and together they walked to one of the open tables. She hovered, watching as the older man carefully lowered himself into his chair, then put his cane on the floor under the table and out of the way of other guests.

"We haven't seen you in a while," she said, opening the first bottle and passing it to him. "Were you off in the Bahamas again?"

Mr. Kazinsky, nearly eighty, with thick glasses and gnarled hands, winked at her. "I wish. I could use a little time somewhere warm."

"Is this where I mention it's seventy-eight outside?"

"At my age, that's chilly weather." He patted his chest. "I wasn't traveling. I had a little cold. I'm fine now."

"I'm glad."

She knew her friend lived in a retirement community nearby.

He'd moved there after he'd lost his wife three years before, which was when he'd started coming into her store. At first they'd only said hello, but a few months ago, she'd started taking the time to have lunch with him.

She gave him a few minutes to eat the first half of his sandwich, telling him about Kai's success at the weekend surf tournament and how Yolanda's oldest wanted to enter the school's spelling bee.

"The word list is twenty-five pages long," Beth said. "She showed me a copy. There are at least a dozen words on each page I'd have to look up."

"So she's hoping he changes his mind," Mr. Kazinsky said with a grin. "I know that's what I'd want."

"I think she's a little nervous about the process. So what's new in your world?"

"It's been six months since my daughter kicked out her no-good husband."

Beth took a second to realize what that meant. "I can't believe it's been that long. Does she still want you to move in?"

When his daughter had thrown out her cheating husband—and what was it about men and being faithful?—she'd asked her father to move in with her. Mr. Kazinsky hadn't wanted her making an emotional decision, so he had insisted she wait six months to see what happened.

"She does," he said. "We talked about it over the weekend. She said she and the grandkids discussed it, and they want me there." He frowned. "But I don't know."

"What about your life at the retirement community? Would you miss your friends?"

"Some, but they'd only be a few blocks away. I'd still see them." He looked at Beth. "I'm an old man. I wouldn't want to be a burden."

"You're kind of not the burden type." Mr. Kazinsky was sweet, thoughtful and funny. "I live with my aunt, and it works for both of us. A friend of mine—" Her chest tightened as she thought of Jana and Teddy.

She cleared her throat. "A friend of mine and her daughter live with her brother and his three kids. Extended families can work." She reached across the table and lightly touched his arm. "But you have to promise, whatever you decide, that you'll still come in here every now and then."

"Are you kidding? I'm still hoping to convince you to run away with me."

They talked for a few more minutes before Beth got him a to-go box for the second half of his sandwich and packed it up for him. She cleared a couple of tables, smiling as she overheard a very nervous teenage boy ask out a pretty girl about his age. The moment got better when she said yes.

Later, she had her new hire finish his paperwork before introducing him to Kai, who would supervise his training. An unexpected and very large sandwich order came in at four thirty for a five-o'clock pickup. She and the afternoon shift scrambled to get it done. As they all worked together, Beth realized that for the first time in several days, she felt okay. Not great or even good, but her chest didn't hurt, and she could go five minutes without wanting to cry.

Yes, she ached for Teddy, and she missed Jana. Yes, she was sad and confused about her brother, and the road to mental wellness seemed steep and daunting. But as she added sliced turkey to bread, she knew that Surf Sandwiches had become so much more than simply a business she'd purchased because she wanted her uncle to help put Rick through medical school.

She loved what she did here. She'd created something wonderful that her customers adored. Her employees were happy. When she'd gone online with a job opening, she'd had over fifty applicants. Nearly everyone had mentioned they knew someone who worked at Surf Sandwiches, and they wanted to be on the team.

That was on her, she thought, fighting against the knee-jerk reaction to put herself down. She waited for the negative thoughts—the voice in her head telling her she wasn't ever going to be enough—to fade. When they didn't, she thought maybe she should listen to her aunt and start journaling.

Once the big online order was finished, Beth made a couple of sandwiches and added a few salads to a to-go bag. She drove to the food bank and parked next to Jana's car, then got out to wait. A few minutes after six, she saw her friend—her former friend—walk outside.

Regret swept through her—for what she'd done and for what she'd lost. She'd sacrificed her friendship with Jana in a misguided attempt to protect her brother. More fool her.

No, she told herself firmly. She wasn't going to beat herself up over Rick. That was the first step in healing. She'd done what she'd done with the best of intentions. Now her job was to figure out when everything had changed and to learn from her painful lessons. After that, she would think about forgiveness—for her sake, not his. But that was for later. Right now she had to speak with her friend.

Jana spotted her and came to a stop. Beth couldn't read her expression. She wanted to rush toward her and hug her. She also wanted to run in the opposite direction and hide. Instead she simply stayed where she was and waited. Finally Jana walked toward her.

"You weren't at your shift," Jana said, her voice neutral, her expression unreadable.

"I changed days." Beth raised and lowered one shoulder. "I didn't know how you were doing or what you were thinking, but I figured seeing me wouldn't be good for you."

"Okay."

They stared at each other.

"I want to apologize," Beth said quickly, before Jana could

leave. "Please, if you'd just let me do that. I know I don't deserve your time, but I'm asking all the same."

Jana nodded without speaking.

Beth hadn't figured out what she was going to say, but she had a general idea of simply blurting out the truth and then dealing with the consequences.

"I'm sorry I didn't tell you Rick was dating Galaxy. At first I had no idea. I thought he wasn't seeing anyone but you. It never occurred to me he was the type of man to cheat." She paused. "Honestly, I didn't think he would know how. I was totally suckered by his act. These past few days, I've been thinking about how he's different now. He's not the kid I grew up with. I'm trying to figure out when it all changed, but he's kept so much from me. I'll probably never know, and I'm not sure my knowing makes any difference to you."

"Probably not," Jana murmured.

"Right. I need to get to the point. I saw him with Galaxy. Her father's an astrophysicist, by the way. I guess that's why she has that name, although honest to God, Galaxy?" She shook her head. "Sorry. Anyway, I saw them together, and I couldn't believe it. I confronted Rick. He said she'd flirted with him, and he'd been shocked and caught up in being popular."

As she spoke, she realized how ridiculous the words sounded. Yet she'd believed him.

"He said he'd been a fool and that you were the woman he wanted to be with. He promised to break things off with Galaxy, and I believed him."

"Because you wanted to," Jana said, her expression unreadable.

But the words were enough of a blow. Beth let her gaze fall as she nodded slowly.

"Yes, I wanted to keep the secret. I was dating Teddy, and I knew if I told you what had happened, I was risking our relationship as well. The two of you were so important to me." She pressed her hands together, twisting her fingers. "I was wrong—I get that. And I don't say any of this to justify what I did. It's just everything was so perfect. You and I were getting close, and I desperately wanted that friendship to continue. At the same time, being with your brother was magical. I'd never felt like that before, so the thought of not seeing him again, of us not being together… I wasn't strong enough."

She felt her eyes burning, but blinked away the tears. "I hurt you. I hurt you so much. I was a terrible friend when you've been nothing but kind to me. You let me into your life. I got to meet Linnie and hang out, and that was so precious. I'm so sorry for repaying you with lies and betrayal."

"You thought he'd broken up with Galaxy?" Jana asked.

"Yes. I swear, I believed they were done. More than once, Rick told me he was grateful I'd made him see what was important. That you were special and he wanted the relationship to go somewhere."

Jana's mouth twisted. "He's good with a line, I'll give him that."

Beth's throat tightened. "I don't understand. I've been trying to figure out how he played me. How could I have been so wrong about my own brother? I thought I knew him, but I don't at all. I keep remembering how when we were kids and our mom was off doing something dangerous, we'd take care of each other. I protected him from bullies and he helped me with my math homework. We were a team. But somehow that all became something else, and I didn't notice."

She squared her shoulders and drew in a breath. Now came the really hard part. "Last Saturday, Galaxy came to see me at the store. I thought they'd broken up, so I was shocked to see her. I thought maybe she wanted me to help her get Rick back, but according to her, all was well with them. I realized he hadn't broken up with her at all. She told me they'd been together for nine months and they were in love."

Jana looked away. "I wasn't the one cheated on. I was the one he cheated with."

"I didn't know," Beth said miserably. "I swear, I had no idea. She kept talking about how great things were with Rick, and I kept thinking about you and how wrong he was and how you were going to be hurt."

She brushed away tears. "She was nice. I think that makes it worse. She works at the urgent care in his Santa Monica office building. He can't even be bothered to go find the women he dates. He picks them up in the building."

Seconds later, she realized that might have sounded bad. "I'm not blaming you."

"I get that. He's an asshole. I'm sorry to dis your brother, but he is. I don't like hearing the truth, but it can't touch me anymore."

"You ended things?" Beth asked. "I'd wondered."

Jana nodded. "He came by to try to—" She made air quotes. "Explain. I dumped him. In a way, his coming by clarified a lot of things for me. He was a mistake from the beginning. I was sucked in by a very practiced liar. I'm still working on not blaming myself, and that's tough, but I'm getting better." She looked at her. "Was there anything else?"

Her cool voice, the disinterested question, cut Beth down to her heart.

"I miss you," she whispered. "So much. I regret losing our friendship."

"How much of that is about me, and how much of it is that you lost Teddy, too?"

"It's both. You were someone I cared about. I admire you and what you're doing with your life. You're an inspiration."

Jana grimaced. "Hardly."

"You are. You're a great mom. Linnie is wonderful, and you're so lucky to have her." There were more tears, but Beth ignored them. "I know this can't be fixed. I accept responsibility for my part in that and how I hurt you. I'm desperately sorry."

She paused. "Stupid words, but they're true."

She opened the back door of her car and pulled out the to-go bag, along with an extra-large shopping bag with a wrapped box inside.

"These are for you."

She passed over both. Jana hesitated before taking them.

"I don't understand," the other woman admitted.

"One's dinner because it's Thursday and, well, I know the kids are with Dex and you're probably hungry. The other is a graduation present. I know it's in a few days. Obviously I won't be there, but I'll be thinking of you, and I wanted to say congratulations."

Jana shook her head and held out the shopping bag. "I can't."

"Please take it. I want you to have it." The tears fell faster. "I screwed up, and nothing can change that. But please know that despite my actions, I really was your friend. I wish you and Linnie every happiness. Always."

With that, she turned and got in her car. In the mirror, she saw Jana stayed where she was, watching until Beth turned out of the parking lot. She carefully drove about two blocks, then pulled into a grocery store parking lot and gave in to the sobs. She wasn't sure how long she cried, but after what felt like hours, there was finally nothing left inside. She wiped her face on a tissue, then headed for home.

All the loose ends were tied up. She'd apologized, and now it was time for her to move on. The lessons learned would stay with her always. In the end, she would be a better person. A stronger person. And next time, God willing, she would do much, much better.

"You okay?"

Jana looked up and saw Dex in the hallway. She sat at her built-in desk, Beth's still-wrapped package in front of her.

"I'm fine." She tried to smile and failed. "Are you heading

out?" Because if he was, she would return to the family room to watch the rest of the movie with the kids.

"Not yet." He studied her, then nodded at the box. "A graduation present?"

"I guess. It's from Beth."

Dex pulled up the spare chair and took a seat. "You saw her today?"

"She came by the food bank." She ran her finger along the silver ribbon that encircled the blue wrapping paper. "I wasn't even sure about taking my shift, but then I went."

"Sure." Dex grinned. "Because you'd never miss a shift."

"I wouldn't unless I had an urgent reason. Being uncomfortable because a friend of mine didn't tell me her brother was cheating on me..." She sighed. "Or with me, doesn't count."

She looked at him. "She wasn't there. I saw her when I left. She said she'd changed days so she wouldn't upset me."

"That was thoughtful."

"Are you being funny?"

"Nope. Stating the obvious. It was thoughtful of her to change days."

Jana eyed him suspiciously. "You're taking her side."

"I'm Team Jana."

"Sorry. I'm a little touchy. I'm also confused, faintly nauseous and feeling incredibly stupid because I miss her. Until the whole Rick cheating thing, she was a good friend." She looked at him. "She was so good with Linnie."

He watched her without speaking.

Jana drew in a breath. "She said she was sorry, then she explained how it all happened. I mostly listened. Then she gave me dinner because on Thursday she always brings me dinner." Her voice shook a little. "And she gave me this."

"How was dinner?"

"Good." She managed a smile. "She makes a really excellent sandwich. There's extra if you want some."

"I'm good. We had Thai food." He grinned. "And mochi ice cream."

"You spoil them!"

"It's part of my job." He nodded at the box. "Are you going to open that?"

"I don't know."

"Want me to do it?"

The offer surprised her, then she felt herself relax as she handed over the box. "Yes, please."

He put the box on his lap and reached for the scissors in the caddy on her desk. After cutting the ribbon, he started to tear the paper, then looked at her.

"Are we saving this?"

She smacked his arm. "Of course not. Just open it!"

"You're violent. I think that scares me a little."

"Dex, come on."

He flashed her a smile, then ripped the paper and lifted the top of the box. She gasped when she saw the beautiful leather messenger bag nestled inside.

"It's gorgeous." She picked it up and felt the soft smoothness of the rich brown leather. "It'll be perfect for nursing school."

"I'm thinking that was her point. Well, damn. Now I have to get you something better than the pencil box I was going to buy."

"Yes, you do." She opened the bag and looked inside. There were side pockets and one big zippered one. She stood and slipped the cross-body strap over her head.

"Looks good on you."

"I love it!"

"I'm glad."

She flung herself at him. Dex pulled her close and wrapped his arms around her, even after she started to cry.

"I'm so confused," she admitted.

"You don't have to decide anything now."

"I miss her."

"That's allowed."

"You're not going to tell me I'm wrong?" she asked.

"You're not. You feel how you feel. I respect that."

His gaze was direct, his face familiar. Dex had been a part of her life nearly as long as she could remember. He was so good with the kids and steady and a great friend.

Find someone who is always there for you. Someone you already like and trust.

Teddy's words echoed in her head, surprising her and making her suddenly feel awkward being so close to Dex. She cleared her throat and quickly took a step back. No way, she told herself. He wasn't talking about Dex. He couldn't be. They were friends, nothing more.

"You, ah, sure about that extra sandwich?" she asked, avoiding his gaze.

"I am." He glanced at his watch. "If you're going to be all right by yourself, I'll head home."

"Of course. Thank you. Have a good night."

He nodded and left. She stared after him. No, she told herself. She wasn't interested in Dex, and he wasn't interested in her. Only now that the thought had formed, she had no idea how to make it go away.

25

"This is Rocky. He's going to be your horse for the lesson."

Beth stared up at the very, very tall horse and immediately regretted her decision. She wasn't athletic, nor was she especially coordinated. Riding was for slender young women with British accents. She was pushing forty and had never been a fan of heights.

"Is he okay with that?" she asked, her voice suddenly dry. "Doesn't the wand choose the wizard?"

Bert, her instructor—a small, weathered man who could be anywhere from sixty to ninety-five—grinned at her. "*Harry Potter and the Sorcerer's Stone*. I loved those books. Great movies, too."

He took Rocky by the bridle and eased the horse closer to her. "Say hello. Give him a soft pat on the neck and greet him by name. Horses like that you know who they are."

She swallowed her fear and managed a faint, "Hello, Rocky. Thank you for being my horse today. I'm terrified, and I'd like very much not to fall off."

"It's fine if you do," Bert told her. "He'll just step over you. Rocky's not the trampling sort."

There were horses who were trampling sorts, she thought frantically.

Bert chuckled. "All righty then. Let's get going. First we're going to learn how to saddle Rocky here, then you're going to ride him."

"Or I could just saddle him this time and ride him next time."

"Where's the fun in that?"

"Oh, I'm not here for fun," Beth murmured. But she dutifully followed Bert and Rocky into the barn and prepared to meet her fate.

Jana stood with her row and followed the person next to her down the aisle to stand by the stairs to the stage. There were only about two hundred graduates in her class, so they were holding the ceremony inside the large auditorium. Family and friends filled every chair and clapped loudly as names were called.

Dozens of emotions battled for dominance. Pride, of course. She'd gotten a B+ in calculus, and would graduate with a 3.75 GPA. A heady number for someone who'd started without being sure she could even complete one class. Now she was headed to nursing school. A hard road, but one she was determined to finish. She was ready for the next phase of her life.

But mingling with the pride was a sense of regret for the paths not taken. If she'd gone to college out of high school, her life would have been easier. She would be settled in her career of choice, rather than being two years from barely starting. Only without her mistakes and tangents, she wouldn't have Linnie, and her daughter was a blessing she could never regret.

As Jana moved closer to the stage, she thought about the past few weeks and all the drama she'd endured. A couple of weeks into the breakup, she found she didn't miss Rick at all. Knowing the real man wasn't anyone she would want to be with had gone a long way to healing her. Yes, she felt foolish and taken advantage of, but so what? She'd been authentic—he'd been the one playing games. She regretted ever being sucked in by him, but more than that, she regretted not having Beth in her life. If she had refused to date Rick, then she and Beth could have stayed friends. Eventually Beth would have met Teddy, and the chemistry or connection or whatever they wanted to call the lightning strike that was their relationship would have happened. Without Rick in the middle, they could have still been together.

She started up the stairs, moving to the pace of the names being called. Her family had arrived early enough to be near the front, where they'd all promised to scream as loudly as possible. Jana had to admit she was looking forward to the noise.

"Jana Mead."

As she started toward the center of the stage, she heard her family shouting.

"I love you, Mommy!"

"Way to go!"

"You're rockin' it, Jana."

The last voice was Dex's. He had professional training and could project loud enough to be heard three states over. The familiar sound should have been no big deal, but hearing him gave her a new and unexpected shiver.

The sensation was so surprising, she nearly stumbled. Jana managed to shake hands with the college president and take the diploma cover from her. She crossed the stage as the next name was called and returned to her seat.

Confusion made it impossible to watch the other graduates. She was too busy trying to figure out what had just happened. A shiver? Over Dex? What was that about? Sure, he was a funny, kind and incredibly handsome guy, but that had never mattered to her before. She'd known Dex all her life and had never once thought of him as more than Teddy's BFF and a part of the family. He wasn't anyone she saw as romantic.

Except ever since her brother had told her to find someone she already liked and trusted, she'd been thinking about Dex. She knew her brother would never set her up to be humiliated, which maybe meant that he knew something about how Dex felt about her. But Dex had never once hinted he had feelings, so maybe she was wrong about the whole thing. Only Dex was kind of the one guy in her life who wasn't Teddy.

When the graduation ceremony wrapped up, she was no closer to an answer than she had been before. She made her way through the crowd to where her family and Dex waited. They all raced toward her and hugged her.

"You did great," her brother told her while Linnie danced in place.

"I saw you, Mommy. Did you hear me?"

"I did. You were very loud. It was great!" Jana turned to Dex. "I heard you yelling, too."

He winked. "I'll always yell for you."

An easy, casual statement that shouldn't have meant anything, nor did it. Not exactly.

They drove back to the house. The late-afternoon graduation was to be followed by a barbecue. Jana was surprised to find a pile of presents waiting on the kitchen table.

"What's all this?" she asked. "You didn't have to do this."

"We wanted to," Magnolia told her. "Milestones need to be celebrated."

They all gathered around the table and watched as she opened her gifts. There was a beautiful gold heart necklace with her name and Linnie's engraved on it. Her daughter climbed in her lap as she put it on.

"That's you and me," Linnie told her.

Jana's heart squeezed tight from all the love. "It is us, isn't it?" She looked at her brother. "Thank you."

"Wasn't me," he said with a grin. "Your daughter picked it out."

Teddy and his kids gave her a folding laptop table for her bed, a bedside shelf that tucked between the mattress and box spring, and a fluffy robe.

"For all the homework," Atlas said. "Dad told us you'd have even more than you have now. So you can study in bed, then take a nap and study some more."

"Very thoughtful. Thank you."

She hugged all three children, then turned to what was obviously a couple of bottles of wine. The label had been customized to read, "Pairs well with graduation." There was a bottle of red and a bottle of white.

"Those will be fun," she told her brother. "Thank you."

"I expect you to share."

"I'm happy to."

The last gift was from Dex. Jana fumbled a little as she tore the wrapping paper on the six-by-nine-inch box. When she opened it, she found a card.

"Good for one spa weekend away, including treatments, meals and drinks. Take a girlfriend. Babysitting included." Underneath was a slender brochure for a very exclusive spa up in Santa Barbara.

She'd never been to the spa but knew the name, of course. It was the kind of place the rich and famous went to, with fancy skin treatments and gourmet food.

"You can't give me this," she told Dex. "It's too much."

"I want you to have it."

"But…"

He shook his head. "Be gracious and say thank you."

"Thank you," she breathed, not sure what the generous gift meant. Was he celebrating the moment or sending her a message?

She supposed the only way to find out was to ask, although she should probably wait for a more private moment.

Magnolia took charge, telling the younger kids to clean up while she started setting the outside table. Teddy collected the food, including the burgers he would barbecue. Dex opened a bottle of champagne and another of sparkling apple cider. Very fancy plastic champagne flutes were put on the table.

"I'm feeling quite special," Jana told everyone. "Can we do this every day?"

Linnie hugged her. "We can if that's what you want, Mommy."

"You're a sweet girl."

Jana got out the Bluetooth speakers and hooked up the music system. The kids went off to play. Dex followed to do his pushing duty on the swings. She walked over to where Teddy was heating the grill.

"Thank you," she told him. "The party is great."

He hugged her. "Congratulations. You worked hard for this. We're all proud."

She studied him, taking in the hint of sadness in his eyes. While she knew she wasn't responsible for what had happened, she couldn't help feeling guilty.

She'd already told him about Beth's apology, so she didn't bother mentioning that. Instead she said, "She never tried to ask me about you. When we spoke? She could have tried to play on my sympathies."

"I'm ignoring you," he said as he walked back into the kitchen.

"And I'm following you." She grabbed his arm, forcing him to a stop. "Teddy, come on. Why are you being so stubborn? In her position, you would have done the same thing."

He stared past her, neither denying nor agreeing. "She hurt you."

"Rick hurt me. Rick was the jerk. Beth was the sister who loved her brother."

"She made a choice."

"Given the circumstances, it wasn't the wrong one."

He glanced at her. "You've forgiven her?"

"I think I have to. I miss my friend." She touched his arm. "If you and I weren't so tight, it might be harder for me to understand, but I would do anything for you, so I get what she was up against. She was just as misled as I was. She wasn't mean or deliberately cruel. She was trapped."

She wished she could shake him and make him see. "You're in love with her, Teddy. And you're the kind of man who doesn't unlove very easily. I appreciate that you've been so supportive, but it's time to think about whether or not you want to be happy for the rest of your life."

He shook his head. "We're done."

"You're a fool."

He shrugged. "Maybe, but this is how it has to be."

Later, after dinner, when the kids were gathered around the fire pit with their dad, Jana and Dex cleared the table and loaded the dishwasher.

"I don't get it," she said when they were done and she'd filled him in on her conversation with her brother. "I know he's hurting. Why is he so stubborn?"

"It's his nature. He's loyal, and Beth betrayed his trust, something he never thought could happen. He can't just get over that."

"But they love each other, and he won't forgive her and move on."

Dex watched her. "You obviously have."

"I miss her, and I want her to be my friend again."

"Do you trust her?" he asked.

A question that required a moment of thought. What Beth had done was wrong, and Jana had been on the receiving end of the pain. And yet...

"I understand why she did what she did. She's sorry for what happened." She looked at Dex. "I'm over him and I'll be fine, but Beth lost her brother."

"She didn't lose him. He was never what she thought. The difference is, now she knows that."

"Which puts her in a worse position."

Jana thought about all the questions she had about Dex and what her brother had said, then tried to figure out how to ask if he had feelings for her. If only there was an easy way to slide into that particular topic.

"What?" he asked. "You have the strangest look on your face."

She opened her mouth, then closed it, hoping for some kind of inspiration. The only thing that occurred to her was the truth.

"Are you in love with me?"

Despite how some people dismissed Dex as simply a brainless action hero, he was actually a gifted actor. In that moment, as silence filled the room, nothing about him changed, and she had no idea what he was thinking. That realization was followed by the horrific thought that maybe she'd gotten it all completely wrong, and he only ever thought of her as Teddy's baby sister.

"Yes."

Wait, what? She blinked. "You're in love with me."

His dark gaze locked with hers. "Yes."

"You never said anything. I don't understand. When did this happen?"

One corner of his mouth turned up. "I wasn't thinking I should send an announcement."

"Why not? It would have been helpful."

"Because you don't see me that way."

He had a point there, she thought. At least, she never had before.

"As to the when, it was when you came back pregnant with Linnie. I took one look at you and knew."

Her mouth dropped open. She consciously closed it. "But that was five years ago."

His expression turned rueful. "Tell me about it."

"But you could have hinted or flirted."

"I was giving you time to settle into being a new mom. Then you got busy with school. Just when I was about to say something, you started dating Paul."

Ugh. And that had gone on for months. "After that I swore off men," she said, more to herself than him. "And then there was Rick."

"No offense, but you have horrible taste in men."

"I know."

Dex was in love with her. Dex. She was going to have to take a minute and think that through. She'd thought maybe he would say he liked her or had wondered about them dating. But love was a whole different thing.

"I'm going to need a moment," she told him.

"No problem. Take all the time you want. I'm used to waiting for you."

Jana sat in her car outside the urgent care center. This was the third time she'd driven over and parked. Previously she'd ended up driving away without going inside, but today she was determined to actually speak to Galaxy.

She'd gone around and around, trying to figure out the right thing to do. She didn't want to be vindictive. Instead she wanted to give the other woman information. If the situation were reversed, she would want Galaxy to come see her and tell her the truth about the man she was in love with.

She grabbed her bag and got out of her car, then walked inside and went to the reception desk. She smiled at the young man standing there.

"Hi. Is Galaxy working today? I need to speak to her. It's personal, by the way. My name is Jana Mead."

He frowned. "She is. Are you a friend?"

"I know her boyfriend and his sister." Jana kept her body language open, her expression relaxed. She didn't want to come across as scary or make anyone think she was going to be a problem.

"Okay. Let me see if she's available. You're Jenny?"

"Jana."

"Oh, right." He pointed to the waiting area. "Have a seat."

Jana did as he'd requested. About two minutes later, he was back at his station.

"She'll be right out."

"Thank you."

Suddenly, what had seemed to make sense when she was safely in her car had her doubting herself and her stomach writhing. None of this was her business, she thought. She wasn't responsible for Galaxy or her relationship with Rick. Only before she could leave, a tall, stunning redhead in dark green scrubs walked into the reception area. The guy at the desk pointed at Jana.

"I'm Galaxy," the green-eyed beauty said, sounding confused. "Can I help you?"

Jana rose. "Is there somewhere we can talk?"

Galaxy led her into one of the treatment rooms. She shut the door and faced her. "What's going on?"

Jana swallowed against nerves and ignored the need to run for her car. She cleared her throat and then offered what she hoped was a reassuring smile.

"My name is Jana. I'm friends with Beth and I, ah, know Rick." She paused, searching for a way to make herself believable. "What Beth can do with a sandwich is practically an art form."

Galaxy relaxed a little. "She's very talented."

"I work in medical billing. Rick's surgical practice is in that building, too."

"Yes, he has two locations. Look, I have to get back to work. Can you get to the point?"

Oh, God. Jana sucked in a breath. "Three months ago, he asked me out, and I said yes. We were dating until about four weeks ago." She pulled her phone out of her bag and unlocked her photographs. "That weekend you went out of town, he and I went away."

Galaxy took a step back, then another. Her eyes were big, her skin pale. She started shaking her head. "No. You're lying. I don't know what sick game this is, but no. He's not dating you. I see him all the time. We've been together ten months. We're in love."

Jana showed her the phone with the selfie of her and Rick out by the hotel room's fire pit. She scrolled through several more.

"I didn't know," Jana told her flatly. "I don't date men involved with other women. He lied about everything."

Galaxy stared at the phone. She continued to shake her head. "It can't be true. He loves me."

Jana thought about saying she didn't think Rick was capable of loving anyone, then decided there was no point in that. Galaxy wouldn't believe her.

"I know how I felt when I found out the truth," she said instead. "I thought you'd want to know what had happened. If you didn't, then I'm sorry."

She put her phone in her bag, stepped around Galaxy and left.

26

Beth shifted gingerly on her desk chair in her small office. She'd just had her fourth lesson with Bert and Rocky, and she was as sore as she'd been the first time. Horseback riding used a set of muscles that weren't happy about the activity, and wow, did they complain. If she didn't want to spend the rest of her life whimpering, she obviously needed to start working out regularly. Maybe yoga or Pilates would help, she thought, making a mental note to find a class somewhere nearby.

She completed her soda order and clicked the send button on the website. Business was brisk, which helped. At least her work life was in order.

As for the rest of it, well, she was getting by. In the four weeks since everything had fallen apart, she'd made some progress. She hadn't seen or spoken to her brother. So far she was fine with that. Agatha had been supportive and loving, always ready to listen. Beth was enjoying the horseback riding, and while it was tough to work at the food bank on a different day and not see Jana, she knew it was the right thing to do.

As for Teddy, well, there still weren't words to describe her pain. She ached for him in ways she wouldn't have thought possible. It wasn't just that she missed him—it was losing out on the promise of what they could have been to each other. While the thought of being a stepmother terrified her, she knew that she'd been willing to give it her all. She missed Magnolia, Atlas and Orchid. And Linnie. Always Linnie.

She drew in a breath and deliberately pushed the sad thoughts away. She'd been doing a lot of reading online about dealing with grief and healing from pain caused by a family member. One of the most helpful suggestions had been to schedule time to feel angry or sad or betrayed. Just twenty minutes a day, at a specific time.

At first she'd been skeptical, but she'd discovered the practice really helped. For her, the window was when she got home from work. She went into her room and did some deep breathing. After that, she had twenty minutes to wrestle with her less positive emotions. During the day, when she found herself wanting to dwell on how her life had gone to shit, she reminded herself that doing that was already on her calendar. Pushing aside the feelings the rest of time was getting easier, and she was feeling lighter and more able to cope.

"Hello, Beth."

She looked up and was stunned to see Jana standing in the doorway to her office. Beth rose.

"Hi. You're here."

A neutral statement when what she really wanted to ask was, "Are you here to yell at me?" Because Jana never had, and it was something Beth figured she deserved. Not that she could tell what Jana was thinking. While she didn't look angry, she wasn't exactly smiling, either.

"Last time you did all the talking," the other woman said. "I figured it was my turn."

That didn't sound good, but Beth nodded and motioned to the chair opposite.

"I very much want to listen." She'd earned whatever Jana wanted to tell her.

But instead of approaching the desk, Jana stayed where she was. "I only have one forgiveness left in me. For what happened, I mean. Not for the rest of my life."

Beth didn't know what that meant, so she stayed quiet.

Jana met her gaze. "It's yours if you want it."

"The forgiveness? You're going to forgive me?" She spoke the words without being able to feel them. Shock immobilized her.

"I miss you," Jana said simply. "I miss us being friends."

Suddenly Beth was up on her feet and racing across the small room. She reached for her friend just as Jana surged forward. They hugged each other, squeezing hard. Deep inside Beth's chest, some of the heavy, cold sadness melted, leaving her feeling lighter and warmer.

"I'm sorry," Beth said when they'd separated. "I'm so sorry about what happened and what I did. Or rather what I didn't."

"No," Jana told her firmly. "No more apologizing. You've already done that. I understand why you did what you did. If it had been Teddy, I would have kept his secret. It was a sucky situation, and now it's behind us."

Once again Jana impressed her. "I don't think I could have been so gracious."

"Oh, I think you would have done way better than me. But I got here." She pointed to the door. "Can you take a half hour or so? I thought we could walk over to the beach and catch up."

"I'd love that."

Beth let Kai know she would be gone for a bit. She and

Jana each took a bottle of sparkling water, and they walked out into the warm, sunny day. Once they crossed the highway, they walked onto the sand. In front of them, the Pacific Ocean stretched out to the horizon. The water was a deep blue. The tide was out, and the wide stretch of damp sand made her feel as if they could walk for miles without touching the water.

Once they were settled facing the waves, they opened their drinks, then touched bottles.

"So what's new?" Beth asked.

Jana laughed. "Oh, you know. The usual. How are you doing?"

Beth suspected her friend was asking about both Rick and Teddy.

"I haven't talked to my brother in nearly a month," she said. "I don't know when I'll hear from him." Or if, but she didn't go there.

"I'm sorry."

"Don't be. Our last conversation was awful. He's not who I thought. I keep remembering the little boy, but the man is very different." She smiled at Jana. "Agatha wanted me to start journaling. She gave me a whole kit. Apparently it helped her after my uncle died. I did try for an entire week, and journaling is so not my thing. But she mentioned telling the story of Rick and me. So I've been writing out as much as I can remember, starting when Agatha and Dale rescued us from foster care."

"That's ambitious. How's it going?"

"Slow." Beth grimaced as she thought of how she tried to write a couple of pages every day. "He said a lot of terrible things to me that I either forgot or didn't want to remember. I'm not sure which. At the time I thought he was being pragmatic and protective, telling me I couldn't make it in college and trying would be a waste of time. He changed, and I have to accept that."

Jana's expression turned sympathetic. "I'm sorry you're dealing with that."

"It's okay, because I *am* dealing. I know that ignoring what

I've learned will only hurt me." She looked at her friend. "At first I thought I'd lost him, but now I understand that he was already gone. I'm seeing the truth."

"He's still family."

"Yes, but he's not anyone who cares about me. I deserve people who love me and support me in my life. If he's not going to be that, then I'm better off with him gone."

Jana nodded. "The words sound good. Do you believe them?"

"Mostly. I have my weak moments when I miss him—or at least the him I thought he was."

"And Teddy?"

The softly asked question still stabbed her in the heart. She looked out at the ocean, wanting the timelessness of the waves to remind her that life went on. People healed and had lives that were relatively happy, even when they'd lost the one man they would love more than anyone.

"I miss him with every breath," she said simply.

"I know, and I want to fix it. I don't know how."

Beth turned to her. "You can't, and what happened isn't about you or your fault. I know that. There's nothing to fix." She paused to gather a little courage. "I'm in love with him." She held up her hand. "Don't say anything. I just wanted you to know because he's your brother, and you might worry that I have a little Rick in me. Maybe I do, I don't know. I hope not. But when it came to Teddy, there was only good."

She swallowed against the tightness in her chest. "So I've said it, and now we're never going to speak of him again." She wrinkled her nose. "I take that back. We're going to talk about him because he's your brother and stuff will come up. Regular 'hey, we played volleyball this weekend,' or whatever. I don't want you to think you can't say his name. It'll be awkward at first, then it will get better."

She squeezed Jana's hand. "I want it to get better."

"Me, too."

"So, what's new with you?" Beth asked, ready to stop talking about herself.

"I went and saw Galaxy today."

Beth stared at her friend. "Holy crap. Seriously? You went and saw her? As in, 'Hi, I'm the ex'?" She frowned. "*Ex* is wrong. This is so complicated. We need new words to describe it all."

Jana nodded. "We do. I'd been thinking about going to see her, but wasn't sure if it was the right thing or not. If it was me, I'd want to know my boyfriend was cheating."

"I would, too." But Beth wasn't sure she would have had the courage to confront Galaxy. "What did you say?"

"I told her what had happened with Rick and showed her some selfies, and then I left."

"Wow." Beth couldn't imagine any of that had been comfortable. "I wonder what she's going to do with the information." While her interactions with Galaxy had been brief, the other woman had been very sweet and genuine. She deserved someone who treated her better.

"I do, too," Jana admitted. "If you hear anything, please tell me."

"I will."

Her friend looked at her. "I also want you to change back to Thursday at the food bank. It's not the same without you."

Beth smiled. "I promise I'll do that today."

"Good. I want us to be hanging out again. Maybe we could do something with Linnie."

Beth nodded. "I'd like that a lot. I'm taking horseback riding lessons."

"What?" Jana laughed. "That's so great. How's it going?"

"Good. I ride a horse named Rocky. He's huge, but very gentle. He's patient with me, which I appreciate. Linnie might like learning to ride."

"She absolutely would. I'm the one who's too terrified. How about if we just hang out here on the beach instead?"

Beth made a clucking sound.

"Yes, I am a chicken, and proud of it." Jana glanced at her. "So, there's Dex news."

"He's been secretly dating Taylor Swift for a year and they're getting married?"

Instead of laughing, Jana looked away. "Not exactly. It turns out he's in love with me."

"What?" Beth narrowed her gaze. "You didn't want to lead with that bit of news?" She tried to grasp the concept. "He's in love with you? Since when? And how did you find out?"

"After the Rick thing, I told Teddy I was done with dating. Every guy I picked was bad." Jana groaned. "Jeez, I just said both their names in a sentence. I'm sorry."

While Beth wanted to take a second and sink into her Teddy sadness, she knew that for her and Jana to regain their friendship, she had to be able to talk about the man without reacting.

"No apologies," she said quickly. "It's totally fine."

"It's not. You practically flinched."

"Maybe, but I'm going to get better, so let's pretend that didn't happen." She shifted on the sand so she was facing her friend. "Tell me everything."

Jana explained about how her brother had told her to find someone she trusted who already cared about her.

"I had no idea what he meant. The only guy we have in common is Dex. But he's never once hinted we're anything but friends."

"I never saw anything," Beth admitted. "But he would be really good at hiding his feelings."

Jana stared at her. "The barbecue at our house. When it was all of us—you, Rick, me, Teddy, Dex and the kids."

"I remember the afternoon. Did something happen? I was so nervous about meeting Teddy's three that I wouldn't have noticed a meteor falling to earth."

"Oh, I'm pretty sure you would have remembered that." Jana

leaned forward. "It was Rick. He told me there was something going on with Dex. Or rather that Dex had a thing for me."

"Rick saw it?" Beth couldn't imagine her brother being that perceptive. Of course, he'd fooled nearly everyone into thinking he was someone different, so maybe he was better at seeing that in another person.

"I told him he was wrong," Jana admitted. "As far as I knew, Dex saw me as Teddy's sister and no one else."

"But it's way more than that. Since when?"

Jana ducked her head. "Since I came home pregnant."

"Five years?" Beth's voice was a shriek. She lowered the volume and the pitch. "Five years? What has he been waiting for?"

"Me to adjust to being a mom. Then I met Paul, who turned out to be a disaster."

"That is not your fault."

"I seem to make a habit of falling for guys who aren't exactly who they claim."

"Then you should stop that."

"It's the plan."

Beth was still trying to wrap her mind around the fact that Dex was in love with Jana.

"Now what?" she asked. "Do you want to go out with him?"

Jana squirmed a little. "Yes, maybe. I don't know. I have to totally change how I see him. He's a great person. I've known him forever, and I trust him completely."

"Is it the sex thing? Or even just kissing? Because if there's no chemistry, then it's not going to work, no matter how hot he is."

Jana grinned. "I'm getting the odd tingle. But I want to give it time. I want to be sure. I think we both deserve that."

"You do. You're being really smart about all this. Did you tell him you need time?"

Jana nodded. "He says he's going to wait."

"That's romantic. I hope it works out."

"Me, too."

Beth reached out and grabbed her hand. "Thank you for forgiving me. I've missed you so much."

"I've missed you more. Let's never fight again."

"Pinky swear," Beth said. "Then it's for sure."

27

Summer sped by. Jana worked an extra few hours a week to pad her savings account. By mid-August she was training her replacement and looking forward to her classes starting. She and Beth had decided that swimming lessons were more Jana and Linnie's speed than horseback riding, and the three of them had signed up for classes at a local swim club. Her second week in the pool, Linnie had announced she was going to be an Olympic swimmer, which would have been funny if the instructor hadn't mentioned the four-year-old seemed to have talent.

But getting serious about the sport was several years off. For now, they were simply learning about water safety and mastering different strokes.

Jana had never heard from Rick again, nor did she know what had happened with Galaxy. Beth had recently mentioned she hadn't heard from her brother, which made Jana sad. She wished the two of them could have been as close as her and Teddy. But Beth was working hard to deal with her disappointment. Writing about her childhood with her brother and how he'd become someone else had started to morph into an actual story. In addition to the horseback riding and the swim lessons, Beth had signed up for a novel writing class. She was keeping busy, but Jana knew her friend still missed Teddy.

She crossed the yard and went through the gate in the back fence on her way to Teddy's studio. The modest bungalow contained two treatment rooms, a waiting area, a bathroom with a shower, his office and a small kitchenette. There was also parking for several cars off the quiet residential street.

She let herself in and called out a greeting, then walked to her brother's office.

"I'm heading out with the kids," she said, then pulled a piece of paper out of her back pocket. "I have the lists."

She'd offered to do the back-to-school shopping. Teddy had many wonderful qualities, but enjoying time at a mall wasn't one of them.

"You sure about this?" he asked. "I can do it later."

She sat down in one of the visitor chairs. "I don't mind. They're really good about it. Plus I plan to take advantage of Magnolia's bossy side. Linnie is practically frantic with excitement about starting school. I'm not sure I'd be able to keep her focused on my own."

Teddy grinned. "Magnolia does have mad skills. You'll take the Suburban?"

She groaned. "Yes, I will drive the world's largest vehicle so there's room for everyone and all the packages." She didn't like borrowing Teddy's car, but sometimes it made sense.

She got up to leave, then sank back down and stared at her brother.

"You're being stupid," she announced. "You're still missing

Beth, and I know she's still missing you. I'm the one who was hurt, and I've long forgiven her. You should, too."

His gaze was steady. "We agreed not to talk about this."

"No, we didn't. You said *you* didn't want to talk about it anymore, but I never agreed." She pointed at him. "You're still in love with her. It's been over two months. You've punished her enough. Now it's time to go be with her and do the happy thing."

"No."

"Why? You're so stubborn. It's ridiculous. You're wasting your life when everything you want is right there in front of you. Or it would be in front of you if you'd go see her. Eventually you're going to figure out she's exactly who you should be with, and you will have blown it."

"I could say the same about you."

Jana glared at him. "We're not talking about me."

"Why not? To quote someone in this room, it's been two months. It's time for you to do the happy thing."

"My relationship with Dex is different. I'm trying to figure out how I feel about him."

Teddy studied her before saying, "If you don't know how you feel by now, maybe that's the answer."

"You're changing the subject."

"I am."

"Fine." She stood. "You're making a huge mistake, Teddy. Beth's great, and it's not going to take very long for someone else to figure that out."

She left before he could say anything and made her way through the gate and backyard. Once she was inside, she paused, then pulled her phone out of her pocket. Because it was possible her brother had a point.

I'm taking the kids shopping for back-to-school clothes, and I know how much you love the mall. Want to join us?

She sent the text before she could talk herself out of it, then went to collect everyone. Seconds later, her phone vibrated with an incoming text.

I'll be there in five.

Three hours and hundreds of dollars later, the shopping was done. All four kids had new shoes, jeans, shirts and underwear, along with hoodies and light jackets. In their part of the world, fall and winter weren't actually cold, although there was a slight chance that it could rain once or twice.

Magnolia had wanted a couple of dresses she could wear to school, but Orchid and Linnie hadn't been interested. A dress might limit their playground activities. Through it all, Dex was a calming force. He'd intervened when the backpack discussion threatened to become heated. He'd helped Atlas pick out the coolest shirts and T-shirts so he would fit in and not have to worry about wearing clothes that looked like they'd been picked out by his aunt. And when everyone had gotten tired and cranky, he'd steered them all to the food court, where they'd split up to buy snacks ranging from pretzels to fried rice to wings and french fries.

Jana found herself both participating in all that was happening and observing it. Despite his declaration at the beginning of summer, she and Dex were still comfortable together, hanging out as they always did. He didn't try to put his arm around her or kiss her, nor did he make pointed comments to hurry along her decision. He was as easy to be with as ever, but with an added element of attraction.

She was aware of him, of how he moved and the way his sexy smile made her insides quiver. Even more important, when he swept up Linnie and set her on his shoulders, she could imagine what it would be like if she and Dex were a lot more than friends. He was someone she could trust with her heart, but more important, she could trust him with her daughter.

Teddy had been right—it was time to make a decision.

She put down the pretzel she'd been nibbling on and wiped her fingers on a napkin.

"Magnolia, can you take charge of everyone for a second? I need to talk to Dex about something."

"Sure." Teddy's oldest barely glanced up from her wings.

Jana turned her attention to Dex, who was watching her with a completely neutral expression. She stood.

"Come on."

He dutifully got up and walked with her.

"We going to knock over a liquor store?" he asked conversationally.

"No."

"Because if we are, I need to let Teddy know he has to pick up the kids."

"Very funny."

"I can be."

She walked to the far end of the food court, then stepped behind a very large pillar. One big enough to conceal them from child-size prying eyes. When they were hidden from view, she stopped and faced Dex.

"You should kiss me."

One eyebrow rose. "Should I?"

"Yes. What if there's no chemistry? That might be a dealbreaker for you."

"I'm not worried about the chemistry."

"Don't you want to be sure?"

"No, but I do want to kiss you."

Before she could respond to that, he stepped close and cupped her face in his large hands, then lowered his mouth to hers.

The second their lips touched, she felt all the air rush out of her. Sparks exploded, and her thighs started to shake. She instinctively leaned in, wrapping her arms around him. He dropped his hands to her waist and pulled her hard against him. The kiss went from family friendly to X-rated in five seconds. Two heartbeats after that, Dex pulled back.

"Not in public," he muttered, staring at her. "Still worried about the chemistry?"

She shook her head, even as she tried to understand the feelings surging through her. Not only had she never felt anything like it, she'd also never felt the sureness that came with whatever that had been. Was this the knowing that Teddy had talked about?

"I thought I'd come over for dinner tonight," she said softly.

"That would be good. Dinner." Although the heat in his eyes made her think there might be less time spent in the dining room than one would expect.

"I'll bring Linnie next time, but not tonight."

"Probably for the best."

They stared at each other for another few seconds, then Dex put his arm around her. "We need to get back to the kids."

"We do."

He smiled at her. "We're going to be great together."

"Yes, we are."

Beth stared at the "Great job! Every week you get better and better" scrawled across the top of her title page. There were also glowing margin notes, along with a few corrections of grammar and suggestions to extend the conversation between Mandy and her mother. Mandy being the fictional heroine of the book Beth was writing.

She smiled. Not only was she constantly amazed she was actually trying to write a book, but judging from all the feedback her instructor had given her, it was going well. Her!

She glanced over at Kai, who sat at the desk next to hers, looking equally stunned. Surprisingly, when he'd found out she was going to be taking a writing class at UCLA Extension, he'd wanted to go with her. Kai, it turned out, wanted to write a spy novel where the heroes were surfers, which allowed them to travel all over the world. The kid had depths.

Their instructor—a part-time screenwriter and full-time psychologist—was pushing seventy and old-school. Assignments were turned in on paper because he claimed he was of a generation that "thought with a pen in their hand." At first Kai had balked, claiming he didn't even own a printer. But after seeing the positive feedback in written form, he'd been excited to join the 1990s. For Beth, she had to admit there was something satisfying about handing in actual papers and then getting them dropped on her desk during the next class.

"Setting as character," Dr. Previn said from the front of the class. "That's our next topic. It's a reading-heavy week. I get that. Do the best you can. Your assignment is to pick a scene to rewrite with the idea of setting as character. I want to see anywhere between three and seven pages from you, and I want both the original version and the new and improved version."

He smiled at the class. "You're all doing so well. Congratulations. I'll see you next week."

Beth collected her things and nearly floated out of class. The praise from her instructor always carried her through the times when she stared at her computer screen with no idea what to do next. Dr. Previn thought she was a natural born storyteller with a readable style. The two weeks they'd spent on plotting had totally rocked her world. She'd started the class with the idea of turning her growing up with Rick into a book, but had quickly realized that real life doesn't plot well. In a matter of days she'd decided to change everything around and was now writing a coming-of-age story focused fully on Mandy and the trials of dealing with her action junkie mother. As of this version, the brother didn't even exist.

Perhaps a metaphor for her actual life, Beth thought with both

sadness and resignation. The summer was nearly over, and she
hadn't once heard from her brother. Not that she'd reached out
to him. Agatha had counseled her to give herself time to figure
out what she ultimately wanted. She supposed that at some point
she would want to know that he was all right—even if whatever
faux closeness she thought they had would never exist again.
She didn't want him in her life on a regular basis—not when she
couldn't trust him to act like a decent, caring person. But cutting
him off completely didn't seem right, either. Which meant listening to Agatha made the most sense. Time would provide clarity.

She and Kai walked to her car. They drove to class together
and split the cost of parking. Sometimes they went a little early
and grabbed dinner at one of the food trucks parked on cam-
pus. They talked about their writing and the weekly lessons.
While she'd always liked Kai, their shared interest had added a
nice dimension to their friendship. He was, in a way, like the
younger brother she could trust. She would guess she was very
much an older sister for him. She knew that he was still estranged from his family.

"Did you see the schedule for next session?" he asked as she
headed west on I-10. When it ended in Santa Monica, she would
drive north to Malibu. Not the most direct route, but they both
liked being near the ocean.

"Yes. I want to take Dr. Previn's next class." Which was a
continuation of his beginning writing series.

"Me, too. I'm learning so much."

"And going to college," she teased. "You were opposed."

"It's not the same."

"Do you ever think about reaching out to your parents?"
she asked. "And we don't have to talk about them if you don't
want to."

"I think about it," he admitted. "But I'm not sure what to
say. They're the ones who threw me out. Shouldn't they reach

out first?" He paused, then sighed. "Every couple of months I get a Zelle deposit from my mom."

"She's sending you money?"

"Uh-huh." He looked at her. "It's not a lot, but maybe that's not the point."

"It isn't. That's her connecting with you. Kai, it means something. You should at least say thank you."

"I do, but she never answers my texts."

Hearing that made Beth's heart ache. What was his mother thinking? Kai was an amazing young man. Where was the win in not speaking to him? He was her son, and Beth knew eventually the other woman was going to see what had been lost.

"I'm sorry," she said softly. "One day she's going to regret that. We can undo a lot of damage, but we can never get back time."

"What about the time you're wasting?" he asked in an obvious attempt to change the subject. "You haven't tried to contact Teddy."

"Nor am I going to," she said, ignoring the automatic ache that occurred whenever she thought of him. "He made his feelings clear. I hurt him and I regret that. The least I can do to make things right is leave the man alone." Jana had forgiven her. She was grateful for that.

"But you're in love with him."

"I am. Even knowing how it ends, I would still want to be with him for the time we had. It was magical."

Even more important, she now knew what love really felt like. Should she ever get involved again—something that seemed very unlikely, because she would be measuring every man she met against the standard that was Teddy—she knew how she was supposed to feel when she was with him. Anything less wasn't going to be worth the effort.

She drove back to the store and pulled up next to Kai's car.

"See you tomorrow," she said as he got out.

"I'll be on time."

"You always are."

She waved and drove home. As she pulled into the drive-way, she saw a familiar Suburban parked at the curb. Her breath caught as her heart pounded in her chest. She only knew one person who drove a Suburban.

Even as she wondered what he was doing here, she told herself the person waiting inside wasn't Teddy. Jana could have borrowed his car and dropped by. Only Jana knew that tonight was her writing class, and she would have texted first.

She grabbed her backpack and hurried to the front door, only to hesitate before opening it. She'd been up since six that morning, had worked all day and had gone to class from the store. She was still wearing her stupid Surf Sandwiches T-shirt over jeans. Not exactly the glamorous look she'd been hoping for should she ever run into Teddy again. Of course, she wasn't exactly the glamorous type, so there was that.

The front door opened, and Agatha grabbed her arm to pull her inside.

"What's taking you so long?" she asked in a low voice. "Teddy's here. He showed up about fifteen minutes ago. He knew you were at your writing class and asked if he could wait to talk to you. I've been doing my best to entertain him, but it's difficult when half of me wants to hit him upside the head with a blunt object and the other half wants to ask his intentions."

Her stomach flipped over a few times, while her chest got a weird floaty hopeful feeling. Teddy wouldn't show up to yell at her. Their relationship was over. As far as her and Jana being friends—he shouldn't have any complaints there.

She dropped her backpack on the floor, smoothed the front of her bright yellow T-shirt and turned toward the family room. When she hesitated, Agatha gave her a not-so-gentle push.

"I'll be in my room," her aunt whispered. "With the door closed and the TV on. I won't hear a thing."

Beth braced herself for impact, then moved into the family

room. Teddy stood by the sliding glass door, staring out into the darkness.

Even from the back, he looked good. Tall and broad-shouldered. His hair was a little long, and she thought he might have lost weight, but otherwise, he was exactly as she remembered.

In the second before she spoke, she thought how much it hurt to look at him and how great it was to be in the same room with him. She'd been so busy trying to heal from learning the truth about her brother that she'd kind of forgotten to fall out of love with Teddy.

"Hi," she managed.

He turned to face her. "Beth!"

He took a step toward her, stopped, then moved again, walking right up to her, putting his hands on her shoulders and kissing her.

The second his mouth touched hers, emotions exploded inside of her. Not just wanting, because that was a given, but so much more. Longing and love, hope and relief, and a thousand other joyous feelings she couldn't name.

He kissed her with a fierce desperation that spoke of loneliness and regret, along with forgiveness.

"I'm sorry," he said when he drew back. "I'm sorry. I've been a complete ass."

"You haven't. I hurt you and Jana. I was so wrong. I'm sorry for what I did."

He shook his head. "I should have talked to you. I should have been willing to listen and understand. Instead I reacted. I was shocked to think you would keep a secret from me." He pulled her close and hung on. "Rick's your brother. You had to protect him the same way I'd protect Jana."

While she never wanted him to let go, she knew they had to get everything said. She reluctantly drew back.

"Rick isn't who I thought. I didn't see it until the whole Galaxy situation. Knowing what I know now, I would have acted differently, but I didn't have all the information."

"I know." He cupped her face in his hands and stared into her eyes. "I've only loved two women in my life. With Valonia, everything was easy." He smiled. "Life is a little more complicated now. I have kids, you have to deal with what Rick did. I guess I expected perfection, and that's unrealistic."

Her mind was still caught back on "I've only loved two women."

"You love me?" she asked, her voice a whisper. Her heart pounded hard in her ears as she waited breathlessly for his answer.

"Yes. I love you, Beth." He grimaced. "I realized I screwed up everything by taking so long to admit it. I've felt righteous in my anger. It's taken me a while to figure out that I've actually been afraid because it turns out, you can hurt me."

He dropped his hands to his sides and gave her a rueful smile. "I didn't know you could. I didn't know Valonia could. We fought, but nothing like this ever happened. Like I said—life is more complicated now. It's taken a while, but I've figured out that pride is lonely and that being without you is the worst feeling in the world. Can you forgive me?"

What? He was asking if she could forgive *him*?

She flung herself at him. "I can. I do. I love you, Teddy. You're the man of my dreams, the one I've been waiting for."

"What about that other guy you've been seeing?"

She pushed away and stared at him. "What are you talking about? There's no other guy!"

His mouth twitched as if he were holding in a smile. "Oh, I don't know. I hear you have a real thing for a guy named Rocky."

She laughed. "Yes, I'm taking horseback riding lessons, and Rocky is my horse boyfriend."

"The kids would enjoy horseback riding lessons," he said softly. "If that's something you'd like to share with them."

"I would love it."

She stepped back into his embrace. The cracks in her heart had miraculously healed. Not just because Teddy had come back but because in the past few months, she'd started to find herself.

He held her close. "I love you so much."

"I know the feeling."

They stared at each other. She smiled.

"So, do you have to hurry home?" she asked.

"Not really. Jana and Dex are with the kids tonight. I'm actually free until morning."

"Better and better." She took his hand in hers and started down the hall. "I'm free until morning, too."

He followed her into her bedroom, then shut the door behind them and drew her close.

"I love it when a plan comes together."

"Me, too."

★ ★ ★ ★ ★

Beach Vibes

READER DISCUSSION GUIDE

Book Club
Menu Suggestion

An assortment of sandwiches, of course! You could even let your book club try peanut-butter-and-breakfast-cereal sandwiches, with a variety of cereal options on hand. Pickles optional.

Or if you want to offer a slightly more refined menu, try the recipe below.

Ham, Brie & Apple Panini

WITH JALAPEÑO HONEY

Recipe for jalapeño honey follows. If you don't feel like making it, you can substitute any brand of hot honey you like. You can also use turkey instead of ham, pear instead of apple, spinach instead of watercress… It's a sandwich! Make it your own.

FOR EACH SANDWICH, LAYER:

Bread (recommended: ciabatta or a hearty whole wheat)
Jalapeño honey
Handful of watercress
Thinly sliced apple
Ham
Brie
Jalapeño honey, or mustard, or mayo,
or any combination of the three
Bread

Brush the outsides of the bread with olive oil. Press the sandwich in a panini press—or on a griddle or flat pan with another pan weighing it down—until the bread is nicely browned and the cheese is melted.

JALAPEÑO HONEY

1 cup of honey
1 jalapeño

Cut jalapeño into four quarters, lengthwise. Put honey and jalapeños in a small saucepan. Heat over medium-low for about 5 minutes, stirring occasionally. Remove from heat and allow to cool for a couple minutes. Discard the jalapeño quarters, then run the honey through a fine-mesh sieve to remove all of the seeds.

Questions
for Discussion

These questions contain spoilers, so we recommend that you wait to read them until after you have finished the book.

1. When *Beach Vibes* starts, Beth is profoundly lonely because she had lost both friends and family in her divorce, as well as losing her husband. Did that feel relatable to you? Why or why not?

2. When Beth saw Ian's billboard proposal, she ran her car up onto a sidewalk. If she's over her ex-husband as she claims she is, why do you think she reacted so strongly? Do you think a billboard proposal is romantic or tacky or...?

3. What did you think of Rick when you first met him through Jana's point of view? Did your opinion of him change when you saw him with his sister, and as you read the book? If so, what did he do or say that made you think differently of him?

4. Why was the friendship between Beth and Jana so important to both women? Discuss the role of friendship in a person's happiness. Do you think it's different for men and women? If so, how?

5. How would you describe the scene in which Rick brings the two women together for dinner, revealing that his sister and his new girlfriend already know one another? Discuss the women's complicated feelings about that dinner.

6. How did you feel when Jana revealed that she doesn't know who Linnie's father is? Did you understand why that made Beth worry that Jana might be after Rick's money? Why or why not?

7. When Beth met Teddy, the sparks were instant. Was that love or lust? Do you believe in love at first sight?

8. Was Beth right to keep Rick's relationship with Galaxy a secret from Jana? Why or why not? Once she realized that Rick was still seeing Galaxy, do you think she would have told Jana the truth, if Teddy hadn't overheard her berating Rick?

9. Discuss the role of these characters in the story: Dex, Aunt Agatha, Kai.

10. Teddy and Dex were child TV stars, took very different paths in adulthood, yet remained close. Which of the men was more appealing to you, and why?

11. Did you find the ending satisfying? Why or why not?

12. One of the major themes of this book is family loyalty—Beth's loyalty to Rick, Teddy's loyalty to Jana. Yet in the end, Beth cut off contact with her brother. Was she right to do so? Why or why not? How much loyalty do we owe our families?